## AN UNREAL PLACE TO MEET THE REAL THING

R.J. was on. Performing, and knowing it, and feeling like a jerk. God, she wanted to be home in her yellow robe. Not here talking to these people, entertaining. One of the starlets who was collecting completed contest forms walked up and put her hand on Jason Flagg's arm. "Um . . . well, are any one of you through with your things that you fill in? Ready to . . . um . . ."

"Not yet," Jason told her and she shimmied away.

"Ahh," R.J. said, watching her, "if only she could speak . . . what stories she could tell." The other laughed.

"Almost show time," the blond woman said, touching the red-haired man's arm. "I'm going to go save us some good seats, darling."

"We'll join you," Jason Flagg said. And he and the two women headed toward the living room, leaving R.J. face to face with handsome David. There was an awkward silence as she looked at him looking at her.

"So," she tried, "aren't you going to ask me what my sign is?"

"Not necessarily," he said. "I know what your sign is. Your sign is *Closed Until Further Notice*. And one-liners are a great way of making sure everybody stays away until then. It'll be nice when you're able to turn your sign over so it says *Open*."

"Nice talking to ya," she said, moving away from the table.

"If you ever get to know me," he said, "you'll learn that above all else, I tell the truth."

BANTAM BOOKS BY IRIS RAINER DART

*Beaches*
*'Til the Real Thing Comes Along*

# 'Til the
# Real Thing
# Comes Along

## Iris Rainer Dart

BANTAM BOOKS

NEW YORK · TORONTO · LONDON · SYDNEY · AUCKLAND

'TIL THE REAL THING COMES ALONG
*A Bantam Book*
*Bantam hardcover edition / October 1987*
*Bantam paperback edition / July 1988*

**Library of Congress Cataloging-in-Publication Data**

Dart, Iris Rainer.
'Til the real thing comes along.

I. Title.
PS3554.A78T55  1987      813'.54      87-47571
ISBN 0-553-27248-9

*Published simultaneously in the United States and Canada*

PRINTED IN THE UNITED STATES OF AMERICA

KR    0 9 8 7 6 5 4 3 2

*This book is dedicated to the memory of
my parents, Rose and Harry Ratner,
and
to my blessings, my son and daughter,
and
to Stephen Dart,
my knight in shining armor*

*THANK-YOUS*

Barry Adelman
Doctor Howard Allen
Sylvia Angel
Ann Beckett
Mary Blann
Hank Bradford
Francois R. Brenot
Joyce Brotman
Ethel Eisner
Sandy Ferguson
Joe Mansfield
Elaine Markson
Doctor Alfred Pasternak
Fanny and Benny Rabinowitz
Elliot Ratner
Joe Singer
Meg Sivitz
Susan Sivitz

and a special thank-you to my
editor, Linda Grey, for the confidence,
enthusiasm, and support she's given
me since the very first day.

# 'Til the
# Real Thing
# Comes Along

# BOOK ONE

# R.J.

*I*t was three o'clock in the morning and a thick gray cloud of cigar smoke hung in the air over the conference table. R.J. took another sip of coffee from a white mug that had the words THE BROAD printed boldly in red on the side, then held the mug next to her cheek, hoping the heat would soothe her pounding headache.

"Patsy's gotta say it right out on the air," Harry Elfand announced. " 'My husband left me for a younger woman.' America is gonna love her for tellin' the truth, so let's run with it."

"How young is the other woman?" Eddie Levy asked, knowing the other writers would rise to the bait.

"She's so young, when he takes her out to dinner he has to cut her meat," Marty Nussbaum offered.

"He has to strain the food."

"He comes home with pablum on his breath."

"The only social disease he worries about is diaper rash."

The voices of the writers were strained with exhaustion.

"You're makin' the girlfriend too young," Harry Elfand said. Then he absently put a lit match to the cigar he was chewing, even though the cigar was already lit.

R.J. wriggled her toes inside her boots. She would never get through another hour of this. She was freezing and sleepy. A younger woman. What's funny about a younger woman? she thought.

"Everyone reads the *Enquirer*. We've gotta make Patsy

come out smelling like a rose. She caught her old man cheating. The girlfriend's eighteen. Patsy's thirty-six."

"How'd Patsy catch him?" Eddie Levy asked.

R.J. put her cup down on the table and answered in a sleepy voice. "She found Clearasil on his collar."

"That's funny," someone muttered very quietly.

"Good one," Harry Elfand said to R.J. "Stay with it."

"Freddy's so cheap, he'll marry the girl 'cause he can get her into the movies for half price," R.J. said. She was so punchy that she laughed a sharp little laugh out loud at that one. No one else even cracked a smile.

"Okay, two jokes about the girl is enough," Harry Elfand said, turning to face R.J. "Now gimme one about why he left Patsy."

Why he left Patsy. Why he left Patsy? Because she was . . .

"Boss, I got a great idea," Marty Nussbaum said. "Since R.J. is on a roll, why don't we all go home and let her stay here and finish it?"

"Because it's gotta be done by nine this morning," Harry Elfand answered, tapping his cigar out—which usually meant he was considering ending the meeting.

"I'll come in at seven," R.J. said, knowing it was the only answer that could get all of them out of there and to their respective homes to sleep, even for a few hours. She stood, hoping Harry Elfand would take a cue from her. As she did, she could feel the stiffness in her neck and back and legs.

Someone sang a few bars of "Thank Heaven for Little Girls," and all the men stood too.

"Well, if you ask me, writing for television is a hell of a way to make a living," Marty Nussbaum said. It was what he always said when a meeting ended at this hour.

"You call this living?" everyone muttered. It was what they always muttered as they searched for their car keys and made their way out the door. When they were all in the hallway, moving, shuffling toward the elevator, too tired to talk—which for them was very tired—R.J. switched off the lights in the conference room, closed the door, and turned to join them.

*OPENING MONOLOGUE*

*(TIM CONWAY, BETTE MIDLER, RAY CHARLES)*

*MUSIC: PATSY OPENING THEME*

*FROM BLACK, THE PATSY SUNSHINE HOUR LOGO
MOVES FORWARD AND FREEZES WHEN IT FILLS FRAME.*

ANNOUNCER (VOICE OVER)
From Hollywood . . . it's the Patsy Dugan
Sunshine Hour!!!!

IMAGES OF PATSY EXPLODE ALL OVER FRAME. DOZ-
ENS OF SHOTS PER MINUTE. LAST SHOT GOES TO
BLACK.

ANNOUNCER (V.O.)
. . . And now, ladies and gentlemen, the rhinestone
cowgirl herself . . . Patsy Dugan!!!

PATSY (SINGING V.O.)
LIKE A RHINESTONE COWGIRL
RIDING OUT ON A HORSE
IN A STAR-SPANGLED RODEO.

DISSOLVE TO: PATSY LIVE

Howdy, everybody.

AUDIENCE (O.S.)
Howdy, Patsy!!!

PATSY
Well, if y'all have been readin' the papers I guess y'all
know by now that my husband Freddy who used ta
be on the show with me has left me for a woman half
my age. Now, ain't that the pits? Only thing worse
was the way I figured out he was cheatin'. (BEAT) I
found *Clearasil* on his collar. And ya *know* how cheap
Freddy is. He'll probably marry the gal on accounta he
can get her into the movies for half price. Ain't it just
awful? Freddy told *The National Enquirer* he left me
'cause I was dumb. Now ya see, that's where me and
him are different. I would never use name-callin' in
the press against that two-timin', lowlife, redneck piece
of trash.

He also told everybody I was a lousy housekeeper. But I proved he was wrong about that. After
the divorce I'm keepin' the house in Beverly Hills,
the house in Malibu, and the house in Hawaii. Hey,
who needs him anyway? There are still some men
around who think that *I'm* a cute young chick.
'Course, most of 'em are in nursing homes and institutions. I'm jokin' because I want y'all to know that
I am not one bit bitter about this situation. I have
me a very positive attitude about my future. As soon
as I can, I'm gonna start goin' on dates and meetin'
people, because I believe it's possible to go out there
and find a man. After all, that young gal found
mine!!!

I'm real glad y'all are here ta keep me company
tonight. We're gonna have us a real good time. My
special guests are Tim Conway . . .

APPLAUSE
The fabulous Ray Charles . . .

APPLAUSE
And my good friend, the Divine One, Bette Midler.

APPLAUSE
So stay tuned, hear? We're comin' right back, with Patsy's Sunshine Hour.

MUSIC: RHINESTONE COWGIRL

PATSY (SINGS)
THERE'S BEEN A LOAD OF COMPROMISIN'
ON THE ROAD TO MY HORIZON
BUT I'M GONNA BE WHERE THE LIGHTS
ARE SHININ' ON ME.
LIKE A RHINESTONE COWGIRL . . .

MUSIC: OUT

DISSOLVE TO BLACK.

$M$ichael had a whole routine that he did with a cigarette. First he'd light one, take a few long drags, and exhale volumes of smoke through his mouth and nose, and, R.J. was sure, sometimes a few bursts even came out of his ears. Then he'd make a kind of nest in the crook of his hand, where he'd cradle the cigarette while he rolled it between his thumb and forefinger and stare at the glowing end. Then he'd blow on the lit end, which would make the orange part look even brighter, and tiny ashes would fly all around his face. After that, he'd take another few drags, let out more raging smoke, and look at the cigarette with distaste, as if he was sorry he'd ever started smoking it in the first place. So he'd smash out what was left of it wherever he happened to be at the time. He'd smash it into a telephone pole if he was walking down the street. He'd smash it into the bricks of someone's pool deck if his host had neglected to provide him with an ashtray. Or—and this was the one that made R.J. cringe—he'd smash it into his half-full drinking glass at a party. At the moment, R.J. was watching him smash the remains of the most recently smoked cigarette into the freshly mowed lawn of the Four Oaks School, not six feet from the sign that said SMOKING FORBIDDEN ANYWHERE ON CAMPUS.

It wasn't that Michael hadn't seen the sign. It was that he just didn't care. He was nervous. Very nervous. R.J. had seen him nervous before, but never this bad. Maybe the loud music and all the kids running and squealing were upsetting to him. Probably he'd never been around this many kids at once. Never at a school fair. But that was all part of what he'd have to get used to, now that he was going to be Jeffie's stepfather in a few days. Five days.

R.J. felt queasy. Probably she was just worried that the wedding plans could go awry. Nothing serious. Michael was lying on his stomach on the grass now. He had a new cigarette going, and he was doing the part where he blew on the lit end. R.J. looked at his carefully combed prematurely silver hair and his perfectly manicured nails, and the queasy bubble in her stomach felt as if it were growing from Ping-Pong ball to tennis ball size. She glanced across the lawn to see if there was a line waiting to get into the ladies' bathroom, actually the girls' locker room. There was. When she looked back at Michael, and saw his contorted face, at first she thought it must be a joke he was playing . . . but no. This wasn't funny. He was sobbing. Silently. His cheeks and the backs of his ears were bright red, and his body was shaking with the effort of holding in what, if he hadn't contained them, would be mighty cries.

"Michael."

He couldn't answer.

"Michael, my God, are you okay?" Maybe she should get him out of there before the children saw him, or before he let go and the children heard him. Her eyes scanned the fairground trying to spot Jeffie. Fifth-grade boys. There were so many of them, and almost all of them were wearing the same red school sweat shirt. It was impossible from this distance to pick out her own son from the rest.

"Michael, let's get you to the car," she said, "and I'll ask one of the other mothers to look after Jeffie. Michael," she said again, touching his shoulder. "Please."

"I can't," he said, moving his shoulder away from her touch.

"Of course you can," she said in a voice she often used to encourage Jeffie. "The parking lot is just across the street."

"I mean"—he narrowed his puffy red tear-filled eyes—"that I can't marry you."

The queasiness bubble was now a medicine ball that filled R.J. from her throat to her groin. She looked back toward the ladies' room, positive that she would have to run over there any second, push all those other people out of the way, scream "emergency," and lock herself into a cubicle and throw up. Instead she took a deep breath and said, "That's fine. Now let's go." She stood and helped Michael, who was still trembling, to his feet.

She took him back to her house after asking Harriet Wallace, another fifth-grade mother, to promise to locate and look after Jeffie. Now she sat in her living room across from Michael, who was blowing on the ash of the current cigarette nested in his hand. In front of him on the coffee table, an ashtray was already filled with the gold filter butts of several recently completed Dunhills.

"This is going to break my mother's heart," he said quietly. "She's not going to believe it when I tell her I couldn't do it. I'm a forty-year-old man, for Christ's sake. You'd think by now I could settle down. But I still can't make a commitment to one woman." His voice broke in a way that R.J. thought sounded as if it had been rehearsed. "It isn't you. You're a hell of a gal. I mean, you must be if I thought I could marry you. Look how close we came. Christ, we had blood tests. We had wedding rings," he whined, as if she didn't know. "I never came this close with anyone. But I can't . . . I . . ." He burst into tears and threw himself at R.J., put his arms around her, and buried his wet face in her neck.

"Oh, God. Forgive me. Please, R.J., say you forgive me. I'm a sick horrible person. My God."

R.J. put her arms around his shoulders to comfort him and patted his back, and as she did, her nose and eyes were overwhelmed with the acrid smell of cigarette smoke. R.J. hated Michael Rappaport, and she hated herself for ever agreeing to marry him, for ever allowing herself to fall for the dozens of clever ways he'd used to win her over.

"Napoleon never waged such a campaign," her friend Dinah would tell everyone, about Michael's courtship of R.J. That line always got a big laugh, because everyone knew that Michael was short. Only five feet what? Three, probably, but it was something he never discussed. After the Napoleon joke, Dinah would be encouraged to go on and regale their mutual friends with tales about poor Michael, so lovesick over R.J. that on top of all the other insane things he did to court her, he actually went to one of those billboard companies that rent advertising space on the Sunset Strip, knowing that Sunset was the route R.J. always took home from work. And "spent a friggin' fortune,"

Dinah would announce, just so he could tell R.J. he loved her.

But how did Michael know that R.J. would even see it? That was what someone invariably asked Dinah when she told the story. And Dinah, who had set the story up perfectly in the hope that someone would ask just that, was ready with an answer.

"Because," she would say, heavily mascaraed eyes aglow, "it wasn't *a* billboard. It was *three*—count them—three billboards. The first one said 'Michael loves'; the second one said 'his beautiful R.J.'; and the third one said—are you sitting down, everyone?—'more than life itself.' "

"No!" People would invariably shriek in amazement, and R.J. would shift uncomfortably in her chair, and they would turn and look at her as if to ask: This can't possibly be a true story, can it? And she would nod weakly and admit it was not only true, but that renting the three billboards was one of the less extravagant things Michael had done in an effort to win her hand. Making her feel as if her life were an episode of *Love American Style*. And sometimes someone would say, "I remember that. I had a meeting at the nine-thousand building and I remember seeing those billboards and wondering what shmuck did that?"

R.J. would always jump to Michael's defense then, remembering how sweet he looked that day, standing on Sunset knowing just when she would drive by because he'd paid someone at her office to call him at a number in a phone booth as soon as R.J. left for the day. He was carrying two dozen roses and had his thumb up as if he were hitchhiking. But R.J. didn't see him at first. ROCKY II: THE STORY CONTINUES. A determined Clint Eastwood punching his fist through the prison wall to ESCAPE FROM ALCATRAZ. R.J. loved the billboards. Later she remembered that she'd once told Michael that the reason she took Sunset home instead of Beverly was to look at the billboards. MICHAEL LOVES . . . HIS BEAUTIFUL R.J. . . . MORE THAN . . . Oh, God.

"No," R.J. said aloud when she read the three signs and her brain put together what they said. "No. Oh, please, no," she said again when she spotted Michael standing at the curb just beneath the third sign. "No." And she pulled up and rolled down the car window.

"Yes, darling," Michael answered, walking to the car and leaning against the door. "Let me be your husband." At least that sounded like what he said, because his words were nearly drowned out by the noise of the passing cars. "Let me be Jeffie's father. You're my life," he said louder. It was sweet. There were tears in his eyes.

"Oh, Michael," R.J. began, but a motorcycle whizzed by, roaring above her words. When it had passed, Michael said, "Don't answer now. Give me some time to prove to you how wonderful our life together can be. Tell me every dream, every fantasy you've ever had, about how you want your life to be, and I'll make it come true."

His eyes were filled with tears. R.J. took a deep breath to stall for time so she could decide what to say to him. She could hear an ambulance in the distance and she waited while it got closer and very loud, then passed and disappeared.

"This is wrong," she said finally. "It's too soon. We've just been seeing each other for such a short time and—"

"I'll quit smoking," he said, as if that would change her mind. "I'll do anything. I'll even grow taller."

Then he laughed a little laugh at that, but she knew it was a touchy subject. He'd always been the shortest boy in his class, in his family too. On his twenty-first birthday his mother had taken him out to dinner to a fancy restaurant, and after the meal had given him a box containing a pair of elevator shoes. Michael had had a few drinks the night he finally felt close enough to R.J. to tell her that story, and when he did, she remembered thinking how sensitive and dear he was. And how hurt he'd been and how much he needed her.

"R.J., I love you. I want to dedicate my life to you and your son. I want to marry you and adopt Jeffie."

Jeffie. Since Arthur's death he'd never been the same. The hopeful glow was gone from his sweet little eyes. Two years. Her friends said two years was long enough and it was time to stop mourning and get on with her life. She would get on with her life, she told them, but she would never stop mourning. That was when the friends always exchanged a look that meant "she's so neurotic" and then told her with a pat on her back or her arm or her hand: "We'll find you someone."

Michael Rappaport had been a fix-up by her accountant and his wife. He was a literary agent at a large show-business agency and a Harvard graduate. "He should have been a lawyer," her accountant, Morrie, told her. She guessed he said that to point out how smart Michael was.

"You're both single, and you're both Jewish. You're petite and he's five something. Three . . . four . . . not a giant, but extremely attractive," Sylvia, her accountant's wife, had told her.

Hardly criteria for a relationship, but it was a beginning. Short men. People loved trying to fix her up with short men. Always she turned them down since the fix-up she'd had once in high school with Phil Stutz, who was even shorter than Michael. Phil took her to a dance, and while they were dancing to Johnny Mathis singing "Chances Are," R.J. overheard someone refer to them as "the puppet couple." Short men. Her accountant's wife, Sylvia, must have heard the hesitation in R.J.'s silence.

"Hey, you'll go," she urged. "It's one evening. How bad could it be? You'll talk. You'll be sitting down and you won't notice."

So she went. On one date with a man to whom Dinah referred for weeks afterward as Michael How-Bad-Could-It-Be Rappaport. And then she went on another because the truth was, he wasn't so bad. And then another because he was very persistent, and then another because she didn't know how to say no, and now . . . She should have known it would go wrong when after only four dates with Michael he told her he loved her. My God. How could he possibly know so soon? It embarrassed and unnerved her.

She had been seeing him for nearly two months when she introduced him to Jeffie and watched the way he had knocked himself out to charm the kid. Jeffie was crazy about airplanes. Michael knew airplanes. Promised to take him out to the Planes of Fame Museum at Chino Airport. Jeffie played soccer in the park. Michael promised to come out to watch him play. Jeffie loved video games. Michael promised to spend an afternoon in a video arcade with him.

When R.J. finally decided to say yes to Michael's proposal, she told herself it was because she had to make a new life for herself and Jeffie. A family for herself and her son. Jeffie seemed excited by the idea, and that convinced her that she'd made the right choice. To be a family. Her son needed that. Some corner of her knew that it was a rationale. A place to hide. Michael promised her—no, swore to her—that he wanted to be part of a family too. That's what he was offering her. In August. Now it was November, and not only had there been no Chino Airport, no showing up at a soccer game, and no visit to an arcade, but now the little shit was backing out of the marriage too.

When he'd consumed and smashed out what R.J. counted as three more Dunhills and made a phone call to his mother to tell her he was on his way over to see her with some bad news—"No, Ma, I won't tell you over the phone. No. No one died, and it has nothing to do with Aunt Minnie's surgery"—Michael begged R.J. once more to forgive him, swore he'd never stop loving her, recited a litany of thank-you's for her patience, kindness, thoughtfulness, charm, sense of humor, and grace under pressure. She responded with all she had left. A numb half-smile. Then she watched him walk to his car and get in, find his dark glasses in the spot where he always kept them, tucked up behind the visor, and put them on. Even from just inside her front door where she stood, she could see him turn the rearview mirror so he could look at himself, and then push the bridge of the glasses down to the middle of his nose, which is how he always wore them. Then he started the car. As he backed out down the driveway he glanced at R.J. over the top of the glasses, puckered his lips, made what she was certain would have been a little smacking kiss if she had been able to hear it, and was gone.

When Jeffie came home she would tell him the bad news. Oh, God. Poor baby. Or maybe not such a poor baby this time. *Bad news* was what she'd told him when Arthur was murdered. *A terrible thing happened last night. A robber came into the house to steal some money and then he killed your daddy.* Is that how she'd said it? She knew she hadn't said *shot him in the stomach.* Killed. Murdered. Words coming out of her mouth that sounded as though they were from some horrible movie or television show. Words that a nice Jewish girl never even imagined she would ever hear someone else say, let alone say herself. Guns, robbery, murder. Those were things they talked about on *Adam 12* or *Quincy,* or in newspaper articles she'd skimmed, shaking her head while she did, with pity for the poor sad people in the crime-filled ghettos.

Now she remembered. "It's okay to cry and scream and fall on the bed and hate everybody," she had told her son, certain from the even look he gave her that he wasn't really sure what she was saying. "You're allowed to be furious and tell the whole world how full of anger you are." Her cousin Mimi's husband, Jack, the psychiatrist, had told her to say that. R.J. and Jeffie were sitting on the flowered bedspreads on the twin beds the morning she told him, in the guest room of Mimi and Jack's apartment in New York. She held her little boy's left hand with her right hand while his right hand played with the fingers of her left, tapping on each of her polished fingernails. She ached, watching his sweet little face as he slowly absorbed what he had just heard. Eventually he sighed a tiny sigh; then he stood, walked out of the bedroom, down the hallway and into the living room. R.J. followed him feverishly, and saw him sit down at Mimi's upright piano, think for a moment, as if to review his repertoire, and then pound out a violent rendition of "Chopsticks" . . . over and over and again. R.J. knew she would never hear "Chopsticks" again without feeling sick to her stomach. For the rest of her life when she heard it, she would remember every detail of those few days. Like the smell of formaldehyde in the morgue, where she had gone to identify the body. A drawer. The body of the man she loved in a drawer.

No. Michael Rappaport's change of heart was not such bad news. This was not like losing Arthur. Nothing. This was nothing. It was simply the loss of a relationship she hadn't even been sure she'd wanted. One she'd been involved in for all the wrong reasons. She would go back to work in two weeks, as planned. She and Jeffie would go back to their lives as usual. It would help when she had to get up early, get dressed, go into the office, think, be funny, be productive, turn out pages, get the show on the air. Maybe she'd even try to find an exercise class to go to every now and then. She hadn't been to one since she couldn't remember when, and her legs were turning to Jell-O. No, they weren't. She still had great legs.

"Are these the legs of a comedy writer?" Harry Elfand would joke on the rare days that R.J. came to work dressed in a skirt instead of pants. "I ask you, America. Are they?" And all twelve of the guys—R.J. was the only female writer on the staff of the show—would have something silly to say, like: "Never mind the legs, honey. Show us your skits."

Her first day back on the show she forced a smile onto

her face and settled into her chair at the morning meeting.
She riffled through her appointment book, hoping to look
preoccupied so no one would ask her any questions. It was
working. The men were filing in, talking to one another,
and no one said a word to her. If only the meeting would
start, there wouldn't be time for personal chatter.

"Say, R.J.," Eddie Levy said. "What happened to the
wedding?" Oh, shit. "The guy musta caught some of your
reruns and decided to marry Gail Parent instead. Now *she's*
funny."

"Thanks, Eddie."

"Poor kid," Artie Zaven said. "First a dead one, now a
no-show." Then he thought to himself. "Wait a second.
Maybe that woulda worked better if I had said: 'First a dead
one, now a dead *beat*'?"

"Thank your lucky stars, R.J.," Harry Elfand said. "The
truth of the matter is, and I know every one of the guys
here will agree, marriage sucks. So be glad that asshole
dumped you."

"Harry," R.J. said, "now that you express it so elo-
quently, I feel much better."

"Marriage," Marty Nussbaum said, getting the faraway
look in his eye that he always got when he was about to say
something silly, "is like a besieged fortress. Everyone on the
outside is trying to get in, and everyone on the inside is
trying to get out."

Comedy writers never laugh. One or two of them muttered a barely audible "funny," and Harry Elfand gathered a
bunch of freshly sharpened Blackwing 602 pencils into his
hand as if they were pick-up stix, a signal that the meeting
was about to begin.

Thank God, R.J. thought.

"The guests are Carol Burnett, Marty Feldman, and
Glen Campbell. Glen's going to sing a duet with Patsy. So
we need a sketch for Marty and Carol, and then a musical
number for Patsy and Carol with a . . ." R.J. stopped listening. She doodled with a pencil on the yellow legal pad in
front of her. She was recovering. She was back at work. The
swing of things would take over and she wouldn't think
about Michael Rappaport. Harry was giving everyone an
assignment now.

"And you do the wraparound blackouts for Patsy and

Carol. Got that, madame?" Harry Elfand said in R.J.'s direction.

And she wouldn't cry anymore as she had been for the last two weeks, since the day of the school fair. After all, even if it had been a mistake to be involved with him in the first place, this was still an ending, dashed hopes, another failure.

"R.J?"

R.J. looked up. "Yeah. Sure. Wraparound blackouts. I'll do them."

"By four o'clock, guys . . . and gal," Elfand said.

The men all pushed their chairs back and stood. R.J. didn't move. Michael Rappaport. How could she let him make her feel this rotten? Why did she ache every time she thought his name? It must be because of the rejection.

All the other writers had left the conference room before she got up and walked slowly to her office, a tiny windowless cubicle, sat down on her creaky typing chair, and looked at her watch. She had to start working. Maybe she should go downstairs to the taping and try to catch Patsy in her dressing room to discuss some ideas. Patsy liked that. It made her feel as if she were a part of the creative process. The wraparound blackouts. Three short sketches that would later be connected by a musical number. Carol and Patsy would sing and Marty Feldman would join them in the sketches. Maybe it should be something about men who can't make a commitment. Yeah, that was funny, all right. Shit, there was an ache inside her that made her feel like an elephant was sitting on her chest. Michael . . . my God . . . how could he?

She picked up the phone and dialed Dinah's number. Dinah would comfort her, and *then*, when she felt a little better, she could start to work. When she heard Dinah say hello, her throat filled with tears and she couldn't speak.

"Hello? Hello? Hey, who *is* this?" Dinah asked.

"Di . . ." She could barely get it out.

"Oh, hon . . ." Dinah said. "Where *are* you?"

"At work," R.J. managed. "But I can't work. I can't do anything. Maybe because, according to my appointment calendar, I'm supposed to be just getting back from my honeym . . ." she couldn't finish the sentence.

"Hey, do *I* know? I'm sitting here staring at the pink dress I was going to wear to be the world's oldest bridesmaid and now I've got no place to . . . R.J.? Ahh, Arj, think back a few weeks. You sat on my sofa and said, 'Di, do I really want to go through with this?' You always knew deep in your heart you were going to marry that little Toulouse-Lautrec for all the wrong reasons. Someday you'll fall to your knees and thank the gods that this happened.''

"I know. I know, but I did a terrible thing to my poor Jeffie. He's been saying to me every day, 'Ma, now I'm gonna have a father at my bar mitzvah.' I mean, he was so glad to finally be a family. . . . Oh, God. Michael promised he was going to have the papers prepared so he could adopt Jeffie as soon as we were married. Oh, God, Di . . .''

"If it makes you feel any better, just recall if you will that my twins *did* have a father at their bat mitzvah. A father and his bimbo girlfriend, not to mention my ex-mother-in-law, the queen of Shaker Heights, who told the rabbi behind my back that I was a—''

The door to R.J.'s office was kicked open as if it were a drug bust. It was the way Harry Elfand always entered a room. He looked at her tear-stained face and the phone in her hand and said, "Ahhh, shit. See what happens when ya hire broads? Insteada workin' they sit on the phone all day cryin'. If you didn't write such good fuckin' jokes, I'd fire your ass.''

"I think I'd better call you back,'' R.J. choked into the phone, and hung up.

"I came in ta tell ya Patsy's sick today. She won't be comin' in for a day or two, so just write whatever you think works and that'll do it,'' Harry said without looking at her.

"Okay,'' R.J. said, and took a Kleenex and blew her nose.

Harry Elfand started out the door; then for some reason he turned back, and this time he did look at R.J.—with the gentlest look she had ever seen on his fat unshaven face. Harry had been a comedy writer for so many years that he liked to say about himself, "I wrote jokes for Caesar. And I'm not talkin' Sid here. I'm talkin' Julius.'' He had enough money so that he only had to work now for the fun of it. *Joey's Place,* a situation comedy he'd created, had been on the air for seven years and then sold into syndication for millions of dollars. Harry loved the fact that everyone in the business knew that. And he also loved the fact that everyone thought of him as a curmudgeon. But every now and then, albeit rarely, he'd let some sweetness shine through. Now he spoke in a voice R.J. knew he meant as sympathetic, though it resembled a bad imitation of Marlon Brando as Stanley Kowalski.

"Hey. You gonna live through this or what?"

"Sure," she said, "I'll live through it."

"Atta girl," Elfand said. He started to close the door behind himself as he left, but turned back one last time. "Hey, I don't want to put the pressure on," he added, "but it better be hilarious." And he was gone.

R.J. sighed, blew her nose again, put a piece of paper in the typewriter, and began to write.

*Garden of Eden. Have Patsy dressed, or in this case un-
dressed, as Eve. Marty Feldman is Adam. Adam tells Eve
he wants to date other people. Eve reminds him there are
no other people. He is stunned. He realizes that's probably
why the song is called "Tea for Two." And why he's never
been in a ménage à trois? (No. Program practices will get
you for that one.) Wait! Here's an idea. Eve notices that
Adam is missing a second rib, which makes her think he
has a woman on the side. (Maybe it's not too late to go
back and get your teaching credentials.)*

"Darlin', when Freddy broke up with me I'd like ta kill
myself," Patsy said. She was lying on the floor, on her left
side, doing leg lifts. Leaning forward so her famous enormous breasts grazed the floor. Her long white-blond mane
of hair was pulled back and caught in a ponytail holder at
the top of her head. "Couldn't leave the house for cryin'.
Couldn't sing a goddamned note. Now look at me. Shit, I'm
beatin' guys away with a stick. So will you. It probably
don't feel like it now, but I guarantee you're gonna be just
fine."

"Thanks, Pats," R.J. answered.

"Hell, I know lotsa guys. I could set you right up with
any one of 'em in no time flat."

"That's okay," R.J. said. Patsy Dugan's fix-ups. R.J.

shuddered inwardly at the thought. After Patsy's husband, singing partner, and mentor, Freddy Gaines, walked out on her for an eighteen-year-old, giving the *National Enquirer* enough fodder for at least half a dozen issues, Patsy bravely went back on the air to do what used to be *Patsy and Freddy's Good Time Hour* alone. No one thought she could handle it. It was common knowledge that Freddy's quips and the way that he teased Patsy about her body, followed by her smart-mouth retorts, were the charm of the show. But Patsy "done fooled 'em all," as she would say, grinning when the producers read her the ratings each week. And once the show was on its feet, she was determined to make a hit of her personal life too. That was harder. She'd been with Freddy Gaines since she was sixteen. Now she was thirty-six and she didn't know the first thing about how to behave with a man. And besides . . . who was going to ask her out? She was the biggest superstar on television. You didn't just call a woman like that and say: "Hey. Feel like goin' out for a pizza?"

Although there were a few men who tried. R.J. had met the latest crop of Patsy's dates as they hung around the dressing room at the tapings. Brick, a New Wave musician with a kelly-green streak through his otherwise royal-blue hair. Ricky, a young, skinny stand-up comic Patsy had met one night at The Comedy Store. Ricky was deadpan and nervous and he was always sweating.

"Isn't he cute?" Patsy would ask everyone on the set about Ricky. "Can't we find a spot for him on the show?"

"Adorable," Harry Elfand would say, smiling a toothy smile at Patsy; then he'd turn to the writers and announce while making a face, *"kenst brechn,"* which was Yiddish for "I could throw up," and the writers would try not to laugh so that Patsy wouldn't know that Harry was making fun of her and her latest love. Behind her back Harry's routines about Patsy's boyfriend the clothing designer of dubious sexual identity, and her boyfriend the constantly sauced and on-the-decline movie actor, and her boyfriend the lawyer with Mafia connections, filled the writers' room with nearly as much raucous laughter as there was cigar smoke. And that was a lot.

"I'm not going to be ready to meet anyone for a long long time. I just hurt too much," R.J. told Patsy, not only to avoid the possibility of Patsy trying to find a man for her, but because it was true. Her depression didn't seem to want to go away. She had taken to wearing very large very dark glasses to work because they covered everything on her face but the red nose she had blown nearly to smithereens during the past weeks. Exercise classes weren't helping, and throwing herself into her work wasn't helping and neither were any of the other prescriptions for behavior she got from the stack of self-help books she devoured night after night. How to recover from a lost love. But the lost love wasn't Michael Rappaport. It was still Arthur, her late husband. Maybe because it had ended so tragically and they had never had a chance to make everything right.

R.J. and Arthur had been fighting for weeks. She had walked around with a filter of pain over her eyes and ears and heart, and was certain he was doing the same. No pleasures, not even her son's smiles and hugs, could lighten the weight of knowing that the marriage was fighting for its life, and losing. Maybe if she got away for a few days, went to stay with some cousins in New York. Had a chance to think about everything. There are certain decisions we make which are only historical in retrospect. Like the decision R.J. had made after she'd packed her suitcase, when she decided that she ought to take Jeffie with her.

"He has lots of cousins there," she announced to Arthur. "They never get to see him. He'd only have to miss a few days of school." She realized that her tone was defensive because she was certain that Arthur would say it was a bad idea. Disagree with her. The two of them seemed to be on the opposite side of every issue lately. Even what to have for dinner.

"Yes, take him," Arthur said, never looking up from the work he was doing. "It's better for me to be home alone this weekend."

Those words would replay themselves endlessly in her head. *Better for me to be alone.* For months afterward in dreams she saw that moment, except sometimes in the dreams what he said was: "Yes, take him. I'm going to be murdered this weekend, and I'd rather my son wasn't there to watch."

A few days in New York. Every night she had called Arthur. She missed him. Missed the old days when they were secure and smug about their love for each other. Now the phone calls between them were cold, businesslike, to pass information, news about their son. Except for that night. Saturday. It was ten P.M. in New York. Everyone in her cousin Mimi's apartment was preparing for sleep. Jeffie was already dreaming away in the guest room, where R.J. would go as soon as she tried to reach . . .

"Arthur?" she said.

"Arj, hi." Something was different in the sound of his voice; the usual coldness was only half there, maybe even less than half. There was a flutter of hope in her chest. "I tried calling you today," he said. "No one was—"

"A matinee. I took Jeffie to see *A Chorus Line*."

"I was cleaning out my desk and found the letter you wrote to me the night Jeffie was born," he said.

She inhaled, wondering what he would say next, and as she exhaled a quick breath, tears rushed to her eyes.

And? she thought. And?

"Arj, I love you," he said. "I need you and we can't go on like this. Whatever it is that's tearing us apart we'll fix, we'll solve. We have to. I don't want any other life than the one we had before things started to go bad for us."

Her tears fell into the little holes on the telephone receiver and she wiped them off, then moved her tongue back and forth across her upper lip to catch the other drops as they fell.

"Arj?"

"I'm here," she sniffed.

"The second you get home I want us to sit down, be together, and figure out how we got off the track, and how to get back on. How to get back where we were."

"Oh, Arthur, my love," she said. "Thank God for you. Thank God you're saying all of this. I've been so lonely for you and for our love . . . I felt so . . . deprived. I'll do anything. I'll quit working if you want me to stay home."

Maybe that would save them, she had thought. She knew how much Arthur hated her working. Writing at home had been acceptable. But taking a full-time job? Out of the question. When she was first offered the job on Patsy's show, he was furious. Full time? What about my son? What about my meals? She'd rushed out and found Manuela, and had begged him not to let it become an issue between them. His acceptance had always been grudging at best. "If it will make us better, I'll quit," she'd said to Arthur that night on the phone from New York. Even though she didn't want to choose, she loved him much more than the job.

"Don't say that, Arj," he told her in a voice filled with more understanding than she'd ever heard from him. "I know you love your work. I know how good it makes you feel. You don't have to quit. We just have to work it out. I think we can. Don't you?"

"Oh, yes," she said. "I want to." Thank God. Thank God. Thank God. R.J.'s cousin Mimi walked into the kitchen, saw R.J.'s tearful face, pulled a Kleenex from the pocket of her bathrobe, handed it to R.J., and walked out.

"Get some sleep, honey," Arthur said. "I love you."

There are certain decisions we make which are only historical in retrospect, R.J. thought again. She had been uncertain that night as to whether or not to call Arthur. As if maybe her constant calling was a bother to him. That was frequently the way it felt.

That night the house in Los Angeles was robbed by four young men. Two black and two white. All were armed. Arthur was awakened by the noise of them kicking in the back door. They took three hundred dollars in cash, two cameras, a watch, and Arthur Misner's life.

Certain decisions we make are only historical in retrospect. If she hadn't decided to take Jeffie, hadn't honored that last-minute thought, he might be gone too. She thanked heaven every day for her precious son, who needed her to help him with his homework and wanted her to cheer for him at Saturday soccer games, and who grinned from ear to ear when she pulled up in her old Mustang to pick him up at Hebrew school. And she was grateful for how much he reminded her of Arthur. That would have to be enough for her.

"Well," Patsy said, sitting up and rolling over onto her left side, her eyes never leaving her own reflection in the rehearsal hall mirrors. "I'll keep an eye out for you just in case. But ya better tell me what yer kinky fer."

"Pardon?"

"I mean what do they have to be? Short? Tall? Young? Old? Jocks?"

"You mean my type?"

"Yeah," Patsy said, then shook her head at her reflection and thought out loud, "goddamned inner thighs are goin' fast."

Now she got up on her hands and knees and was thrusting her bent leg to the side, like a dog at a fire hydrant. R.J. watched her do a few more knee lifts, then caught sight of herself in the mirror, sitting in the back of the rehearsal hall wearing the same jeans and black turtleneck she'd worn all through college, a sure sign she wasn't at her best. Jesus, was she so needy to be understood that she'd been pouring out her heart to this travesty of womanhood who couldn't possibly understand? Or could she? Maybe R.J. was being unfair. Maybe underneath it all she and Patsy really were alike. After all, the real reason Harry Elfand had hired R.J. to write *The Patsy Dugan Sunshine Hour* was because Patsy wanted at least one writer on the staff who had "a woman's point of view." Maybe all women had similar needs when it came to what they wanted in a man.

"Personally," Patsy began—the thigh lifts must have been difficult, because her words were accompanied by labored breaths—"all I care about is if they got great big dicks."

R.J. watched herself in the rehearsal hall mirror as she picked up her purse next to the folding chair where she was sitting and then got to her feet.

"Yeah, well . . . I left the new material over on the table with your stuff, Pats," she said. "I'll be in my office if you want to go over it."

"Thanks, babes," Patsy said. "Jes remember what my daddy sez. They can kill ya, but they can't eat ya." Certain that meant something obscene, too, R.J. kept walking.

Dinah loved that story when R.J. told it to her on the phone later that evening. R.J. could tell by the way she made her tell it over again that Dinah was memorizing every detail of it so she could tell the story at parties.

"By the way, Robert has a guy for you," Dinah said. Robert was Dinah's sometime boyfriend the endodontist. Or, as Dinah liked to describe him, "on again off again." Then she'd always laugh and say to R.J.: "And *you're* the one who's the comedy writer."

"Not interested in being fixed up anymore, Di. Thanks anyway," R.J. said, turning Jeffie's hamburger on the griddle with her right hand, putting the bun in the toaster oven with her left hand, and holding her head uncomfortably to the side to secure the telephone receiver between her ear and her shoulder.

"His office is in the same building as Robert's. R.J., don't say no so fast. He's a gorgeous, brilliant, Jewish psychiatrist. Thirty-nine. Never married."

There was a long silence.

"What are you thinking?" Dinah asked.

"I'm thinking: I wonder which one of those qualifications you just named is going to be the one that hangs him up the most."

"You're so cynical."

"No shit, my friend."

"If you sit at home brooding do you know what you're doing?" Dinah shouted into the phone.

"Yeah," R.J. answered, opening the refrigerator and pulling out the ketchup and relish bottles. "I'm sitting at home brooding."

"You're giving that little no-talent mayor of the Munchkins—who calls his mother every time he takes a leak—power over you and your feelings."

"Dinah, don't try to shrink me. Please. I don't want to go out with the gorgeous brilliant psychiatrist from Robert's building because I'm not interested in looking for, or meeting or getting involved with, any man. Maybe it's just for right now. Or maybe it's because I just don't believe I want to go out into the dating world, since I frankly don't think there's anyone out there. And you don't have to worry. Michael Rappaport isn't even in my mind. He doesn't have one drop of power over me at all."

"I'm starvin' to death," Jeffie hollered down from upstairs.

"It's ready," R.J. shouted back. "Gotta go, Di," she said, and hung up the phone, which rang again so immediately it made her jump. " 'Lo?"

"Hi," said the man's voice. Then nothing. R.J. hated that. Arthur, practical no-nonsense Arthur, had once told her after she'd received a slew of obscene phone calls one month, that if the caller didn't identify himself immediately she should hang up. "If it's someone who needs to reach you, he'll call back," Arthur had cautioned her.

"Hi," she said. The voice was familiar, but the question in her own voice told the caller she had no idea who it was.

"It's Michael," he said. Michael? Michael! Michael

Rappaport, her former fiancé. Ah, yes. *That* Michael. Hah! She hadn't even recognized his voice. Michael. See, Dinah? He doesn't have power over me one bit. Then why was her heart pounding and why were her palms sweating and, Christ, why was her son's hamburger burning on the grill?

"Ma," Jeffie shouted.

"Michael?" R.J. asked, praying her voice wasn't betraying her shakiness. "Uhh, can I . . . I mean . . . where are you? I mean are you at home? Can I call you back? I'm fixing . . . I mean I'm in the middle of . . ." It was six weeks since she'd heard his voice. That familiar voice. And now there he was. But she couldn't do this to Jeffie. She had rules, and one of them was that Jeffie's needs came first.

"I understand," Michael said sweetly. Sweetly. Not whining, the way she remembered he could sound so often. "Buzz me back, hon. Soon as you can. Okay? I'll be home all evening."

"Great." R.J. hung up the phone, flipped the burger into the air with the spatula, and watched as it landed perfectly on Jeffie's plate, pulled the bun out of the toaster oven without a mitt, and her fingers didn't feel a thing.

"Come on, sweetie," she called out to Jeffie, then did a little dance step as she pulled a container of yogurt out of the fridge for herself. "Hon," Michael had called her. I'll be home all evening, he'd said very clearly. Not on a date. Home all evening. Probably brooding over her. Probably realizing what a colossal error he'd made by ending it with her, hurting her, letting a woman like her go.

He had, after all, been the one who was so madly in love. Insisted, even though they weren't kids anymore, that they have a huge engagement party. What a party it was too. At their favorite Italian restaurant on a Monday night when the place was closed to the public, with every friend either of them had in attendance. An evening filled with romantic surprises, her favorite flowers on every table, a five-piece band that played only old love songs. And the ring.

"Hey, Mahh," Jeffie said, biting into his burger. "Any chips?"

R.J. put the yogurt down and went to the pantry for the chips. The ring that had belonged to Michael's late grandmother. His mother's beloved mother who had left it to Michael's mother, Sadie, who had kept it in a little jewelry box on the top shelf of her closet. The ring Sadie Rappaport had promised Michael from the time he was a little boy, the ring she would give to him for his fiancée when he grew up and fell in love.

"Regular or taco?"

"Taco," Jeffie said. R.J. brought the whole bag to the table.

Just after everyone had finished the perfect Italian feast, Michael had made a toast to the woman who had made him the happiest luckiest man in the world, "my beautiful R.J.," and Dinah had cried and R.J. remembered being a little weepy, too, with relief, and Michael's older sister Sarah, who everyone said practically raised him, was dabbing at her eyes too. Everyone was surprised when the mother of the about-to-be groom, Sadie Rappaport, stood and tapped on her wineglass with her knife. She was so tiny that some of the people who were sitting at tables in the back couldn't even see her as she began her speech.

"I'm sixty-four years old," she began, then added with a twinkle in her eye, "although I'm sure I look much younger." Everyone applauded, and someone yelled, "Hear, Hear."

"So far I've had a terrific life. My Harold, may he rest in peace, was a good provider. And even though I lost him too soon, I managed to live a nice life anyhow, and have mostly anything that I want. But one thing I've never had was a daughter-in-law." Everyone laughed. Sadie paused for the laugh just long enough, and R.J. remembered thinking that her future mother-in-law's timing was better than Patsy's.

"Because," Sadie went on, loving her own performance, "my son was too picky. Now, thank God, he decided enough was enough and he'll break down and marry R.J." Everyone laughed again. "So, Mikie, honey," she said—and now she sounded like Ralph Edwards telling the guest on *This Is Your Life* which person from his past was about to emerge from behind the screen—"here is the surprise your mother has promised you all your life." And at that, Sadie pulled a ring box out of the purse that was standing next to her plate on the table.

"Ahhhs" went up from everywhere. Everyone, especially the women, craned their necks to see what the surprise was. Sadie turned to Michael and looked deep into her son's eyes. "With *my* love for *your* love," she said. Michael stood and hugged her, and the man and his mother remained locked in a tearful embrace that was applauded by everyone, especially R.J., who at that moment remembered being told: "You can tell a lot about a man by the way he treats his mother." But Sadie had been sitting between R.J. and Michael at the round table, and now when she opened the box and showed the ring to Michael and he oohed and ahhed and she wept and neither one of them even looked at R.J., R.J. felt a little awkward.

Michael held the box up and showed the ring to the gathered group, and everyone said "oooh," but R.J. still couldn't see it because Sadie was still standing and blocking her view. She just smiled to cover her discomfort. Then Sadie took the box back from Michael and, after what seemed a very long time, handed it to R.J., who stood, trying to ignore the fleeting thought that the three of them probably looked like "the puppet family."

Then R.J. looked at the ring, looked at Sadie, and could get out only the words *thank you* because she had to put her face into her hands to cover her reaction, which was so overwhelming that it embarrassed her. Everyone thought she was crying. Thank heaven they thought that, because really what she was doing was laughing like a lunatic. She had never seen anything so appallingly gaudy in her life.

After the party, when Michael took her home, the two of them laughed in the car until the tears came. About the ring. The cocktail ring from Grandma, with clusters of tiny diamonds set in platinum, arrayed in some strange disorder that made it look, as Michael described it, like a chandelier in a Miami Beach condominium.

"Michael," she said, "I don't mean to be ungrateful. Your mother was so sweet, and she meant so well . . . but what do I do?" R.J. opened and closed the ring box, hoping each time that maybe when she opened it next, the ring would have changed.

"You take it to a jeweler and have the stones taken out," Michael said. "Then he puts them into a plain band, and we get me a gold band the same width, and we're all set." They had pulled up in the driveway of her house and he stopped the car. Now he moved toward her, took her in his arms, and kissed her.

"Did you have a wonderful time at our engagement party?" he asked, kissing her all over her face.

"I did," she answered. "Thank you so much, Michael. It was so romantic and wonderful. Are you sure it will be all right?" she asked again.

"What?"

"Changing the ring. Taking the stones out and starting again. Are you sure?"

He had laughed. "Of course I'm sure."

The next day on her lunch hour she had gone to a jeweler named Jay Marden, who was highly recommended by Dinah. The jeweler shook his head when he opened the box and saw Sadie Rappaport's mother's ring.

"They don't make 'em like *this* anymore." Then he looked at R.J. and said, "No offense."

He liked the plan of using the diamonds to make a plain wedding band, even made R.J. a little drawing of how it would look, and told her he would use the platinum from the existing ring to make the band for the new one. R.J. signed a paper saying she had left her diamonds there, gave him a deposit on the work, and went back to the office. Ten days later when she got the call saying that the ring was ready, she was ecstatic.

Mr. Marden stayed open a little later than usual so R.J. could pick up the ring after work. She decided to sneak out of the office a few minutes early, feeling so guilty that when she passed Harry Elfand in the hall she coughed a fake cough just in case he was about to ask her where she was going.

"Feel better," Harry mumbled.

"Thanks," she said.

The new ring was perfect. So beautiful it made R.J. melt when she saw it. Married. She was going to be married again. Be a part of a family again. And Jeffie would have a father. Maybe eventually she'd even have another child.

"Want to try it on?" Mr. Marden had asked her.

"Oh, no." R.J. was too superstitious to put the wedding ring on before the wedding. If she did, the wedding could come to some bad end. Bad end. After Michael's smoky announcement to her that day at the school fair, R.J. had taken the wedding list and she had telephoned everyone on it one by one to tell them that the plans had been canceled. Somehow she managed to get through all the calls without crying. "Better to find out now," she heard herself saying to them. And fifty out of sixty people actually said, "It's really for the best," back to her.

"Hey, thanks for dinner, Ma," Jeffie said, wiping some ketchup from the side of his mouth. "C'n I be excused?"

"Sure, baby," she said, picking up his dish and her empty yogurt container and carrying them to the sink.

Michael. Why had he called her? She was afraid to think what she was hoping. That he missed her. Wanted to apologize. He would have to apologize. Profoundly. He had hurt her so much. Hurt Jeffie too. And left R.J. alone to give once again the news of another loss to her little boy.

"Jeffie," she had said that day when he'd returned from the school fair. She had watched as Harriet Wallace's car pulled up in the driveway and the back door flew open and Jeffie, laughing heartily at something Matt Wallace had obviously just said to him, leaped from the car and ran to the front door. The odor of Michael's cigarettes still hung in the living room air, although immediately after he'd left, R.J., on some automatic nice-Jewish-girl instinct, had emptied the ashtray and washed it with hot soapy water, dried it, and put it away.

"Honey, sit down," she had said to Jeffie.

"Uh-oh," was his reply. He recognized bad news on her face. He sat on the living room sofa with the same look he wore in the orthodontist's waiting room.

"Michael and I aren't getting married," she had blurted out, certain afterward that there were probably dozens of better ways of telling him. Maybe she should have started out by saying: "This doesn't have anything to do with you," or "This isn't your fault," the way some parents did when they informed their children of their impending divorce.

"Okay," Jeffie said. The lack of expression on his face was eerie.

"I'm sorry," R.J. offered. "He told me today that he just can't do it. I'm sorry," she said again.

There was a moment when neither of them spoke or moved; then Jeffie asked, "Can I be excused?"

No, R.J. thought. Don't run away from this. Or from me. Let's talk about it. You need to and God knows *I* do.

"Yes," she said. "You can be excused."

He stood and without looking at her walked out of the living room into the hallway.

I have to be strong, have to be strong, R.J. said to herself. Dinah was right. I was going to marry him for all the wrong reasons—it wouldn't have been right. Better to find out now instead of . . .

"Ma," she heard a little voice say. When she turned and saw the look on her baby's face, all her resolve vanished. He was running toward her, his arms extended, and when he got to the sofa he collapsed on her lap, his arms around her neck.

"Oh, honey, this will pass. We've made it through so much worse than this. And this is happening for a reason, which is that it was wrong. A mistake. I was stupid and made a wrong choice. But something good will come of it. You'll see." She felt his body shaking with sobs, and the wetness of his tears on her face. Or were they her tears against his?

Jeffie. Her baby. Tonight, after she heard him go back to his room and turn on the television, she called Michael.

"Hello?"

"It's R.J.," she said nervously.

"Hi," he said. "Thanks for calling back. Listen, I need to talk to you."

"What about?" she asked.

"It's important," he said. "Too important to talk about on the phone. I'd like to come over."

Come over. No. Jeffie would still be awake for a while. Seeing Michael walk in the door would only confuse him.

"Not a good idea."

"After he's asleep," he said, obviously knowing what she was thinking.

What did he want? Not just to chat, or to see if she was surviving. *That* he could do on the telephone. And why did she care so much? She realized now as she caught sight of herself in the mirror above her bedroom dresser that she had actually put on makeup before she returned his call, as if he would somehow be able to tell through the telephone line whether or not she looked good.

"Okay," she said. "At ten."

By nine-thirty she had completely redone her makeup, changed her outfit four times, and finally ended up back in the jeans and work shirt she'd been wearing to make dinner, so she called Dinah for a pep talk.

"It's none of my business, obviously," Dinah began.

And then she and R.J. both said the word *but* in unison, because they both knew Dinah couldn't help but try to interfere.

"But what, Di?" R.J. said. Maybe, she thought to herself, the red sweater was better than the blue work shirt. Her black hair always looked great against bright colors.

"But don't let him seduce you. Don't go to bed with him no matter what he says. Even if he begs your forgiveness and has a rabbi with him to perform the ceremony tonight."

"Di, he's probably just coming over to make sure I haven't slashed my wrists or anything."

"Don't kid yourself," Dinah said. "That little stand-in for Herve Villechaize is probably just horny so he figures—"

"I won't go to bed with him, Di, I swear. I'll call you in the morning."

"What morning? You'll call me when he leaves. Which better be a half hour after he arrives."

"Later," R.J. said, and hung up.

She peeked in on Jeffie, who was peacefully asleep, then walked around her quiet house trying to figure out how she felt, what she should say to Michael. What if he'd changed his mind? Could she ever take him back after the crazy exit he'd made? Why would she want to? His breaking up with her had been God's way of telling her she wasn't supposed to marry him in the first place. That thought made her laugh out loud.

Michael's headlights in the driveway brought her to her feet, and she was at the door before he was even out of his car. Before she could think about it he had taken her into his arms and was kissing her all over her face the way he used to, and her body was responding, not just to the kisses but to the familiar feel and smell of him, some cologne that she remembered he sometimes wore, and the gum he chewed in the mistaken notion that Trident cinnamon covered up the smell of the cigarettes.

"I'll get you a drink," she said, reluctantly breaking free of his embrace, so confused, wishing she'd never said yes to his visit but excited that he was here. Maybe just as an antidote to her loneliness. Please, just as an antidote to her loneliness.

She poured wine for each of them. He raised his glass to her.

"You're still my beautiful R.J.," he said.

She forced a smile. She knew him. His expressions. This one she'd seen him use in business. With writers or producers he was trying to woo. She'd be with him when they'd bump into one of them when they were out to dinner or walking on the beach, and he'd get that forced sincere look on his face and say sweetly, "Don't forget . . . I'm you're biggest fan." Now the look was there for her, and he asked her ever so sweetly: "Are you okay? I mean you look fabulous but I've been worried about you. Tell me you're okay."

She took a long sip of wine so she could decide what to answer. Yes, goddamn you, I'm more than okay, because I've survived a fortunate escape from your sniveling little clutches? Yes, I'm okay because I really didn't love you? Or should she tell him the truth—that she felt so alone and so cheated out of the dream she'd been harboring about making a new life that even though she knew what a mistake it would be, she wanted to curl up in his lap and have him hold her and tell her that he was back and really would make everything in her life work?

"I'm fine," was all she could manage.

In one swift move he pulled a Dunhill from the maroon-and-gold box and extracted his gold Dunhill lighter from his shirt pocket. He lit the cigarette. He took a few long drags until he was surrounded by a smoke cloud. When it cleared, he looked long at R.J.

"You're a survivor, kiddo," he said, still with the sincere look. "You're tough. It's what I love about you the most."

Love about you. That's what he said. Not *used* to love about you. Not *loved* about you.

Now he cradled the cigarette in the crook of his hand, rolled it between his thumb and forefinger, and blew on the lit end. Tiny ashes flew all around his face.

"And you have values. Good strong values. Not like most of the girl— women in this town. You *know* what's important." He sucked hard on the cigarette again, then exhaled. There was another cloud, and then, as if it were a pronouncement, some information she could live on forever, he said, "You are *not* a bimbo."

"Thank you, Michael," she actually found herself saying.

"I've been so depressed since we broke up," he said,

looking everywhere but at her. "I've been a mess. I haven't gone to my office in weeks. They'll probably can me."

What was he getting at? Of course. It was just what she thought. Six weeks ago he had allowed a rush of the pre-wedding jitters to get to him, and now he was sorry. Now he was regretting his outburst so much that he was back to try and reconcile with her. Back to tell her what a mistake he'd made. And the weird thing was that, in spite of what a jerk she knew he was, she was actually sitting there flicker-ing back and forth between wondering how she could ever have loved him, and aching for him to come back. To make it okay. To stop her from having to go out into the world again alone. Back to dating. Back to courting. Back to going through the long process with someone else.

"I don't eat," he said to her, and put the cigarette out. "Hardly eat at all," and then he looked at her with big tormented eyes.

Doesn't eat. Poor thing. God. He *did* miss her. Maybe she should . . .

"Want me to fix you something?" she offered. Dinah would kill her for that one. "The shmuck treats you like garbage and you're gonna cook for him?" she would say. But now, when Michael's face lit up the way it used to when they first met, R.J. decided not even to mention it to Dinah.

"You know," he said, leaning forward as if he were going to tell her a secret, so close that she could smell the cigarettes on his clothes, "I've really missed your ome-lettes." Any minute he was going to beg her to get back together. He was just too embarrassed to do it right off the bat.

"You got it," R.J. said as she smiled and practically skipped into the kitchen, where she ripped open the refrig-erator door. Once he launched into his spiel about getting back together, she wouldn't say anything at first. She'd just listen. Let him explain away all the crummy things he'd done. Give him the opportunity to win her over. Eggs, cheese—ah, she even had some mushrooms. She'd tell him that it would be difficult. That she and Jeffie would have a hard time trusting him again and that he'd have to promise to work hard to regain their trust. Butter. It was true. Especially for Jeffie, her baby. He'd had enough hurt and she had to protect him.

For weeks after Arthur's death, Jeffie had refused to go to school no matter how much she encouraged him. After a lot of encouraging, R.J. decided that maybe the best thing for her to do was just to back off. Her cousin Mimi's husband the psychiatrist said, "Everyone has his own mourning time. Jeffie will go to school when he's ready."

"Do the other kids know about my dad?" he had asked R.J. one night.

"Yes, they do," she told him, knowing, by the way he lowered his eyelids when he heard her answer, that this was why he was afraid to go back. He was probably afraid that not having a father would set him apart from the others. Make him weird.

"Mrs. Liebman calls me all the time to say how much everyone misses you," she said. That was a little bit of an exaggeration. The teacher had called twice.

"Yeah, sure," he said.

R.J. was afraid of what the children might say to him. The questions they might ask him. Children in their innocent but eager curiosity could evoke thoughts that might never have entered his mind. Did your dad's stomach get ripped open? Did he bleed to death from the bullet? Did you see him when he was a corpse? Who are you gonna make something for when it's Father's Day? Maybe that was why she didn't push him to go back. Jeffie.

One day, in the middle of the morning, he had called her at work to tell her he couldn't find the red-and-blue Lego truck he'd made a few months before. He said he needed it very badly and he sounded worried. He said he thought maybe he had left it in his cubby at school. She asked him if he'd like to go over to the school and look for it, and when he said yes, she told Harry Elfand she had an emergency and rushed home to pick Jeffie up. When she and Jeffie pulled into the school parking lot in the Mustang, and Jeffie saw all the cars and realized that it was a regular school day and everyone was there, he looked nervous. "Maybe," he said, "this was a mistake." Probably he had left the truck at Jamie Eisner's house and not at school at all. He wanted to go home.

"Why don't we check your cubby?" R.J. had asked gently but firmly, in the tone her cousin Mimi's husband the psychiatrist had suggested she use. She pulled the Mustang in between a green Volkswagen bug and an old red

Cadillac. Then she had a long panicked moment when she was sure she'd been too firm and not gentle enough, because it looked as if he were about to cry and insist that she take him home. Instead, he opened the car door, got out, and looked over at the one-story building for just a second. Then he slammed the car door and ran with a kind of combination gallop and hop toward his homeroom. By the time R.J. had reached the door of the schoolroom, he had already gone inside. So she stood on her toes and looked in through the one tiny window set into the top of the door.

It was an odd moment she was seeing. Frozen in time. No one moved. Jeffie was standing very still just inside the door, looking nervously at the group of children and the teacher, all of whom looked back at him with great silent surprise. No one moved. R.J. bit the inside of her lower lip. Then the teacher said, "Jeffie." That was all, and as if that was their cue, all twenty children leaped from their seats and ran to him, their arms open wide, shouting his name, hugging him, holding him, tickling him, tackling him lovingly to the ground. They were a pile of joyous friends, and the most joyous of all of them was Jeffie, who R.J. could see was filled with relief as two of the boys now helped him to his feet. That was when R.J. opened the door and entered the room. None of the children even looked at her. They were all still surrounding her son. But Mrs. Liebman came over.

"How is he?" the teacher asked R.J.

"Fine now," R.J. said, fighting back tears of gratitude as she watched her son being led around the room by friends who were showing him projects that he had missed on the walls and shelves.

"I hope we didn't disrupt you too much," R.J. said to the teacher.

"Not at all," Mrs. Liebman said.

"I mean, he's not really back to stay," R.J. apologized. "It was just that he forgot his Lego truck and I . . ."

Then Jeffie's eye caught R.J.'s and he smiled a little happy smile at her and waved a little wave. The kids were all jabbering away. Some to Jeffie and some to one another, and the noise level was very high. Even so, R.J. was able to make out the words her son was saying to her over the din.

"Ma, you can go now. I'm gonna be okay."

The mushrooms were just soft enough for her to add

the eggs. She grabbed a plate, and by the time she'd pulled the popped toast out of the toaster and buttered it, it was time to flip the omelette in half and slide it onto a plate. My God, it looked great. Michael would be . . .

"Michael," she said, carrying the tray into the living room. Coffee. She should have put some coffee on the tray. That would have been good. Or at least some orange juice.

"Michael?"

He must have gone into her bedroom. Maybe he'd gone through there to use the bathroom, or . . . "Michael?" No answer. He couldn't possibly think she would follow him into her bedroom and then . . . Maybe this *was* a seduction. Maybe Dinah was right. Maybe Michael just came over to try to get her into bed. It sounded from where she was standing as if drawers were being opened and closed. Maybe she should walk right in there and . . .

"Michael!"

Michael stood wild-eyed and red-faced in the middle of her room.

"Where is it?" he demanded. He looked silly. Like some impersonator on television doing a Dr. Jekyll and Mr. Hyde routine.

"Where is what?" R.J. asked. She was afraid. What in the hell did he want?

"The ring," he said. "The ring my mother gave you. I want the ring back." If he hadn't been so serious, the contorted enraged face would have made her laugh.

"Michael, the ring your mother gave me doesn't exist anymore. Remember? We called it the chandelier and I had it all changed around?" Laugh, she prayed, but he didn't.

"Give me the ring right now or I'll find it myself. That ring is a family heirloom, and you're not going to be in my family," he said through clenched teeth, "so give it to me."

He walked toward the armoire where she kept her jewelry box.

"Michael, stop this," she said.

"Give me the ring!" he screamed.

"Get out of this house, you crazy son-of-a-bitch! If you weren't so crazy you would have gone into your office where I sent the ring by messenger three weeks ago, with a lovely note that said I'm sorry it didn't work out. Well, I'm not sorry. I'm thrilled. I thank God every day for saving me from the brink of disaster by making you too nuts to get married. Because I was so stupid and wanting to get married so much that I would have married you. A mama's boy who is so hung up on his mother that he'll never get married until she dies."

"Shut up," he said menacingly. "Shut up." Now she was really afraid, because she could see she had really touched a nerve with that one. "I'm not hung up on my mother," he said. "I'm not. And she's never going to die, do you hear me?" he screamed, jumping up and down, his fists clenched. "Never, never, never."

With each word he bent his knees and took off from the ground with both feet and landed hard again and again and again. R.J. looked on in shocked silence, and suddenly, when the absurdity of what he had just said registered and at the same time it occurred to her how much he reminded her of what she was sure Rumpelstiltskin must have looked like when the princess guessed his name, she couldn't control the huge laugh that rolled up out of her chest and into his face. It was a combination of relief that she finally saw him as foolish instead of romantic, and the absurdity of what he'd just said, and the way he'd said it . . . She's never going to die. Rumpelstiltskin. Agghhh. Like a child at a solemn event she tried to hold it in, but that made her laugh even harder. Oh, God, she could tell by Michael's flared nostrils that the laughter made his rage even hotter. His face curled into a sneer.

"You're a mean bitch," he said with a little stamp, and then he stormed out of the bedroom, through the living room, and out the front door, which he slammed behind him.

She was shaking, still laughing and simultaneously fighting off tears as she went into the bathroom, washed her face, and ran a brush through her hair. After a few minutes she noticed Jeffie reflected in the mirror. He was wearing his football pajamas, standing sleepy-eyed in the doorway.

"Hi, baby," she said.

"What was all the yellin' about?" he asked.

"Um, it was me. I mean, I just had the TV up too loud," she lied. "I'm sorry I woke you, baby."

"Jeez, what in the heck were you watching?" he asked.

"Oh," she said, putting an arm around him and walking him back to his room, "some really bad show."

*Have Patsy say: I was having a relationship with a great guy, but we broke up because of religious differences. He was a devout coward. He gave me a gorgeous diamond ring and then he wanted it back. Can you believe it? Next time some guy asks for my hand, I think I'll just give him the finger. (Censor will delete, leave it in for now, Patsy will laugh.)*

"Eyyy, R.J.," Harry Elfand said, kicking her door open as usual. His brow was furrowed and he was carrying some typed pages in his right hand and a Styrofoam cup filled with coffee in his left. The steam was rising from the coffee. R.J., never able to shake her role of Nice Jewish Girl, made it fresh for the guys every morning. When she first started working on the show, she occasionally brought in home-made cookies, until one of the other writers accused her of trying to "bake her way to the top." For a minute she thought that Harry was coming in to complain about the coffee. Then he handed her the pages.

"Could ya quit pourin' yer friggin' personal life all over the goddamned script?" he said. "First you give me guys who can't make a commitment, then lines about broken engagements. Lighten up, will ya? Besides, program practices will chew your ass off."

"Sure, Harry," R.J. said.

"I mean, they're sort of funny ... but enough is enough," he said, turning to another page. "Now this one was for Patsy to do with Jerry Lewis. Right?"

"Right."

"Well, he's out. He's got another gig, so can ya rewrite his part for the guest we got to replace him?"

R.J. nodded. "Who is it?"

"The Pointer Sisters."

Harry went back to his office and R.J. stared at the sketch for a few minutes, until the intercom on her telephone buzzed. It was Harry.

"Did I mention that the Pointers will be here at two o'clock to see the pages?"

R.J. looked at her watch. It was one-fifteen.

"Thanks, Harry."

Every day of every week was like that. The staff of writers were all bananas. The pressure to be creative on deadline was getting to them all.

"What's the ending, the goddamned ending of the sketch?" she heard Iggy Richmond say, frantically pacing up and down the hallway.

"Do what you always do," Marty Nussbaum yelled out the door of his office. "Have the guy jump out the window."

"The window," Iggy Richmond hollered back, excitedly. "Brilliant idea! The guy could jump out of the window except for two small factors. The first factor is that there *is* no guy in the sketch. There's two gorillas. And the second factor is that the sketch takes place in the jungle."

"Nuance," Marty Nussbaum replied.

There was a chuckle from one or two of the other cubicles.

"If you guys would shut the fuck up out there and do your work insteada cockin' around," Harry Elfand shouted from his office, a double cubicle because he was the head writer, "maybe we could go home at a decent hour tonight."

R.J. got up from her typing chair and closed her door. Not that it would help very much. The worse the pressure, the louder they got.

Patsy hated the current script. After the read-through she'd been very quiet; then with a flick of her wrist she'd tossed it across the reading table. As it landed in a nearby wastebasket she announced, "This script sucks the hind tit."

Then she stood, aimed her famous breasts toward the door, and marched out.

The writers were surprised. They'd all been congratulating themselves for days about how funny this week's script was. All of them looked down at the table in disappointment, except R.J., who looked at the group of them, amazed at how much they resembled a bunch of little boys. Their expressions reminded her of a group of Jeffie's friends at a birthday party when she told them there would only be birthday cake because she'd forgotten to buy the ice cream.

"Hey," Harry Elfand said. "At least ya can't say our star ain't elegant. I mean, what a way with words that cunt has—no offense there, R.J."

"So what do we do?" Sherman Himmelblau asked.

"We start again."

"From scratch?"

"Unless you want Madame Patsy to say she's not showin' for rehearsals on Wednesday," Elfand said, sucking on an unlit cigar.

"Wednesday—Christ, that's forty-eight hours from now."

"That's right, kiddies. So call your wives and boyfriends, and your wives' boyfriends and your boyfriends' wives, and tell them not to hold dinner for you . . . or anything else for that matter, 'cause we got our work cut out for us."

That was Monday. On Tuesday they came back with little or no sleep and stayed until two Wednesday morning. Finally abandoning the idea of working alone or in teams, they decided they'd get more work done if they all worked together. Wearily, they moved into the conference room. R.J. had inhaled as much cigar smoke in the past day and a half as if she'd smoked a box of stogies herself. And the food that the constantly browbeaten office runner brought in to sustain them throughout the long days was, as Harry Elfand aptly described it, "as tasteless as the jokes get at half past midnight."

By Wednesday at nine A.M., R.J. had chills from exhaustion though she wore her jeans and her black turtleneck sweater. The script had to go to be Xeroxed at noon. She wore no makeup and her hair was limp and dirty. And the worst part was that all of them would probably have to stay all night tonight. Thank God she had Manuela to look after Jeffie.

"So all right," Harry Elfand said. "Where *are* we?"

"We're on the funeral home sketch, Harry," R.J. said. "Where Redd Foxx goes to his father's funeral and the guy in the casket is white."

"Oh, yeah. Okay, let's see ... Nussbaum, this was your sketch. What've you got? Nussbaum!"

Marty Nussbaum's face was on the conference room table and it was clear to all of them that he was asleep. Poor Marty. Of all the writers on the show, he was R.J.'s favorite. He looked like those dolls they used to sell when she was a kid, the ones that were called troll dolls. He had wild long hair that stuck straight up all over his head, and a big belly. And he always wore a silly little smile. The sketches he wrote were invariably bizarre—strange but wonderfully clever. He would write a whole piece in what he called "Nussbaum insults Shakespeare," in which all the characters spoke in iambic pentameter, or he could write a nonsense dialect so cleverly that you were sure the characters were speaking a foreign language. Unlike the other comedy writers, who never laughed at one another's jokes but rather nodded in appreciation if they liked one and mumbled a barely audible "That's funny," Marty Nussbaum laughed when he liked your joke, until he had to pull a handkerchief out of the back pocket of his jeans to wipe the happy tears from his eyes.

"Eyyy, Nussbaum, ya *putz*," Harry Elfand said, but Marty Nussbaum didn't stir. "You doin' the Redd Foxx shit or what?"

Nothing.

"What *is* this asshole? Dead or something?"

No one moved, especially Marty Nussbaum.

"We'll get back to ya, Nussbaum," Harry Elfand said to the top of Marty Nussbaum's long curly wisps of hair. "Who's got the sketch with the Pointer Sisters?"

"Harry," R.J. said. "Shouldn't one of us see if ... Marty's okay?"

"What are you, Florence Jewish Mother Nightingale over there? Sure, why dontcha give him mouth-ta-mouth resuscitation too?"

R.J. stood and walked over to Marty Nussbaum's chair. "Marty," she said softly, touching his back.

"He's out like a light," Eddie Levy said.

"What about the Pointer Sisters?" Harry Elfand asked. "I need someone to write the intro to their song. Now who's it gonna be?"

"Holy shit," Iggy Richmond said, as R.J. gently lifted Marty's head and the others were able to see his face. "Nussbaum is dead."

"Christ," said Sherman Himmelblau.

"Well then," Harry Elfand said, lighting his cigar, "I guess that means he's not writin' the Pointer Sisters' sketch. Levy, why don't *you* take a pass at it?"

Marty Nussbaum's funeral was held at the Writers Guild theater, and the eulogies were funny and moving. "Marty Nussbaum was a method writer," Harry Elfand said, standing at the podium wearing a solemn face. It was the first time anyone had ever seen Harry in a tie. "I mean, he really threw himself into his work. I asked him to write a funeral sketch for this week's show, and just to get the essence of it, he died."

R.J. sat in the last row of the theater watching as the various comedy writers, each one trying to top the one before, paid silly, zany, sometimes brilliant tributes to the funny little man. The writers, usually so critical of one another, were laughing at each other's Marty Nussbaum stories in spite of themselves.

At Arthur Misner's funeral no one had laughed. The service had been punctuated by Jeffie's anguished cries as he held tightly to R.J. His tiny face, soaked with tears, was pressed against her skirt. Yiskadal v'yis Kadosh, the mourner's prayer. "My daddy," he cried every now and then. "My daddy." The sound of the little boy's pain bounced off the walls of the sanctuary and pierced the hearts of the onlookers, who clucked their tongues, making pitying noises.

The coffin had been closed for Arthur's service, but before it was closed, the funeral director advised the family that they could go into a private viewing room, "to say their last goodbyes." Arthur's parents had gone in first. R.J. had stood frozen, watching them, knowing it would be her turn, and Jeffie's, next. Should Jeffie go? She was afraid the sight of Arthur in a coffin would be more than *she* could stand. How could a little boy. . . ? Arthur's parents emerged from the viewing room weeping, arms around each other's waists, as if to hold each other up. Arthur's mother was moaning quietly.

"Maybe you should take Jeffie in now," someone said to R.J.

Slowly, feeling everyone watching the two of them, R.J. held her son's hand and moved toward the door of the room where Arthur lay dead. But before they reached the doorway, Jeffie squeezed his mother's hand tightly. When she looked down at him his eyes held hers, and with great conviction he said, "I don't need to go in there. I know what my dad looked like."

"One time Nussbaum wrote a blackout that kind of summarized his point of view," Eddie Levy said from the podium. "It was a family sitting around at a dinner table, and all the food was on the table, and the father of the family said, 'Thank you, God, for the food we're about to eat, and for the roof over our heads.' And all of a sudden, the roof collapses and falls onto the food."

A giggle fluttered through the audience.

"I'm worried that when Nussbaum got up there, the big guy mighta held that against him."

A bigger giggle.

"My son told me, a few nights before he was murdered," Arthur's father had told R.J., taking her aside at Arthur's funeral, "that you two were having problems. Maybe if you'd been at home instead of running off to New York, this never would have happened." R.J. had frozen in her tracks. Wasn't the loss of Arthur pain enough for all of them?

"Either that or your grandchild would have been dead too," she snapped, but then her own grief replaced her anger and she wanted to explain. To somebody. To anybody. Even this poor sad man who was so stunned by the loss of his son that he wanted to lash out at everyone. "I wasn't really running off. I thought that maybe if I . . ."

Arthur's father had turned his back and walked away. He rarely spoke to R.J. now, except to ask her if he could speak to Jeffie when he called the boy every month or so.

"Will those of you who have to go back to work please sign the guest book for Mrs. Nussbaum, and for those of you who would like to come to the Nussbaum residence for a nice piece corned beef, there are printed directions being handed out in the lobby."

That night R.J. quoted as many of the funny remarks from Marty Nussbaum's funeral as she could remember to Dinah. Robert the dentist was at some convention in San Francisco, so Dinah brought the twins over and joined R.J. and Jeffie for dinner.

"You look awful," Dinah said. "No man, a job that takes up your whole life. What in the hell are you going to do with yourself, R.J.?"

"Di, it's a terrific job," R.J. said.

"So terrific it kills people. Besides, I'm more concerned about your social life than your work. Ever since Willie-Shoemaker-without-the-horse dumped you, you haven't so much as gone to the movies with a member of the opposite sex."

"I don't want to," R.J. answered. "There's no one out there. Why should I bother?"

"That's what *I* said until one day I had a toothache that required endodontia. And poof. I made an appointment and there was Robert with his cute furry fingers in my mouth, and we were both in love."

"Inspiring," R.J. said, wishing she hadn't given Manuela the night off as she looked at the sinkful of dishes.

"Tomorrow, any day, any minute you could meet someone. But not if you stay cooped up at the office and then come back here and lock yourself in. You have to get out into the world."

"Ma, I have homework," one of the twins whined.

"I know," Dinah said. "We're leaving."

Cooped up. That's exactly what she was. At the office and then at home, R.J. thought, and it was just the way she wanted it. She didn't want to date. She didn't want to have to tell her story to some new guy and then have him tell his story to her and then go through all of the first date politeness and then ... no. She was going to wait a while—a long while—before she put herself through the horrors of dating again. Maybe forever. Maybe she'd just become one of those women who was so driven by her career that she didn't even think about romance. Yes. She liked that idea. Except for the bleak outlook it offered her son. Jeffie deserved to have a man in his life. Someone constant. Someone who would be there for him. Not someone who, if it didn't work out with R.J., would be gone. And never again would she introduce him to someone who made false promises.

Once, a few weeks after the engagement party, Michael, Jeffie, and R.J. had gone out to lunch. R.J. had looked on happily as Michael and Jeffie talked about airplanes. C-49's and F-18's. Things she knew nothing about. She could not have been more delighted that her son and her fiancé seemed glad to be with each other. After lunch all of them, wordlessly reluctant to have their time together end, piled into the car, and Michael took a drive out toward Malibu. For some reason he took a right turn off the Pacific Coast Highway into the Serra Retreat neighborhood. At the end of one street there was a house with a FOR SALE sign stuck into its front lawn. What a house. Red used brick and a shake roof, and green grass that was dotted everywhere with brightly colored flowers. All of it framed by two enormous oak trees. It was so perfect it didn't look real. More like a symbol. The dream house for the dream family.

"Maybe that's the house we'll be buying soon," Michael had said.

R.J. remembered looking at Jeffie in the rearview mirror. He was gazing at the house with such longing it pained her. The memory of it still hurt her because she'd failed him. She had failed to make everything okay.

Friday afternoon was brown with muddy rain, and the car-pool line crept forward inch by inch. R.J. had been there for thirty minutes and at last her Mustang was three cars from the front. Finally she saw Jeffie separate himself from the sea of yellow hooded slickers and run, splashing water around him, toward her car. Breaking the school's rules of an orderly exit.

"Jerry Vogel's mother came, and Lefty went with them," he announced, cheeks red, and tossed his books into the back seat. As he sat, his wet slicker squeaked against the seat of the beat-up yellow Mustang. "So we can go straight to our appointment."

He was excited. R.J. could tell. The appointment was at Big Brothers. R.J. had made the call asking for the appointment yesterday. She and Jeffie would be interviewed by a social worker who matched men who had volunteered their time, with fatherless boys.

"Whaddya think she'll ask us, Mom?" Jeffie asked, as

if he feared there would be a test he might not be able to pass.

"Just questions about your interests and hobbies, I guess." That answer seemed to hold him for a while. He looked out the window at the rain, quiet for a long time.

"Will my big brother be there too?"

"Not yet, honey. It may take a while for them to find one for you. We may have to wait."

The United Way building was a funny-looking two-story Fifties-style structure. The rain started coming down in a torrent as R.J. pulled into the parking lot. She found a parking place and maneuvered the Mustang into it. She stopped the car and left the radio on, and she and Jeffie sat listening to the Beatles singing "Michelle" until the rain slowed. Then they got out of the car and ran to the front entrance. R.J. felt the welcome warmth and could smell the overworked heating system as she pushed open the glass doors. Jeffie ran ahead of her, following the arrows drawn on cardboard and tacked haphazardly along the hallway on the way to the Big Brothers waiting room. It was a tiny room. There were two chairs with wrought-iron armrests and orange plastic seats, and there was also a Formica side table on which a chartreuse lamp sat.

Jeffie took his slicker off, hung it on the back of one of the chairs, and sat tapping his damp-sneakered foot on the linoleum floor in an impatient gesture, glancing every few seconds at the door of the social worker's office. Now they could hear voices on the other side of the door and the knob turned, as if someone was about to open it. When someone did, it was a small man in his sixties. He was wearing a damp-looking plaid raincoat and carried an umbrella over his arm. He was followed by a smiling red-headed woman of fifty.

"Bye, Abe," the woman said. "Thank you."

Jeffie stood nervously as the woman turned her attention to him and extended her hand. "Jeff," she said, "I'm Anne Schaffer." He took the woman's hand and shook it, and R.J. thought to herself that Jeffie looked younger and more vulnerable than ever. Anne turned to R.J. and said, "Welcome," and mother and son followed her into an office furnished in the same wrought-iron and orange plastic decor.

"Well," the woman said when they were seated. It was

an opening for conversation but Jeffie was uncomfortable and he looked down at the floor. As if she knew to go on talking instead of waiting, Anne Schaffer said, "When she called me on the phone, your mother told me she thought you should have a big brother. What do *you* think?"

Jeffie shrugged and didn't look up. R.J. could tell that he was afraid. Afraid that if he said the wrong thing they might not give him a big brother at all.

"Guess so," he answered.

"You know that big brothers come in all shapes and sizes and types," Anne said gently. "Like that man Abe who just left here. He's a big brother." Jeffie's lower lip protruded a bit at that and R.J. knew it was because That Man Abe was not what he had in mind.

"So just for the sake of imagination let me ask you this. If you could create him," Anne said, "make him anything you wanted, how would you like your big brother to be?"

Jeffie shrugged, and still wouldn't look up. R.J. wanted to rush over and hug him, but her eyes met Anne's and she sat very still.

"Good athlete," he said softly. Arthur had been a wonderful athlete. "Likes video games. Fun. You know." Now he looked up.

"I do know," Anne said, "and I'm going to try to find you one. Right now there are lots more boys who need big brothers than there are big brothers. But I'll see what I can do."

She asked him questions about school. What classes he liked and disliked. His friends. When he seemed to begin to warm up to her, to relax, R.J. relaxed, too, and thought about Arthur. For months after he died she had continued to feel his presence in the house. She would be cooking or reading, when suddenly, from nowhere, she would be certain that she'd caught sight of him just out of the farthest corner of her eye. But when she turned, of course, he was gone.

"Arthur," she had said aloud one day, feeling foolish but eerily as though he were really around. "Don't rush away. I could use your advice about so many things. Like how to handle your father, and what to do about a medical insurance policy for Manuela, and whether or not I should sell the house to pay off all the debts from the business." That particular morning it was chilly outside, the chill that comes right after a rain, and she had stood in her living room hugging herself to keep warm, looking out at the view of the hills. "Arthur, it's hard not having anyone to talk to. No one to share all the questions I have about Jeffie. I mean, sometimes I wonder if I'm doing a good job with him and I wish that . . ." Then she sighed. This was bananas. Over the edge. Probably her cousin Mimi's husband the psychiatrist would tell her it was something every widow goes through. She should go and turn up the heat and sit for a while and read. Arthur was murdered. Dead. Gone. And she was left. Left to make the decisions about his father and medical insurance and the house alone. That was just how it was. And as far as whether or not she was doing a good job where Jeffie was concerned, no one else could tell her that. She would just have to continue to do her best and hope it was enough. Then, just as she had been about to turn away from the window, right above the houses on stilts that jutted out on a nearby hillside, there appeared the beautiful arc of a rainbow. R.J. had looked at it for a moment and then smiled. She was sure it was her answer. From Arthur.

"Thanks, Art," she had said. "I miss you so much. Thanks for stopping by."

Now, Anne the social worker was summarizing.

"Your big brother won't ever really replace your dad, or make you not miss him, but he can be a great friend to you, so that's what we'll try for. Okay?"

Jeffie nodded.

"Remember, too, that it may take a long time for us to find the right match for you," Anne warned. "But when we do, it'll be worth it."

They all got to their feet.

"I'll be on the lookout for a nice warm man who will come over and take you out once a month, and you can talk things over with him, and call him if you need a friend at any time, and know that he's reliable and there for you."

Jeffie nodded, and R.J. smiled and said, "While you're at it, could you find one of those for me?"

They all laughed.

Jeffie galloped down the steps ahead of R.J. and through the lobby, pushed the door open, and in a gesture she'd never seen from him before, held it open for her. The rain outside had slowed to a fine mist, and Jeffie walked ahead, deliberately and happily sloshing through puddles like Gene Kelly in *Singin' in the Rain*. In fact, as he reached the Mustang he extended his arms and did a happy twirl.

Thank God, R.J. thought. This is the happiest I've seen him in years. Thank God I thought to do this for him. Why did it take me so long?

Jeffie pulled the passenger door open and slid into the seat. R.J. opened her door, shuffled through her purse for her keys, found them, and was about to get into the car when something caught her eye in the sky above Westwood. It was a rainbow.

*Have Patsy say: It seems to me there are two kinds of single
men in the world. There's the kind that can't make a
commitment to a woman. Who fears gettin' married like it
was the plague, and . . . (SHE THINKS ABOUT IT)*

*Actually, now that I think about it, there's only one
kind of single man in the world.*

*You think I'm suspicious of men? The other day I was
in the doctor's office and when the doctor told me to take all
my clothes off, I said, "I'm not that kinda girl," and
stormed outta there. Now how could I do that to kindly old
Doc Milgrom? He's a fine man and a wonderful podiatrist.*

*I told my girlfriend Sally that I wanted a man who
could make me hear bells ring, so she fixed me up with a
guy who looked like the Hunchback of Notre Dame.*

*I wanted to meet a man who was safe and stable. So
far the ones I meet are only safe in a stable.*

*I met a man at a party who was like fine French food.
Heavy on the sauce. (You need a vacation, girl. You're
losing your grip.)*

Hobart Fineburg was a voice-over actor. That meant he
did radio commercials and the voices of Mattel toys that
talked. He starred in two Saturday morning cartoon series
at Hanna-Barbera studios. In one he played a dog, and in
the other he portrayed a villain of a thousand disguises.

Despite Hobart's alleged brilliance, however, R.J. thought they all had the same voice. And she'd been in show business long enough to know going out with an actor was a big mistake.

"Hey, it's just dinner. You don't have to marry the guy," Eddie Levy said. Hobart was Eddie Levy's friend. He came to have lunch one day with Eddie and spotted R.J. He had dark curly hair that needed a haircut and nervous eyes, and even though he wore a coat and tie and some reasonably nice gray pants, with them, probably for effect, he wore dirty sneakers. One of the laces on the sneakers looked precariously loose. As soon as R.J. noticed it, she began to worry that it would come untied any minute. She could tell right away that Hobart liked her when he and Eddie stopped by her office to ask if she wanted to join them at Canter's for lunch, because Hobart, whom Eddie called Hobie, laughed at everything she said, and none of it was funny.

"C'mon, R.J., it'll do you good," Eddie said.

"No thanks, Eddie. I'm on a huge diet. If I went to Canter's, I'd just order a number eight, and then be sorry later."

Hobie laughed.

"So you'll just have a salad," Eddie said.

"What's the point of going to a deli and having a salad?" R.J. asked as she rolled a piece of paper into the typewriter. She had work to do. Hobie laughed at that too.

"You'll keep us company," Eddie urged.

"Nope. Anyway, I have to finish Patsy At Home."

Hobie only giggled at that.

"Nice meeting you," R.J. added, hoping that would give them the hint and they would leave her office.

"Want me to bring you back a number eight?" Hobie asked, grinning. He was sort of cute in a stupid way.

"It's just dinner. Hey, you don't have to marry the guy," Eddie Levy reminded her when he got back from lunch alone. "So I gave him your number."

Hobie called her that night, and they met for an early dinner in a restaurant that was halfway between their houses.

"You're great," he kept saying. "I mean, you're so terrific. What I mean to say is"—and then he sang, full out, with no self-consciousness and in a very pleasant voice—"In this world, of ordinary people, extraordinary people, I'm glad there is you." She smiled. Maybe Hobie was okay. He ordered a nice French red wine and they talked. They'd both been poor as children. They both thought they'd picked show business as a way to escape drab childhoods. "Small world, isn't it?" Hobart sang. He knew the lyrics from every song imaginable. He fit them into whatever they were talking about, and sang them into the conversation. It was sweet. Once he looked long into her eyes and said, "When we have a baby, let's name him Irwin. I always liked the name Irwin." There was something endearing about that.

After the third glass of wine he told her that when he was very young he'd been a loser on *Name That Tune.* The original *Name That Tune,* where you had to run up and pull a bell cord before the other contestant in order to win the right to answer. Though he'd been certain that the song was "Sailor Boys Have Talked to Me in English," he tripped on the way to the bell cord, and his opponent, an elderly kindergarten teacher, beat him to the bell. "Sailor Boys," screamed the schoolteacher, jumping up and down as the mortified Hobie lay on the cold studio floor. The old lady won. He'd never told that to anyone, he said to R.J., who put a conciliatory hand over his to soothe him. He took her hand and kissed it and said, "Thank you." After the fourth glass of wine he admitted that the *Name That Tune* story was a lie.

He called her five times after that night. Every time he did she turned down his offer of dinner. He was too crazy. Certifiably *meshugge.*

"Go have dinner with him," Eddie Levy said to her before the meeting started on Monday. "Because every time you turn him down he calls *me.*"

"*You* have dinner with him," she answered.

"Me? What are you? Crazy?"

"Hey, Eddie. It's just dinner. You don't have to marry the guy," she said, and stood to get him to leave her office. But when Hobie called her for the sixth time, he caught her on an off night and she accepted.

"Let's tell each other things about ourselves that are really intimate," he said to her over the salad.

I'm a comedy writer, R.J. thought. I should be able to get out of this one.

"You first" was all she could think of.

"I like to live dangerously," he said, and then drank

some more wine. She knew he was going to tell her some story, so she didn't say a word.

"When I was in my teens I used to go down to the Lower East Side to score a nickel bag of dope. And after I had it hidden inside my coat, I'd purposely walk past a policeman, just to feel my heart beat, thinking he might catch me and it would ruin my whole life."

*Oy vey*, she thought. Why did I agree to see him again? She could see in his eyes that he knew she thought his story was nothing, and that he was going to try again.

"I go out with a lot of women, and each time I meet a new one I always tell her I want to have a baby with her and what we should name the baby. Then I try and remember which woman goes with which baby name, without screwing up. Like you're Irwin. Right?"

The next time he called her she lied and told him she was seeing someone else very seriously and it wouldn't be fair to the new guy. It was another few months after that, that she accepted the fix-up from Dinah. With the psychiatrist from Robert's building. She met him at a sushi restaurant on Pico Boulevard. He was gorgeous. There was no doubt about that. Tall and blond and tan with aqua eyes. He drove a black Mercedes and wore a black leather jacket, and he smelled great, and when he smiled he had a mouth full of gorgeous straight white teeth. He was, he told her proudly, a sensational tennis player, an avid skier, and a long-distance runner. This was no mere psychiatrist. He was a Jungian analyst. And he loved children, and he hoped to meet hers one day. And most of all to have some of his own. Oh and by the way, he had eschewed (his word) current popular literature to read the classics, most of which he was rereading, since he'd been an undeniably great scholar in both undergraduate and graduate school.

R.J. had a headache. She was grateful when the psychiatrist excused himself to make a phone call. The headache was pounding and she had a screaming urge to run outside, jump into her car, and leave before he came back. A fat man at another table—whose wife was obviously nagging at him about something—was looking over at R.J. When his wife turned away from him, pouting, he winked a conspiratorial wink at her.

He knows, she thought. The fat man knows that I'm sitting here as miserable as he is. When the psychiatrist returned, before he could lift his arm to gesture to the waiter for another round, R.J. grabbed it.

"Listen," she said, "you're great, you really are, but I've got to . . . I'm not feeling very . . . Would you mind if I . . ." and she turned and was out the door of the restaurant, into the cool evening, and finally inside the safety of her old Mustang, driving home. Laughing. A panicky laugh.

"He was perfect," she said to herself out loud. "The perfect man, and I hated him." And that made her laugh even more, certain that she was probably going over some edge of sanity.

Then there was the guy who called because he'd noticed her at the Writers Guild meeting. He wrote movies of the week and had seen R.J.'s credit roll by on Patsy's show, and would she meet him for a cup of coffee? Sure, why not? He looked like Woody Allen, and later, when she thought about it, she realized that he was probably trying to be funny. People always tried to be funny with her because they knew she wrote comedy, so when she walked into the Hamburger Hamlet and said, "Hi, I'm R.J.," he said, "Let's get this out of the way right now. Do you have herpes?" She never even sat down, just turned and walked out the door to her car, wondering if he'd call after her apologetically, saying that he'd only been trying to make a joke. He didn't.

The divorce lawyer who asked her to come over and "do psychedelic mushrooms." The studio executive she went to lunch with, who asked if she would make love with him on the floor of his office while he talked to his wife on the speakerphone.

"You'll love it," he told R.J., his breathing changing audibly at the thought. "She has no idea. Sometimes I tell her I'm lifting weights. Of course *you* can't make a sound, but that's what's great."

No more. She wouldn't put herself through it again. She'd give up dating. Become the world's first Jewish comedy-writing nun. It was hard enough getting through a day at work. The ratings were slipping and Patsy was defensive and edgy, and "the boys," as Harry Elfand referred to the writing staff, were getting more and more neurotic. Patsy was threatening to fire everyone. Though it was a threat she'd made in the past and never carried out, it was unnerving to the staff, all of whom had families to support.

Thank God for Jeffie, R.J. thought. He kept her sane, and responsible and laughing. She didn't need anyone else in her life but him. And then she met Barry Litmann.

Barry was round and bearded, with lots of bushy hair, and he dressed in silly outfits. Costumes. Like a tux jacket over a Six Flags Magic Mountain T-shirt and jeans. Harry Elfand had hired him to replace Marty Nussbaum, only Barry would be in a higher position than Marty had been. He would co-head-write the show with Harry. Take on some of Harry's responsibilities—"So I can dust off my golf clubs," Harry Elfand said. The thought of Harry playing golf made R.J. laugh. Barry Litmann said he liked her laugh. When she handed her sketch in at the end of the day, he liked that too.

"You're funny," he said. "Not just pretty."

R.J. nodded, a kind of thank-you nod. Coming on. He's coming on to me, she thought. He called her on Friday night and asked her if she'd like to come over for dinner on Saturday. Only he didn't say *dinner;* he said something like "dinner and dancing," and soon they were giggling on the phone like old friends, and she asked him what he was going to cook, and when he described the few things he was able to cook, she said she'd make the dinner and bring it. Chicken in a pot. It was her specialty.

Jokes were his, and boyishness, and he made her laugh so much while they were sitting in his tiny kitchen, eating the chicken in a pot by candlelight, that sometimes she had to put the fork down and cover her face with her napkin because she knew her cheeks must be flushed and her eye makeup must be running and she was embarrassed. And before she left at ten o'clock he held her hand and asked her if she'd come back for dinner another night. She promised she would and drove home remembering all the funny things he'd said, grinning.

Every evening that week they stayed at work after the others had left, and talked. And laughed. He had grown up in Hollywood, the youngest in a family of five brothers, all of them funny. Their father, a former silent film comic, would dispense the most love to whichever brother told the best joke last. It was probably apocryphal, he told her, but an older brother swore that when he learned to talk, Barry's first sentence was "Didja hear the one about the rabbi?"

Always on. That was the only way to describe him.

Always performing. Sometimes it was exhausting. But it was a welcome change from every man she'd ever known. Especially Michael Rappaport. Silly. Barry would say anything that came into his head. And most of it was hilarious.

One night after everyone was gone and she was leaving the office, he came in and closed the door and took her in his arms. He was wearing a Mickey Mouse sweat shirt with a tie.

"I want you to come over for dinner and dancing this Saturday night. Will you?" he asked.

"You bet." She grinned. So darling. As he gave her a hug, she tried to remember what day it was, and how long she'd have to wait until Saturday. Three days? Two? It felt good to be held. Very good.

"Oh, and by the way," he whispered into her hair, his beard tickling the side of her face and her ear, "I'm cooking."

"I can tell," she said, and they both laughed.

On Saturday night after Jeffie had gone to sleep she drove to Barry's house, where Barry was waiting with a spaghetti dinner and low lights and music. After dinner they made love. This man was not a candidate for marriage, or fatherhood, and she wanted marriage more than ever, and a father for her boy. But he was silly and sexy and exciting to be with and maybe this was a necessary respite from her pursuit of forever relationships.

The following Monday at work, Patsy was on the warpath. Something about the writers always making her look like a dumb broad in all the sketches and she wanted to look smart.

"Hey, we're writers, not Svengalis," Harry Elfand said. Everyone held his breath. "The reason you look like a dumb broad is because that's what you are," he blurted out. A few of the writers closed the doors to their cubicles to block out the sound of the fight in Harry's office.

"I'm too rich for this, bitch," he shouted. "I don't need you, or this show, and I'm not puttin' my writers through this anymore. So do this script or *I* walk."

The writers heard a long silence. Harry saw a tense forced smile on Patsy's face.

"Then hit the road, and take your writers with ya," Patsy said.

"Yeah?" Harry said, talking directly into her perfectly made-up face. "And what're you gonna do? You're gonna stand there on television with nothin' to say, like the dumb dipshit broad that you are. So you know what I'm gonna do now as a favor to you? I'm gonna walk outta here, Patsy, like you and me didn't have this discussion, see? And then you can go talk to your lawyer and talk to your agent and talk to your squeeze of the moment, and when you figure out what it'll cost to replace me you'll reconsider and apologize." He walked out, went to lunch, and left Patsy standing in his office.

For the next two weeks the office was filled with tension. No one was getting any work done. The writers were on the phone with agents and producers of other shows, putting out feelers for jobs. Everyone was depressed. Except for Barry and R.J. Neither could repress a smile when the other walked by. This man was a real wacko, now R.J. knew for sure. To begin with he drove to work every day in what used to be a school bus. He lived with three dogs in a huge house in the Valley that had a tennis court, even though he didn't play tennis, "because," he told R.J. one night, "one of the dogs is thinking of taking it up." From the street the house looked as if it were haunted, or at least abandoned, because Barry never mowed the lawn, and the living room drapes were always drawn.

Inside, the house was all whimsy. *Battlestar Galactica* sheets on the bed, a working telephone booth in the hallway outside the kitchen, and on the grand piano, which nobody ever played, there was a neon sign spelling out his name that blinked on and off all day and all night. Barry. Barry. Barry. Still, R.J. was glad to be there with him. At least she knew he was never going to make promises to her and Jeffie that he couldn't keep.

On the Monday after their last date, which had been on a beautiful Saturday afternoon at the Venice kite festival, R.J. sat at the office working on the monologue for Patsy when the door burst open, Harry Elfand-style. Harry had a strange look on his face.

"Listen, I know this is real unfair, and I know you've been through a lot of shit in your life," he began. Then he closed the door behind him and sat on the corner of her desk, and in R.J.'s stomach she knew this was serious. "Anyhow, you didn't do nothin' wrong," Elfand said. "But you're a scapegoat. See, Patsy decided a long time ago that the reason we needed a woman writer on the show in the first place was so she wouldn't come off lookin' like what a bunch of guys think a woman is like. If you get my meaning. She said she wanted a woman's point of view, so we hired you. Well now she hates the scripts and she's gotta blame somebody, and *I've* got a long-term, run-of-the-show, ironclad contract . . . so it ain't gonna be me. And shit—''

"Harry, didn't you stick up for me? I write better jokes than any man on your staff."

"She doesn't care."

"You didn't defend me," R.J. said. "You didn't." Now she was standing and pulling open her desk drawers, emptying the contents into her briefcase. "And I suppose Barry didn't either."

"Barry ain't here. He's out with the flu or somethin'. Hey, the Writers Guild says she has to pay you for the next two months anyway."

"Big deal," R.J. said, slamming drawers. "I've got a kid to support. A career to worry about."

"Aww, c'mon," Harry said. "Everybody knows your old man left you a bundle when he kicked off."

"Get out of here, Harry," R.J. shrieked, collecting the framed photographs of Jeffie she had placed on every windowsill and shelf. In his soccer uniform, in his Little League uniform, with her at Disneyland, with Arthur at the Santa Monica pier.

Arthur. Left her a bundle. What a joke. She was still going to court nearly once a month at her own expense to fight greedy business partners and numerous associates who were trying to attach the estate for fees R.J. was certain were trumped up. And now she was out of work with—big deal!—two months' pay. Harry Elfand took one last look at her. "Sorry," he said, and backed out, closing the door.

R.J. sighed and sat on her typing chair for a moment to sort out her thoughts. The spring creaked as she swiveled back and forth, wondering what in the hell she was going to do next. There was no doubt she'd keep writing. That's all she knew how to do. So she'd get another job on another show. Start again with a new staff of people, a new star. She'd be fine. And she wouldn't take it personally. It was just business. Then why was she ready to cry?

Was it because the romance with Barry was starting to go bad too? For some strange reason, while she was in the water with Jeffie at the beach on Saturday, he just disappeared. Without saying goodbye. She thought he'd gone for a walk or to the men's room or to get something to drink, but hours went by and he didn't come back. And he hadn't answered her phone calls since then. She had even considered calling the police, but she was afraid if it was nothing, if it was just that being at the beach with her and her son made him nervous, then he would think she was an hysteric.

Now she knew that he hadn't been kidnapped, because he had obviously called in sick to Harry. So it was she he was avoiding. Never mind. It didn't matter. He didn't matter. What mattered was her child and her work. She was good at her work and nobody could take that away from her. So she wouldn't write for Patsy Dugan. Maybe she wouldn't even write for television anymore. She would take a shot at writing fiction. A novel. The thought was overwhelming. Maybe she'd start with short stories. Yes, she would, she thought, as she pulled a folder of her sketches out of her file drawer and put it into her briefcase. She'd try writing short stories first and see if she could sell one.

When her things were all packed, she stood in the doorway of her little cubicle of an office and stared. She had loved that job. Loved being one of the few women writers in town who could sit in a room and write gags with the best of the guys. And now, she was out on her ass.

Maybe she should call Dinah. Dinah would tell her it was all for the best; now she could start writing real things. Big things. Like movies and books. She picked up the phone. Short stories, she thought. About what? Something that really moves me. Arthur's death. No. She knew she wasn't ready to write about that yet. Instead of dialing Dinah's number she dialed Barry's number at home. It rang three or four times. Then Barry answered.

"Barry?" R.J. said. "Thank God. I've been so worried." He told her he'd had to leave the beach suddenly on Saturday because he didn't feel well. He sounded very cool and distant, and as if he couldn't wait to get off the phone. By the time he told her what had really happened Saturday, she knew what the first sentence of her short story would be.

# CHICKEN IN A POT

## a short story by R.J. Misner

The only problem with Jackie Schwartz was that he couldn't go outside. Inside, though, he was great. Cute and sexy, warm and nice, with the best sense of humor she had ever known.

When Molly first met him he lived in a big house in the Valley where the grass on the lawn had grown very tall because Jackie couldn't go outside to mow it. He had three Chihuahuas, Patty, Maxine, and Laverne, and he drove an old school bus to work. During the first two months Molly knew Jackie, the school bus was vandalized, Maxine the Chihuahua was run over by a hit-and-run driver, and Patty the Chihuahua was eaten by a raccoon. Molly thought it was a string of real bad luck. Jackie knew it was life's way of telling him that the world was a dangerous ugly place, and that he was right to stay indoors. So he did. The grass on his lawn grew taller and Jackie Schwartz felt certain that inside his house was the only place to be.

The truth was that he really did go outside. Five days a week. As long as it took him to get to the school bus, which he parked in the driveway at the side of his house, and out of the school bus and into the office building where he worked. And then again out of the office building in the evening, and directly into his house, which he never left on the weekends. Just stayed inside until it was time to go back to work again on Monday.

He earned lots of money at his job, so he never had to go out to everyday places like the market or the cleaner's. The cleaning lady who came to his house three times a week was paid extra to do that for him. Also, there were many girls at work whom he could phone and ask to come over to his house for "dinner and dancing," as he called it. And they did. So Jackie never lacked for company or someone he could "laugh into bed," which is how he described his technique, since his funny personality was his ultimate charm and he knew it.

Then one day at work he met Molly. She had sad eyes, as if she had just been through some terrible disaster, and he met her when she came into his office to ask a question of his partner Martin. But when she opened the door her eyes met Jackie's, and even though she talked to Martin, asked him her question, got her answer, and left, the whole time she was in the office her eyes had been locked with Jackie's. After she walked out and the door was closed, Jackie said to Martin: "I'm in love with that girl. Who is she?"

Martin gave Jackie Molly's telephone number and Jackie called her and made her laugh on the phone, even though he knew that he didn't really have to work that hard because he could tell that she liked him already. Soon Molly became one of the girls who would drive over to Jackie's house for "dinner and dancing."

It was wonderful for both of them. Molly was not only a great laugher at Jackie's jokes but she had a few jokes of her own to tell him, and of all the girls who had cooked dinner for him over the years, her dinners were the best. Especially her chicken in a pot. She had learned to cook when she was married, she told him. And her eyes, which were sad even when the rest of her was laughing, told him not to ask what had happened to her marriage.

Usually she crept out very early in the mornings because she had a son who was being cared for by a housekeeper, and Molly liked to get home before her son woke up and have breakfast waiting for him and then drive him to school on her way to work. And after she was gone, Jackie would lie alone in the bed and think about marrying her. And what it would be like to have her move out of her house and into his house. She would, of course, bring her son. There was lots of room for him. He was eleven years old and would probably love Laverne, the only surviving Chihuahua. And they would all be busy at work and at school every day, and every night they would have chicken in a pot and laugh at Jackie's jokes and Molly's jokes. It was a good idea.

One night when Jackie and Molly were in bed together after making love, clinging happily to each other, telling jokes and laughing, Molly said, "Tomorrow, Bobby and I are going to pick you up at two o'clock and we're going to drive down to the kite festival at Venice Beach." Bobby was Molly's son.

Jackie tried to keep the smile on his face and not reveal to Molly what he was thinking, which was that there wasn't a chance of his going to Venice Beach, or any beach for that matter, because beaches were outside and he didn't go outside except to get in and out of his car to go to or from work.

"I'm busy tomorrow," he told her.

"Oh," she said, her sad eyes looking even sadder. "I thought it would be a good chance for you to meet Bobby."

If Jackie was going to marry Molly someday, he really *ought* to meet her son. Maybe Molly thought that his not wanting to go to the kite festival meant that he didn't want to meet her son, and that wasn't true at all. But all he said was: "Sorry. Busy tomorrow."

She didn't pressure him. Not even one question. She just kissed him a little kiss on the cheek and soon they were asleep.

In the morning when Jackie woke up, Molly was gone. He looked at the clock and knew that by now she must be at her house having breakfast with Bobby, probably talking excitedly about the kite festival.

Kites. Jackie had never even owned one, but in the days when he was still going outside he used to see them in the sky at the park and imagine what it would be like to be able to lie on top of one while it floated around. Then, after he imagined that, he pictured looking down at the park from the kite and that thought made him dizzy and nauseated and afraid. Dizzy and nauseated and afraid with a very dry mouth and throbbing palms. The way he felt now at the thought of going outside, to the beach, to the kite festival. His heart was pounding and he put the pillow over his head to stop the images that came and made him feel panicky.

Molly. She was so sweet and so beautiful. Light-years better than any woman he'd ever known. Why would she ever marry him anyway? A man who spent his life locked in his house or his office. This was a test, he thought. This was God's way of seeing if Jackie could and would take some steps to make himself well.

Venice Beach. To go to Venice Beach with Molly and her son. Maybe he could handle it. Try to relax, look straight ahead . . . No.

At noon the phone rang. It was Molly. Even her voice was sweet.

"Ooh, good," she said. "You're home. Thought I'd call to see if you'd change your mind about coming with us. I'm packing a picnic."

A picnic with sweet Molly and her son.

"No," he said. "I have a meeting. I was just on my way out."

"Ahh, sorry, hon," she said. "We'll miss you."

After he put the phone down, Jackie walked all around his big house. In and out of each room. Into his den, where he sometimes worked on projects at home, and into the guest bedroom, which was the room he was thinking would make a great room for Bobby, and into the living room, where the drapes were always drawn. He opened them now. Just a crack. It was the first time he had looked out that window for a long time, and he was surprised to see how tall the grass on the front lawn had grown, because he hardly ever looked at the front of the house. Almost always he drove his car into the side driveway and entered through the side door.

Molly, he thought. Her laugh. Her jokes. Her chicken in a pot. The way she liked to sleep at night curled up so close to him. He was in love with Molly.

"Molly," he said into the phone when she answered, wishing for an instant that he had made an error in dialing and the voice on the other end would now tell him: "You have the wrong number," so he would be able to change his mind.

"Jackie, hi! Was your meeting called off?"

"Yes," he got himself to say. "Pick me up at two."

"Hooray," she shouted. "See you soon, sweetheart."

Sweetheart. He had made the right choice. He would handle it. He knew he could. This was God's way of telling him it was time to leave the house.

He dressed very carefully. Madras Bermuda shorts and a T-shirt that said HÄAGEN-DAZS on the front and RUM RAISIN on the back. Shorts and T-shirts were what people wore to the beach. He remembered that from the days when he still went out. When it was nearly two o'clock he went to his closet and found a hat. A blue baseball hat that had a white D for Dodgers on it. A girl named Joanne, who used to come over for "dinner and dancing," had brought it to him one night as a gift. Wearing the hat made him feel a little safer. As if, in case the world caved in, at least his head would be protected.

Molly honked the horn, and when Jackie peeked outside he realized that this was the first time he had ever seen her car. It was an old yellow Mustang convertible, and she and her son sat in the front seat, looking at the house. They were both smiling. A convertible. Jackie hadn't counted on a convertible.

He walked to the car. All the time monitoring himself, telling himself he would be fine and that he could handle it.

"This is Bobby," Molly said, and her usually sad eyes looked a little less sad today. "Bobby, this is Jackie." The boy and the man nodded at each other.

"Mind sitting in the back?" Molly asked Jackie.

"Not at all," he said. Thank God, Jackie thought. If he sat in the back, neither Molly nor Bobby would know that his eyes would be closed all the way to Venice Beach.

"What a day," he heard Molly say.

"Beautiful," Jackie agreed from the back seat. *I*

*will be fine. I'm not afraid. I'm not,* he said to himself. But he was. He didn't open his eyes until he could tell that they were in Venice because he heard the man in the parking lot ask Molly for two dollars, and then he heard Bobby say, "Ahhh, man, look at the sky. There must be a million of 'em."

*I am fine. I will look now.*

There *must* have been a million of them. Kites. Every shape and color. Filling the sky. Soaring, gliding, spinning. Some tied in groups of five or six or eight that moved together like a flock of birds or airplanes in formation. And he was looking at them. Sitting in the back seat of a convertible looking at the splashy gay spectacle of them, and he was fine.

His heart felt as light as one of the kites for the first time in years. Maybe since all of this started. Since the time he'd had to leave the Rose Bowl because suddenly, during a football game, he'd looked around at the thousands of people in the stands, and then up at the sky, and he'd felt small and feverish and panicky. Certain that the sides of the Bowl were about to collapse and he would be trapped there. So he told the people he was with that he had the stomach flu, and then he ran for the schoolbus and vomited all over one of the back seats before he drove himself home. That was the first time. There were dozens of others. In a movie theater in Westwood. Walking on Wilshire Boulevard. At the Music Center. The Forum. Panic. Heart pounding. Dizziness. Overwhelming nausea. Gasping. Gasping for breath. No more. Finally he promised himself never again, and it was right after that promise that he started his whole new life style. Work and home. Home and work. Swearing he would never go out again into an open space and be afraid.

But now, today, here he was, thanks to Molly. As if nothing had ever happened. His breathing was fine. His heartbeat was regular. He looked at her smiling face as she opened the car door.

"Wait 'til you see what I've packed," she told him as she walked to the trunk to get the picnic basket. Bobby ran onto the beach.

"Ma," he yelled back. "Look at that one that looks like a sailboat."

Molly nodded and waved and let him know she'd seen it. Jackie stood slowly, got out of the car, and walked to the trunk to help. The air. The sea air was wonderful, and he felt so good and so proud. Not that he could tell Molly why he was proud, but it didn't matter.

"I'm so glad you came," she said, handing him the picnic basket. "Bobby will warm up to you. I think he's probably a little nervous about you, because"— and then she flushed a little before she said—"because I talk about you so much."

Molly. Molly. Molly. There was no one like her. When he looked into her eyes he saw what his future could be and it filled him up. Made him feel lucky. He was lucky to have found this gentle, loving girl.

"Come," she said, taking a blanket out of the trunk and hanging it over her arm. "We'll find a spot near the water. That way if Bobby wants to go in I can watch him."

Jackie was fine. Fine. Fine. Happy. Joyous even. Walking along the beach with a vital, spirited, fun-loving woman who danced a little dance step as part of her walk to show him how happy she was that they were all at the beach together.

"This good?" she asked, as she stopped walking.

He shrugged. "Sure." They were a few yards from the shoreline. The shoreline. Imagine. He hadn't seen the ocean, except on television, in more years than he could remember.

Molly handed him one end of the blanket and held on to the other end. They moved apart and spread it out on the sand, put the picnic basket on top, and sat.

"It's hot," Molly said. "You were smart to wear a hat."

Bobby ran up and down the beach, his head thrown back so he could watch the splendid kites in motion. Here and there on the beach the kite flyers sat or stood or ran, playing their bolts of string like puppeteers, as the kites rose and dipped and soared in response.

The beach. Jackie was at the beach. Molly pulled off the sweatshirt dress she was wearing and she had a red-and-white one-piece bathing suit on underneath. A bathing suit. He didn't even own one.

"Think I'll go into the water," she said, and gave him a little wave. She was beautiful and he loved her, not just for being beautiful but for picking him up in a convertible and bringing him to the kite festival. He watched her as she stood. When Bobby saw that his mother was in her suit, he ran up to the blanket, stripped off his own shoes and socks and shirt, and grabbed her hand, and the two of them ran playfully into the surf.

*I am fine. I am fine. I'm at the beach and I'm fine,* Jackie thought.

Molly splashed Bobby with a big two-handed splash and he shrieked and spun and leaped on her and they both fell, laughing, into an oncoming wave.

Jackie took a deep breath, leaned back on his elbows, and rested the back of his head against the side of the picnic basket. Molly and Bobby were moving deep into the water now, hand in hand, and suddenly Bobby looked up at the sky. Something he saw, one of the kites, must have excited him, because he pointed and made an excited sound that Jackie could hear from the sand. Then Molly looked up in the direction where Bobby was pointing and made the same excited sound.

Jackie checked his own breathing. Looking up was not the easiest thing for him to do. Other swimmers had stopped in the water and were staring at the same spot in the sky as Molly and Bobby. It must be something special. *I am fine.* He could handle it. After all, he had braved a convertible, and now this wide-open expanse of beach.

His eyes still on the people in the water, Jackie took off the blue Dodgers hat. That was a good start. The sun was hot on his scalp but he liked the feeling. He leaned his head back again on the basket, and he knew now that all he had to do was tilt his head upward and to the right and he would be able to see what it was the others were watching. He took another long look out into the ocean. Bobby was cling-

ing to his mother's arm. The place where the two of
them stood must have been a sand bar, because even
though they were far out, the water was only up to
Molly's thighs. Molly's thighs. They were reason enough
for Jackie to brave anything.

Slowly he moved his head back. Some of his
bushy hair got caught in the fibers of the basket but
he didn't notice, because he, Jackie Schwartz, was
looking at the sky for the first time in years. And not
an ordinary sky. A sky that was dotted with . . . my
God. No wonder the others were agog.

Filling the sky was a kite the size of twenty of the
others combined. It was gleaming. Shining so brightly
that at certain moments it was nearly impossible to
look at it. Yellow and flaming orange like the sun.
That's what it was. The sun. The kite of the sun.
Bobbing. Dancing. Rising higher than all the others,
then suddenly dipping toward the beach as if it could
fall, then suddenly rushing skyward again and floating.

Jackie wondered who the owner of such a kite
could be, and he moved his eyes to the beach and
looked around. There were many more people on the
beach now than when he and Molly and Bobby had
arrived. All of them watching the sun kite. All of them
looking up at the sky. But he didn't, couldn't find the
kite flyer among them.

The sun kite was up very high now. It was at its
highest point so far, and Jackie was leaning back
against the basket, squinting against the brightness of
the day to try to locate the string, when the sun kite
began to move toward the earth. Slowly at first, then
faster, as if the kite flyer had lost control. Too fast.
Toward Jackie, he was sure. Moving in his direction.
And the sky behind it was spinning, too, and he knew
that the sun kite, which looked so large so high up in
the sky, must be overwhelming up close . . . and, my
God, he was sweating and his heart was pounding,
and the kite and the sky and all the other kites were
going to close in and . . . Molly! Any minute he would
be sick, panicky and vomiting, and Molly would see
him and so would her son and they would hate him.

There was nowhere to go. Why hadn't he thought
of that? Why hadn't he said, "I'll meet you there," to

Molly. He could have driven his school bus and met Molly and Bobby at the beach. Then he would have had an enclosed place to hide. But now, nothing, nowhere. The men's room. That little cinder-block building at the corner. No. God. He pictured himself in there gagging and sick like some wino. The sun kite. It was coming. He had to look away. Somehow he took his eyes from the sky and covered his face with his hands.

He was soaked with sweat. Eyes still closed, he felt around on the blanket for the Dodger hat and put it on. Then, opening his eyes but steadfastly staring only at the sand, he moved up the beach, through the crowd of people, toward the men's room.

The odor in the men's room made him reel, but it was better than being outside. No one else was there, so he pressed his forehead against the cinder block. Just to cool himself. His breathing was beginning to slow down. Thank God. Becoming more regular. *I'm fine*, he told himself. *I'm inside now and I'm fine*. But he wasn't fine. He was afraid. So afraid that he knew he couldn't go back to the beach and let Molly and Bobby see him this way.

After another few minutes in the men's room, he was feeling well enough to walk slowly outside. He looked around so he could decide what to do. Then, his shoulders hunched protectively, his hat pulled as far down on his head as it would go and his eyes fixed on the sidewalk, he began to walk as quickly as he could toward the bus stop.

That night, after his headache subsided, he sat in a hot bath. From the tub he could hear the phone ringing.

"Molly," he said aloud, but he didn't get out to answer it.

Early Monday he called in sick to work. After that he put the phone down, went back to sleep, and slept all morning. At twelve-thirty in the afternoon the ringing of the phone woke him. It was lunchtime at the office. It would be Molly.

"H'lo?"

"Jackie? Thank God," she said. "Are you okay? I've been so worried."

"I'm okay," he said. *I am fine*. What could he tell her? "I'm sorry," he said. "But I had to leave the beach because I didn't feel well."

"Is there anything I can do? I mean, can I bring you anything?" she asked, and he heard in her voice that she was really concerned. "Shall I come over?"

"No."

There was silence. The truth is your best friend. His mother had told him that many times when he was a boy. His best friend. The truth. He would tell the truth.

"I'm . . . you see, Molly . . . I don't . . . I mean . . . I should have told you. There's something wrong with me—has been for years. I mean . . . I can't . . . go outside."

Now there was an even longer silence as Molly thought about what he'd just told her. Finally she spoke.

"You mean you're agoraphobic?" she asked. When he didn't answer she went on. "I've read articles about that." Still Jackie said nothing. "They have therapy for it now," she said. "And it works. Behavior modification clinics. Have you thought of—"

"No. No therapy. I'll be all right. No. Thanks for calling," he said, and hung up the phone.

He didn't go to the office for the rest of that week. Just stayed in bed. When the cleaning lady came, she cleaned around him. The only phone call he made was to a gardening service to ask if they would come and mow his lawn on a regular basis.

On the following Monday, when he did go to work, he heard from his partner that for one reason or another, Molly had been fired from the company.

"She left those for you," Martin said.

On Jackie's desk, in a manila envelope, Molly had left copies of several magazine articles about the treatment of agoraphobics. He glanced at them, then threw them into the wastebasket.

At about four o'clock that day the door to the office Martin and Jackie shared opened. Standing in the doorway was a girl named Shelly. She was a new girl in the department. She had some papers for Martin. Although she completed her transaction with Martin, it was easy to see by the way she smiled at Jackie that he was the one who interested her.

After she left, Jackie said to Martin: "I'm in love with that girl. Who is she?"

That night Jackie called Shelly. When he asked her to come over for "dinner and dancing" she said she was on her way.

*C*ompared to the mean black IBM she used at the office, the little blue Smith-Corona portable R.J. used at home looked like a toy. It was sitting on top of the folding card table she had treated herself to, fifteen years ago, with her last remaining books of Blue Chip stamps. The dining room chair she'd pulled up to use as a desk chair made it look as if some child were "playing office," but this setup was going to have to serve her for a while. At least, she thought, she didn't have to worry about maintaining her wardrobe. She could wear her old faithful yellow terry-cloth bathrobe every day. The one she'd worn so endlessly, practically to tatters, that Arthur had fondly named it The Yellow Robe Of Texas.

Six magazines. While R.J. was running from job interview to job interview, her agent had sent "Chicken in a Pot" to six magazines, but there hadn't been so much as a nibble. Her first short story. And she was nearly out of money. Maybe it was time, she thought in the middle of the night, every night, for her to take a job. Any job. A reader. A secretary. She had applied for work as a staff writer on various shows. One was about a lady cop. Cops. She'd had enough of cops to last her a lifetime. There had been dozens of them around after Arthur's death. Plainclothed, deadpan, probing again and again. Cops.

"Now, Mrs. Misner, can you think of any reason why anyone would have wanted to kill your husband?"

"Yes, I can."

Police Detective Finucan had brightened. "And what reason would that be?"

"He cheated at Scrabble."

The policeman had pockmarked skin and dandruff. His fingernails were bitten down to the quick. He was five foot six, and not one of the items of clothing he was wearing fit him properly. The shirt was too wide in the collar, the pants were too tight in the waist and too short, the socks sagged down toward his ankles, and the sleeves on the sport coat were so long they came almost to his knuckles.

"He always took nine letters instead of seven out of the bag. God, it was annoying. I first caught on when I noticed the letters falling off the rack and onto the bed—"

"Izzat supposed to be funny, Mrs. Misner?" the irritated officer interrupted. "I'm tryin' to solve a murder here. The murder of your husband, and the father of your little boy, and you're makin' jokes? Am I supposed to think you think this is a humorous situation, Mrs. Misner? Because the L.A.P.D. isn't laughing. Now let's proceed with my questions and dispense with your jokes, if ya don't mind."

R.J. bit her bottom lip.

"I'm sorry," she said hoarsely. "It just came out. Sometimes I say silly things by force of habit. I think it's because I'm a . . ."

"Pisces?" Detective Finucan guessed. "My ex-wife was a Pisces. They're very emotional."

"No," R.J. said. She had felt one of those uncontrollable sobs rising again, and she held her breath in order to stop it. When she could finally speak again, she finished the sentence: "Because I'm a"—and then, after a huge intake of air, she was finally able to say—"I'm a comedy writer."

"A what?"

"Comedy writer," she managed, and then the sobs came.

Finucan the detective unwrinkled his brow, and his eyes got wide with what looked oddly like awe.

"No kiddin'?" he said. "No kiddin'." R.J.'s revelation had made a new man out of him, and with an almost courtly gesture he produced a handkerchief from the pocket of the ill-fitting jacket and held it out to her, thrusting it practically under her dripping nose. The handkerchief was a color R.J.'s mother would have called tattletale-gray, and it had Finucan's scent on it, which R.J. thought she remembered, from boys in high school, was English Leather. Nevertheless, she took it, emitted a word that sounded enough like "thanks" to get by, wiped her eyes on the handkerchief, and looked back at Finucan, who was now gazing at her in a way that seemed almost flirtatious.

"You know, a lot of people think I remind them of that there Columbo," he said, striking a pose that R.J. knew he thought made him look like Peter Falk. "And I got stories I could tell the people who do that show that they wouldn't believe. Do you know any of those producers or writers on that show? How 'bout Columbo? Do ya know *him*? See, I was thinkin' maybe I could just be sort of like a technical adviser. Start small."

R.J. was speechless. The policeman who had come to question her about her husband's murder wanted to be in show business, and to use *her* as his connection. Years from now he would probably run up onto the stage of the Music Center to announce to a cheering crowd: "Thank God for small blessings. If Arthur Misner hadn'ta been shot to death, I never woulda won this Emmy."

"Of course I wouldn't just *tell* them my stories," Finucan had added hastily. "I'd sell 'em for a couple of grand each. Let's see. I've got ten or twelve of them, at let's say two—no, let's call it three grand apiece, so that comes out to . . ."

That was when R.J. lost it. "No," she had shrieked at him suddenly, with a rage that was not only in her voice but smeared all over her face. "No, no, no, no, no."

"Okay," said Finucan, "so I'll ask for fifteen hundred and work my way up to three grand, after I whet their appetites."

R.J. had put her face in her hands. She dug her fingernails into her scalp, hoping to create an external pain so she wouldn't feel the one that was gnawing away at her insides.

"I mean," she said softly, finally, "no, I don't know anyone who would want to murder my husband."

Enough cops. No cop shows. When the lady-cop show hired two men who had written *Charlie's Angels*, R.J. told herself that she didn't want to be on the staff of another television show anyway. Didn't want to go into an office every day, and then not be home after school for Jeffie. Especially now. If only she could work at home, that would be better. That was why she'd written and sent out her short story, "Chicken in a Pot." Six magazines. Not even a nibble.

Her little at-home office. She'd better use it well. Her mother would have asked did she think Blue Chip stamps grew on trees? What ever happened to Blue Chip stamps? she wondered. She was still a writer even if she didn't have a job. Pick up a piece of typing paper. Or maybe she wasn't. Maybe the real reason she'd been fired was that she was awful. Roll it into the typewriter. Maybe Harry Elfand was just trying to be nice, telling her it was because of Patsy's craziness, and the real reason was that she was just not funny. Type something at the top of the page. Anything. Something to keep it from looking so empty. At least when she'd been working on the show; she could always start the day by typing the words OPENING MONOLOGUE at the top of the page, or PATSY AT HOME.

"What are you doing?" Jeffie asked. He had probably been standing in the doorway of her room for a long time.

"I'm writing. What does it look like I'm doing?" R.J. asked.

"Sitting there staring," Jeffie answered.

"Well, that's part of writing," she said.

"It is? Boy, that's weird. Somebody gives you money to sit there and stare? If that's true, then I should have that job. I'd be president of the company in no time."

"The staring part comes when you're trying to decide what to write about."

"I think you should write about us."

"What about us?"

"Our life. Like those other dumb shows about families that are on TV, only good instead of dorky."

"You mean a situation comedy?"

"I don't know. Just a show. Only it's real instead of dumb. A mother who goes into her room to cry, and a maid who talks Spanish only nobody understands her, and a kid. And real stuff happens. Like the father dies and the mother dates these stupid guys who keep dumping her, and then she gets fired from her job, and the kid's failing math."

"How could you be failing math? Don't tell me you're failing math. I'll call a tutor. I'll get a tutor to come once a week to catch you up. Why didn't you tell me before?"

"See how real it is? You already believe it and it hasn't even been on yet."

"Jeffie, go back to bed. And don't worry about my work, okay? I'll come up with something, and if I don't I'll get another staff job. I love you, honey, but I need to sit here for a while and—"

"Stare?"

"Yeah. I'll see you in the morning."

"Love you, Mom. 'Night."

A pilot. Maybe she could sell a pilot. Maybe if she came up with something, she could get a meeting at the network and . . .

"Mom?"

"Mmm?"

"If you write about us, don't make me one of those TV kids who knows all the answers. Okay? 'Cause that's what they're always like and it's so jerky. If you don't mind, make me a real good athlete, and thirteen instead of twelve." And he was off to bed.

He was right. They were funny. Laughable maybe. Even at their saddest moments. Like right after she was fired from Patsy's show, when she'd tried to fire Manuela. Using her nonexistent Spanish, she'd sat the housekeeper down and tried to explain to her that she could no longer afford her services. *"Yo no tengo dinero,"* she tried. Manuela didn't blink. "And I don't know when I will again. We love you, but we can't . . . I can't afford you."

Manuela took a deep breath and then spoke to her rapid-fire, and R.J. just sat there shaking her head because she didn't understand one word. But Manuela was vehement. She stood and paced back and forth as she talked, angrily, gesturing the way Ricky Ricardo used to when he was mad at Lucy, and finally R.J. put up a hand to stop her.

"Wait," she said. "One minute." And she picked up the phone and dialed Dinah. Dinah's phone rang and rang, and R.J. was about to hang up when Dinah answered.

"Di?"

"Hi, hon. Just ran in. What's up?"

"I have to fire Manuela. I can't afford her. I'll help her find another job, and I want her to know all that, but I don't have the language for it. Please help me," she said to Dinah, who was fluent in Spanish, and handed Manuela the phone. Manuela listened, nodded, listened, nodded, and then, arms waving with the same gestures she'd used as she'd paced in front of R.J., she assailed Dinah with her answer, then handed R.J. the phone.

"Hi," R.J. said to Dinah. "What'd she say?"

"She said she knows you'll have good things happen to you, and when you do, you'll pay her. And meanwhile she'll stay on for just the room and food, because she believes in you, and she can't stand seeing you having this downbeat attitude because you're no fun the way you used to be, and she asked me to ask you if you've ever seen *Imitation of Life*?" Dinah was laughing, R.J. started to laugh too. Manuela laughed. R.J. put down the phone and hugged her.

"*Gracias*, Manuela, *gracias*," she said.

"You welcome," Manuela said, hugging her back.

Good things would happen. Not if she didn't get something down on this page. Type something.

ABCDEFGHIJKLMNOPQRSTUVWXYZ. Once upon a time there was a . . . shit. Michael Rappaport. Mrs. Arthur Misner.

Mercifully, the phone rang.

"You surviving?" It was Dinah. She didn't wait for an answer. "Come to a party with us next Monday night. We have to be there at six o'clock."

"No chance." Dinah's parties. No chance.

"My girls will stay with Jeffie."

"Absolutely not. I don't want to go to parties. Dinah, I know you mean well, but there is absolutely no point in my going to some party where everyone is drinking too much and pretending to have fun, when all they're doing is checking one another out to see who they can get into bed. I know I've said this before and then gone back on it, but this time I mean it. I'm not on the market anymore. My life is about my son, who's the greatest kid in the world and needs my attention, and it's about my work, such as it is. I no longer believe in fairy tales or fantasies. You told me to date—I dated. An agoraphobic, a pathological liar, an adulterer, a narcissist, a paranoid, and a serious doper. You're right I probably should be more open. I haven't been out yet with a manic depressive or an ax murderer. Why close the door to those possibilities? Dinah, I've had my share. One nice sweet man who loved me, which is probably more than many women ever have, so I'm not going to be greedy. After all, we come into this world alone and eventually we go out the same way ... so why the big panic to couple up? You know what I mean? Noah's ark isn't leaving yet. So, my friend, party or not, I'm going to stay in my house and sit at my Blue-Chip-stamp table and write, Dinah. Write something I can sell in the commercial marketplace so I can make a few dollars and stay afloat. And if I do sell it, after that I'm going to use my time to write something I care about. Something some dyspeptic head writer won't sneer at, and to which some illiterate star won't forget the punch line, and some holier-than-thou program practices dimwit won't decide is too sexy. No, Dinah, I will not go to a party with you, because I'm going to sit home and write. Every night, including Monday."

There was a long pause on the line before Dinah said, "So what time should I pick you up?"

R.J. hated herself for answering. "Five forty-five," she said.

But when Monday night came she didn't feel any more like going to the party than when she'd first heard about it. She stayed in the shower until there was no more hot water, then got out and stood looking in the mirror at her wet naked self. A drowned rat. Once she'd been pretty. All right, maybe just cute. But now she was a drowned rat. A small dark damp creature. She used to joke when people would ask her if writing for television was difficult, by saying: "It's so hard that before I did it I was tall and blond." But it wasn't a joke. Those endless days with Patsy's show had taught her how to write funny, how to think funny, how to take ideas and turn them into comedy material, how to be unafraid to say anything in a meeting, even if it sounded stupid, and how not to care when twelve men said, "That idea's a piece of crap." How not to wince or get tearful, but to forge ahead until the right words came into focus. Because sometimes good ideas came out of bad ones. Once she overheard Marty Nussbaum talking about her and he said, "She can pitch jokes in a room like a man." He'd meant it as a compliment. Earning that compliment had unequivocally toughened her up.

So had being single. In Hollywood. A place where people pretended to be other people and got paid big money for doing it. Escaped into fantasy. All of them caring more about the illusion than the reality. About how things appeared. My God, maybe she was one of those people, and meeting the kind of men she'd been meeting since she'd decided to go back into the world was a reflection of who *she* was. Not a statement on the condition of men at all. No. She hoped that wasn't right. Anyway, it didn't matter. What mattered was Jeffie, and making a decent living to support him, and making certain his life was comfortable. And as for romantic love? It looked as if she just wasn't meant to have it anymore.

When she was dried, made up, and dressed in an emerald-green silk blouse and black silk pants, she looked in her jewelry box for her pearl earrings. She thought she had put them away in the concealed compartment underneath the shelf. Yes. They were there, just next to her high school ring, and a strip of four pictures from one of those photo machines. Those pictures. She hadn't looked at them in a long time. There she was, squeezed onto the little adjustable stool in the booth next to Arthur. In the top picture the two of them were grinning at the camera; then, in the next one, both of them, unplanned, were somehow making the same goony face at the camera. Then the next, where with the spontaneity of two toddlers they were sticking their tongues out at each other, and at the bottom, the two of them kissing. Kissing. Oblivious to the final flash. R.J. remembered that the kiss had lasted a long time. Lasted until the clunk of the photo machine signaled them that the pictures were ready. Arthur.

I quit, Arthur, she thought as she looked at the strip of pictures and noted sadly that they were beginning to fade. I thought that maybe I'd meet someone and get married again, but I don't have the energy, the time, or the interest anymore to look, to date, or to get involved with flakes, which I've decided is all there are out there. I wanted to find someone for me, naturally, but I wanted it for Jeffie, too, because we both need to be a family so badly. So badly I nearly married someone I tried to talk myself into loving. But more and more I'm convinced it isn't in the cards. Maybe you're glad, because if I never fall in love with anybody again, I'll always be yours. Then she smiled, wondering what Arthur would say to all this. I'll bet up there where you are, you have a big laugh every time I get involved with one of these bozos. Well, it's okay. I always used to love making you laugh. She smiled a tired smile and put the pictures back, next to her high school ring. As she

closed her jewelry box she heard Dinah honking the horn.
She put on her pearl earrings, grabbed her black-and-white
checked coat, ran into Jeffie's room to give him a quick kiss,
and as Dinah honked for the third time, she was out the
door. Dinah's car reeked of Opium, the perfume she always
wore, and she was dressed in some outrageous leopard-skin
print dress. Dinah always looked turned out, no matter
what the occasion. Her ex-husband was an accountant who
had insisted she dress conservatively. The minute they separated she had gone on a shopping spree to "make my closet
rival Liberace's," she'd declared. Free of the accountant's
tyranny, her imagination soared. Even when she stopped by
an early-morning soccer game to cheer Jeffie on, she'd
stride across the park, her blond permed hair done up in
combs, her eyes shadowed, her lips lined, and the glare of
her flashy outfit would be enough to wake up the sleepy-
eyed R.J., who invariably wore her jeans and black sweater
under a hooded sweatshirt with the hood up to protect her
cold ears. R.J. never ceased to be amazed.

"You work every day, all day. How do you do it?"
she'd asked one shivery damp morning in the park.

Dinah, defensive, answered, "How can you *not* do it?
I'm in the people business. I see dozens of people every day.
Frequently stars. I have to look good."

"Di, this is a soccer game. In the Valley."

"Do you know how many actors live in the Valley?
Who could have sons who play soccer?"

"Hi, Dinah," someone had said that very minute. It
was Mike Farrell.

"I rest my case," Dinah said to R.J., waving an effusive
wave at Mike Farrell.

Tonight, Dinah was excited about the party. R.J. could
hear it in her voice. Dinah loved parties. Her breathing
changed just talking about them.

"Robert's coming from the office, so he'll meet us there.
I heard it's going to be fabulous," Dinah said. "A major
party."

"Great," R.J. managed.

"Attitude," Dinah said. "You have to do something
about your attitude. Maybe you'll meet someone."

"Di, you've been living in Studio City, which is precariously close to Hollywood, for too long. That's why you still
believe in the Someday-My-Prince-Will-Come school of love.

Well I don't. I mean, let's get down to cases. Even your beloved Robert gets queasy when you mention combining your families. Doesn't he?"

"You get very shrill every time the discussion of men comes up," Dinah said, making a right onto Sunset.

"Well, doesn't he?"

"Robert's not even divorced from Joanie yet," Dinah said.

"They've been separated for twelve years," R.J. reminded her. "And he's been going with you for four of those years. Don't you think it's time he made a decision?"

"He has to do things in his own time," Dinah said. "Anyway, it's not as bad as Richard Lavin. He's living with his ex-wife, and they're both dating other people."

"Oh, spare me, Dinah," R.J. said. "Spare me from having to hear these stories. What happened to good old-fashioned wanting to be together, like my parents had? It no longer exists. That's why I've thrown in the towel."

"No you haven't," Dinah said. "If you had, you wouldn't be going to this party."

"I'm going to the party because for the last four days and nights, while Manuela fed my son, who stopped in every now and then for a hug, the only time I left my writing table was to eat the following: one baked potato, one container of cottage cheese with an expiration date stamped on the bottom that was somewhere around the time of my senior prom, some grapes that were so wrinkled I think they were up for the part of raisins in a Sun-Maid commercial, and eight ounces of V-8 straight from the can. I'm hoping there's some food at the party. I'm too smart to hope for a man. The ultimate thrill for me would be to spot the chip dip of my dreams across a crowded room."

Dinah drove through the Bel-Air west gate.

"How's the writing going?" she asked.

"Okay. I've got a pilot idea I'm going to try to sell to a network this week. Actually it was Jeffie's idea. Whose house is this anyway?" she asked as they drove up the long driveway toward what R.J. could now see was an elegant Bel-Air home.

"Some friend of Robert's. The guy has a party like this every year. You know. With three or four TVs, and everyone puts money into a kitty for the person who guesses all the winners."

"What winners?"

"Oscars."

Oscars. It was Oscar night. R.J. hadn't known. Didn't care. Didn't want to watch. She certainly didn't want to sit down with a piece of paper and match her movie consciousness with everyone else's. She hadn't even seen some of the nominated movies. The red-coated parking attendant took Dinah's car, and R.J. looked at the open door of the house and knew she'd made a mistake. If only she'd met Dinah here instead of coming here in Dinah's car, she could have munched a few hors d'oeuvres, had a glass of wine, and gone home after half an hour. Back to the Yellow Robe of Texas.

There were about thirty people milling around, carrying wineglasses. Talking that kind of high-pitched cocktail party chatter that's usually punctuated by throaty forced laughter. Maybe, R.J. thought, she would just call a taxi. Say she had a headache. An older gray-haired man in a suit walked smiling toward where R.J. and Dinah stood in the foyer.

"Dinah? I'm Jason Flagg. Do you remember me?"

Obviously Robert's friend. Dinah remembered him.

"This is R.J. Misner," Dinah said. Jason Flagg shook R.J.'s hand, looked her in the eye sincerely, as if he had learned to do it that way in a Dale Carnegie course, and then proceeded to introduce R.J. and Dinah around the room. Despite R.J.'s attempt to listen and follow along, the names were a blur, as if that comic, the one who was the master of doubletalk, Al Kelly, were making the introductions. But she nodded and smiled at each of the guests. A tall thin girl with high cheekbones. A fuzzy-haired man in a plaid blazer. Two starlet types, one in tight jeans, one in a silk charmeuse jump suit. A pudgy man in his fifties wearing a velour sweat suit. A handsome-looking couple: The woman was very tall, with waist-length blond hair. She wore tweed pants and a silk blouse. The man was a blue-eyed redhead with lots of freckles. Handsome. Obviously an actor. The couple looked as if they'd just stepped out of an ad for Ronrico rum.

R.J. smiled and nodded at everyone, having no more knowledge of what their names were than when she'd walked in. Ahh. She spotted the buffet table, took Dinah's elbow, and turned her in that direction.

"Food," she whispered, while Dinah looked back over her shoulder at the crowd. When they were out of earshot of the others, Dinah said, "There are a few single guys here."

"Mmmm," R.J. said and devoured a piece of quiche, a strawberry, and a chicken wing. One of the starlets, who passed out the forms for the contest with the smiles and gestures of a game-show prize girl, handed R.J. hers and said, "Good luck." R.J., who hadn't had a chance to wipe off her hands, got sweet-and-sour sauce all over the form.

*Coal Miner's Daughter,* Sissy Spacek, *Raging Bull.* Who cares? she thought. "Is it okay if I don't enter?" she said, thinking she was talking to Dinah. Then she realized that Dinah had slipped away.

"Oh, sure, but it's just for fun." The woman from the Ronrico ad was standing between R.J. and the man from the Ronrico ad. R.J. spotted Dinah across the room, talking to Jason Flagg and a dark-haired woman who had just come in.

"Jason tells us you're a television writer," the man said.

"Yes," R.J. answered.

"Would you have written any show I've ever seen?" he asked.

"Patsy Dugan," R.J. answered. An actor. The guy must be an actor. They were always nice to writers. Figured writers could get them acting jobs. Boy, were they wrong. "I mean, I wrote her television show. Now I'm free-lancing, which is my way of telling you I'm out of work."

The man smiled.

"Comedy writing. God, that must be fun," the woman said.

Yeah. A laugh a minute, R.J. thought. She would go home. As soon as she could get out of this conversation she would go home.

"Is it hard to do?" the woman asked.

"Let me put it this way," R.J. said, now on automatic pilot, giving her clichéd answer: "Before I wrote comedy I was tall and blond." The woman and the man both laughed.

"How did you get into comedy writing?" the woman asked.

"Too short to act, too silly to write drama," she said.

The handsome freckle-faced man had one freckle on

his chin that was a little larger, a little darker than the others.

"What's Patsy Dugan like?" he asked. "Is she really as dumb as she comes off on the show?" R.J. had answered that one dozens of times.

"That depends on what you think of as dumb. For example, she thinks that the moon is the back of the sun." The couple laughed. "Honestly," R.J. said, straight-faced, doing her usual bit about Patsy. "Until recently she thought that Mount Rushmore was a natural phenomenon."

The man laughed. "I don't understand," the woman said.

"She thought it was formed by the weather over the years," R.J. explained. "That if things had gone differently it could have been Washington, Lincoln, and Jerry Lewis."

Both the man and the woman laughed at that. Jason Flagg, hearing the laughter, walked over, his arm draped around the brunette's shoulder.

"We were just hearing about what it's like to be a comedy writer," the blond woman explained.

"Who's a comedy writer?" the woman with Jason asked.

"I am," R.J. answered. God, she wanted to go home.

"Isn't that usually thought of as men's territory?" the handsome man asked, looking long at R.J., who dropped the carrot stick she was holding. She watched it sink irretrievably into the spinach dip. "I mean, is this an example of how women are now breaking into fields that were formerly thought of as being controlled by men?"

"Oh, the men I work with are extremely liberated. If there's some sketch having to do with women that they don't understand, they always say, 'Let's ask the broad what to do.'"

Now the four people laughed.

R.J. was on. Performing, and knowing it, and feeling like a jerk. God, she wanted to be home in her yellow robe. Not here talking to these people, entertaining. One of the starlets who was collecting completed contest forms walked up and put her hand on Jason Flagg's arm. "Um . . . well, are any one of you through with your things that you fill in? Ready to . . . um . . ."

"Not yet," Jason told her and she shimmied away.

"Ahh," R.J. said, watching her, "if only she could speak . . . what stories she could tell." The others laughed.

"Almost show time," the blond woman said, touching the red-haired man's arm. "I'm going to go save us some good seats, darling."

"We'll join you," Jason Flagg said. And he and the two women headed toward the living room, leaving R.J. face to face with handsome. There was an awkward silence as she looked at him looking at her.

"So," she tried, "aren't you going to ask me what my sign is?"

"Not necessary," he said. "I know what your sign is. Your sign is *Closed Until Further Notice*," he said. "And one-liners are a great way of making sure everybody stays away until then. It'll be nice when you're able to turn your sign over so it says *Open*."

Oooh. Who was this guy anyway? Nasty. You talk to someone at a party and right away he thinks he's got a right to be your shrink. Next thing she knew, he'd be sending her a bill for his services. Time to get out of here.

"Nice talking to ya," she said, moving away from the table, but his voice stopped her.

"I calls 'em as I sees 'em," he said, and when she looked back at him he smiled a wry smile.

"If you ever get to know me," he said, "and judging by the look on your face I'd say that's highly unlikely, you'll learn that above all else, I tell the truth."

Who cares, R.J. thought. Her luck. The one party she agrees to go to and she has to end up talking to some hostile, arrogant jerk. When they're that handsome they think they can say whatever they want. What a mistake. Dinah's parties. She would find Dinah and tell her she was going home.

"Don't think it hasn't been a pleasure." She glowered at the man.

Dinah was now regaling a group in the corner with stories R.J. recognized as being about her ex-mother-in-law. When R.J. took her aside to tell her she was leaving, Dinah shook her head in disbelief. "Did somebody say something wrong? Are you okay? Can't you wait until the show is over? There are so many nice people here, R.J., and after the show they'll probably sit and talk and you might like one of them and one of them might like you, and you could . . ."

R.J. knew she was behaving like a child. That it wouldn't kill her to stay for the few hours it would take to watch the television show, to smile and be sociable and not go home and pout because of one superficial thing one superficial man said to her. After all, she'd been cooped up like a hermit for weeks, and just as an exercise she ought to see if she could last out the evening. But she didn't want to. Didn't want to fake being interested.

"I'm sorry," R.J. said, and as everyone moved toward the living room, where the television sets were already on full-blast, she walked into the kitchen, asked one of the kitchen help for a phone, and called a taxi.

# A LAUGH A MINUTE

a treatment for a half-hour
television pilot submitted
by R.J. Misner

This is an idea for a pilot called A LAUGH A
MINUTE. It's about a single, female comedy writer
who works on the staff of a television show where she
is the only woman, and even though some days she'd
like to quit, she can't because she's supporting her
thirteen-year-old son who's a great athlete. Molly is
short, neurotic, and Jewish, looks kind of like a short,
neurotic, Jewish Marlo Thomas.

The characters are MOLLY; her son; her housekeeper, ESPERANZA, who Molly suspects speaks perfect
English and who won't admit it, so with whom Molly
communicates in sign language. And the staff of the
television show on which Molly ekes out a hard-
earned, very insecure living—i.e.:

The comedy writing team of FELZER and BOW-
MAN. Felzer is claustrophobic and Bowman is agoraphobic, so they can't get together to write inside or
outside. The dilemma is solved by their taking offices
on the first floor so that Bowman may sit inside their
little cubicle of an office with the window slightly ajar,
communicating with Felzer, who sits outside on the
grass keeping track of everything on his portable
typewriter.

ALVIN KARP, a lovable old veteran who tries to
teach Molly all of the rules of comedy writing, who
when Molly asks him if a joke she just wrote is funny,
says, "Yeah, and it was funny when I wrote it for

Miltie in fifty-one and a few years ago for Hope at the Oscars and right after that for Johnny. Now was your question is it *still* funny? The answer is yes."

MURRAY DEEMS, the show's head writer, who says of himself that he must be a liberated guy because, after all, he did hire Molly, whom he calls "the broad."

AT HOME, Molly is living the life of a single Hollywood woman. Raising her son, JOSH, who would argue that *he's* raising *her*. Especially when he sees her dating the crazy men who go by. Wanting to get married so badly she proposes to every man she meets. So far the mailman has given her a strong maybe. Her best friend is LEONA. Also single, with a teenaged daughter CISSY. CISSY starts every sentence with the words "Okay, like." Leona is outrageous and outspoken. She has a boyfriend and she is never without a fix-up for Molly. The fix-up unfailingly turns out to have some bizarre problem and is always more trouble than he's worth.

AT WORK, Molly wants so badly to fit in that before she exits the one restroom that she shares with all the other writers, she puts the seat back up. The guys take a fatherly interest in her, and like Leona they are always trying to fix Molly up with guys. Much of the series will be based on Molly trying to find one man in the whole big wide world to whom she can relate. But no luck. Short, tall, fat, thin, old, young, there isn't one who's right for her, and she's worried, because all the independence in the world can't take away her longing to find a guy who wants to come home after work and be a family with her and her son. And maybe even start a new wing of the family. In Hollywood? No chance. It's an updated "Courtship of Eddie's Father," with a harder edge.

The two sets are the office and Molly's apartment.

### SAMPLE STORY

Josh calls Molly from school and says he isn't feeling well. It's Esperanza's day off and Molly doesn't want Josh to go home from school and be alone, so she picks him up at school and brings him to the office. By the end of the day Josh is covered with chicken pox. By the end of the week, so is most of the staff of the show.

"*N*ice pitch," Arvin Podvin said. He was the manager of comedy development at the network.

"Very nice. Funny. Good idea. We don't have anything else like it right now that I can think of," Sheldon Milburg offered. He was the director of comedy development at the network.

"But the problem is," Howard Colson said, and he was the vice president of comedy development at the network, "that it's about show business, because your character Molly is a comedy writer for a living. And shows that are about show business don't work."

"*The Dick Van Dyke Show* was about show business, and so was *The Mary Tyler Moore Show* about show business, and so was *WKRP in Cincinnati*, and so was—" R.J. began, but she was interrupted by Howard Colson's tone of voice.

"Let me put it this way. *We* don't want a show about show business. Peter says that America doesn't understand show business. And I have to agree." Peter was the executive in charge of all programming at the network, and Howard Colson was right. He did have to agree. Peter fired network underlings for showing the least bit of individuality. Peter Tavaris was the one who was credited for the network's current first-place status, and all programming decisions were left to him. The job of the men R.J. was meeting with today was simply to sift through all the material that was submitted to the network and pick out the proposals that complied with Peter's rules. Peter never went to meetings. Not the ones with writers on R.J.'s lowly level anyway. R.J. had met him once when he'd come to a taping of Patsy's show.

She'd been sitting in the makeup room that day in a seat next to Patsy's makeup chair, trying to work out next week's monologue with Patsy. The seating area of the adjacent dressing room had been filled with the usual hangers-on. Patsy's latest boyfriend, Patsy's hairdresser, the wardrobe lady, Patsy's ex-sister-in-law, who had dropped by to report on how miserable the eighteen-year-old girl was making Patsy's ex-husband Freddy. R.J. knew something strange must have happened because they'd all been yakking away just a moment before and now not only were they all silent, but when she peeked out of the makeup room to see why, every one of them was standing, heads kind of bowed in awe as if they were at a religious service. Peter Tavaris had just walked into the room.

"She decent?" Tavaris called in to the makeup room.

"No, I ain't," Patsy had yelled out. "And if yer here ta tell me ta tuck my tits in on my opening number, you kin just go right back to yer big fancy office, 'cause they're my stock in trade, Mister Network Biggy."

Tavaris didn't even crack a smile.

"Just stopped in to say hello, Patsy," he said.

"Be right out," Patsy answered.

R.J. came into the seating area and extended her hand to Tavaris. "I'm R.J. Misner," she had said.

"I know exactly who you are," was the reply. "The opening monologues and 'Patsy At Home,' " he said. It was chilling the way he said it. There were dozens of writers on the shows his network produced. He knew exactly which one of them wrote what. "Nice to meet you."

R.J. and the others left the dressing room so Peter Tavaris and Patsy could be alone. An hour later, when they were ready to tape the opening monologue, the blue-sequined low-cut dress Patsy had been supposed to wear was nowhere to be seen. It had been replaced by a green-sequined dress with a high mandarin collar.

"It's not really about show business," Arvin Podvin suggested now, albeit somewhat softly. "I find it to be more about single motherhood than it is about show business. Show business is just the arena in which this particular single mother spends her time." By next week Arvin Podvin will be working somewhere else, R.J. thought.

"Maybe she could still use the same single mother and kid, because the kid is funny. I like the kid. And the mother could do something else instead of being a comedy writer. Like a teacher," Sheldon Milburg said.

"We have three teacher pilots in development," Howard Colson reminded him.

"True," Sheldon Milburg said, and looked embarrassed that he'd forgotten the three teacher pilots.

"Well," Howard Colson said, pushing his chair away from his desk, standing and offering his hand to R.J., "we really like your work, but no sale today, I guess. Please come back another time."

R.J.'s mind raced. Maybe she should offer to rewrite the woman's profession. Not to teaching. They did, after all, have three teaching pilots, but to something else, because they liked the kid. The kid is funny. And she could come back with it. What could she change the woman's profession to? She ran through the alphabet. Aviator, boxer, call girl, dancer . . . no. Dancers were in show business. Executive, farmer . . . Sheldon Milburg and Arvin Podvin were standing, too, and R.J. stood.

"Thanks," she said, only there was a frog in her throat and it sounded like "hinks," and she walked to the door that was now being held open by Arvin Podvin and out into the reception area of Howard Colson's office. And even though when she thought about it later she knew she must have exaggerated the number in her mind because she was feeling so lousy about her meeting, she would have bet she saw, sitting and chatting loudly, competing for one another's attention, at least fifteen comedy writers she knew, waiting for their turn to pitch their ideas to Howard Colson, Sheldon Milburg, and Arvin Podvin.

A bath—that's what would make her feel better, she thought as she pulled the Mustang out of the network parking lot. A nice hot bath. She would sit in the tub, then make a little dinner for herself and Jeffie and sit down at the typewriter and come up with more ideas. More ideas. Hah. She said that as if it were like *bake another pie*. The way people who didn't write thought about writing. That it was easy. That it didn't cost in time and energy and head-beating against the wall. Especially if you had to write to

other people's specifications. Easy. Just something lucky
people sat around and did every day. Marty Nussbaum had
once told R.J. that when he was writing episodes for television, his wife came to him and said, "Marty, we need new
outdoor furniture."

"Gloria," Marty had said to her, "I'm sorry, but right
now we can't afford outdoor furniture." Marty's wife had
the answer. "So why not just whip up an episode of *Sanford
and Son*?"

R.J. missed Marty Nussbaum. Poor Marty. She missed
all the guys from Patsy's show. Episodes of the shows she
had worked on were still airing, and she would sit by the
television on Sunday nights, watching them and feeling
homesick for her crazy friends. She was still hurting from
the firing. Not just hurting. Shocked too. For weeks she had
tried to get Patsy on the phone, hoping maybe in a confron-
tation she could get an answer out of Patsy about what
happened, find out if it had really been Patsy's idea. But
Patsy wouldn't take her calls. R.J. had even dropped her a
note, but Patsy hadn't answered it. How could it be that one
minute Patsy was her buddy, offering to fix her up on dates,
and the next she wouldn't even call her back?

A bath. After her bath she would begin again to think
of ideas to sell. That was her life now. Writing. Writing.
Every idea she could think of. With an occasional visit from
Dinah, who would breeze in, engulfed in a cloud of Opium,
wearing another of her outrageous outfits. "You have to get
out of this place and have a life," she would say in a voice
so loud that it was still ringing in R.J.'s ears after she left.
Jarring R.J.'s usual silence. She loved the quiet times with
Jeffie, talking about his father. Arthur. And how much they
missed him. And laughing about the good times the three of
them had shared. Arthur. That guy at the Oscar party had
been right on the nose. R.J. Misner was closed. Unavailable.
She had tried to open up and come back into the world.
Starting with Michael Rappaport. Granted, an unfortunate
choice. But she'd made what Arthur would have called "a
good college try." She just wasn't ready and might never
be. One day they would come with a little white truck and
cart her away, because she stood around sometimes, talking
to rainbows as if they were signs from her dead husband.

Closed. Was it so obvious that even a stranger at a
party could pick up on it? A stranger who looked right into

her eyes and told her in so many words what a jerk she
was. Won't it be nice when you're able to turn your sign
over so it says open? How precious. Probably the guy just
stumbled accidentally on the truth. It was what he said to
all the girls at parties when he was trying to pick them up.
Hah. Pick her up. Why would he want to do that? He was
with a tall gorgeous blonde who called him darling. He
didn't need to pick up an exhausted out-of-work comedy
writer.

"Dinah called you," Jeffie said with a mouth full of
something he'd just taken out of the refrigerator. R.J. was
sorting through the mail. "But you missed her, 'cause she's
goin' outa town," he added. Yes, she'd forgotten that this
was the day Dinah was leaving to visit her mother in
Florida.

"Thanks, honey," she said absently.

Maybe a shower. The water pounding on her back
would break up some of the tension that had taken over her
neck since the meeting with those network creeps.

"Getting into the shower," she announced.

She dropped her clothes to the floor and stepped into
the silent cold space of the shower cabinet. She was so lost
in thought that she stood for a long time without even
turning on the water. Every morning she and Arthur used
to take showers here together. And fight. And when they
made up, Arthur would joke that it was a good thing the
water had been running so the neighbors couldn't hear
them. They would fight about her working; they would
fight about his traveling so much on business; they would
fight about whether or not to have more children.

She wanted them, little lambs with soft squishy cheeks
to bite and secret little spots under their chins to kiss—the
way Jeffie was before he became a big boy and was no
longer a baby. Arthur didn't want any more children. Expensive, demanding, time-consuming, he said. He adored
his son, really adored him, but one child was enough. And
to make that clear, every time Arthur made love to her,
which was not very often, he always asked without fail:
"Are you wearing your diaphragm?" Sometimes she would
be in the heat of passion, and it infuriated her, insulted her,
because he was asking that as if she might try to trick him
and get pregnant without his consent. Consent that he
would never give.

Then why did she miss him, canonize him, the way people frequently did with the dead? Rewrote them, punched them up, made them more grand or more glamorous or more lovable than they could possibly have been? Maybe because, despite those fights over what her father would have called honest disagreements, Arthur had been wonderful with her so much of the time. Fun. Someone to laugh with the way she remembered her parents laughing together. And the early struggles had been romantic. Arthur liked to tell friends that when he and R.J. first got together they were so poor that they registered for Styrofoam. He liked to describe his favorite French meal by putting on a Pepe Le Pew French accent and raving over what he called *fromage chaumière dans ma robe de bain*. Cottage cheese in his bathrobe.

She realized she was shivering, and just as she turned the water on full blast, she thought she heard the phone ring. Whoever it is will call back, she told herself and lathered up.

"Some guy," Jeffie said, as she emerged wearing her yellow robe. "He left two numbers—one's his office and one's his house. He says he'll be at the office number for a while." He handed R.J. a corner of his lined notebook paper where he'd written the name, David Malcolm, and a number. Later—she'd call him later. David Malcolm. She had no idea who that was. Would have bet that she'd never even heard the name before. Maybe it was a Dinah fix-up. Shit. She'd made Dinah promise never to do that again. She opened the refrigerator and looked for something to munch on while she cooked dinner. Maybe she should call this guy back, whoever he was, just to get it over with so she could have her dinner in peace and not have to think about it any more or wonder if he was a bill collector.

She dialed the phone in the kitchen, nibbling on a piece of Parmesan cheese she'd found in a Ziplock bag in the cheese drawer of the fridge, and waited while the phone on the other end rang. Four times, five times. R.J. looked at the kitchen clock. It was after six. This Malcolm guy must be gone for the day.

Not gone. There. A secretaryish voice answered.

"David Malcolm's office." A direct line.

"David Malcolm, please," R.J. said.

"May I say who's calling?"

"R.J. Misner," she answered. "I'm returning his call."
David Malcolm. David Malcolm. There was a long silence,
and then a man got on the phone.

"R.J.," he said enthusiastically, like an old friend
who hadn't seen her for a long time. David Malcolm. David
Malcolm. She had no idea. Not even a vague picture in her
mind. "I met you at that party a few weeks ago. At Jason
Flagg's. Oscar night. We talked just before you left. I asked
Sarah to get me your number from Jason —but this is the
first chance I've had to call."

Who was this? It had to be the Ronrico rum guy. My
God. Handsome. The one who told her she was closed.
What could he possibly want?

"Who's Sarah?" His wife.

"The woman I was with. You remember, you told her
that before you wrote comedy you were tall and blond. I
thought that was adorable."

His face. R.J. tried to conjure up a picture of his face.
All she could remember was handsome. So attractive-looking
she was certain at first that he must be an actor. Freckles.
What in the hell did he want from her?

"I saw the Patsy Dugan show and watched your credits
go by. What parts did you write?"

"What parts did you like?"

"The opening."

"I wrote that."

"The part where she's alone in her apartment."

"I wrote that too."

"The part where I saw your name go by," he said.

Cute, she thought.

"I'm calling because I'd like to have dinner with you
one night," he said.

Huh? R.J. thought. "Who's Sarah?" was all she could
say, aware she'd asked him that already.

"Just a friend," he said.

She didn't know what else to say.

"What about dinner?" he asked.

"I don't think so," she said. "I'm sort of busy these
days." Not a lie. She wouldn't tell a lie—she was working
on her writing and she was sort of busy. "And I, well, I
don't think I'm really . . . I don't really want to go out and
have dinner with anyone and I . . ."

God. She sounded like an idiot. And felt like one too.

But it was better to feel that way now and not have to sit in a restaurant somewhere with this guy one evening and tell him her life story and have him say, "Oh, yes, I read about your husband's death in the papers. Did they ever catch the man who shot him?" And she would have to say, "It wasn't one guy—it was four, and they caught one, only he wasn't the one who pulled the trigger, and he was underage and . . . no, they never really . . ." Arthur, she thought. How did this happen? How did I walk down the aisle with you at age twenty-three, full of idealism about love and marriage and the future, and here I am at age thirty-seven, sad and tough and not interested in or believing in the very thing I wanted most all my life. A marriage like my parents had. With passion and mutual support and friendship and laughing, lots of laughing. This guy on the phone wouldn't know about that kind of thing. He was probably afraid that if he laughed, his handsome face would crack. He didn't seem to have much of a sense of humor at the party. In fact he was insulting. Very insulting. What did he want from her?

"No" was the last thing she said to him. He said, "I understand," in a voice that meant he didn't, and they both hung up the phone.

R.J. opened the refrigerator, took out a package of chicken breasts, washed and seasoned them and put them into the oven to bake. Washed and dried the lettuce leaves, cleaned and cut up some vegetables, put them in the steamer and turned on the fire and, while her dinner cooked, walked into her bedroom to check for any dirty coffee cups she might have left there from her morning work time. Arthur used to tease her about talking to herself, something she used to do a lot. Since Arthur's death she didn't talk to herself so much anymore, but she did find herself talking a lot to Arthur. She tried to confine it to times when she was out of Jeffie's earshot. Now, here in her bedroom as she gathered a coffee cup, the plate that had held her morning toast, the wrapper from her packet of megavitamins, she said, "Arthur, I turned this guy down for lots of reasons but the biggest was because I just don't want to be bothered anymore. A bad way to be, at the tender age of thirty-seven, but it's true. I no longer know the good guys from the bad guys, or even if there are any good guys. And it's not some feminist issue about men being the enemy. I'm just meeting all the bad ones," she said, picking up a crumpled Kleenex that had fallen to the floor next to her bed last night. She sat on the bed. "I mean, this guy sounded okay, you know, a nice person and all . . . but I don't want to date anymore. I want to get married. I want to be married. I want to stay married forever. And I don't even meet anyone I even want to have a conversation with. I don't think I should go out with him, because the truth is he isn't even a candidate. He's too handsome to have a sense of humor, and I'm sure he's not Jewish and . . . Arthur, I'm starting to sound like some neurotic yenta, and I don't know what to do."

The phone rang again.

"A drink," David Malcolm said before R.J. could even produce the word *hello*. "A drink on a night when you already have another date later. So you can't even be tempted to make it longer than it takes to drink one drink. And you'll already be dressed for your real date so you won't have to worry about wasting all that effort for me in case you hate me."

Cute. A cute approach. But Hobart had been cute. And so had Barry Litmann.

"I can't," R.J. said. And that was how she felt. It was not even so much that she didn't want to, but that she couldn't. Didn't have the wherewithal to be hit over the head anymore.

"One glass of wine. I'll even meet you there so you can exit gracefully. Arturo's. In your neighborhood, R.J."

No. Everything told her to say no.

"How's Saturday?" he asked. "A good night. A date night. Tell your date to come for you at eight and meet me at seven."

"Saturday," R.J. said, simply repeating what he'd said. He took it as acquiescence.

"See you there."


"Handsome," R.J. thought as she sat at the little cocktail lounge table across from David Malcolm. Like the paper-doll groom in bride-and-groom cutouts she'd had when she was little. Great haircut, square jaw, nice clothes. Similar to the coat and tie the groom paper doll wore to the rehearsal dinner. But she didn't care about handsome. Never had. She cared about constant, which she was certain handsome men never were, and she cared about sense of humor, which handsome men probably never took the time to develop, and the fact was that she cared a lot about a man in her life being Jewish. She had never been out with a man who wasn't Jewish.

Even all these years later, at age thirty-seven, with both her parents gone to their final resting place so that neither of them could tell her she shouldn't do it, as they surely would have if they were alive, this date felt as if it were against the rules. They both ordered white wine. The first few minutes were nice. Small talk. Dancing around kind of small talk. The usual. I'm from Pittsburgh. I'm a native Californian. Carnegie Tech. Wharton. I'm a writer. I'm in manufacturing. Nice to meet a civilian. Pardon? Someone not in show business. The wine came. "To you," he said. All she got out was "yeah." They both drank; then there was a long silence. R.J. broke it.

"So what do you want from me?" she said.

"Is that how you learned to start a new relationship?"

"Pretty much. Yeah. I mean, what's the point of small talk. I'm too old and way past it. You told me at the party I was closed. You're right. We both agree. Now you're knocking on the window. How come?"

"I like a challenge."

"*Meshugge*," she declared.

"God bless you," he answered.

"I didn't sneeze. I said *meshugge*, which means—"

"I know the definition of *meshugge*." He smiled.

"Oh, yes? What is it?"

"*Meshugge*," he said, "is when a charming twenty-nine-year-old WASP takes out a defensive, terrified thirty-seven-year-old Jew, and tries to convince her if she puts her dukes down they could have a good time."

"Oh, please," she said. "You're not twenty-nine? That part's a joke. Right?"

"Not a joke," he said. "I'm twenty-nine." And he put his hands up in a gesture of mock guilt.

R.J. raised her index finger and said into the air, "Taxi."

"You're calling a taxi?"

"Only because my other choice of what to say was 'check, please,' and I don't have any cash on me."

"I'll cover the drinks."

"Why even finish them?" she said brusquely. "We have about as much chance for romance as the coyote and the roadrunner."

"An interesting choice of analogy," he said. "Two creatures in combat. Why do you automatically assume that there has to be conflict? Why not opt for mental health? Try optimism. You might get a pleasant surprise. Ever read a book by Norman Vincent Peale?"

This guy can't be for real, R.J. thought. He's not going to talk about Norman Vincent Peale.

"No, but if he's a writer I probably dated him," she joked.

"I doubt it," he joked back. "He's too healthy for you and probably you'd think he was too goyish."

That was funny. Coming from him it was funny. He was a nice kid. Attractive and smart for a kid. He was a kid. Twenty-nine. And for some reason he saw something behind her flippant answers that he liked. No, she told herself. See how you're getting sucked in again already with the faint hope that the guy is human. That he's some handsome prince who can save you from yourself. From turning into an even crustier old broad than you already are. You are grabbing on to that last shred of hope you keep pretending you don't have, that there really is a man who wants sunset walks and happy ever after. No. Every time she'd held on to that hope she'd been fooled, hurt, defeated. And Jeffie had suffered in the wake of her stupid decisions. She wasn't going to make another one. Not for what was simply some handsome kid.

"My God, it's nearly eight," he said, looking at his watch. "I've really gotta run. I'm going to be late if I don't."

He put a ten-dollar bill on the table, took a last sip of wine from his glass, and helped R.J. to her feet.

"Thanks for meeting me," he said. "It was nice having the opportunity to talk to you like this."

So tight-assed and formal. So polite. And it hadn't been nice at all. She'd been a giant pain and they both knew it. David Malcolm looked even better in the bright lights of the parking lot than he had in the soft illumination of the cocktail lounge. Like a boy, though, R.J. thought. A handsome boy. If Dinah saw him she would say, "Use him up, honey. Have a little fun with him and when he leaves to marry some debutante, which is who he's looking for, wish him well, wish the debutante well, and keep moving."

"I'll talk to you," David said when they were standing next to R.J.'s Mustang.

"Mmmm," R.J. said, wondering what odds Jimmy the Greek would give for his ever calling her again, let alone a relationship flowering. After she got into the car and rolled down the window she realized David was still standing there smiling at her.

"You're tough," he said. "Real tough."

Tough. Arthur had called her that many times. Years ago when they first met. And when he died, everyone told her that's why she would survive, because she was tough. David Malcolm leaned against the door of her car and said, "Tough is good for gun molls, street punks, negotiators at a bargaining table, and all-weather shoes. But it's not so great for steaks, abalone, or women who don't want to scare away potential friends. Lucky for you, I see right through it." Then he squeezed her nose and walked away to his car. Squeezed her nose?

She drove home, went to her room, and sat down at the card table. The words *he will never call me again* repeated themselves over and over in her head, and she tried to remember all the dumb things she'd said to him. So what do you want from me? Wonderful. He was right. She sounded like a gun moll. Norman Vincent Peale. If he's a writer I probably dated him. Ugh. It wasn't even funny. Just mean and defensive. Shitty. And he could see through it. Lucky for her. What did that mean? That he wouldn't hold it against her? Maybe not. But he wasn't ever going to call her again. She rolled a piece of paper into the Smith-Corona, having absolutely no idea why. She didn't have an idea in the world. When the phone rang she said, "Thank God," out loud, meaning *thank God something had saved her from having to write anything*, and she answered it.

"H'lo."

"I'd like to speak to the funniest, sexiest, most exquisite woman who was ever involved in the television industry in America."

R.J. grinned. It was Eddie Levy.

"I did dial the number for Cher, didn't I?"

"Leeee-veee," R.J. shrieked. "Where have you been hiding?"

"Hey, I got a gig that is so elegant and so sophisticated, it's the next best thing to writing for *The New Yorker*," he said. "I am now on the staff—are you sitting down, my darling girl?—of *Three's Company*."

R.J. laughed. "No!"

"Would I kid you? Every night an old Jewish man eyes his wrists and his razor with longing, hoping they'll get together. Elfand dumped me too. So, R.J., what about you?"

"Nothing, Eddie, zero. Pitched a pilot to the network and they hated it."

"So you've got two networks to go."

"Maybe. Or maybe it's just no good," she said.

"Nah," Eddie said. "If it was no good they would have bought it. Listen, I heard a good place to pitch pilots is Meteor productions. ABC loves them. They've got lots of shows on the air. The lady in comedy development is Beth Berger."

"Yeah?" R.J. said, "Beth Berger. Maybe I'll try her."

"Hey," Eddie said. "I don't want to hear in your voice that you think you'll never work in this town again. I've been at the table with you at four in the morning. You're good and you're funny, *maydele*, and also you're tough."

There it was again. While Eddie did a pep talk that R.J. was sure was from a parody he once wrote of *42nd Street*, she thought about David Malcolm. Tough was good in women comedy writers, but not in women men fall in love with. He would never call her again. And nobody else would either. She had given up men and vice versa.

"So get out there and do it," she thought Eddie said. "And if worse comes to worst, I'll see if they can use a funny broad on *Three's Company*."

"Thanks, Eddie," she said. "I appreciate the call."

"Don't be a stranger," Eddie Levy said, and he hung up.

On Tuesday she had a meeting at Hemisphere Studios. Her agent told her that Norman Ginsberg, a producer she'd met a few years before, was looking for a woman writer to do a pilot about three young girls living in a loft while they were trying to get into the music business. When R.J. got to the studio, the guard at the gate didn't have a pass for her, so she had to wait a long time until he was able to reach the office of Norman Ginsberg. Finally Norman Ginsberg's secretary told the guard that it was okay for him to let R.J.

drive onto the studio lot. But when R.J. arrived at the office, heart pounding, ideas flooding her brain, Norman Ginsberg's secretary, who looked a lot like Loni Anderson, apologized and said that Norman Ginsberg had been called out of town. The meeting was canceled.

"We tried to reach you this morning," the secretary said, smiling a big toothy smile at R.J. R.J. had been home all morning, and not on the phone. "Sorry, hon. We'll call you to reschedule."

R.J. stepped out of the office, stopped at a drinking fountain, took a long swig of the water, and regretted it. The water tasted metallic. Her car had been overheating on the long ride here on the freeway. This was obviously not her day. She stood quietly for a moment. At least the corridor was air-conditioned. Her car would be as hot as an oven and she would have to take it in today for servicing before it got worse and more expensive to fix. She certainly couldn't use another expense. She held her breath to steel herself against the day, and walked out of the building, feeling the burning sun on her arms as she made her way toward the parking lot.

The handle was already so hot she had to open the car door gingerly. She threw her writing pad, pen, and purse on the passenger-side seat and got in. She was glad she was wearing pants so her legs wouldn't burn on the vinyl seat. She was afraid that when she turned the key something terrible would happen and she would be without a car.

"Hi," she heard someone say, and she turned, surprised to see David Malcolm standing by the car window.

"What are you doing here?" she asked.

"Hey, it's nice to see you too," he said, grinning. He grinned a lot. A kind of smug grin that bothered her.

"Oh, just putting some things together," he said.

"Didn't you tell me you weren't in show business?" she asked.

"I'm a legacy," he said. "My mother worked at this studio for a few years."

"As what?"

"Actress."

R.J. couldn't think of any actress she'd ever heard of whose last name was Malcolm.

"Had lunch?" he asked.

"Nope."

"C'mon," he said, opening her car door and taking her by the hand toward the studio commissary. Maybe it was her day after all.

"The Cobb salad is the only thing that's good," he said, and then looked at the waitress as she walked up to their table. "Two Cobb salads," he said before R.J. could utter a word. The waitress didn't even write the order down. Just walked away.

"So meanwhile," R.J. said, "back to my question. What are you doing here?"

Before he could answer, R.J. spotted Norman Ginsberg, the executive with whom she was supposed to be meeting at that very moment, walking into the commissary with a beautiful girl who looked like a model. Ginsberg wore rimless glassses and looked like a mole, and even when he stood still his hands were always in motion. His eyes were scanning the room. When they met R.J.'s, they blinked in embarrassment.

"Oh, God. Oh, God. Oh, R.J. Hi. Oh, God. Hi," he said, and then he whispered something to the model and came rushing over to the table where R.J. and David sat.

"Um, I really was called out of town," he said. "I mean, that's really the truth. But I'm not leaving here 'til after lunch and I had to meet with this woman about casting. So my secretary tried and tried to get you this morning to tell you but you . . ."

Bullshit, R.J. thought.

"Norman, this is David Malcolm," she said.

Norman Ginsberg's eyes got very wide behind the rimless glasses, and he pushed his hand out for David to shake.

"I am so delighted. I am really delighted. I am so glad to meet you. Listen, R.J., maybe we shouldn't wait until next week to reschedule. Maybe we should meet on Friday."

"Fine," she said. "See you then."

Norman Ginsberg walked away. No *goodbye*. No *excuse me*. No *nice meeting you* to David. Just walked away.

"Nice guy," David said, and both he and R.J. laughed. "Warm, honest, friendly. Certainly a man I'd like to do business with." And they laughed again.

R.J. drummed her fingers on the table and chewed the inside of her cheek. The truth was that Norman Ginsberg's secretary would call her later to reschedule the meeting for Friday and that she would come rushing back because she needed the job. Needed to do business with him, even if he was a lying creep.

"You seem nervous, roadrunner," David said. He remembered. "Is it this place? If it is, I can cancel our salads and we can go elsewhere for lunch."

"I'm okay," she said. Her car. She was worried about her car. Worried about it and she wished she could stop worrying about it and just enjoy lunch with this lovely man. She was worried about everything. Jeffie and his bar mitzvah. It was coming up within the year and she didn't know how she would be able to pull it off. Afford a party. He deserved to have a nice party to celebrate. She was worried about . . .

"What's on your mind?" David Malcolm asked. Sweet. It was sweet of him to ask. This stranger. She'd seen him twice before in her life. She wasn't going to start telling him her problems. He probably didn't even know what a bar mitzvah was.

"Maybe you're just tense because of work and you ought to get out of town and have a vacation," he said.

R.J., who was ripping a border around the edge of her paper place mat, exhaled a little breath of air from her nose. It was a laugh. A vacation? From what? Not getting jobs? With what money? A vacation. She couldn't remember the last one.

"With me," he said, and when her eyes looked up to meet his, his danced, as if enjoying her surprise.

"You're bananas," she said. "I don't even know you."

"That's the beauty of it," he said. "By the time we get back, you will."

"My son . . ."

"Your housekeeper can take care of him for a few days." This was funny. He was asking her to go away for a weekend with him. And after the way she'd behaved on that first night, she was amazed he was even talking to her.

"Can we have separate rooms?" she asked, certain that the invitation was a joke. You didn't go off with somebody you barely knew.

"If you like."

"I mean, what if we get there and find out we hate each other? I'm very sloppy. I once lost a first draft of a script under clothes from last Thursday."

He smiled.

"Don't you think—" she began.

"R.J.," he interrupted. "Unlike some of the people at this table, I think you're great. In fact I don't think you should want to go back to being tall and blond. I think you're wonderful-looking."

"What happened—you left the cane and the German shepherd at home?"

He didn't smile. "I told you the other night that I think your compulsion to be funny is a cover. So, to vacation or not to vacation. What do you say?"

The waitress brought the Cobb salads. R.J. was thrilled with the interruption so she'd have time to think. How could she go away with this guy? Who in the hell was he? Going away would be a mistake. She should have at least a few dates with him before she even thought about . . .

"Iced tea," he told the waitress.

"Two," R.J. said. The waitress walked away. "Gee," she said, "we're having tea for two. Next we'll be having a girl for me and a boy for you." He smiled a little smile.

Norman Ginsberg and the model were being seated at a table next to R.J. and David's. Norman waved a funny little wave and mouthed the word *Friday* to R.J.

"Why don't you tell him you won't be there on Friday, because we're leaving on Friday morning?" David asked.

"Oh, I can't," R.J. said. "Not just because the meeting could be important. But because, I mean, I can't."

"Okay," David Malcolm said sweetly. They both dug into their salads and ate wordlessly. The waitress brought the check, and when they both had finished, David put cash on the little tray and he and R.J. stood.

As they started toward the door, Norman Ginsberg called out, "R.J.," and R.J. turned to look at him. "Kiss, kiss," the little mole said in an effort to make up for not showing up at the meeting and then lying about it. R.J. tried not to wince, then forced a smile and walked closer to the table.

"Norman," she said. "I forgot, but I won't be able to make it on Friday. I'm going out of town for a few days with David."

Norman Ginsberg nodded, and David took R.J.'s hand as they walked together out of the commissary.

\*       \*       \*

On Thursday night R.J. tried on every outfit in her closet, then stood in front of the mirror, hating every one. If Dinah were in town she would be sitting on the bed now, telling her: "This one's too dowdy. That one's too flashy. The black one's perfect. Put that sweater with those pants and that one with these and you've got it." But Dina was still in Florida with her mother, and R.J. was in a panic. She hadn't bought herself anything new in ages and nothing seemed to fit or look right or . . .

This had nothing to do with clothes. She was thirty-seven years old. The mother of a soon-to-be teenager. She was an older woman with six very prominent gray hairs. Okay, eight. And she was packing up to go on a trip with some twenty-nine-year-old honey. That's what he was after all. And she was doing exactly what she'd promised herself not to do. Wasting her time on someone who was an impossibility. The biggest impossibility so far. Just because David Malcolm seemed more sane than the other men she'd met, he certainly wasn't more available. Not for her anyway. Maybe for some girl of twenty-three who was blond and just out of the convent. She laughed at that thought and then moved closer to the mirror to look at her hair. The gray count was more like eleven or twelve. Finally she chose a few things that would have to do, threw them into a suitcase, and crawled into bed.

Tomorrow night at this time—if she didn't come to her senses and cancel—that freckled face could be next to her. This was a mistake. It would end up to be just another hurt. She stared at the ceiling for hours, thinking that when the day broke she would call David Malcolm and tell him she couldn't go away with him, and fell asleep deciding exactly how she would tell him. The sharp jangle of the phone ringing startled her awake at nine.

"H'lo?"

"Why don't we take your car?" he said.

"Huh?"

"It's a gorgeous day and a convertible would be great."

R.J. sighed, remembering the promise she had made to herself last night.

"David, listen," she began. "I've got to say this—"

"R.J.," he interrupted, "excuse me for interrupting, but I know this is awkward. We've just met and I'm whisking you off to drive up the coast to a place you could hate, and you're liable to end up thinking I'm a bore. But what the hell? Nothing ventured, nothing gained. And despite your pugilistic attitude, I can tell that you already like me, so what's the worst-case scenario? I reserved a two-bedroom cabin so we'll each get some reading done. Now what did you have to tell me?"

R.J. rolled over from her stomach to her back and looked out at the brightly lit day.

"That my car overheats," she said.

"Then we'll stop at a gas station on the way," he told her. "I'll be by in an hour."

He parked his Jaguar in her driveway and brought tapes to play on the way up. Kenny Loggins, Jobim, and Frank Sinatra. He threw his duffel bag and her hanging bag into her trunk, took her keys, helped her in, got into the driver's seat, and they were off. As soon as she let herself relax, knew there was no turning back, R.J. felt as if she were in a movie. Watching the coast go by as they drove north, looking at the view just past his face. That handsome face that kept smiling at her and laughing at her dumb jokes. The jokes she couldn't stop making about everything: the scenery, the music, her nervous preparations to leave town, why the two of them were together to begin with. He laughed an outraged laugh at those jokes.

They stopped in Santa Barbara for lunch at the Biltmore. The valet took the Mustang, and R.J. and David walked hand in hand through the cool tile-floored, high-ceilinged lobby to the dining room.

"This is a special place for me," he said after they were seated at their table. "My parents used to bring me here when I was a kid."

"You mean last year," she teased. He smiled. R.J. looked around at the elegant dining room and thought about her own immigrant father, who had probably never even seen a room like this. There were lots of older people having lunch. Ladies with hair that looked tinted blue, and men wearing brightly colored golf pants. The waitress brought the menu.

"No chance there'll be a bagel on here," R.J. said, opening it. She was right.

Back in the car after lunch, as they moved up the coast, he asked her a lot of questions about her childhood, and when she answered them she could tell by the comments he made that he was really listening to her. Interested. After a while he put a tape in the tape deck, and they sang along with the music: Jobim's "Quiet Nights and Quiet Stars," and Kenny Loggins singing "Celebrate Me Home." And when David put the Frank Sinatra tape on, they were somewhere around Big Sur and he turned the music louder.

"I'm surprised," she teased him, "that at your age you even know who this is."

"Are you kidding? Old Blue Eyes?" he said, and his own blue eyes danced.

He knew every word of every song, and as the introduction to "You Make Me Feel So Young" played, they were just approaching Big Sur. He pulled the Mustang off the road, got out of the car, came around to the passenger side, took her hand, pulled her to her feet into his arms, and with Sinatra playing at top volume, they danced. Slow-danced. Close together. With the ocean smashing against the rocks below. Drivers of other cars passing on the road honked in amusement, but R.J. didn't hear the ocean or the horns. Just her own voice in her head, warning herself: Don't melt. Don't let this feel so good. It feels this way because it's a seduction. Know that and accept that and don't fall for this boy. He's a boy. This can't work. And you'll want it to, because you're wanting it already and . . . "Songs to be sung, bells to be rung, and a wonderful fling to be flung," Old Blue Eyes sang. A wonderful fling to be flung. That's what it was. Why couldn't she just let it be that?

The Ventana Inn was rustic and the cabin was luxurious and cozy. David had checked in with ease, and minutes later, he and R.J. sat on the porch of a two-story cabin set into the side of a green hill, with the ocean far below. They sipped wine and watched the sunset. And though David didn't ask, R.J. began to tell him about her life. How her father and mother both came over to America from two different places in Russia when they were very young.

They were poor struggling Jews who had escaped oppression to live in a strange new place. And she was their only child, who came to them late in life. For many years her elderly grandmother lived with them and raised her while her parents worked. The stories about what R.J. thought the world was like from her vantage point as a child growing up in Pittsburgh, Pennsylvania, were so strange and unusual to him that several times he had to shake his head and laugh. A long time later, when she thought about it, she realized she had told him those stories to prove to him immediately how totally wrong they were for each other.

Then he told her about working in the paper business and a little about his mother, who had been an actress and very beautiful but of whom he had very little memory because she had died when he was very young. And then they held hands quietly. When it was night, they walked down the long path from Ventana to the highway, and down Highway One about a quarter of a mile to Nepenthe. It was a funky, casual burger place where the people who sat around the outdoor rock fireplace waiting for their tables to be ready inside, looked as if they'd just stepped out of the sixties. R.J. and David waited by the fire, too, drinking red wine and talking. David told her about his work and how he had begun in the paper products division. A few years before he had started the company's computer paper department, though the bulk of the company business, which had started with one small lumber mill, was still from their various newspaper and magazine accounts and from their sale of pulp.

"I always thought that meant dirty novels," R.J. told him and he laughed.

"We're a perfect pair," he said. "I work for a company that makes paper and you write on it."

She told him about her days on Patsy's show, and the things the men said in meetings, and what it had been like working with Patsy, and how she'd been fired. By the time they'd walked back to the cottage at the Ventana Inn, and he held her and kissed her a kiss that had so much sweetness and warmth behind it, she knew that the second bedroom he'd so politely paid for was a nice gesture but a waste of money. Because she only wanted to be in his arms all night long. Even if it was dumb. Even if it was a fling. Another kiss and yes was all she could say when he lifted her and carried her upstairs. Yes. And at two in the morning, after endless hours of lovemaking, she said, "You know, a woman of my age is at the peak of her sexuality, but men peak at eighteen. So maybe I was wrong about your being too young for me. I think the real problem is that you're too old for me." He giggled and kissed her on the nose, and then proved to her before they finally fell asleep that he was not at all too old for her.

She woke up in the morning with a start. David was wrapped around her and in a very deep sleep. Even when he slept he was handsome. She slid out of his arms and stood, then looked at her watch on the night stand. Eleven-thirty. So late. They probably hadn't fallen asleep until God knows when. She tiptoed into the bathroom and . . . good God. She hadn't taken her makeup off the night before, and her face was a mess. Her head was pounding too. She washed her face and brushed her teeth, wrapped a towel around her naked body, walked downstairs to the living room of the cabin, looked outside at the leafy green view, and worried. Why had she let herself do this? Steal away for a weekend with this boy? Yesterday with him had clearly been more than she'd hoped for, but once again there was nowhere to go. Big deal, Dinah would say. Life is short and so are you. Live it up.

She sat sleepily on the wicker and white-canvas chair with her feet curled under her. To this man she was an attractive oddity, she thought. An older funny person in show business. Fun to slip away with for the weekend. That's what this is. So she had to stop doing what she was already doing. Thinking about every couple she'd ever heard about in which the woman was older and how happily married they were. That was crazy. That was self-destructive. That was how she could insure herself getting hurt. By wanting marriage and a family so much that she'd try to fit any face into the picture where the husband/father is supposed to be. The way she had with Michael, or Barry, crazy after crazy, ad infinitum. No, kiddo, she told herself. This boy is not for you. Get your act out of here and on the road back to L.A.

"It isn't even noon yet," she heard David say as he walked down the steps. "What are you doing up?" He was naked. The soft golden hairs on his chest and arms and legs glowed in the sunlight that poured in the window. Unless there was some deep dark secret he was keeping—a horrible temper, a shady past—he was without a doubt the sweetest, most attractive man she'd ever encountered in her life. She felt an enormous rush of feeling for him. A longing not just to press herself against him, but to hold him, learn about him, feel close to him, and . . .

"I want to go home," R.J. said, and the words *better now* fluttered through her head. Better now, before she cared too much. David didn't look surprised but his jaw tensed.

"Looking to cut your losses?" he asked. He understood. She nodded, he shrugged, and they were checked out, in the car, and on the road south in minutes. They spoke only to exchange strained polite conversation about restroom stops. At San Luis Obispo it started to rain and when they stopped to put the top up, R.J. said, "I'll drive." When she got behind the wheel she felt a little better, as if taking control of the wheel had given her control of the situation, but when he slid the Frank Sinatra tape into the tape deck, and Frank sang the songs they had listened to on the way up the coast, and she remembered how it felt to be close to him . . . no. She was doing the right thing now. Making a mature decision.

The freeway into Los Angeles seemed uglier and more congested than she'd ever seen it. R.J. drove the Mustang up her street and into the driveway, parked, and got out. David got out, too, and opened the trunk so he could take out his bag. He took hers out as well, and carried it to the front door. The drive had taken them all day. It was dark. Finally they stood at her front door. He looked into her eyes and she felt foolish and sad for feeling the way she was feeling and handling it all with so little finesse. But what he had said was right. Cutting her losses was exactly what she was doing. There was no percentage in hoping this would turn into something other than a hot love affair with a younger man. That might have been the right thing for many other women, but not for her. Not now.

"I'm sorry," he said, "but you must have been so hurt down the line that you can't see past your pain. And you've really got some negative self-fulfilling prophecy going about the two of us. So I want you to know that I had a great time with you yesterday and last night, and I hope for your sake you work out your problems one of these days."

R.J.'s face burned. She didn't know what to say. He was right, but he was wrong, for her. If only. The door opened and a sleepy-eyed Jeffie looked at the two of them.

"Hi, Mom. I could hear you guys talking out here, so I—"

"This is David Malcolm," R.J. said. "And this is my son, Jeff."

"Nice meeting you," David said.

"You too," Jeffie said, eyeing David closely.

"I've got to go," David said. He walked to his car, threw his duffel bag into the trunk, got in, and backed up to pull out of the driveway.

"Neat," Jeffie said, looking at the Jaguar.

"You mean the guy or the car?" R.J. asked. The right thing, she kept saying to herself. I'm doing the right thing. Then why did she feel so rotten about it? So much so that she wanted to run out to the driveway and say "Wait! I'm a jerk and I'm changing my mind."

"Neither," Jeffie said. "I'm talkin' about his license plate."

R.J. looked at the personalized license plate on David Malcolm's car. There were no numbers. Just seven letters. R-A-I-N-B-O-W.

# BOOK TWO

# DAVEY AND ROSIE JANE

1939–1962

*L*ily Daniels pushed the food nervously around on her plate with her fork, and every now and then took a bite that she could barely swallow. She knew she should eat, because later when she got to her room she'd be starving if she didn't. She was trying very hard to hear and remember every word everyone at the table was saying, so the minute she got home she could tell it all to her mother. But it wasn't easy because so much of it was a dazzling blur of clever conversation, at this big long table that was supposed to be elegant. Lily's mother would laugh out loud when Lily told her that the ketchup and mustard were sitting on the table still in their factory bottles. And there were paper napkins instead of cloth. Because that was hardly the way either of them had imagined it would be having dinner at San Simeon with William Randolph Hearst and Marion Davies.

Marion Davies was darling and witty and Mr. Hearst was obviously mad about her. Earlier today she had sat by the tennis court for nearly an hour with Lily, asking her questions about her acting career, honestly interested in all of the stories about what it was like to be a contract player at Hemisphere Studios with Mr. Hearst's friend Julian Raymond as the studio boss.

"I've only had the teensiest parts so far," Lily told Marion—as she insisted Lily call her instead of "Miss Davies." And Lily made a mental note to tell that to her mother when she got back to Los Angeles, to prove that

Marion was a very warm, nice person despite the fact that she was Mr. Hearst's "misstresss," which was the way her mother had hissed it this morning while she watched Lily pack. Sitting on a chair in Lily's room in that way she did so that her back never touched the back of the chair. Knowing her twenty-one-year-old daughter wouldn't pay any attention anyway if she tried to stop her, but obviously hating the idea that Lily was actually going to spend a weekend in the home of that brazen couple who lived in sin.

Marion Davies also wanted to know—and it didn't feel as if she was just making small talk either—how Lily had become a studio contract actress to begin with. And Lily, who had told the dumb story over and over to every one of her girlfriends, to everyone in her family on both sides, and even to one reporter from a fan magazine, told it again. How she was working as a receptionist in Dr. Beeler's dental office when Julian Raymond came in with an abscessed tooth and saw her there and offered her a movie contract. And the way Dr. Beeler, who had been Mr. Raymond's dentist for years, warned her that the devil was in show businesss. Marion Davies had loved that part. Laughed a hearty laugh.

"I'll bet you're going to be a big star," she said to Lily, who said thank you and stopped herself from telling Marion Davies the truth, afraid it might seem hurtful to this woman who was only a Mistress and not a Wife. What Lily really wanted was to be married and have what she called "tons of children." Stardom really didn't mean much to her. In fact she had told Mr. Raymond that, when he was trying to woo her away from Dr. Beeler. He had perched on her reception desk in Dr. Beeler's waiting room, laughed, and said:

"Dear girl, if you come and work at my studio, I promise you'll stand a much better chance of finding the man of your dreams than in a shabby dentist's office on Wilshire Boulevard. You'll meet producers and movie stars and cowboys and politicians. You're so pretty you'll be able to take your pick of the lot. And in the meantime I'll make old Alfred here sign a paper swearing if you change your mind he'll take you back."

In the two years she'd been at the studio, Mr. Raymond and his wife, Vera, had become a kind of aunt and uncle to Lily. Escorting her to premieres. Making sure she was home safely at her widowed mother's tiny home when she returned from a location shoot. It was only because the Raymonds had built a bank account of trust with Lily's severe mother that Colleen Daniels had agreed, albeit grudgingly, to let Lily join them for a weekend at San Simeon.

San Simeon. After dinner Lily went to the tiny loft bedroom she'd been assigned just off the projection room. The room had been brought to California piece by piece from a monastery in Europe. She sat on the bed and thought about her day. The way at lunchtime Mr. Hearst out of nowhere had said, "I feel like some Welsh rarebit," and everyone, all the guests, had trooped into the kitchen to cook one up. Vera Raymond grated cheese, Lily made toast points, and Julian buttered the toast. Everyone pitched in except for that stodgy friend of Mr. Hearst's from Chicago. The one with two last names. Malcolm Rand. No. Rand Malcolm. The man sat there the whole time reading the newspaper. The newspaper! Lily couldn't believe it. And someone said after they'd all been cooking and chatting and he'd been behind the paper for at least an hour, "I only hope that's a Hearst paper," and everyone laughed. Lily would have to remember that. Her mother would think that was funny. Especially since Rand Malcolm never even looked up. Just turned the page.

The next day was Sunday, Lily's last day at San Simeon, and of all things, with her rotten backhand, she was asked to be Mr. Hearst's tennis partner. At his direction she played the net while he, dressed in a white shirt and white trousers, stayed at the base-line. Hitting the long balls again and again until he and Lily easily beat Vera and Julian Raymond. Marion Davies was watching the game, and when it was over she waved to the others, took Mr. Hearst's hand, and they walked off.

Lily, wiping the sweat from her freckled face and then rubbing the towel hard through her bright-red hair, looked after them dreamily. "He is so in love with that woman," she said to the Raymonds.

"Goddamned if *I* know why," she heard an unfamiliar voice say, and when she turned, she realized that the Raymonds had gone, too, and sitting at a table under a nearby tree was that Malcolm man. With a start, Lily realized he'd probably been there the whole time.

"*Why* is because she's the perfect woman for him, no

matter what my mother says about their marital status," Lily snapped, then felt silly because she probably sounded like some dumb lovesick girl to the man from Chicago. By way of response, he picked up his newspaper from the table next to him and began reading it as if Lily weren't standing right there.

Well, nice talking to you, too, she thought. Mr. and Mrs. Raymond had told her they'd be going out for a drive at two and it was a few minutes before. She'd go to their room and find them and join them. She had just turned to go when she heard the man's newspaper rattle and his throat clear. When she turned back he'd lowered his newspaper just enough to reveal his eyes, which she noticed were very blue.

"What makes her so great?" he asked.

"She's full of beans," Lily said, using an expression of her mother's which, when stoic Colleen used it, was one of enormous praise. "And with all due respect, he's dull. She lights up the rooms here and he knows it." How could anyone, even an old fogy like this guy, not see that? "I mean, when I first saw the two of them together yesterday, her so beautiful and him with that big head and funny voice, I thought she can't really love him. It must just be all the money. And that made me mad, but then when I watched them I realized that she brings him out. That's what a partnership is for. That's what my father always said about it. Because people would say Cal and Colleen Daniels are like night and day, and you know what he would answer them? 'That's why the night *needs* the day.' My parents were like that. You see, my mother is kind of like Mr. Hearst. Not *that* serious, and certainly not that rich, but a person who keeps things inside, and my father, God rest his soul, was the life of the party. He could sing 'Danny Boy' until you cried your eyes out. 'Cal Daniels always has something to say, whether he does or not,' my mother would tell me. But she loved that about him. Every couple needs one person like that. And my dad could talk without end," she said, smiling at the memory of her father.

"Obviously," Rand Malcolm said, "it's in the genes." Lily, realizing from his tone that she was being insulted, was about to say something about his rudeness, but it was too late. He already had the newspaper in front of his face again. The boor.

"It's been a pleasure," she said, and walked up the path, having no idea that the turning point of her life had just taken place. At San Simeon.

Within a few years, audiences all over America had fallen in love with Lily Daniels when she appeared in her first leading role in *Boarding School*, in which she played a young teacher at a girl's school who is accused of murder. The cop who investigated the case and fell in love with the young woman was played by Jack Welles, a craggy-faced hard-looking actor who made his living playing tough guys. The contrast between Welles's world-weary attitude and Lily's dauntless love of life was so electric and sexy that Julian Raymond ordered three more scripts written in which they could play lovers.

The first one took place in the old West and was called *The Sheriff's Daughter*. That was Lily, and Welles played an outlaw in the jail. When they fell in love and she wanted to help him escape, he refused unless she agreed to run away with him. At the last minute she couldn't go with him and he couldn't go without her, so he died on the gallows, but not before telling her that where he was going now, "They'd never let your kinda gal in."

The next one, *Dear Suzy*, was a comedy about a newspaper on which Lily was the editor and Jack Welles wrote the lonely-hearts column. It was full of snappy repartee and love scenes and jokes, and the biggest hit yet. Then they made *Woman on the Run*. Jackie Welles played Gino, a no-good mobster who had only one soft spot and that was for his gal "Red," a beautiful but shy girl who wouldn't give up her job in the five-and-dime and take money from him, " 'cause it ain't right." When Gino was shot down in the street, leaving Red alone in the world, audiences cried—and vowed to see any picture starring Lily Daniels and Jackie Welles together. Those two were magical. What sex appeal. In real life, off camera, they were probably madly in love.

They weren't. Jack Welles had been happily married for the last twelve years. To three different wives, for three years each, with a year off—an intermission—in between. And Lily was still hoping to meet the man of her dreams, and starting to think she wouldn't. And that maybe she would have been better off staying in Dr. Beeler's office. Certainly the work in a dental office was a lot easier than this. And the people she met seemed a lot more sane. And at least in a dentist's office you knew what you were doing. Not like making movies. Never quite feeling she was getting the hang of it, she took acting lessons even on the days she was shooting. At least once a month in frustration she would march into Julian Raymond's secretary's office and insist that she be allowed to see Raymond right away. And when Raymond called her in he'd be all smiles and tell her how many letters came to the studio every day praising her work, and she would invariably tell him: "Mr. Raymond, I just don't know how much longer I can keep doing this. I'm not very good at it, and I don't have the patience for it, and frankly I'd rather go get a *real* job."

She was using most of her earnings to put two of her brothers through college and to help support another and his wife. She didn't want to give that up, but she didn't know how much longer she could keep convincing herself that this silly carrying-on she was doing in these movies was acting.

Somehow Julian Raymond would calm her down. With reports from her acting teacher about how well she was doing. With reviews from newspapers all over the country on how moving her performances were. With news of the rumor that for *Woman on the Run* she could be nominated for an Academy Award. And though none of those things mattered very much to her, eventually she would feel bad about taking up so much of Julian Raymond's valuable time and leave his office assuring him that she would keep making pictures for him. That she wouldn't run back to Dr. Beeler's office or just up and quit.

Then the airplane landed on the back lot—a private plane, unheard of in wartime, but there it was. It was a Lockheed 12, someone told Lily later. When it finally touched down on the big open field behind the western set, people rushed out of offices and dressing rooms and sound stages and ran out toward the field excitedly, as if it were not just a fancy airplane that had landed but a spaceship. When the propellers stopped turning, the plane was very silent for a moment, and so were all the people standing in the field. Then the door opened and out of the airplane came the pilot.

He had high cheekbones and blue eyes and thick wavy strawberry-blond hair and a very serious expression, and he looked familiar to Lily but she couldn't quite place him. He didn't even acknowledge the people in the ever-increasing crowd, all of whom were looking at him nervously. This had to be some kind of gimmick. Some kind of publicity stunt. Some out-of-work actor who knew how to fly a plane and was landing it here at Hemisphere just to get attention with the hope that that would help him get a part in a picture. He was certainly better-looking than any actor this studio had under contract. Finally he stopped and looked around at individual faces in the crowd, as if he was trying to spot someone, and then he spoke.

"I'm looking for that girl."

Julian Raymond was nowhere in sight. He must have been at a meeting somewhere off the lot. The crowd remained quiet, as though no one knew what to say. Finally Barney, a cameraman Lily liked, spoke up. "What girl is that, mister?" he asked. Lily thought Barney's voice sounded very afraid.

"That actress named Lily Daniels," he said, and Lily's insides jumped when she heard it. She tried to make herself very small and to hide behind one of the makeup men who had run out onto the field just ahead of her as the plane was landing. Maybe this was some crazed fan who wanted to meet a movie actress, and this was his way of doing it. He could be violent or have a gun on him. Lily wished she had stayed in the safety of her dressing room and watched the airplane land from her window. Now she prayed silently that no one would tell the crazy fan that she was standing there, shaking. Everyone was silent until the man from the airplane spoke again, to no one in particular. "My name's Rand Malcolm."

Rand Malcolm. Rand Malcolm. No. The stodgy guy she'd met a few years ago, maybe five years ago, at San Simeon? Impossible. The one who was always reading the newspaper. Could he have been this handsome?

"Rand Malcolm from the Rainbow Paper Company?" asked Charlie, an accountant from the front office.

"That's who I am," Malcolm said, walking toward the crowd.

Of course, Lily remembered, her heart pounding. Someone at San Simeon had told her that was why Rand Malcolm had been visiting Hearst that weekend. Waiting to talk business with Mr. Hearst. Malcolm owned a company that manufactured paper. Probably he sold it to the Hearst newspapers.

"Read about you all the time in the Business Section," Charlie the accountant said, with what Lily noticed was great respect in his voice.

"I always use your plates and cups when I don't feel like doin' dishes," shouted Sadie, the woman who ran the studio kiosk and sold newspapers, candy, and gum.

"Well, God bless you, madam," Malcolm said, nodding at her.

"Hell, no," Sadie said. "God bless *you*. Who wants to do the goddamned dishes?"

Everyone laughed. Lily thought about making a run for it, back to her dressing room. What did Rand Malcolm want from her?

"What do you want from Lily?" Harry, a grandfatherly electrician, asked shyly. Lily realized now that everyone in the crowd knew she was standing out there among them. They were protecting her.

"I want to marry her," Rand Malcolm said. Now everyone was smiling and chatting, exchanging looks, because all of them felt the glamour and the romance and the fun and the drama in this moment—which was more than in any movie any of them had ever worked on. And many of them had been around for a very long time. And then, as if they'd agreed on it, they all parted to clear a path, and Lily, who had been studying lines in her trailer, wearing baggy trousers and one of her brother's old shirts and not one drop of makeup, moved out of the crowd and down the path toward Rand Malcolm.

Malcolm didn't say a word as she walked toward him. Just nodded. A businesslike nod. Almost as if this was exactly the way he had pictured it would happen. Never thinking Lily Daniels might be at home when he landed his airplane at the studio, or out of town, or that she could be outraged at his audacity and not interested in speaking to him, or that someone as pretty as she was, was probably engaged to another man or, worse yet, married to someone who would tell him to get back into his goddamned airplane and go home to Chicago. No. He felt positive, as he always did, that things would work out exactly as he hoped. And when Lily arrived at his side he said, "Let's go somewhere and talk."

For the next three weeks Rand Malcolm stayed in Los Angeles. There was lots of talking. And there were long dinners and walks in Griffith Park, and an evening spent with Lily's mother and brothers carefully looking him over.

"I'm a damn good man," Rand Malcolm told Colleen Daniels. "The right man for Lily." Above his bed at the Rainbow Orphanage, where he had lived until he was fourteen, he'd had a sign, a quote from Emerson: DO WHAT YOU'RE AFRAID TO DO. He'd lived by that and been successful because of it. Now when he realized he was nearing forty and that maybe he hadn't married because he was afraid of *that*, he decided to find the right woman. Lily was twenty-six; Rand Malcolm was thirty-eight. Colleen was worried about that.

"Means I have more experience," he said. "More time to get situated." Indeed, he had done that very well. His paper company was the largest in the world. "No partners and no ex-wives." He'd never been married, though lots of women had tried. He was "not interested and too busy." But the memory of that little Irish girl he'd met at San Simeon had stayed in his mind.

"Fred," he had said, calling in Fred Samuels, the associate who had been his childhood friend, "find me that girl Lily. The one who's in movies."

"Boss," Samuels had said, using the term that was more of a nickname for Rand Malcolm than anything else. "She's starring in a double bill at the Bijou. Why don't I come by and get you later, and the popcorn's on me?" By the time the first reel of *Woman on the Run* was over, Rand Malcolm was in love.

The home offices of the Rainbow Paper Company were in Chicago. Lily's mother was worried about her only daughter moving away.

"I'll move my company here," Malcolm said.

Lily watched her mother respond to him. Colleen usually liked men with more of a sense of humor, but Lily guessed that her mother noticed, the way *she* had, that even though Rand Malcolm's words were serious, there was an unmistakable twinkle in his eye. As if there were someone inside longing to be helped out. This was the man she had waited for. And he had come out of the sky to marry her, as if life were a fairy tale.

That night, when her mother and brothers had excused themselves and she and Rand sat alone, Lily looked around at the shabbiness of the house. The tiny living room, where the arms of the sofa and of every chair were frayed down to the stuffing. She had begged her mother for the last few years to please let her buy or rent the family a newer, better house, some better furniture, but Colleen Daniels always refused. So even now, Lily Daniels the movie star still slept in the same tiny bedroom she'd slept in all through grade school and high school.

"Will you marry me, Lil?" he asked, and when she looked up, she saw him next to the chair where she sat, on one knee. He took her hand in his and looked into her eyes.

Lily had always known what she would answer a man when he finally said those words to her, so now she gazed deep into Rand Malcolm's eyes and said, "For me that would all depend on how you feel about children."

"I want twenty of them," he said. He knew he'd given the right answer when Lily's beautiful arms went around his neck and she kissed him sweetly. And her big green eyes, which always looked wet, looked even wetter when the kiss broke and she said, "Then I accept."

Julian Raymond sat in his office reviewing the latest box office figures. Jack Welles and Lily Daniels were like magic. The grosses for *Woman on the Run* were the highest he'd ever seen in the history of Hemisphere Studios. Christ, he was the smartest son of a bitch in the movie business. And he had three more scripts in the works that would be just perfect for the two of them. His biggest problem—and this thought made him laugh out loud, breaking the silence in his high-ceilinged, elegantly furnished studio office—was which one of the three to make first, since they were all sure-fire hits. A tap on his office door made him look up from the numbers.

"Yeah?"

The door opened and there was Lily Daniels herself.

"Lily!"

"Sorry," she said, "but your secretary was out so I . . ."

Still so humble. If she ever figured out how she had him and the whole world by the balls, she'd probably become a bitchy prima donna like the rest of them. Or maybe not. Now he and Vera had known Lily for nearly seven years—Christ, was it that long? That meant her contract could be up any time now. He'd have to remember to have his secretary check that as soon as Lily left.

"Lily," he said, jumping to his feet, seating her in a chair. "Can I get you anything?"

"No, thank you, Mr. Raymond. I—"

"Lily, what is it? Is something wrong?"

"Oh, no," she said. "Far from it." And then she blushed. She actually blushed. Julian Raymond had been in Hollywood so long, he couldn't remember the last time he'd seen anyone who was still innocent enough to blush. "It's just that I . . . I'm coming to remind you that my contract with Hemisphere is up next week."

Is that sweet, Raymond thought. Lovable and naïve and sweet. She probably was afraid that the studio wouldn't pick up her contract and she was coming in to talk about it.

"It's hard to believe," she went on, "that it's seven years since that day we met in Dr. Beeler's office, and you said that I would meet the man of my dreams at Hemisphere Studios. Well, I've met him and I'm leaving. In fact I've spent the morning emptying my dressing room, so that you could move someone else in there right away . . . and, well . . . I'm so happy . . . and I wanted to come by and thank you for making it possible for my dreams to come true because you were absolutely right. If I had stayed in Dr. Beeler's office, this certainly never would have happened."

Raymond's mind was racing. This wasn't possible. The biggest asset this studio had was saying this to him?

"Lily," he said. "I have three pictures lined up for you and Jackie to make back-to-back. The first one starts shooting next month. You can't just walk out on me to get married because your contract is up." God, how had he forgotten? How had everyone in the legal department let this get by? It didn't matter. He would talk her out of this guy anyway, whoever he was. Who could he be anyway to get her to give up the best career any movie actress could ever wish for? Some gigolo, some hotshot producer—maybe Jack Welles was looking to make her his fourth wife. He was about due for a change, and a vulnerable little girl like Lily might get roped in by a guy like that. Why was he worrying?

There wasn't a man around who could offer her what this studio could—the money, the glamour—and Julian

Raymond couldn't wait to sit back and start explaining that to Lily. To tell her what he'd give her in a *new* seven-year contract. The kind of deal a star like her was eligible for now. She wouldn't be able to resist, and instead of marrying whoever this clown was, she'd just do something smart, like secretly move in with the guy.

"Lily," he began, "I don't know where you met this guy or who he is but whoever he is he can't—"

"You won't believe who it is!" Her face, glowing with love, was more beautiful than usual. "His name is Rand Malcolm, and we all met him together in San Simeon."

"Rand Malcolm from Chicago?"

Lily nodded. "Yes," she said.

"The guy from Rainbow Paper? Vera said she thought his *face* was made out of paper because we never saw him for two days behind *The Wall Street Journal*. That's who this is about?"

Lily nodded.

"Oh, shit," Julian Raymond said, then added, "Excuse me," when he realized by Lily's face that she was offended by his language. "Lily, you can't leave me. The studio. Surely Rand Malcolm knows how important your movies have become. He's not going to deprive you of making one or two more. Okay, maybe three."

"Rand has nothing to do with this decision," Lily said. "It was all mine. And I made it long ago. When I was a little girl." Lily stood to leave and extended her hand. "You've been very good to me, Mr. Raymond, better than almost anyone, except my parents and Dr. Beeler, and I want you to know I'm grateful."

Julian Raymond's face was pale with defeat. If she were a man he'd be threatening right now to sue her ass. A man, hell. If she were marrying someone he thought he could beat in a court case, he'd threaten to sue her ass. But with Rand Malcolm's money . . . Lily was at the door now, looking at him expectantly, as if she thought he was going to give her his blessing or something.

"Good day, Lily," was all Julian Raymond said, as Lily Daniels Malcolm bounced happily out the door. It had been all she could do to keep from pouring out every detail of the tiny but perfect wedding which had taken place in her mother's living room only the night before. And how afterward, in their room at the exquisite Ambassador Hotel,

Rand had held her gently and kissed her sweetly and told her: "I'll give you everything, Lil," and she told him that just by loving her he had already done that.

But though both of them had meant what they said, they soon discovered that he couldn't give her everything she wanted, and what he *could* give to her would never be enough. Because after a year of trying they discovered that Lily couldn't, and probably would never be able to, become pregnant.

For the next five years every attempt they made was futile. They flew all over the country seeking advice, hoping against hope that this doctor or that might have the answer. From medications to unique positions in their lovemaking to potions of herbs and flower petals. Lily even went secretly to a psychic healer, knowing Rand would think it was nonsense. But nothing worked. And each time Lily would get her "monthly," as she called it, she wouldn't allow herself to cry, because that "didn't solve a darn thing." It would just serve to make her more determined to find an answer.

Their life together was filled with love and great excitement. The opening of the Rainbow Paper Center in Los Angeles. The day they found their dream house in Hancock Park. The huge parties they threw to celebrate each event. Rand insisted on having Lily with him on every business trip. She would chatter gaily to all the wives, thrilled to be in Rand's world, which was populated by such fascinating people. Rand Malcolm's friends and colleagues. Not only politicians and princes but giants in the business world. And as dazzled as Lily was by meeting all of them, they were more dazzled to be in the company of Lily Daniels, the stunning former movie star all of them had seen and fallen in love with on the screen. And she was even better in person because she sparkled when she was on the arm of her beloved Mal, as she and his close friends called Rand Malcolm.

And there were many close friends. Each wanting to tell his beautiful young bride tales about the many years of Mal's life when he hadn't had Lily around.

"Mal's a man of few words," someone had said. Had it been General Eisenhower who told her the story about how when you played cards with Mal he didn't talk all night, just concentrated on his cards? Then at the end of the night he'd say, "I win and you lose," rake in his chips, and go home.

Fred Samuels, who had been his friend since college, said that at Stanford, Mal had been known as Mister Five Words Or Less. "Mal figures if it takes more than five words to make his point, why bother?" Fred enjoyed telling Lily how changed Mal was since he'd married her. "Now sometimes he gets up as high as ten words."

Lily knew it was true. Mal had changed. Laughed with her, and was playful. The other morning in the shower he had sung to her. "Lucky in Love," his favorite song.

Mal. He was so patient and giving with her. Gazing at her across the dinner table, "I'm a goddamned lucky man," he'd say. But always she could see the pain in his eyes when a fertility experiment didn't work, and his increasing disappointment when each passing year made it more and more clear that he would never father a child. At least not with her.

Not with her. Mal. How she loved him. More every day.

"Maybe we should adopt," Lily said one morning, after awakening in a hotel in Paris with a heavy period that was eight days late. The lateness had given her such false hope, she had already been thinking about where she would send their child to school when he was five. Now she felt depressed and weepy.

Mal was shaving and she saw the reflection of his furrowed brow in the bathroom mirror.

"We have to keep trying," he said.

"But there are so many homeless babies out there who would be lucky to have us and—"

"I want a blood relative," he said, turning to look seriously at her from the bathroom. Five words or less. She never mentioned adoption again.

Late one night, after Mal was asleep, Lily sat looking out the bedroom window of their Hancock Park home. She hadn't been able to sleep properly for weeks. Earlier, Mal had made love to her, but it seemed halfhearted, as if without even the shred of possibility that they might create a child together, some part of the passion was gone. The moonlight streaming in the open window shone on Mal's face, and when Lily's eyes followed its path and looked at him she shook her head in disbelief, the way people do when they can't believe their own good fortune. More than good fortune. This man, this extraordinary creature. Could she even hope to give him back a small percent of the joy he gave her?

Of course she knew he loved her, was proud of her beauty, her charm at dinner parties, but almost any pretty girl with any sense could look good and say the right things in a crowd. She wanted to be more. To give more. Mal had turned forty-four last week and was still without a child. Dear God, if Mal had married someone else, he'd probably have at least four children by now. Married someone else.

The night was warm, and while Lily watched, Mal, turning over in his sleep, moved the sheet from his upper body and Lily could see the pattern of golden-red hairs on his hard naked chest, that chest that she loved feeling against her own. And the tears came. Married someone else. In the silence of the night, Lily walked into her closet and began to pack her things.

$F$or the first time in twenty years, Rand Malcolm didn't go to work. He showered, dressed, then sat in the living room of his home, alternately looking at the portrait of Lily that hung above the mantel and at the hastily written letter he held in his hand.

My dearest Mal,

I couldn't face you to tell you this, so instead I just left. Forgive my cowardice and please forgive a lie I told you six years ago that I can no longer live with. I have to have my career back, Mal. I miss the hard work of making a movie, the thrill of escaping into another character's skin, the importance of being Lily Daniels the actress. I tried, Mal, but as much as I love you, being a wife just wasn't enough for me, and pretending it was has been a terrible mistake for both of us. And being an actress, giving it the kind of dedication I need to give it, means to me that I can no longer be your wife.

I hope some day you'll forgive me for this, and understand. I am going today to Julian to ask him to sign me and give me another chance. I've heard about a script that's perfect for me, so maybe I can convince him that a comeback would be worthwhile.

Thank you, Mal, for six wonderful years. Please let's proceed with our parting without malice.

Lily

All his life he'd prided himself on having perfect instincts about people. Even from a distance. Like when he met Lily at San Simeon and again when he saw her on the screen. There had been such an enormous honesty about her work as an actress, he was certain that Lily Daniels the woman had to be just that honest. Well, this time he'd really missed the boat. Amazing. Lily leaving him. His own Lily wanting to go back to an acting career. And she had seemed so happy. Loved the travel. Loved the luxury of work-free days when she could drive her convertible to Culver City, pick up her mother, and take her to the beach for lunch. More than all of that, loved him. But not enough, and now she was gone. Why? Why in the hell would she go?

Lily sat in the guest parking spot at Hemisphere Studios hating what she was about to do. Her head was still pounding with her mother's admonishments from this morning. She was a foolish ungrateful girl and leaving that man was the dumbest thing anyone ever did and . . .

"Lily, is it really you?"

Jackie Welles looked tan and fit, and flashed her what he used to tell her, when visitors came on the set, was his "fan smile."

"God damn it's good to see you. What in the hell are you doing slumming around here?"

"Jack," Lily said, getting out of the car to give him a hug. All those pictures together, and yet when she looked at him, hugged him, he felt like a complete stranger to her, and the memory of all their work together seemed like a dream she could only vaguely remember.

"I've come to see Julian," she said. "I don't have an appointment. I guess I was afraid if I called and asked him to see me he'd refuse. He wasn't exactly happy with me when I left six years ago. But . . ."

"Well, truth be known, dollface, neither was I. You practically blew my whole career right into the crapper," Jackie said, still smiling, his capped teeth catching the noonday sun. "I mean, I'm surviving nicely without you, but—"

"Do you think he'll take me back, Jackie?" Lily asked, and she had to turn her face away as if she were looking around the lot, because she was afraid she would cry if she didn't. My God, she thought. I'm about to go in and beg for the last thing on earth I want.

"You mean that's what you're here for?" Jack Welles asked. "Kiddo, if you mean it I'm the happiest man in the world. I can take that place at the beach I've been longing for, and get rid of Lulu! She's been a goddamned albatross lately, and I met a girl last month—"

"I'd better go inside before Julian goes to lunch," Lily said.

"Lil," Jackie said to her, putting his hands on her shoulders and looking beseechingly into her eyes, the way he had done in *The Sheriff's Daughter* when he was begging her to run away with him. "Let me come in with you. Raymond loves me. I can help your case. I mean, just seeing the two of us together again, his little gold mine. That could help your case."

"No, Jack," she said. "I'd better go alone."

He took his hands from her shoulders and gave her a little pat on the cheek. And then, as she walked toward the building that housed Julian Raymond's office, Jackie's final words caught her and made her turn and give him one last look of pain.

"Marriage not working, huh?" he asked.

She turned back and kept walking. Julian Raymond's secretary Stella, who had always oohed and ahhed and gushed all over Lily, nodded coolly in greeting and said she would see if Mr. Raymond was in. Lily bit the inside of her cheek. To begin with, if he *wasn't* in, Stella would certainly know it, and Lily had seen his car outside, so of course he was. . . .

Stella returned quickly after a moment in Julian Raymond's office and told Lily: "Have a seat, and he'll get to you as soon as he can," in a voice that sounded as if she wanted to add, "even though I don't know why he would."

Nervously, Lily thumbed through some magazines. Her stomach ached. Colleen had tried to get her to eat breakfast before she left the house this morning, but Lily had been too queasy. Too afraid, because she knew what she had to do as soon as she unpacked the few things she brought with her to her mother's. Get Raymond to take her back. Under contract. That way she could make a clean break with Mal. Not have to take one cent from him. Be independent and let him leave the marriage with everything that was his. Mal. Oh, please, she didn't want to think about how much she loved him or she would fall apart. Lose her resolve, and she mustn't. This was right. She was barren. Incapable of conceiving. Could never give him what, because she loved him more than anything, she knew he must have. Blood relatives. Offspring. An orphan, left by an unwed mother at birth, never knowing one blood relative of his own, Mal had to have a child that was his.

When she thought about her own mother and how close they were, and her angelic father and how much he'd meant to her, and even her brothers who bragged to their friends about "my sis the star," and knew that Mal would never feel the power of that kind of connection because of her, it broke her heart. Soon, when Mal realized that she was serious, wasn't ever coming back to him, he would divorce her and eventually remarry, someone who could have children, and that would be the best thing. For him. Because she loved him she had to leave him.

"Good day, Lily," Julian Raymond said, in what sounded like the same voice in which he had said those same words to her six years before. She dropped the magazine and stood.

"Mr. Raymond."

"Please come in."

Julian Raymond's office looked exactly as it had on the day Lily had come to tell him she was leaving, and for a minute she had the eerie feeling that her life with Mal hadn't existed in reality at all but instead was just another role she'd played on the screen. Raymond was barely in his chair when Lily spoke.

"I want to come back to Hemisphere," she began, hating the childish sound of her own voice. "I know I made you angry when I left and I'm sorry for that. I was swept off my feet and couldn't help myself, and I know I acted irresponsibly toward you and the studio . . . but I think that it hasn't been so long that the moviegoers have forgotten me, especially the pictures I made with Jack, and if you'll forgive me and sign me again I'll—"

"Let me stop you," Raymond said. "Is Malcolm's business failing? Did you find him with another woman? What's really going on here, Lily? Try and keep in mind that you're talking to someone who knows you very well. And knows you're not here because of your concern over the moviegoers' loss. So before I tell you that I welcome you back—which of course I will because I need the money—tell me the goddamned truth."

"Mal and I are going to get a divorce," Lily said, shuddering at the sound of her own words.

There was a pause until Raymond spoke again. "His loss, my gain," he said. "I'll have the contracts ready by Wednesday at noon. For another seven years. Where are you living now?"

"At my mother's," Lily answered.

"Fine. I'll send a few scripts over for you to look at this afternoon."

"You won't be sorry," Lily said. But I will, she thought, and she nodded a kind of humble nod to Raymond, who didn't stand as she walked to the door and left.

"He's called every hour for the last three, and finally some guy who works for him dropped off this envelope for you," Colleen said.

Mal. He was looking for her. How Lily longed to run to him, burst into his office and tell him it was a joke, a lie, a crazy stupid idea she'd thought of in the middle of the night but now wanted to forget about. Instead she got undressed and slid under the covers of the bed in her old bedroom. The bed where she had spent so many nights dreaming and praying to meet a man like Mal. And now she was giving him up. She opened the envelope slowly. Maybe the letter would say "I know you left because you can't have children but I don't care about that anymore, because I don't really want children anyway. I only want you. Forever." But it didn't. It said,

> Lily,
>     I understand. And I guess you have to do what you have to do.
>
>                                            Mal

For the next few days Lily left the bed in Colleen's house only to come downstairs and eat, or to take an occasional shower, or to come out to the front porch and say hello to her brothers when they came by to visit Colleen. Mostly, she stayed in her old room and read the scripts Raymond had sent over. She didn't know or care if they were any good; she only knew that Mal wasn't calling to try to change her mind, and that she had this horrible queasiness she couldn't shake which she knew was fear. Fear that she couldn't pull this off. Fear that once she signed the contract she wouldn't even remember what to do in front of a camera. Fear that she would hurt so much, trying to live without Mal, that soon she wouldn't care about life at all.

"Gonna make yourself sick," Colleen said, entering Lily's room on Thursday morning.

"Am sick," was all Lily could get out before she had to throw the blanket off and run for the bathroom.

Friday morning she could hardly move from her bed to the shower, but she had to. Had to wash her hair, had to look good. Julian Raymond had told her on the phone the day before that the entire board of directors of Hemisphere would be at the meeting to welcome her back. She could hear in his voice that he had forgiven her, and he told her that everyone at the studio was delighted about her return, and that he was being treated like the hero who had made it happen. Had to get out of bed. Had to look good. Dear God, she was so sick.

"You're going to see the doctor," Colleen said as her daughter stepped out of the shower. "You look like a corpse."

"Can't. Meeting." Lily said, drying her hair with a towel. "I have no time for a doctor." She sighed as she caught sight of herself, emaciated and awful, in the bathroom mirror. All for losing Mal, her beloved Mal. She wouldn't blame the Hemisphere people if they laughed when they saw her and ripped the contract into pieces.

"Fortunately the doctor *does* have time for you," Colleen said, and as soon as Lily had slipped her robe on, Colleen opened the bathroom door and there stood Alvin Brockman, the family doctor. Holding his black bag and smiling his gentle smile at Lily, just as he had when she'd had tonsillitis and the mumps so long ago.

"How a be?" Dr. Brockman asked, the way he did to all his patients.

"I'm fine," Lily lied. "My mother's an alarmist. There's not one thing wrong with me, Doc," she said, and then her body went limp and she kind of folded in the middle and fell into a heap on the floor.

The doctor knelt, lifted Lily, and carried her to her bed to examine her.

Rand Malcolm's limousine pulled up on the tarmac at the Santa Monica airport. Fred Samuels got out first. The company plane, *The Lily*, was ready for takeoff. They would be in Chicago by nightfall, then a brief business dinner and back to the penthouse to rest for the board meeting tomorrow. Rand still sat pensively in the back of the car, as though he didn't realize that they had arrived at the airport. This was how he'd been behaving for the last few weeks, since Lily's departure. Samuels couldn't believe it. He'd known this man for twenty years. Watched him build a multimillion-dollar business, face down the giants of industry, never ever make a business deal that wasn't startlingly to his own advantage, and here he was, devastated by the loss of this woman. Granted, Lily had been a lovely charming girl but . . .

"Boss?" Samuels said.

"Mmm." Rand Malcolm looked out. "Oh. Right." Still distracted, he got out of the car, walked out on the tarmac and up the steps and into the airplane. Samuels made a few jokes as they sat in the cockpit about not being sure if he wanted to put his life in the hands of a guy who didn't even know they had arrived at the airport, but Rand Malcolm didn't smile, just took off the jacket of his suit, put on his headset, and began checking his instruments. He was very absorbed with the instrument panel and later, when he thought about it, wasn't even sure what it was that made him look out the window, to see the blue convertible come tearing around the corner, pull aggressively into the airport gates, and race toward the plane, where it came to a screeching halt. Its driver emerged.

Lily. The airport winds were blowing her bright-red hair wildly around her head, and the skirt of her pretty print dress blew against her legs. Those legs. Rand stood and moved to the heavy door, released the steps, and ran down them to her. Her face was pale and gaunt, and he saw a wildness in her eyes that unnerved him. She didn't say a word, just threw her arms around his neck and held on tight. Sobbing. Weeping. Pulling him tighter and tighter to her. What was wrong? What could have happened? Maybe her mother had died, or one of her brothers. Maybe *she* was the one who was ill. My God, she looked awful.

"Lil," he said, wanting at once to hold and kiss and protect her, but also to tell her to be damned because she'd caused him so much pain. "What is it?"

"Oh, Mal, thank heaven I can come home now," she said, looking at him with swollen red eyes. "You see, I left because I was so afraid . . . that you'd stay with me, be saddled with me . . . a woman who could never have . . . but it's different now. Now I can come home because I'm . . . Mal, I'm pregnant," she said, holding him at arm's length, praying she would look into his face and see that he understood. That he'd know she had left only because it had been the best choice. That now she could go back home to Hancock Park. And he did seem to understand everything now. She could see him putting it all together as he looked at her. Now he would make it okay. Or not. Instead his eyes looked cloudy. His face impassive. His jaw steel.

"I'm sorry, Lily," he said, "but I don't know what to tell you. It bothers me that you're a leaver, a quitter, a person who runs away from a problem when it gets to be too big. That doesn't give me a lot of confidence in our continued future. I know that your being pregnant is what you wanted. It's what I wanted, too, but this episode showed me a side of you I'm afraid of, because bigger issues than this one may surface, and then . . . where are you? I don't know," he said. "I don't think we can work it out. I have to leave for Chicago now—I have a meeting there this evening and another tomorrow—and then I'll be back and we'll have to decide what to do about the baby."

Lily was shaking and queasy. The doctor had told her to cancel her meeting this afternoon at the studio and stay in bed, for her sake as well as for the sake of the baby. The baby. Mal's baby. She'd waited for this moment all her life, and now he . . .

"Mal," she said, "I left because I thought maybe you would be better off if I . . ." But he had turned and was walking toward the plane. So she retreated to her car, turned the key, and drove off the field.

From the window of *The Lily*, Mal watched her as she drove away. He waited until her car was completely out of view before he called the tower.

"Meeting canceled," Colleen said. "Postponed, I should say. Raymond's secretary called here and said they can't do it until next Friday. I figured that was okay with you 'cause once you told Rand that you were pregnant he'd . . . "

There was something about the look on Lily's face that made Colleen stop talking.

"He won't take me back," Lily said.

"Of course he will," Colleen said.

"No. I did a wrong thing. A bad thing by leaving when the going was rough. He never would have done that. It's just that I thought I was doing right, Mother, and I . . ."

Colleen Daniels held her daughter while she cried, the way she had when her daughter had shed all her adolescent tears. Only this time Lily was crying very grown-up tears.

What in God's name was she going to do? She was pregnant at last, and Mal would have none of it. She would have the baby. Maybe the pregnancy wouldn't show and she could make a movie or two; then she'd take a few months off. Just a few months that Julian Raymond could add on to the end of the seven years, and she and Colleen would raise the baby and . . .

"Maybe I ought to send one of your brothers over to Hancock Park to pick up some of your things," Colleen Daniels said.

"No," Lily said. "I'll go. The servants are off today, and Mal's gone to Chicago. I won't have to see anyone. It'll be all right." She felt awful. Queasy. Desperately sad. She wouldn't be all right going there alone. To the house she'd lived in with Mal. Their room, their bed. But she steeled herself and made the drive to Hancock Park, alone.

The big house was silent as she opened the door into the foyer. Her feet tapped along the wood floor as she walked to the stairway, but before she went up even one step, she turned to look around the house. The portrait Mal had commissioned of her, which was hanging above the living room fireplace, caught her eye.

"I need to look at it when you're far away from me,"

he had said, by way of explaining why he had to have a portrait of her, then added, "like when I'm in the living room and you're in the kitchen." They'd both laughed. For six years the kitchen was as far away from him as she'd allowed herself to be. Until now. Mal.

Steel-jawed and stubborn. She knew he behaved that way in countless business deals. Relentless, unyielding to emotion or need. But where she was concerned he'd let that posture go. More and more. Until she breeched a rule she knew she shouldn't have. A rule he was right about. Staying in and fighting to the end was what he always did. What winners did.

In her closet she stood and stared at her clothes. Each dress, suit, blouse, brought back a memory of the occasion on which she'd worn it. Inaugural ball, political fund-raiser, that night in Bermuda when the stars glittered on the waves and they'd walked on the beach so in love. She couldn't touch anything. Just stood there for ages. Then she sighed and walked back into the bedroom and gasped when she saw a man's shadow in the hallway. And then the man.

"Mal."

He extended his arms to her, then took her into them and held her, thank you, dear God, held her and kissed her hair and her face and her tears.

"Mal," was all she could say. Her joy was shaking her. Finally he moved her to arm's length and looked seriously into her eyes.

"Don't ever leave me again," he said.

"Oh, I won't," she said. "I promise, my love. I never will. Never. Ever. Ever."

It was a promise that would be broken in a very few years.

# ROSIE JANE'S STORY

## 1956

*B*ubbe died on Pesach, and the rabbi said at the funeral that people who died on holidays were the most blessed. Rosie Jane looked into the open coffin and was sure that Bubbe was only playing a trick on all of them and that any minute she would sit up and start singing *"Oyfn Pripitchuk"* the way she did when she sat up in bed every morning, before she put her teeth in. Of course you had to already know it was *"Oyfn Pripitchuk"* she was singing, because when she sang it without her teeth, even an expert couldn't make out the words. But today there was no singing.

Long after they closed the coffin and carried it out of the tiny chapel to the cemetery, Rosie didn't stop praying that Bubbe would give a big knock. Like the knock she gave on the bathroom door the day she turned the doorknob too hard and the long part fell out into the hallway and the short part fell into her hand and no one was home. So, finding herself trapped inside the bathroom, Bubbe, who was not one to waste time, took a very long bubble bath. Then she tried on all of Rosie's mother's makeup, which was in the upper right-hand drawer next to the sink. And at three-thirty, when she heard Rosie come in from school, gave such a knock that Rosie came flying down the hall to let her out. And they both laughed until they cried at how silly Bubbe's ninety-two-year-old face looked wearing mascara and lipstick and a penciled beauty mark on her chin. Today, there wasn't one little knock to be heard.

The Russian cemetery on Fort Pitt Boulevard echoed with the sad voices of Aunt Sasha and Uncle Benny, Uncle Gershon and Aunt Malke, rich Uncle Shulke and even Aunt Chana, who hadn't spoken to Bubbe in two years since the fight they had over which of them knew the best way to cook chicken for Uncle Munish, who of course was also there. All of them were mourning the loss of Bubbe, their sweet mother, who, in order to support herself and her nine children and to be able to afford the passage to America for all of them, had built a still in the floor of the family house in a *shtetl* near Kiev, and made moonshine whiskey that she sold to the goyim. "Chaike Kaminsky," the rabbi said now, and his big quivering voice sounded to Rosie like an announcer on a radio show when he'd said the part about how she was "a beloved mother and grandmother," and now again as he recited the prayer for the dead, "*Yiskadal v'yis Kadosh. . . .*" And every one of the aunts and uncles and cousins nodded and tapped one another on the arm to point out that little Rosie, Bubbe's youngest grandchild, Rifke and Louie's girl, was crying the hardest of all.

Ay, ay, ay. Such devotion, they all thought. It must be because Rosie loved her Bubbele so much. After all, Bubbe had been sharing Rosie's teensy bedroom in Rifke and Louie's apartment, upstairs from Shulke's grocery store, since Rosie was born. So who could be closer? And everyone knew that while Rifke was so busy running the grocery store and Louie was so busy working at the Settlement House that it was Bubbe who raised Rosie. That must be why the poor little *meydele* wept so bitterly. Wasn't it? How could any of them suspect that what was making Rosie cry was not just grief but guilt and terrible remorse over something she could never tell the others. That *she* had killed Bubbe.

Bubbe was eighty years old when Rosie was born. And the reason the old woman had moved out of Uncle Shulke's fancy-shmancy house in Squirrel Hill, and in with the "poor relations" who lived upstairs from the grocery store, was because one morning her smiling bubbling dentures in the glass on the bathroom sink had scared Shulke's skinny little son Barry, who had to go to see a psychiatrist because of it. And Bubbe refused to apologize to Barry and refused to say she'd never do it again.

Well some things are "*bashert*," as Bubbe liked to say, which means they are meant to be, because for Rifke and

Louie, who had no children and who both worked like dogs, it was perfect to have Bubbe around. It gave them pleasure to find her waiting there with a nice piece of cooked brisket or a boiled chicken when they came from work at night. And more important was that Bubbe had been there only a month when Rifke found out, after years of being unable to conceive, that thank God she was pregnant. That's when it was decided by Uncle Shulke, who decided everything about everything in the family, that while Rifke continued to work in his store, not only would Bubbe take care of the cooking but the new baby also.

Everyone in the family said later that the responsibility of having to take care of Rosie gave Bubbe twelve more years of life. In fact, Bubbe had so much zeal and energy, and such a sense of fun, that she became not only the little girl's caretaker but her best friend as well. And why would a girl need anyone else? Bubbe played jacks and ball better than any kid on the street. Her wrinkled hands somehow knew exactly how high to throw the little rust-colored ball so she could magically scoop up the jacks as she counted them off in Yiddish. *"Eynts, tsvei, dray, fir . . ."* Bubbe never spoke English. She didn't have to. Everyone in her family spoke Yiddish as well as English and she didn't speak to anyone who wasn't in her family. Why should she? She had nine children, they had nine spouses, and there were twenty-two grandchildren. That was enough people for anyone to have to speak to.

Bubbe knew fabulous card games, even though she didn't know the names of the cards. For example, she always called the king the tsar, and the queen the tsarina, and the jack Yossl. And she taught all the games to Rosie. By the time she was five, Rosie could shuffle like a riverboat gambler. But the best thing about Bubbe was the way she always managed to dig up some money to take Rosie to what had become their mutually favorite place, which Bubbe tried to say in English, since she had no idea what the Yiddish words for it could be, or even if there were Yiddish words to describe the "moon pitchkes."

Bubbe would stare at the big screen, watching the actors and not understanding a word they said, and then, afterward, as she and Rosie walked home from the Manor Theater, Rosie would explain to her in Yiddish the "moon pitchke" they had just seen. And Bubbe would laugh at the jokes in all the right places and cry at the sad parts when Rosie told it, just the way the audience had laughed and cried at the actual movie in the theater. Except when they saw *Woman on the Run*, and Lily Daniels, who played the part of Red, rushed into the street where her gangster boy-friend Gino lay, full of bullets. "I love you more than anything," she said. "And now it looks as if you're going to leave me." For that one, Bubbe cried in the movie theater with everybody else, because what Lily Daniels was saying was in her big green eyes and it needed no translation. Rosie and Bubbe went to the Manor Theater every time there was a new movie to see. But that was their only luxury. Everything else they treated themselves to was free.

They went regularly to the Carnegie Museum to see the dinosaur bones, about which Bubbe told Rosie that if she could take those bones home and get the rabbi to kosher them, she could make a great soup. They went to Schenley Park to ride the swings, on which Bubbe pumped higher than any of the children. And when she flew back and forth through the air, her long skirt catching the wind, her dark-stockinged legs flying out and then in, her crocheted shawl floating behind her, she looked like a Halloween witch, and she screamed with laughter like one too.

Who could kill such a Bubbe? Well it wasn't because Rosie didn't love her. In fact, in many ways Rosie seemed to model herself after the old woman. For example, when Rosie carried her books to school she always carried them in a shopping bag. When she packed a lunch for herself it usually consisted of a piece of herring and an end slice of black bread. When the kids in school were asked to name their favorite entertainers seen on television, and most of the other kids picked the Video Ranger or Buffalo Bob Smith, Rosie picked Menasha Skulnik.

Rosie knew she was different from the other kids, and for a long time she didn't care. She would come home from school and do her homework and then put poppy seeds into the hamantashen dough Bubbe had rolled out, or hold a skein of wool while Bubbe wound it into a ball.

But one day that stopped being enough. Maybe it was when Rosie began to change. A bust. The place where a bust should be growing was very sore, and the rest of her body was getting hair in places that had always been smooth. And at night, when she was sure Bubbe was asleep, she

touched herself where she was afraid she shouldn't be touching herself, and sometimes while she did she kissed her
pillow hard and pretended the pillow was James Mason. It
was behavior she was certain that even if she knew the
Yiddish words to describe it, or any words for that matter,
she would never talk about with Bubbe—a woman about
whom Rosie had once overheard her mother confide to
Aunt Sasha: "Imagine. They had nine children and our
father never once saw our mother naked."

Rosie stole curious glances at the other girls in the
crowded dressing room at school as they took off their skirts
and blouses and put on their royal-blue cotton gym suits to
go outside and play field hockey. A few of the girls already
wore brassieres. Rosie wore the same undershirts she'd
been wearing since the fourth grade. Bubbe got them for
her by the package at the wholesale store downtown. They
were called "seconds," just like her underpants and socks.
And her clothes were all hand-me-downs from her cousin
Ruthie, who was a slob, so despite Bubbe's efforts to fix
them, every blouse had a stain that would never come out,
and every skirt was all stretched out around the middle
because Ruthie had a fat belly.

Now she came home from school, went to her room,
looked at the collection of yarn dolls Bubbe had made her,
put her face against the face of Bubbitchke, the doll that
had always been her favorite, and cried. Bubbe had a nickname for people who were misfits. She called them "Kuni
Lemmels." Rosie knew the girls at school thought that *she*
was a Kuni Lemmel. And why wouldn't they? She was
twelve years old and her only friend was her grandmother.
And she still wore pigtails.

And never mind the girls. What boy would ever like a
Kuni Lemmel? Want to dance with her the way Fred Astaire
danced with Judy Garland in *Easter Parade*, or look into her
eyes the way Gene Kelly looked into Leslie Caron's eyes in
*An American in Paris*, or tell her that he waited for her kisses
all day, the way James Mason—oh, God, that James Mason—
told Judy Garland in *A Star Is Born*? Or said, the way Jackie
Welles did to Lily Daniels, in *Woman On The Run*: "Do you
love me . . . ? Well then, maybe my life was worth something after all?" Not one boy would ever say that to her,
unless she could change. Be like the others. And she didn't
know how. Bubbitchke's face was soaked when Rosie set

her down on the bed, wiped her own face on the sleeve of Cousin Ruthie's blouse, and tried to figure out what to do to fix her life. Maybe it was too late. Maybe some people stayed a Kuni Lemmel forever. Rosie shivered at the thought. No. She wouldn't. She would do anything she could think of to change.

There was a seventh-grade barbecue coming up on Saturday night. Maybe she should make herself go to that. A ticket was only fifty cents. She had fifty cents in her sock drawer left over from Chanuka *gelt* her father had given her. She would go to the dance and then what? Talk to herself? What if there was dancing? Who would ask her? And what would she wear?

For a week before the barbecue, after she did her homework, Rosie would hold up one or another of Cousin Ruthie's hand-me-down outfits, trying to decide which one would look the best. None of them. Finally she chose a beige cotton blouse with a ruffle around the top three buttons, and a brown plaid skirt. It would have to do.

The night of the barbecue she showered and washed her hair and let it hang dry; then, instead of braiding it she pulled the sides back into two white barrettes. Then she put on a clean undershirt and underpants and the least-yellowed pair of socks she had in her drawer. She had ironed Cousin Ruthie's beige blouse and the brown plaid skirt by herself the night before and hung them in the front of the tiny bedroom closet she shared with Bubbe. She could hear her mother and Bubbe laughing about something in the hall-way outside the bathroom. That was odd. Her mother rarely came up from the store at this hour. Just before dinner. This was usually the time when the store was the busiest, with shoppers who were buying last-minute ingredients for their dinners. Rosie opened the bathroom door. Compared to the steamy bathroom, the chill of the hallway gave her goose bumps. Her mother and Bubbe stood there expectantly.

"All ready?" her mother asked, smiling a strange smile at her as if she expected Rosie to say, "Yes, I'm ready. I'm going to the barbecue in my underwear." Bubbe was wearing the same strange smile.

"Have to get dressed," Rosie said and walked into the bedroom. Her mother and Bubbe followed her. What was going on? As she opened her closet door to get out Cousin Ruthie's skirt and blouse, Rosie's mother and Bubbe giggled and a bright-red flash caught Rosie's eye. There on the back of the door hung a skirt and sweater in her size which had obviously been made for her by Bubbe as a surprise.

"She made it in three days," Rosie's mother said, beaming. "When I told her you were going to go to the seventh-grade barbecue, she felt so bad that you had nothing to wear but Ruthie's used things that she went to Mr. Zagerson's store and told him she would teach his daughter to knit if he gave her the wool for cheaper."

Bubbe was nodding at all of this, as though she understood, though Rosie's mother was speaking in English.

"She would wake up at night and do some, and then do the rest while you were in school," her mother said, with awe in her voice the likes of which Rosie had never heard. "In between making the meals and cleaning the house."

Rosie forced a smile. She was afraid to look back at the red skirt and sweater, because the first time she'd looked at them, only one word had gone through her mind. *Yechhh.* It was the ugliest outfit she had ever seen. Horribly out of style, bulky and strange. And the color. It was sort of red but sort of orange, and oh, God, what was she going to do? How could she tell her mother, who obviously thought this was the greatest gift anyone had ever given anyone, and Bubbe who had slaved night and day and even bartered her knitting talents to get the wool—how could she tell them she didn't want to wear the skirt and sweater? Couldn't wear it. Would be laughed away from the barbecue if she did.

"Try it on," her mother said. "We know it's perfect because she measured it against the *shmattes* you wear every day."

*Shmattes.* Rags. It was true. Rosie had never once been in a clothing store even to try on a new dress, let alone buy one. But at least Ruthie's hand-me-downs had once been store-bought, not made feverishly from begged-for "for cheaper" yarn by an old woman who had no idea about today's styles.

"*Nu?*" Bubbe said. "*Teet dos un.*" She wanted Rosie to put the horrible thing on so she could see how it looked. Rosie glanced at the clock. Six forty-five. She should be leaving for the school by now. She couldn't leave without at least trying the outfit on. Maybe she would be lucky and when she got it on it wouldn't fit. It would be too late now for Bubbe to alter it, and Rosie could say, "Some other time, Bubbe. Maybe to the next barbecue." Then she could put on Ruthie's skirt and blouse and go. She reached up and took down the hanger, stepped into the skirt while her mother held the sweater, and then both her mother and Bubbe helped pull the sweater over her head, the way she had seen wardrobe people in the movies help the star get dressed.

"*A zey sheyn,*" Bubbe said. So beautiful.

The only way Rosie could get an entire mirrored view of herself was to stand on her bed and look at her reflection in the mirror that hung over the chest of drawers she and Bubbe shared. Her first glimpse of herself in the outfit made her weak. Not only did the orangeish-reddish-colored outfit make her olive skin look deep green, but the way it hung on her body made her look lumpy in all the wrong places.

"*A zey sheyn,*" Bubbe repeated.

"Say thank you, Bubbe," her mother said.

"Thank you, Bubbe," Rosie managed.

Five minutes to seven. Rosie looked longingly over at the open closet at Cousin Ruthie's beige blouse and brown plaid skirt. Never before had her fat cousin's hand-me-downs looked so good to her.

"You'll be late, Rosele," her mother said, helping her daughter down from the bed. "Here's your pocketbook. Your father left an extra dollar this morning in case you should maybe need anything, so I put it in already."

"Thanks Ma," Rosie said. Trapped. She was trapped into wearing the orangeish-red outfit. What could she do? The only way out was to tell the truth, and that would hurt Bubbe terribly. Not just a little hurt, like the time Rosie told her how when she didn't have her teeth in she looked like Gabby Hayes. No, this outfit was the result of very hard work, with love in every stitch. She was probably already a little upset that Rosie wasn't squealing with excitement over the outfit.

"I love you, Bubbe," Rosie said, hugging the ancient, wrinkled woman. She gave one last shake to her unbraided hair, and headed for the front door.

*     *     *

Mrs. Gallagher, who was the seventh-grade music teacher, stood in front of the big brick barbecue pit, turning pieces of chicken over and over with a long fork. Her face was sweating and she kept pushing a lock of her auburn hair away from her wet forehead with the hand that wasn't turning the chicken. All the girls Rosie admired and feared were standing together on one side of the courtyard, laughing and talking. All the boys she longed to have like her and was afraid to talk to stood on the other side doing the same. Rosie felt certain that the orangeish-red skirt and sweater would cause an immediate outburst of ridicule, but not one of them even noticed her entrance. Or if they did, they didn't acknowledge her. If she had been afraid just to go over and talk to the others in the past, now she felt so self-conscious she wished they couldn't even see her. She was orange and bumpy. Maybe she would just go and talk to Mrs. Gallagher.

"Rosie dear," Mrs. Gallagher said. "How nice you look." Rosie could tell that Mrs. Gallagher was surprised to see her at the barbecue. It was the first school function she'd ever attended.

"Thank you," Rosie said. "I just thought I'd come over and see if you needed any help with the chicken." She couldn't tell Mrs. Gallagher that she was afraid to talk to anyone else.

Mrs. Gallagher's sweaty face lit up. "Rosie," she said, "you are the only person at this party even to bother to offer any help. And you know what? I'll take you up on it, because I'm desperate to go to the little girl's room. Please keep an eye on the chicken for me and I'll be back as fast as I can."

And she was gone. Rosie held the big fork and turned the pieces of chicken again and again over the fire. Now she felt a little better. Important even. As if she were doing this because she didn't have time for the silly giggling and carrying on that the others were doing. Besides, it gave her a great vantage point from which she could watch the others. Plaid skirts. Practically every one of the girls was wearing a plaid skirt.

A big burst of laughter erupted from the boys' group and the girls all turned toward them in unison to see why. But the boys' circle remained closed, and even from where Rosie was standing she could see only their backs. Especially the one that belonged to Ricky Lesser. He had dark-black thick hair—like James Mason—and a blue Ivy League shirt, and those big shoulders, and . . .

"Rosie." She jumped, afraid Miss Gallagher had heard her thoughts. "Thank you," Miss Gallagher said. "Maybe you would like to continue turning the chicken while I pour the punch."

"Yes, Miss Gallagher," Rosie said, spearing a piece of chicken and watching as the juice spurted out of it and rolled onto the coals, where it sizzled. Maybe one of the others would see her over here and walk over to talk to her. But no one did.

When everything was ready, Miss Gallagher used the same method she used when she was trying to get her music classes to be silent. She picked up a triangle and hit it with a little stick. When everyone stopped talking she said, "Soup's on," and then laughed a little laugh at her joke, since they weren't having soup. She walked over to the long metal all-purpose table that the school had used the day all the students came to get their Salk vaccine. Tonight the table was covered with a paper tablecloth, on top of which was a giant bowl of cole slaw, another of potato salad, some knives and forks, paper plates, thirty-five cups filled to the top with red punch, and the huge platter of chicken. Miss Gallagher stood next to the platter. She would serve each person a piece of chicken, and then they would move down the line to get their salads.

The boys and girls raced hungrily toward the table. Now the two groups, the boys and the girls, merged, and they laughed and flirted with one another playfully. Not one of them even said "hi" to Rosie. Giggling and teasing, some of them began to push. Rosie still stood quietly at the barbecue, waiting.

"Do not push," Miss Gallagher said, enunciating her words in the same rhythm that she used in music class when she said *do-re-mi*, but the boys and girls continued to push anyway.

"Now," Miss Gallagher said, as if she were about to make an important announcement. "I think that fair is fair and that the first person who should be served tonight is the only person who walked into this barbecue and, unlike the rest of you who are too busy to care about others, said, 'May I help you, Miss Gallagher?' *May I help you.* Four words which all of us could use more often, for if we did we could make a better world."

A voice like a monster's came from somewhere in the line. "Hoooongrrry," it said, and all the seventh-graders laughed.

"Now that's just the kind of selfishness I mean," Miss Gallagher said, "which ultimately causes the downfall of civilizations."

A groan went up from several of the kids. Rosie felt panicky. Miss Gallagher was talking about her. A finky drip, which was what Rosie once heard Joanie Goldberg call a boy in tenth grade whom everyone hated. A Kuni Lemmel, who instead of laughing and talking with the others, offered help to a teacher. *Oy*, please, don't say it.

"So the person I am going to serve first, and she certainly deserves it is—"

"The Virgin Mary," someone yelled.

"No, Stanley Goldman," Miss Gallagher flared, "and we certainly don't need your comments. The person is Rosie Jane Rabinowitz."

Rosie felt heat in her feet that moved through her like lightning and directly into her face.

"Come up to the front of the line, Rosie Jane, please," Miss Gallagher ordered. For a split second Rosie considered saying "no, thanks," but Miss Gallagher looked very upset and Rosie didn't want to make it worse, so she walked to the front of the line. The journey seemed endless. She knew they must all be snickering at the orangeish-red outfit, and when she finally stood at the head of the line, and Miss Gallagher handed her a paper plate and asked her which part of the chicken she would like, she had to swallow hard to keep the nausea down.

She looked at the platter. The charred black and brown and gold of the barbecued chicken was a blur, and she wasn't the least bit hungry, but she was standing there, and everyone was waiting for her to answer.

"Uh, lets see . . . I'll have the, uh . . . I think I'll take the uh . . . fleegle."

Hysteria. Every one of the kids in the seventh grade was laughing. A big laugh. At Rosie. Like the kind of laugh Jack Benny got when he said something funny on his show. Miss Gallagher smiled, a tiny forced smile, but her face looked confused.

"The *what*, dear?"

There was something wrong. Something wrong about asking for the fleegle. Maybe there weren't any fleegles on the platter. But there had to be. Rosie had turned the fleegles over and over on the barbecue herself. And now when she looked down at the pile of chicken, she could see at least six, maybe more of them. She sensed the restlessness behind her in the line, but she didn't know what to say next.

"Hooooongggry," came the monster voice again, and all the kids laughed. When the laughter subsided, Miss Gallagher took a deep breath and looked closely at Rosie.

"*Which* part, dear?" she asked, through clenched teeth. The friendly look she'd had on her face for Rosie earlier in the evening was now all gone. Not the fleegle, Rosie thought. There had been something wrong with asking for the fleegle. Something that made the others laugh. That was a mistake she wouldn't make again.

"Well," she tried, "maybe instead I'll have the poulke."

The laugh from the group was twice as big as the last one. Even Rosie giggled a little giggle because she was so nervous.

"The poulke," someone from the line shrieked out, and the laugh rose once more. Miss Gallagher's face was starting to sweat again, the way it had when she'd stood over the barbecue. Only now there was no hot barbecue. Now the sweat was angry sweat.

"Why don't you point to those two parts, dear?" she asked. The word *dear* was dripping with anger.

Rosie had never been more confused in her life. She wanted to drop the paper plate and run out the door and home, but she was afraid if she did she'd be known as the biggest Kuni Lemmel in the world forever. So instead, still not understanding what the laughter was about, she pointed first to the chicken wing and said, "This is a fleegle," and then to the chicken thigh and said, "and this is a poulke."

There was more laughter, this time dotted with applause.

"Have both," Miss Gallagher said, putting one of each on Rosie's plate. "Next!" Miss Gallagher said, in a voice so loud it made Rosie jump. Rosie was so eager to get away from the others that she didn't even stop for cole slaw or potato salad, but simply took her knife fork, napkin, and plate of chicken to a table, sat down, and began to try to eat, though her head was throbbing with the memory of the kids' laughter and the anger on Miss Gallagher's face.

Fleegle, poulke, what had she done wrong? It didn't matter. She would have a few more bites of the chicken, and when everyone was busy eating and laughing, she would catch the streetcar home. She wasn't even sure now why she'd come to the stupid barbecue. She didn't like any one of these kids to begin with.

"Rosie yanked Gallagher's chain," she heard someone say. "And did you hear Gallagher? The downfall of civilizations."

"Giving Gallagher her chicken order . . . in Yiddish."

Yiddish. *Oy vey. Fleegle* and *poulke* were Yiddish. Not English. In her house, in her whole life, Rosie had never heard another word for those chicken parts. If someone asked her now to say what the English was for them, she wouldn't have known. *Fleegle* was . . . what? Yiddish. She had no idea. There were probably lots of words like that for her. For most of her life, except when she was in school, she nearly always spoke Yiddish, probably because she was with Bubbe. And so many of the kids in her class were Jewish that they knew the word *fleegle* and the word *poulke* and knew what they were. . . .

Positive she couldn't hold her tears inside for another second, Rosie walked out of the school yard still carrying her paper plate with the fleegle and the poulke on it. *Fleegle, poulke,* orangeish-red outfit, helping a teacher, I can't, oh, God, *oy vey.* Why had she said that? When she got to Murray Avenue she could hear the streetcar bell clanging a block or two away, but she decided to walk. She needed to walk, to feel the cool April air on her hot face.

She would get home and her mother would ask how the barbecue was, and she would have to pretend it had been okay, and then she'd go to her room and Bubbe would be asleep so she couldn't turn on the light in the bedroom. She'd have to undress in the dark and slip under her covers, all the while listening to Bubbe snore, the way she had to every night, unless she happened to fall asleep first. Bubbe. This was all her fault. If it wasn't for her, Rosie could have her own room. Maybe even have friends sleep over, if she ever made any friends after this. Bubbe. She was ninety-two years old. That was enough already. Why did she have to stay around so long? Making ugly bumpy clothes for Rosie and talking Yiddish. Maybe she would live until she was a hundred. Then Rosie would be twenty. Old enough to get married, and she'd still be roommates with Bubbe. God forbid. Poo poo poo, as Bubbe would say. No. It was time for Bubbe to die. Big tears rolled down Rosie's cheeks as she quickened her pace, moving toward home, wishing—and hating herself for it—that Bubbe would die. Die. Die. Bubbe, please die already. Rosie fell asleep that night thinking those words.

Usually on Pesach morning Bubbe woke up very early to make the gefilte fish for the seder that night. When she was still sleeping at nine o'clock—which was very unusual, since the first strains of *"Oyfn Pripitchuk"* were usually heard at seven—Rosie's mother came to see why. Rosie was still asleep, with the covers pulled over her head. And Bubbe— Bubbe was dead.

After the funeral everyone came to sit shiva at Rifke and Louie's house. Aunt Chana brought honey cake that was kosher for Pesach. Aunt Malke brought macaroons. Rosie's mother put out coffee and tea. Nobody wore shoes. When it looked as if everyone had arrived who was going to, and people were talking and eating cookies and making jokes about how if it wasn't Pesach they could be eating corned beef sandwiches instead of Streit's macaroons from a can, Rosie's mother got a look on her face as if she'd just remembered something, and she got up and left the room for a few minutes. When she came back she was carrying an envelope, which she handed to Rosie.

"Bubbe gave me this for you a few months ago. But she said I should wait to give it to you until after she was gone. Until you didn't have her around to take care of you."

In the envelope was a hundred dollars. It was the most money Rosie had ever seen all at once in her life. With it was a note. The note was in Yiddish. Rosie could speak Yiddish but she couldn't read it. She gave it to her mother, who read it and then told her what it said. *Mayn kind.* My child. *Ich loz dir iber di gelt zolst dir keyfen cleyder.* I left you this money so you can buy some clothes. *Ich hob dir zeyer lib.* I love you very much. *Dayn Bubbe,* Chaike. Rosie excused herself and went into the room she had shared with Bubbe for her whole life. Then she lay down on Bubbe's bed, where she could still smell the familiar smell of her Bubbe, and hugged the pillow very close to her chest.

"*I*'m forever blowink bobbles
. . . Priddy bobbles in de air . . ."

For three weeks after Bubbe's death, Rosie Jane stayed
home from school. Every morning when she opened her
eyes she looked over at Bubbe's empty bed, and loneliness
ripped through her. Bubbe was gone forever. The only
friend she'd ever had. Now Rosie would have to go back to
school and face the other students in the seventh grade who
had heard her ask for the barbecued chicken parts in Yiddish. Even as Rifke, in the childlike handwriting she had
worked so hard to learn in night school, composed Rosie's
excuse note ("Please forgive my Rosie for being absent due
to our terrible tragedy and loss"), Rosie tried to think of
excuses to stay home for another week.

Her perception of the poulke-and-fleegle incident, as
she was to call it years and years later, was that she had
humiliated herself so completely in front of everyone in her
grade that she might as well not go back to school, because
no one there would speak to her anyway. But when she got
there she discovered that the story had been interpreted by
the kids as Rosie's irreverent way of teasing that dried-up
battle-ax Miss Gallagher. Instead of being laughed at, she
now found herself with the reputation of being funny. Very
funny. She was congratulated for her outrageousness so
often that she started to forget that the reputation was a
fluke, and began cracking the jokes aloud that she would
ordinarily have kept in her head. Some of them actually
were funny.

"Dey fly so high, nearly rich da sky . . ."

Her social life had begun at last. The girls befriended her, because everyone knows it's beauty that threatens other girls, and though Rosie was kind of cute, she was first and foremost funny. And the boys liked her, too, because funny was friendly. It wasn't forbidding or frightening like pretty.

The other immediate result of Bubbe's death was that it brought Rosie closer to her parents. With Bubbe no longer waiting for her after school, Rosie would find herself downstairs in Uncle Shulke's store, putting the groceries in bags for people and ringing the cash register. During the slow periods when no one came in, she and her mother would talk and laugh. Sometimes on a Sunday she would go with her father to the Settlement House where he worked. He said he went in on Sundays, his official day off, because that was the only day when he could get some paperwork done because nobody else was there and it was quiet. When he said that, Rosie's mother would wink at Rosie behind her father's back, a wink that meant the real reason he had to go to work on a Sunday was because being a group worker at the Gelman Community Settlement House was the most important thing in Louie's life.

So important that Mr. Katzman, his boss, had to insist—insist, mind you—that Louie take a week off and have a vacation. The first one he'd taken that any of them could remember.

"Den like my drimz, dey fade and die . . ." Louie sang with the stub of his Marsh Wheeling cigar stuck in the corner of his mouth as he drove along the Pennsylvania Turnpike. The windows of the 1953 station wagon were rolled down, allowing the summer heat to rush through the unwashed car. And other drivers, hearing Louie singing at the top of his voice, grinned as they passed the Plymouth, which chugged along in the far-right lane. "Fortune's alvays hidink . . ." Louie had come to America as a little boy in 1907, and now it was 1957, but the traces of his Russian dialect still lingered.

"I've looked everyvere," Rifke chimed in from the back seat. Whenever the family went anyplace in the car, Rifke sat in the back seat. That was so her Rosele Jane could sit in the front seat, and not, God forbid, get carsick. "I'm forever blowink bobbles . . ."

Now Rosie's voice joined her parents' and she added

the harmony for the last line: "Pretty bubbles innnnn theeee airrrrr." The three singers stopped to take a breath after the last note rang through the car. After they cheered hooray for themselves, the way they always did, Louie, who had to sing a little louder because a moving van was passing them, segued into "Ven you vore a tulip, a big yellow tulip, and I vore a big red rose . . ."

They were all elated to be going on a family vacation. To go to Atlantic City and stay in a hotel. For free. Not that it was such a big-deal hotel. It was only The Seaview, a hotel that was owned by Itzy Friedel, who, Louie explained to Rosie, was his *landsman*, which meant that Itzy Friedel had come over to America from the same town in Russia as Louie. But big-deal hotel or not, it *was* a hotel. And the only time Rifke and Louie had stayed in a hotel in their lives was on their honeymoon in Niagara Falls thirty-one years before. And Rosie had never set foot in one.

Itzy Friedel let out a yelp when he saw the Plymouth parking on the other side of the street, and came bounding down the wooden steps of The Seaview. "I vas doing a little shmoozing with the customers," he said, grinning and looking to Rosie like Bert Lahr as the Cowardly Lion. "Velcome, velcome," he said, taking the suitcases from Louie and doing a happy little dance. Rosie noticed that he had the same accent as her father. Rosie and her parents were tired and their clothes were wrinkled after the long drive. They had eaten the corned beef sandwiches they'd brought from home as they drove, and made only a few of what Louie called "pish stops" at occasional Howard Johnsons. Itzy hugged Rifke and Louie again and again and pinched Rosie's cheek, calling her a *"sheyne meydele"*—pretty girl—and a *"zise punim"*—pretty face. And then, beaming with pride, he insisted on taking them all on a tour of The Seaview.

The Seaview. Rosie loved it. The smell of it, a combination of Coppertone and fresh laundry, would stay in her memory forever. There were six hotel rooms on each floor. Each had a bed, a dresser, a tiny closet, and a ceiling fan. There was a bathroom at the end of the hall that everyone on that floor shared.

"Such a view of the sea The Seaview has," Louie teased, looking out of the window of the hotel room at the window of the hotel next door. The Seaview was on a side street three blocks from the boardwalk. Itzy Friedel raised his eyebrows.

"*Shmendrick,*" he said, with mock anger at Louie, then winked at Rifke and Rosie. "Come here and lean out the window and I'll hold your foot so you shouldn't fall," Itzy said. Then Louie gave a wink at Rifke and Rosie, and he leaned. Itzy held his foot.

"Nothing doing," Louie yelled back in the window.

"*Shmeikel,* lean further," Itzy yelled back out the window.

"*Oy,* no!" Rifke said, and laughed so hard she started to cough.

"Now, if you please, my boy, look toward the boardwalk," Itzy said. "And *zug mir. Vus zeystu?*" Tell me, what do you see?

Louie was laughing now, too. "Oh, yeah," he said. "Now that you mention it, I think maybe out there I caught a liddle glimpse from the ocean."

"Dat's right," Itzy said pulling Louie back into the room. "And that's vy I'm called The Seaview."

Rosie loved seeing her parents laugh. They had both been in wonderful moods for the last few days since Joseph Katzman, her father's boss, had told Louie he really ought to take a vacation. That he "richly deserved one" were his words, which God knows was true, and Louie's family deserved it too. The minute she heard about the vacation, Rifke, probably figuring unless she talked about it Louie would change his mind, told everyone who would listen about the vacation. Where they were going and when they were leaving. Especially her brother Shulke, whom she had to tell so he could give her time off from her job of managing the grocery store to make the trip.

"And Katzman himself said he so richly deserves it," Rosie heard Rifke saying into the phone in a voice that had awe in it. After all, she was talking about the big boss Joseph Katzman, and she was talking to her older brother Shulke.

"And why so richly?" Rifke was never a woman to brag, but today, even though she was speaking on the phone, Rosie noticed her mother stood taller with pride in her husband. "Because he worked so hard and never took a vacation before in all these years."

Work was the only thing Louis Rabinowitz believed in taking the time to do. Eating was something you did in order to refuel for work. Sleep was a way to gain enough energy to work the next day. The only maintenance the old Plymouth station wagon ever had was when he took it to a gas station, where they washed the windows while they were filling the tank. Many times the car would run on empty for a few days, because he hated to take the time away from work to stop at a gas station.

He was a group worker in a settlement house. That's what Rosie wrote on forms where it asked for FATHER'S OCCUPATION. Over and over she had heard Louie tell the story about how he wasn't even planning to be a social worker. He had wanted a graduate degree in architecture. In fact, he had been on a scholarship majoring in art at Carnegie Tech, and after he got his bachelor's degree he would go on to get his M. Arch. degree. Meanwhile, he was earning his tuition by assisting at the local settlement house. The Gelman Family Center was a place where the Jewish immigrants who lived in the Hill District were able to congregate and socialize as well as commiserate about this strange place called Pittsburgh. Louie moved easily among them. He spoke their language, literally and figuratively. Not only could he converse in Yiddish and Russian and English, but he had been a stranger himself not so long ago. He saw the fear in their eyes turn to hope when he showed them by example that soon they would settle in and be happy here. It was in 1922 that Joseph Katzman had called the boy into his office that first day.

"Pop," Katzman said. Louie was surprised to hear the boss call him by the nickname the Settlement kids had given him. Although the job was temporary, he had taken it seriously and become a wise fatherly organizer and friend, and he couldn't remember who started it but every kid in the place now called him Pop.

"I'd like to propose that instead of going on to graduate school, which I hear is what you're planning to do, you come here and work for me full time."

Being around Joseph Katzman always made Louie nervous. The man was American-born, and his wealthy family were friends of the Gelman family who had founded the settlement house. He wore fine suits and had buffed nails and lived in a beautiful neighborhood with his wife and children.

"Your work with the Jewish community impresses me, and I'd hate to lose you to graduate school."

Louie wasn't planning to leave his after-school job as an assistant. He needed it to stay in school and to help out at home. But Katzman sounded as if he wasn't talking about after school.

"I'd like you to come on as a full-fledged social worker as soon as you get your bachelor's. Now I want you to know that if I announced that this job was available, I'd have a hundred applicants in my office by this afternoon. But because I see the way the kids take to you around here, I'm offering it to you."

Louie was torn. Social worker. Architect. Both wonderful professions. But if he chose social worker, he would have a job immediately and not have to go back to school. He could start making money and contribute more to his family, and maybe even meet a nice girl and settle down. Rosie liked the part of the story where her father was so confused about what to do that he walked all the way to downtown Pittsburgh and stood looking into the river for hours. His own father, a peddler, had bad feet because of diabetes and worked only one or two days a week. More and more of Louie's earnings were going to the family household. There wasn't a day when he didn't worry if he would have enough for tuition for graduate school. The people who came to the Settlement needed him, knew he was on their side. It was hard to make an adjustment to living here. Not so long ago, many of them had lived in Russia in houses with dirt floors. It made him feel good to take these people through the marble halls of the Settlement House to the big swimming pool and the cafeteria and the theater and to tell them: "This is all yours."

Standing by the Monongahela River that day, Louie decided to tell Joseph Katzman yes. He would forget about the degree in architecture he had wanted so badly and work at the Settlement House full time. Art and drawing could be a hobby for him instead of a career. Then, instead of going back right away, he walked to Frank and Seders and bought himself a straw hat. A social worker, he decided, should have a hat.

"I think you'll make a fine addition to our staff," Joseph Katzman had said, shaking Louie's hand.

Louie was more than fine. When the Irish boys in the

neighborhood accused the Jewish boys of putting blood on their matzos, Louie found a former boxer to coach the Jewish boys in self-defense. Many of the neighborhood kids in those days worked long hours in the stogie factories or shirtwaist factories to help their families eke out enough money to survive. For those teenagers Louie organized dances, so at the end of a grueling workweek they could relax and socialize, and feel as if they were still kids, though many of them looked like haggard, overworked, world-weary adults. And for the little children he helped institute the "milk well," a nutrition program that served them milk and graham crackers and allowed them to weigh in to make sure they were growing big and strong.

He formed dozens of teams for neighborhood athletes and gave them the chance to play in first-class facilities with quality equipment and the best volunteer coaches he could find. He formed a theater group called Thespians, which he pronounced "tezbeyintz" in his Russian-accented English. Most of the people who signed up wanting to act spoke only Yiddish, so the plays they put on were in Yiddish. *Di Mishpoche,* and *Der Vilder Mensch* were two of his favorites. Louie was at every rehearsal and every performance of every one. He was glad he had decided not to be an architect.

Especially when he was chaperoning a dance and he met Rifke Kaminsky. Rifke was one of nine children who had come over from a little *shtetl* near Kiev. "Come over" is what she called it. What she meant was "escaped." Her family home in Russia had been one large room with a straw roof and an earthen floor. Rifke's mother, Chaike, kept chickens inside the house behind the brick oven and a goat outside, and fed her nine children as best she could with the eggs and the milk. Sometimes they could buy a few extras with the money brought home by Rifke's father, who worked for a miller. In 1914, Rifke's father left Russia to go to a place Rifke and her sisters laughingly called Pittsburgh Pa. He promised to send money and tickets for the family within months. But then came the Great War, and the remaining family learned that immigration was closed. There was no mail from their father. No news. No money. No tickets.

For the next seven years their life was a nightmare. Not only because of their dire poverty, which Chaike managed stoically to rise above, but from the bloody pogroms of the

Russian civil wars. Rifke watched her best friend's father shot to death. Played with a little boy one day, and on the next, found his body in the street.

In order to survive, Chaike and her son Shulke built a still in the earthen floor which they covered over during the day with a rag rug. When the night curtains were drawn, they brewed moonshine whiskey to sell to the goyim. Of course. Who else would drink such garbage? Years later Rifke still had nightmares about the night the soldiers broke into the house and beat her brother Shulke so badly, when they found the still, that when the vile monsters left they were certain that the boy was dead. The very next night after the still was destroyed, Shulke, bandaged and limping in pain, helped Chaike and the other children bury themselves under straw in a wagon headed for the border.

Rifke loved the Settlement House. She loved everything about America. It was exciting to live in a house that had wood floors, running water, and an icebox. To walk down the street on pavement instead of dirt. To borrow her older sister's dresses and go to the dances wearing them. She spoke very little English, and most of what she knew was from popular songs. Her favorite was "Always" by Irving Berlin. Only because of her accent, she called it "Alvays." Rifke's sisters said Pop Rabinowitz was too old for her, because she was nineteen and he was twenty-eight, and her older brother Shulke threatened to come and beat Pop up if he tried to date her, but Rifke was flattered by the attention of such a "big shot" in the world of the immigrants, and when Louie gave Shulke a complimentary membership to the Settlement House to appease him, he agreed they could be married. It was 1926.

Two years later they had a son, Eugene. Eugene died of pneumonia when he was three. Rifke tried for many years after his death to get pregnant again, but she couldn't. Her mother, whom everyone called Bubbe because by now she had ten grandchildren, told her: *"Folg mich, mayn kind."* Listen to me, my child. "When you least expect it you'll conceive again. After all, you did it once before." Rifke had given up on children. Her life was happy anyway. She studied English at night school, though she rarely used it, since her sisters and her mother were her friends and they all spoke Yiddish, and Louie spoke Yiddish at home too. Rifke was very much in love with Louie.

By the early forties the colored people were moving into the Hill District of Pittsburgh, and many of the Russian immigrants moved from there to Squirrel Hill. Among them were Rifke and Louie. For the two of them, however, it wasn't an upward move. It was so that they could live in the tiny apartment upstairs from her rich brother Shulke's grocery store, where Rifke worked full time as the manager. Shulke paid his sister a meager salary and charged them very little for rent, which was good because Louie, who suddenly found himself working in an interracial community, was making little more than the salary he'd started out with at the Settlement House, and life was far more expensive. The arrangement had served Shulke well by giving him a place to put Bubbe instead of having her live with his wife and children, who were embarrassed by her old-world ways.

In 1944, when Rifke was thirty-seven years old and reconciled to being Aunt Rifke but never Ma—as Eugene, her poor precious Eugene had always called her—she became pregnant and gave birth to Rosie.


"So vere's da bading soot?" Itzy Friedel asked Rosie, a twinkle in his eye. "I got us some sanoviches packed up and ve'll go to da beach."

Rosie's father changed in the bathroom down the hall, and Rosie and her mother changed in the room. Rosie wore a navy cotton suit with white polka dots and a little skirt, and it was kind of stretched out because it had belonged to her cousin Ruthie, but not too bad, and she knew she looked cute in it, her long black hair cascading almost to the line of the suit at her thighs. Her mother wore an electric-blue one-piece elasticized suit borrowed from Aunt Chana, over which she wore a white terry-cloth beach robe borrowed from Aunt Sasha. Rifke's huge breasts bubbled over the elastic at the top as if they were trying to escape. Rosie noticed for the first time that her mother's legs were covered with blue bulging veins.

Her father wore plaid trunks that were Itzy Friedel's, and the same shirt he'd worn in the car on the road from Pittsburgh, and the same shoes and socks too. They met Itzy Friedel on the porch of The Seaview, where he stood waiting, dressed in a flowered shirt that matched his flowered bathing suit. He was carrying a giant black inner tube on his left shoulder, and a smaller bright-green one with a sea horse's neck and face rising from it on his right shoulder. The day was bright and hot and the four of them made a strange parade as they moved up the street toward the boardwalk. Rosie couldn't wait to see it. "On the boardvalk in Atlantic City, ve vill valk in a dream." That was another song they had sung in the car. "On the boardvalk in Atlantic City, life vill be pitches and cream."

Rosie thought how lucky Itzy Friedel was to live in a place as exciting as Atlantic City instead of gray old Pittsburgh. As she and her mother walked behind the two men, pieces of their conversation drifted back. "So richly deserved," she heard her father say, in a voice that sounded as if he was bragging. Rosie had never heard her father brag. His white hairless legs looked silly sticking out of the too-large plaid suit. They were the same milky-white as the bald spot on the top of his head.

"No kiddin'? Richly deserved? *Mazel tov*," Itzy Friedel said, patting her father on the back, and when he did, Rosie noticed he was wearing a gold watch. Rich. He must be rich. To own a hotel *and* a gold watch.

"Maybe a raise?" Rosie heard Itzy Friedel ask her father.

"Vy not?" Rosie heard her father say. A raise. That might mean her mother could have a day off now and then, instead of working seven days a week in Uncle Shulke's grocery store. Selling, packing, marking, shlepping, standing on her feet. Rifke never complained, but on the way to Atlantic City, Rosie had seen a light in her mother's eyes that had never been there before.

The boardwalk. Rosie turned in a circle to take it all in. It was the most exciting place she'd ever seen. To begin with, it smelled like fresh roasted peanuts. It was just opposite the beach and the huge blue ocean. There were stores and arcades, all wide open. No windows or doors. A person could just walk right in. Skee-Ball, saltwater taffy, and agggh—look at that. A peanut. A life-size peanut. Well, really a person dressed up like a peanut, handing out free little packs of peanuts.

"Look, Rosele," her mother said.

Rosie watched the peanut bowing and handing little bags of Planter's peanuts to the children who were brave enough to approach him. It was like a dream. If Bubbe were alive she would have said, "Only in America."

"We'll come back to the boardwalk tonight," Itzy Friedel said to Rosie and motioned them all toward a stairway that led down to the beach. The ocean. The sand was burning under her feet but Rosie, seeing the water for the first time, ran toward it as if it had some magnetic pull. Along her way, she took in everything her eyes could devour. The tanned men hitting the multicolored beach ball back and forth and up into the sky, the women in two-piece bathing suits lying on their stomachs with their tops undone, and the little naked baby at the shoreline who shrieked when the surf nibbled at her feet, then chased it when it turned to go away. A family vacation.

Maybe now that Joseph Katzman had opened his eyes and realized her father's true worth, there would be lots of family vacations. That night the three members of the Rabinowitz family, all of whom had very painful sunburns, were treated to dinner by Itzy in a restaurant called Shumsky's.

Before Rosie fell asleep on the cot that the old deaf bellhop put at the foot of her parents' bed, because Itzy could afford to give away only one free room, she looked up at the whirring fan and wished the vacation would last forever.

The next morning, while Rifke slept, Rosie and Itzy and Louie took a six A.M. bicycle ride all the way to Margate, along the empty boardwalk. All the stores and games were closed, and except for some other bicycle riders they could see far down the boardwalk ahead of them, there wasn't another person in sight. The only sounds as they rode were the rush of the ocean and the squeals of the seagulls. Rosie smiled at the sight of her father riding a two-wheel bicycle. Even at this hour he had the stub of the Marsh Wheeling cigar stuck into the side of his mouth. Vacations.

One night Itzy took them to the Steel Pier to see the diving horse. Afterward they played Skee-Ball, and though they didn't have enough coupons when it was time to go home, Itzy Friedel flirted with the prize lady and she gave Rosie a Kewpie-doll bank. Then they watched a man demonstrate a gizmo that chopped and shredded and riced and diced who had a spiel that reminded Rosie of Sid Stone, the man on the Milton Berle show. A lady in a booth was selling a tonic called Vitalac that was supposed to make old people feel young. And when they got back to The Seaview that night, Rosie did her imitation of the lady for the three grown-ups, who screamed with laughter as they all sat rocking in the wicker rocking chairs on the porch of the hotel. Little by little their terrible sunburns were turning into tans, and Rosie loved the way she looked now. So different when she was all brown and healthy. But tomorrow was Sunday and time to leave.

Sunday morning, after Louie packed the Plymouth and cleaned off the windshield, which had been thick with the residue of the sea air, he looked at his boyhood friend. Itzy Friedel wiped away a tear, put a big loving hug around all of them, and Rosie was reminded again of how much he looked like the Cowardly Lion, especially at the end of the movie when Dorothy was saying goodbye to all of them. "Every year," he said. "You'll come back every year." Louie smiled a smile that meant he wished that would be possible and then they were back in the Plymouth on their way home. Home. None of them wanted to go there. Rifke would be back on her full-time schedule at the grocery store the minute she walked in the door, and Louie had fall classes to get started, the athletic activities to organize. Vacations. Why were they so short?

It was the very next morning that Louie went into work to be called into Joseph Katzman's office. A raise, Louie thought. Now he'll tell me about a raise.

"Pop," Joseph Katzman said. Katzman, despite his seventy years, was still dapper. He was a fine man and Louie was proud to have been chosen by him all those years ago. Louie had been standing in front of Katzman's desk for a long moment before he realized there was someone else in the room. A boy who was sitting on the sofa against the wall, under the huge family portrait of the Gelman family, the rich people who endowed the center.

"I'd like you to meet Larry Zeitman. Larry is going to be your new boss." Louie turned to look at Larry Zeitman and for a second a smile flickered across his face, because he looked at this *pisher*, green behind the ears, a boy who didn't seem to be much older than his Rosie, and it seemed as if Katzman had just said . . .

"Nice meeting you," the *pisher* boy said to Louie. "We'll get together in a few days, as soon as I've had an opportunity to assess the program and decide how we should proceed."

Louie looked from the boy to Katzman and back to the boy again. They both stood stiffly, and he realized that he had been dismissed. The two of them were waiting for him to leave Katzman's office now so they could go about their business assessing the program and deciding how to proceed. His boss.

Of course. It was no longer important for them to have someone who spoke Yiddish and had a way with the immigrants, because the immigrants had all moved to better neighborhoods. The new man was experienced in dealing with the colored element, and that was what the neighborhood had to deal with now. When Louie went to Joseph Katzman the next day to tell him he was leaving the Settlement House, that's what Katzman told him. Then, with simply a nod, Katzman accepted his resignation, after thirty-five years of service. Louie started for the door.

"Pop," Katzman said. For the first time the name made Louie cringe. "You understand that things have changed around here a great deal, and the boy, he comes from Chicago. And he has a master's degree."

Thirty-five years, and not only wasn't there a party for him or a going-away present from anyone, but on the day he left, no one even came to his office to say goodbye. Just Clarence Schroeder, the janitor, who came up and said, "Too bad, Pop. Too bad." And Louie, with tears in his eyes, moved the stub of the Marsh Wheeling cigar from the right corner of his mouth across his bottom lip to the left corner of his mouth, took a deep breath, and walked out of the Settlement House forever.

He tried to get other jobs as a social worker. When he applied to the State of Pennsylvania, they told him he was too old; at the community center in McKeesport, they hired someone else; and after nearly three months of looking, he was working for Uncle Shulke too. It made Rosie sad for him, especially after Cousin Mottie's wedding to Sol Befferman's daughter. Uncle Shulke had been sitting at a nearby table, and Rosie overheard him say to Uncle Munish, who was in the button business in downtown Pittsburgh: "If he's so smart, a goddamned college graduate, so how come he has to work for me? And he believes in Communism. You know why? Because Communism is for poor people.

So is equal rights. Equal shmequal. Equal rights is their way of saying I'm equal even if I'm poor. I guarantee you I write Louie Rabinowitz a check for fifty thousand, he wouldn't give a good goddamn about poor people. Of course, I ain't writing so fast. . . ." he added as a joke, and he and Uncle Munish laughed, and Rosie was glad her father was at the buffet table and didn't hear them.

One night when the store was open late, and Rosie had finished her homework, she came downstairs to help her parents. Just as they were ready to close the doors, a man entered. Dirty and unshaven, he had one shoe that was ripped open so you could see his filthy toes. And the man said to Rosie's father: "I've been out of work for a year, because I'm sick, and I don't have enough money to provide for my family." There was a long silent moment and then Rosie's father handed the man a big basket and said to him: "Fill it up. Take what you need. It's free." And when Rosie's mother put her hand on her husband's, as if to remind him that the food belonged to Uncle Shulke and not him, he said, "Let Shulke take it out of my pay."

Unfortunately, the dirty man, who lived in the neighborhood, thought he was doing a good thing by telling everyone how generous the man in the grocery store was. When the news got back to Uncle Shulke, he fired Rosie's father too. Now Louie sat in the apartment above the grocery store every day and read the *Jewish Daily Forward* and didn't talk much. He was only fifty-nine years old, but he rocked in the chair while he read, like a very old man, and he ate too much, and he had heartburn so bad that one night they thought he was having a heart attack until he took a Bromo Seltzer and it went away.

Now they had less money than ever. Rosie would have to get a job after school and on the weekends and in the summer. She was thirteen, and very shy, and it was hard for her to go into the stores on the same block as Uncle Shulke's grocery store and ask the merchants to hire her, but she did.

Teitelbaum the fish man laughed and said Rosie was so little his customers wouldn't even be able to see her over the counter, and besides, his son Jakie helped him after school. Rosie was relieved. The smell of Teitelbaum's fish store always made her sick to her stomach. Mr. Hyman, the owner of the children's store, said she was just a child herself and that the mothers wouldn't want her to wait on them. Schwartz the cleaner did everything himself. Mineo's Pizza had all the help they needed.

So when Rosie's mother went to talk to her brother Shulke, her heart ached. She wanted Rosie to have time after school to enjoy her life, not to be in the dreary grocery store the way she herself had been for the last fourteen years, dealing with all the *meshugge* customers and their demands and complaints.

"She's very responsible," Rifke told Shulke halfheartedly, hoping he would say "I don't need her."

"Sold," he said instead. "Sold American. Every day after school until closing time at ten. Every Saturday all day. In the summer all day every day. That way she'll learn the stock. Otherwise I don't need her."

And so Rosie worked beside her mother every day after school, selling, marking, packing, shlepping the groceries. And after much bargaining and many tears from Rifke, Uncle Shulke agreed that instead of giving Greenberg the sign painter, who was a stranger, money to paint the signs that were taped into the storefront windows once a week, he would give the same money to Louie for painting them.

So the kitchen table became Louie's workshop, and using his drawing talent, the signs became his source of pride. ROKEACH BEET BORSCHT 39 CENTS, he painted in red on white posterboard. SCHAV 39 CENTS, he painted in green on yellow posterboard. In September he did a beautiful one in Hebrew that said L'SHANA TOVA—Happy New Year. And when Rosie came up from the store to do her homework she would peek in, see him there, and she would come in and give him a kiss before she started her homework. While he painted he always kept the cigar in the side of his mouth, and always he would sing the same song.

"I'm forever blowink bobbles, priddy bobbles in de air. Dey fly so high, nearly rich da sky. Den like my drimz, dey fade and die. Fortune's alvays hidink. I've looked everyvere. I'm forever blowink bobbles, priddy bobbles in dee airrr."

*B*y the time he was five years old, Davey Malcolm had seen all his mother's films at least twice. Except for *Woman On the Run*, which he'd seen seven times because that was his father's favorite, and that was the one his parents showed most often after dinner parties, in the screening room. And when they did, Davey in his Little Slugger baseball pajamas would curl up in his mother's lap and put his face near her sweet perfumed neck and watch. Unless the party was just for grown-ups and Davey was hurried off to bed. In which case he would wait in his room until he was certain the screening room was dark, tiptoe back downstairs, slip into the back row, and watch anyway.

Davey knew at exactly which moment he should slip out of the screening room, too, and that was right after his mother took Gino in her arms, while the dying gangster was lying there in the street in a puddle of blood, right where they'd shot him, and she said, "Ahhh, Gino, why did you have to let this happen? I thought we were going to have our whole lives ahead of us. . . . I love you more than anything, and now . . . it looks like you're leaving me." Boy, she was beautiful when she said that, holding onto Gino's coat like she didn't even mind the blood.

And then Gino, who was played by Uncle Jackie Welles, picked up his head just a little bit and looked at her, and even though he was wincing with pain he still managed to say, "*Do* you love me, Red? Do you really? Well then, maybe my life was worth something after all."

Right after that there was that real close shot of Davey's mother. Her sweet freckled face looking so pretty that when it filled the screen like that, Davey got a warm runny feeling in his chest as if he'd swallowed honey. In the movies her eyes were always so wet that even when nobody was dying in a scene she looked as if she were about to break down and cry.

At any rate, Uncle Jackie Welles saying "Do you love me, Red? Do you?" was always Davey's cue to leave the screening room, because after that his mother just said something like "You bet I do, Gino, and I always will," and maybe a few more mushy things, and then there was a siren and an ambulance and lots of people rushing. And the camera was moving up and away like it was going to sit in a tree to watch what was happening, and then there was some real gooey music and the movie was over.

By then the guests would be saying the kind of thing they always said when the movie was over: "My God, Lily. How could you ever give it up? There hasn't been an actress like you since." And then they would say the other thing that they always said, which was something like: "Mal must be quite a guy for you to have given up your dazzling career just for marriage." His mother would smile her pretty smile at his dad, and his dad would smile his special smile in return, and by that time Davey would be in his room, in his bed, sound asleep. Sometimes dreaming of his mother. And when he did, in the dreams he was Gino, or he was Lance Caulfield, the soldier of fortune Uncle Jackie Welles played who was in love with Lily in *Diamond Key*.

Lily. There wasn't anyone else like her. Everyone knew that. Even his teachers in school asked him about her when the other children weren't listening. "Lily Daniels is your mother," they would exclaim, as if he didn't already know that. Their eyes would burn with admiration and curiosity and they would ask, "Isn't that exciting? To have her as a mother?" Davey didn't know what to compare it to because he'd never had anyone else as a mother. "Will she ever make another movie?" they would ask, sometimes in a whisper as if the answer were a secret and Davey could reveal it to them. He would shrug an "I don't know," because what he did know was that she still got lots of telephone calls from people in the movie business trying to get her to come back, and scripts in the mail from people who wanted her to star in their movies, but so far she was still saying no.

"Is she just like she was in those movies in real life?" they would ask, and Davey would nod a definite yes to that, because she was. "Full of spunk," his father always said about her and her spirit of adventure. Taking flying lessons, organizing trips all over the world for her group of friends, and traveling everywhere she could with his father. Except for the last few months. She'd been staying home a lot. Not going anywhere. Davey was glad to have her around because some nights, instead of her hurrying out to some dinner party the way she mostly did when his father was in town, she and Davey had dinner alone together in her room on snack tables. And one night, when all the servants were off, she even ordered Chinese food that was delivered right to the front door. But there was something about the way she was staying home so much lately that worried him. Never leaving the house. Never even going out with friends to play golf. Sleeping very late and often staying in her dressing gown to eat dinner. Once, when Davey came home from school he thought he saw Dr. Weyburn's car pulling away from the house.

Kan, sir. Cancer. My mother has cancer and she's going to die. He overheard it in the kitchen, where he overheard all the important news, so it was probably true. He was sitting where he liked to sit, under the big kitchen table playing with his trucks. It was the same place Davey had been sitting the time Rico the chauffeur told Yona the maid that his divorce was final, then put his hand under her skirt and she squealed and then they kissed a kiss like Davey had never seen before. Making noises in their throats like people never made when they kissed in movies. Under the table was also where Davey was sitting when Yona told Rico she was going to have a baby and Rico looked real nervous and gave her some money and then Yona told Davey's mother she had the flu and stayed away for a few days.

Today, Yona was folding the sheets she had just washed and, when they were folded, putting them on the chair next to the table under which Davey sat running his cement truck through the obstacle course of table and chair legs. Davey could smell the fresh smell of the detergent in the sheets, and Yona rustled them so much while she folded that the rustling noise drowned out some of what she was saying. *Gonna buy*, it sounded like. Rico must have not heard her either because he was running the water at the sink, but then he turned it off and said, "Who's gonna buy? Buy what?"

Davey turned to lie on his stomach now. That way his face was closer to the floor, which made the tiny trucks look bigger and more real.

"Not buy. Die," Yona said. "Lily. She has cancer. The doctor says she's gonna die. Soon. Maybe a few months." Die. The only person Davey had ever heard of who died, except for people in movies, was Grandma Colleen when he was very little. And Lily had told him it was because Grandma Colleen was very old. Lily wasn't old.

Davey put his face down on the kitchen floor. The red-and-yellow cement truck sat touching his nose. He couldn't move. Ever again. Maybe, he hoped, maybe they were talking about a different Lily, an old Lily who was supposed to die, not his mother. There must be lots of ladies around named . . .

"Poor little Davey," Yona said. "What will he do?"

"Poor little thing," Rico said, and then again: "Poor little thing. What will he do without a mother?"

It wasn't a different Lily they were talking about. It was his mother and later that night when he went to her room and looked at her, there was no doubt. She looked worse than she had in the death scene of *Captive Hearts*, when she played a nurse who caught some terrible disease in a Japanese prison camp. At least in that death scene she'd worn makeup. Now she wore only a gray, pain-filled face.

And soon his father, who had never been home a lot, was home every minute. Sitting by Lily's bed, which was now a hospital bed, in the darkened bedroom next to the big double bed they used to share, holding her hand and kissing her gray face, which Davey was afraid to do, and hated himself because he knew his mother knew he was afraid.

"It's okay, Davey," she would say. Even her voice was different now. As if it was hard for her to talk. "You don't have to come close to the bed if you don't want to."

And Davey would think to himself the only thing he wanted to say. But he couldn't say it because his mother would probably laugh, since they weren't his words—they were from the movie *Woman on the Run*. They were the words Red said to Gino at the end. "I love you more than anything, and now it looks like you're leaving me." Over and over he thought those words but couldn't say them.

Two days after Davey watched them take his mother's body from the house, Yona woke him and told him that even though it was Monday he wasn't going to school. Instead he was going somewhere with his father. His father. The thought of going somewhere with his father made his stomach hurt. In the last two months, since his mother's sickness, his father had changed. Not that he had ever been silly or funny the way Lily could be, but sometimes he would read Davey a story, or watch a baseball game with him on TV, or ask him about school. Now he said nothing. The only time he spoke to Davey was right after the doctor pronounced Lily dead. Rand Malcolm strode outside where Davey was lying on his stomach by the edge of the pool driving a tow truck along the precipice of brick.

"Come over here now, fella," his father said.

Davey had been so startled by the sound of his father's voice that he dropped the tow truck into the deep end of the pool, watched it sink to the bottom and then stood.

"Sir?"

His father was more handsome than ever today. His blue tie was the color of his blue eyes. And the way his hair was brushed made him look just like the portrait of him that hung in the Rainbow Paper Company building downtown. When he got almost to where his little son was standing, Rand Malcolm stopped walking and squatted so he would be closer to the boy's size when the boy came to him. When he did, the man put a hand on each of his son's shoulders.

"Your mother is dead, son," he said. He smelled bad. The way Lily's room had smelled for the last few weeks, and Davey held his breath so he wouldn't have to smell it. "And do you know what her last words were?" his father asked. The man's eyes were red and veiny. Last words? How could he possibly know? *Do you love me, Red, do you?* were the only last words Davey could think of, so he didn't answer. Just shook his head.

"She said, 'Don't forget,' " Rand Malcolm said to his son. " 'Don't forget Monday's Davey's birthday,' and then . . ." The man took a deep breath and stood. "So we'll go and celebrate. Somehow we'll go and celebrate."

Today was Monday. So it must be the day of the birthday celebration, Davey thought. By the time he was dressed and downstairs his father was already in the back of the limousine reading the newspaper.

"Morning there, fella," he said. "Happy birthday."

Davey opened the folding seat and climbed on, so he could ride backward with his feet up on the back bench seat, which was the way he liked riding in the limousine even when he was the only passenger. His father didn't look up from the paper until they got to Santa Monica Airport. The car drove out onto the airfield and right up to *The Lily Two*. Hooray, Davey thought. They were going for a ride in *The Lily Two* to celebrate his birthday. A man who worked for his father, named Fred Samuels, opened the car door and let Davey out. When Rand Malcolm stepped out of the car, the man put an arm around him. Mr. Samuels looked very sad too.

"At least there's a nice day for it," he said to Davey's father, and they all boarded the airplane.

Davey loved *The Lily Two*. It wasn't the only airplane he'd ever been on. He'd flown in commercial planes too. But this was his father's own DC-3, so he didn't have to stay in some boring seat for the whole flight. There was a sofa, and a folding table for cards, and a bar that always had a full refrigerator with soda pop and juices and fruit. And there was a little sliding-door closet under the bar, and when you opened it there were jars and jars of salted nuts, and packs of every different kind of chewing gum. And there were playing cards that had the Rainbow Paper Company insignia on the back of each card.

"Got your seat belt on there, fella?" his father called back to him.

"Uh, huh."

Davey could hear the voices from the air traffic control tower talking to his father and Fred as they taxied *The Lily Two* down the runway, then lifted into the Santa Monica sky. Always before when Davey had flown in *The Lily Two*, his mother had been sitting next to him and she would hold his hand during the takeoff. This time he held tightly to the armrest. After a few minutes, as they leveled off he looked out the window. The ocean was waveless, calm. Davey remembered how last year his father had flown very low as they traveled north so Davey and Lily could try to catch sight of the migrating whales. And the time they flew inland and looked down at the grounds of the huge Hearst castle, where his mother and father had met each other a long time ago.

This was a great way to celebrate his birthday, Davey thought as he took a toy fire truck and a small white toy ambulance with a red cross painted on it out of the pocket of the blue blazer he wore, unfastened his seat belt, and lay down on his stomach so he could run his toys around the carpeted floor of the airplane. The fire he was imagining was a big one and there were lots of injured people. Davey had two other ambulances at home and he wished he'd brought them so that more of the injured people could be cared for at one time. But he'd have to make do, and the one ambulance would just have to take as many trips back and forth as possible.

He was so involved in his play he didn't even notice that Mr. Samuels had walked past him and was standing on the left side of the door of the plane, fiddling with the latch as if he was about to open it. In fact, all at once he did release the heavy catch and the sound of the rushing wind startled Davey away from his fantasy fire and he clutched the leg of his seat in fear.

"That's got her," Mr. Samuels said, and when he did, the airplane suddenly swooped very low. They were still over the water, and Davey watched Mr. Samuels sit back down in the cockpit and his father get up and walk toward the door. He carried a brown paper bag in his hand that looked as if it was probably heavy. When his father got to the door he held the bag to his chest and spoke aloud, but very softly, and the noise from the wind and the sound of the plane made what he said nearly impossible to hear, but it seemed to Davey as if he said, "Lil, I'll never love again." Finally, he threw the bag out the door, leaned heavily on each side of the opening with both hands, and looked down after it, his hair blowing wildly, his tie flying back over his shoulder. After a second or two he stepped back, pushed his weight against the heavy door, and closed it with a loud thud. Then he turned, walked past Davey toward the cockpit, and took his seat again at the controls.

What was in the bag? When people died did they

shrink up so small that you could just put them in a bag and throw them away like that? Maybe it wasn't all of his mother in the bag. Maybe it was just some part of her. Like her face. That beautiful face. And why in the ocean? She wasn't even a good swimmer. This was the strangest birthday celebration Davey had ever had. Now he could feel the plane descending, so he put the fire truck and the ambulance back in the pocket of his navy blazer, got back into his seat, and fastened his seat belt. A few minutes later they were on the ground in Santa Barbara.

"Back in an hour, Fred," Rand Malcolm said to Mr. Samuels. "Taking my boy to lunch."

Lunch at the Santa Barbara Biltmore was a chicken sandwich and no conversation. And Davey, sitting silently across the table from his father, whose mind was a million miles away, remembered all the times he'd been in that same dining room for lunch with his father and Lily together, and the way the waiters had fluttered all around her. And the way the chatter was nonstop, about everything they had seen from the airplane on the way up, and about everything they were going to explore around Santa Barbara, or about what they had planned for that evening or tomorrow. How happy they had all been.

This time, after lunch there was a walk on the pier together to take a closer look at the ocean. The sun was hot and Davey wished he could take off his blazer and tie—maybe even all of his clothes and play in the surf. In the ocean. Or maybe not. The ocean was where that brown bag was that had his mother in it. Maybe the ocean water would make his mother come alive again. Like those ads in the back of comic books for what looked like baby sea horses. INSTANT LIFE, the ad said, JUST ADD WATER. The ocean should certainly add enough water to whatever it was in the bag to bring his mother back. Davey looked out toward the horizon, but sadly there was no sign of his mother.

"Time to get back, fella," his father said, and took his hand as they walked back toward the hotel, where a limousine was waiting to take them back to the airport.

A lot of people were waiting at their house in Hancock Park. The people had come to visit and tell his father how sorry they were about Lily's death. The house was filled with them. There were some faces Davey knew, like Uncle Jackie Welles and his wife and maybe one of his ex-wives.

Two of Davey's mother's brothers, Uncle Phil and Uncle Pat, and some ladies who used to play golf with his mother. And pretty Aunt Norma, who was in some of the movies with his mother and on television every now and then. And there were a few of the men from Rainbow Paper.

Poor little Davey. At least twenty people said that. Some said it to his face when they came over to give him a hug; some just said it behind his back but he heard them anyway. He heard every word they said: Looks just like her. What in God's name will Mal do with a five-year-old? Six. Turned six today. Some birthday. Poor little thing. Mal will probably remarry just to get him a mother. Not Mal. Didn't marry Lily 'til he was thirty-eight. God I hate to say this before the body's even cold but I know a woman who would be perfect for him. Who wouldn't be? With his money? She'll have to get in line. That poor little boy. Look, he's crying, and that dark-haired woman is comforting him. Isn't that sweet? She was Lily's laundress. Really? Hmm. I need a good laundress. Wonder what she'll be doing now.

Late that night he sat on his bed, wondering what would happen to him. Would his father go out and get another wife right away? Were you allowed to do that? And would Davey have to call the woman Mother? Probably. Uncle Jackie Welles had had three wives just since Davey was born, and a few before that, and Davey was expected to call them each Aunt so-and-so. One was Helen and one was Arlys and one was Lulu, but Davey never could remember which was which so he was never sure what to call them. And the funny part was that Uncle Jackie, who sometimes tried all three names before he got the right one that belonged to whoever his wife was now, wasn't sure either. No. Davey would refuse to call anybody else Mother. He would tell his father that right off the bat.

No, he wouldn't. His father was so busy all the time, and he ruffled Davey's hair and called him "fella" on those nights when they sat down at dinner together, and he brought him toy trucks and cars from everywhere in the world, but still it was never easy just to go up to him and say something important like *Don't get married to someone else*, or to ask him a question like *What was in the bag you threw off the airplane?* or *What are you going to do about me?* Davey decided he would have to think of some other way to find out what his father's plans were. But just as he turned on his tummy to go to sleep, the bedroom door opened. Only a crack at first, but when Davey turned to see who was there, a voice said, "You're awake," and then the door opened wider to reveal his father standing in the doorway.

"Just came to say hello," Rand Malcolm said. His voice sounded hoarse, as if he'd been coughing a lot, or crying. Davey didn't answer, and his father came into the room and sat at the end of his son's bed. He was wearing a white open shirt and carrying a glass of wine. The light from the moon made his face look as white as his shirt, and he sat quietly for so long that Davey thought maybe he was going to just sit there all night and never say anything. Davey was getting really sleepy, but he didn't know how to ask his father to leave. Finally the man spoke.

"You'll go to boarding school," he said.

Davey said nothing, but he was screaming inside. *No, I won't. I want my mother back.* It wasn't that he was so used to being with his mother. Lily had gone on many trips with his father when Davey had stayed home with Yona and Rico, but always he could get through those times because he knew that soon Lily would come flying through the front door, her arms already extended to hug him. She'd be carrying a shopping bag over her arm filled with dozens of gift-wrapped goodies, and she would sit down with Davey and unwrap each one and squeal with delight as they did, as if *she* were the one who hadn't seen each toy before. But this time she wasn't coming back and he would have to go to boarding school. The thought filled him with fear.

His father put the empty wineglass on the floor, got to his feet, walked to the window for a minute, and leaned on the molding around it, looking down at the front lawn the way he had looked out of the airplane this morning. As if he wished he was jumping instead of looking. Davey put part of the satin end of his blanket into his mouth and bit down hard on it to keep himself from crying. What would become of him? Why was he even alive? If he could be dead, he would be able to be where all dead people go and find Lily there. Then he remembered the brown bag. Thrown into the ocean. The deep part. Maybe he would think more about it in the morning.

"Let's both get some sleep," his father said.

Davey pulled the edge of the blanket out of his mouth just long enough to say good-night.

KIDNAP SUSPECTED IN MALCOLM BOY'S DISAPPEARANCE. BIL-
LIONAIRE MALCOLM'S HEIR STILL MISSING AFTER FOUR DAYS.
MALCOLM KEEPS VIGIL WHILE HUNT FOR BOY CONTINUES.

Edie, the switchboard girl at the Los Angeles offices of Rainbow Paper, sat reading the newspapers. It wasn't that she was dying to keep reading those articles about the Malcolm kid. Frankly it was just that she was bored. The phones hadn't been ringing at all for the last few days. Probably, people were afraid to call. I mean, what was there to say about all this, after all? The kid was gone. At first the boss figured he must have run away on account of being shook up because of the mother dying and all. But after a while they had to rule that idea out, 'cause let's face it, the kid is six years old. And how far can a six-year-old run? Well, since then, police and detectives had been around every minute of every day. Asking everyone questions, in-cluding Edie. As if she'd ever have something to do with a kidnapping, for God's sake.

Well, if ever there was a kid to kidnap, that rich little brat was a prime candidate. The only heir to the Malcolm fortune, and Mr. Mal feeling so vulnerable after his fancy movie star wife kicks the bucket. Well, another day another dollar, Edie thought, yawning and looking at the wall clock. Six forty-nine. Eleven minutes and she could get out of this place. Go home and make dinner for her kids. Eight to seven was a long day, but she shouldn't complain. Ben, the guard, had to stay 'til nine to lock up.

"Hiya, Ben," Edie said as he walked by her desk.

"Edie," Ben said, nodding, and continued on down the hall.

The sound of Ben's keys jingling was always the signal to Davey to hold his breath for as long as he could while Ben made his rounds in the basement of the building. The basement was where Ben always started, and where Davey had been hiding, he wasn't certain for how long, but a couple of days for sure. Davey already had it figured out that within about fifteen minutes of the guard's look-around down there, during which Davey hid behind some big filing cabinets that the company was storing, Ben would be finished checking the other floors. Then at last he would lock the building from the outside and go home. That was when Davey could do what he'd been doing for the last four nights, which was to hurry up to the kitchen next to the executive dining room, tear open the refrigerator, and eat all the leftovers from the lunch the men had eaten earlier. He worried if Lena the cook noticed that her carefully sealed Tupperware containers had been raided, but he wasn't worried enough to stay away from the yummy cold lasagna or the tangy lemon chicken that he'd wolfed down the minute he was certain the building was empty.

Davey had planned to run away much farther than this. Maybe to another country, or New York or someplace . . . but he didn't have any money, and he wasn't sure if they'd sell an airline ticket to a six-year-old, and it took him only an hour and a half to walk from his house to the Rainbow Paper building, where nobody even noticed him come in. And there was food there, so there was no reason to go anyplace else until he figured out what he was going to do. Only that could take forever, because he didn't have a choice. Boarding school. He hated his father—that was all he knew for sure. And he knew his father hated him too. Wished he wasn't stuck with poor little Davey, which was what everyone had been calling him since his mother got sick. The only thing about this running away that he wasn't sure about was just how bad it would make his father feel.

After all, if his father wanted to get rid of him in the first place, send him off to school, maybe when he found Davey's bed empty on Tuesday morning and Davey nowhere in sight, maybe he was glad. Real glad, and never even mentioned it to anybody. Just went about his business, going to the office and to meetings, maybe even flying to Chicago, hoping Davey wouldn't come back at all. That thought made Davey's stomach hurt, because if he couldn't go back to his father's house on Rossmore, where could he go?

Today's lunch was meat loaf and the men must not have liked it very much 'cause there was a lot left over. Davey was happy about that because he was starving, and he washed several slices down with a Coke. While he drank he looked around the huge stainless-steel kitchen, remem-

bering when Lily used to bring him to the executive dining
room to "visit Daddy," and how Lena and the other kitchen
help would fuss over him and bring him back to the kitchen
later for an extra scoop of ice cream and say to one another:
"Isn't he the picture of Mrs. M? Same red hair, same
freckles. A handsome one." And Lily would always beam
and say, "Thank you. We're a little bit crazy about him
around our house." And the help would all laugh and smile
at that. Lily. His mommy. He missed her so much.

When he'd finished his Coke he did what he always
did next, and that was to tiptoe into his father's office, sit in
the huge room—which was lit, off and on, by the neon sign
on the building next door to the Rainbow Paper building—in
Rand Malcolm's big chair behind the desk. And he would
turn on the television set that sat on the shelf next to the
desk. It was eight o'clock. First he watched *Adventures of Jim
Bowie*. Then he watched *The Life Of Riley*. Then he put his
face down on his father's desk and fell asleep. In his dream
he was with his mother, playing in the swimming pool,
splashing and paddling back and forth the way they did lots
of times, only now Davey looked around and didn't see his
mother anywhere. She wasn't sitting on her favorite lounge
chair, or anywhere around the pool that he could see. So he
held his nose and dove underneath the water, and there she
was, sitting cross-legged at the bottom of the pool, just
pretty and smiling as if that was the place she always sat.
"Mom," he told her, "you can't just sit here. You can't stay
underwater, because people can't be underwater and stay
alive," and she just nodded and smiled as if to say *I know*,
and then he remembered that she didn't have to worry
about staying alive because she was already dead, and he
started to cry. And he was still crying when the funny
choppy music they played to introduce the eleven o'clock
news came on and woke him up.

Eleven o'clock. Usually long before this time he was
back downstairs and curled up behind the filing cabinets,
because he knew that some time after midnight the all-night
cleaning crew came to the offices and he had to get out
before then. "Two die, forty are injured as Springfield,
Illinois, is hit by a tornado. Actress Ava Gardner sues Frank
Sinatra for divorce. And in Los Angeles, the son of million-
aire industrialist Rand Malcolm is still missing. More after
this." His father. They had just said something about his

father on television, only . . . He stared at the commercial and then the newsman came on and said, "Industrialist Rand Malcolm today called the press to his Hancock Park home and asked that they help him reach the person or people who might be holding his six-year-old son in custody." There was Davey's house. The house on Rossmore was on television and then there was his father's face on the screen. For a second, Davey wasn't even positive it could be his father, because his face looked real skinny and terrible. Even worse than it looked the other day when he was throwing the paper bag with Lily in it out of the airplane.

"I want my boy back. Please, don't hurt my boy," he said. "You can have anything." And his voice broke.

Then the newsman came on, and he looked really sad, too, when he said, "Anyone with any information regarding six-year-old David Malcolm can call . . ." And then he gave some telephone number, and then there was some more music and a beer commercial. Davey sat staring at the television, not hearing the sound. Not even hearing the office door as it slowly opened, and then the dark-skinned man with the black moustache grabbed him.

Rand Malcolm knew the kidnappers wouldn't get anywhere near his home. The entire neighborhood was swarming with police and had been for days, though he'd begged them to leave, make themselves inconspicuous, help him to make it look to the kidnappers as if he were accessible so that maybe they would approach him with their request for ransom. And of course, with the police around, the press had closed in, and now he was feeling overwhelmed by his powerlessness. Finally he decided, since there was no way to work against the press, he would work with them. Maybe it was a way to get through to the kidnappers. He hadn't slept in days, always sat near the special telephone with the number he had given out on television. They could call at any time, day or night—probably night, so he had to be alert. He meant what he said. No demand was too great. That helpless little boy. Spirited away in the middle of the night. If only the bastards who did the deed would . . . Dear God, please let them bring him home.

"Boss," Fred Samuels said, coming into Rand Malcolm's den. "You have to get some sleep. Let me sit by the phone for you. Just for a few hours."

"Not until my boy's home," Malcolm said. Samuels knew there was no point in arguing with this man, so he started for the door.

"Freddy," Rand Malcolm said. It made Samuels turn. Mal hadn't called him that name since they were in college together. Malcolm was drawing circles on the green blotter with a black fountain pen that was leaking on his fingers. "He has to be alive," he said.

Then he raised his head from his drawing. The two old friends looked into each other's eyes for a long time in silence. When the phone rang, the noise startled them. Rand Malcolm looked at the black phone, and his usually stern, strong-jawed face was soft with pain.

"No," he said, putting his hand on the phone. "I don't think I can . . ."

Fred Samuels picked up the telephone receiver.

"Yes," he said, then listened. "Thank God," he said, and put an arm around Rand Malcolm. "He's safe and well. Rudy the janitor found him in your office. He ran away and he's been hiding there. They're on their way here right now."

Rand Malcolm pushed his lips together hard until they were white.

Then he said, "Excuse me, Fred." And Fred Samuels, understanding, closed the door and left the room. As soon as the door was closed, Rand Malcolm wept. Sobbing the way he never had in his life, even when his beloved Lily died in his arms. He had just dried his eyes when his son, his boy, his only blood relative, his heir, quietly opened the door and closed it behind him and looked with his big blue eyes at his father. He was rumpled and tired and afraid.

"'Why did you run away?" the father asked.

Davey couldn't look at him. Instead he looked down at the dark wood floor.

" 'Cause . . ."

"Because," his father corrected.

"Because . . . I don't want to go to boarding school."

"You should have said so."

"I was ascared."

"Afraid. Of what?"

"If I said I didn't want to go, the only other thing to do was you ending up being stuck with me."

"So you ran away instead."

Davey nodded and then he couldn't hold his tears in any longer. They filled his eyes and nose and he stood there, not making a sound, just letting them come.

"Just like your old lady," he heard his father say, and he extended his hand toward his son, who walked over and extended his own to shake. But before his father could object, the boy threw his arms around the man's neck and embraced him. He couldn't see his father's face trembling as he struggled to hold back the tears of relief and of joy.

*F*rancie Goldman had a big bust and a bad reputation. The first was the cause of the second, because in the tenth grade, boys weren't sure exactly what to do about big busts. And even if they had been, it wouldn't matter, because in 1960 most girls who had big busts wouldn't let them do anything anyway. So the boys in the tenth grade at Taylor Allderdice High School had fantasies about Francie Goldman and were embarrassed by the fantasies, which made them uncomfortable. And that's why they made up stories about her and gave her a bad reputation. But the truth of the matter was that Francie had reached the age of sixteen and not one boy had ever touched her big bust. Even over her clothes. In fact she had never had a date.

Rosie Jane knew that and she didn't care what the boys said. She knew the real Francie. The girl who made her laugh with her imitation of how Milton Berle twitched his lips and how Sid Caesar said "Whoa boy," and best of all did imitations of Victor Borge on her baby grand piano, which took up the entire living room of the Goldmans' tiny house. The piano was a Steinway. It had been a gift from Francie's grandfather, who called it a "Steinberg." Rosie loved to sit and listen to Francie play anything on the piano, even her exercises. And when Rosie was there, after Francie finished playing the classical pieces she was working on, she would play popular songs and show tunes, and she and Rosie would sing every Judy Garland song from *A*

*Star Is Born* and *Meet Me in Saint Louis* until they were both hoarse.

"R.J.," Francie would say, calling Rosie by the nickname she had given her, "I think Garland can sleep well tonight. Her career is safe."

When Francie was asked to join the drama club because they needed someone to play the piano for their productions, she begged R.J., whose other options were Entre Nous, the French Club, and the home ec cooking club, to join with her. The two girls had some funny ideas for the Follies, the show the Drama Club put on every year to poke fun at the school, and when they told the ideas to Mrs. Joseph, the drama teacher, she asked them to write them down. By the time the Follies was assembled in the spring, most of it had been written by Rabinowitz and Goldman.

"The famous team of . . ." Francie called them that morning when she flopped herself down on her bed, her big bust bouncing up and down under her baby doll pajamas, one pink rubber curler falling out of her short silky hair onto the bed.

"Shit," she said, feeling the piece of hair from which the curler had fallen. "Straight as a stick." One at a time she pulled out the other curlers she'd stoically slept on all night. Her hope had been that the discomfort of the little clothespin devices would pay off in a glamorous hairdo. But they hadn't. "Shit," she repeated, and ran a hand through her slightly bent straight hair. "Now that I'm famous, I really ought to start looking better. I mean, we may even have to take a bow for the audience on opening night of the Follies." She rubbed her cheeks hard with a towel. "I need rouge. I need outfits. I need to start being a woman. I've had my periods for two years already. I could have babies and be a mother now. Except for one crucial element. No one even asks me out." Then she grinned that big Francie grin she always grinned before she said something she thought was funny and said, "I've discovered a new form of birth control. It's called unpopularity."

Both girls laughed.

"Francie, I know any minute you're going to meet somebody," R.J. said.

"That's what you said when we went to New York," Francie told her, rifling through a box filled with various makeup containers she'd bought for herself at Kresge's five-and-ten, used one time, and then thrown, disappointed in their results, into the box. The month before, when Francie's brother Marshall was scheduled to play a recital at Juilliard, Francie's parents had offered to take R.J. along to New York to see Marshall's performance and share Francie's room in a hotel. R.J. had been out of Pittsburgh only once, to go to Atlantic City with her parents. In New York the Goldmans and R.J. would stay at the Commodore Hotel. Francie and R.J. would have their own room with a bathroom. R.J. was dying to go to New York. Francie, who hated her virtuoso violinist brother, was hoping to get out of it.

"Maybe you'll meet someone at Juilliard," R.J. had urged, hoping to get Francie excited. "A musician, so you'll have something in common. Francie had made a face. As it turned out, Marshall had the flu and after they arrived in New York and just missed being in a car pileup with three taxis, they got to Juilliard to find out that the recital was canceled. So the Goldmans bought theater tickets from a scalper for themselves and the girls, and on Friday night they saw *Gypsy* and on Saturday night they saw *West Side Story*. Francie and R.J. were first wide-eyed and then in tears over both shows, and all the way back to Pittsburgh in Sam Goldman's new Ford, they sang the songs over and over again.

"Do you know," Francie said, now at the big round mirror over the dresser, penciling dark eyebrows over her blond ones with a red Maybelline pencil, "the only time I've ever even seen a man's thing was one time when I was, get this, on my way home from Hebrew school. I was waiting for the Squirrel Hill bus, and I looked into my purse and I realized that—"

"There was a man's thing in it?" R.J. asked.

Both girls laughed. Francie's laugh always began with a shriek, then became a cackle. R.J. loved it.

"Francie, tell the truth. Where did you buy that purse?" R.J. asked.

"No," Francie managed finally. "When I looked into my purse I realized that I didn't have the right change for the bus. I think I had a dime and a quarter and I needed a nickel and a quarter, so I said to this guy who was standing there waiting for the bus too—"

"Excuse me, sir, can I see your thing?" R.J. said, and Francie laughed again.

"R.J., shut up," she said. "So I said to this guy who was standing there in the snow—by the way, it was snowing—I said, 'Excuse me, do you have two nickels for a dime?' We were all alone on that corner there, and he turns and opens his coat and there's his thing sticking out at me. Right outside the Hebrew school."

"France, I don't want to hear the rest of the story if the punch line is that the guy was the rabbi."

"R.J., have you ever seen a man's thing?" Francie asked, eyes wide. R.J. hadn't.

"They're big. They're extremely big. At least this guy's was. I gotta tell ya. I was scared."

"My God, that isn't funny," R.J. said, seeing the fear in Francie's eyes. But then Francie started to laugh, and R.J. laughed with her.

"Anyway, I was so scared, I dropped my Hebrew books on the ground and I ran. A few minutes later, while I was still running, the Squirrel Hill bus passed me. You know. The bus I'd been standing there waiting for, for twenty minutes before the guy showed me his thing. And when the bus went by me, there was the guy sitting in the back of the bus as if nothing had happened, just sitting there reading—"

"Not your Hebrew books?"

"The newspaper," Francie said, slapping R.J.'s arm. "Arj," she confessed, getting suddenly serious, "I haven't told that story to anybody because I'm embarrassed about it, and I think it's kind of why I've been staying away from boys a lot, and don't ever talk to them. I worry so much every time I look at a boy that he has a thing like that man's hidden in his pants that I can't say a word. Maybe that's why even though I have the boobs that ate Chicago I don't ever get asked out."

Before R.J. could say anything, Francie had thrown her chenille robe over her baby doll pajamas and was tugging at R.J.'s arm. "Let's go sit down at Steinberg and make up some more songs."

It was a few days after Francie told that story about the flasher that she met Avery Willis. He was a senior who was on the stage crew for the Follies. At night he worked in a gas station. Every day at rehearsal, Avery and Francie would kid around. Francie seemed comfortable with him, and seemed to be over her fear of men's things. Avery wore Aqua Velva aftershave, and Francie went and bought some in the drugstore, and when she was home alone, she opened it and took a whiff because it reminded her of Avery. When he asked her on a date, something she'd been praying for, she had to say no, because Avery Willis was a *sheygets*, not Jewish, and she would never dream of asking her mother, who was president of her B'nai Brith chapter, or her father, who went to synagogue every Saturday morning, if she was allowed to go. She just told Avery no, then came to R.J.'s parents' apartment over the grocery store, and when R.J. came up from work, Francie sat on the bed that used to be Bubbe's bed and cried.

"I love him, Arj," she said through her tears and trembling lips. She wasn't wearing any makeup and when her face was this bright red, her eyebrows disappeared completely.

"France, he's the first boy in your life," R.J. reminded her. Thank God, she thought. Thank God this isn't me. My parents would kill me. Louie and Rifke had made it very clear to her that the only acceptable boys to bring home were Jewish boys. And even when she was a tiny girl, Bubbe had told her again and again: Stick with your own kind. No matter what. In Russia they had had a saying for it that Bubbe repeated again and again. *"Besser der eygener bedder vi der fremder Rov."* Better your own bathhouse attendant than somebody else's rabbi. Goyishe men drank too much and beat their wives. And some day, even though they might pretend to love you in the beginning, someday they would call you a dirty Jew. And now Francie, her best friend, was saying she loved a boy who was a candidate for that kind of manhood.

"You'll get over it," R.J. said, thinking how much she sounded like her own mother when she did. "Your mother told me she had a friend who might pay us to make up some songs for her. Let's think about that."

"Arj, I have to see him," Francie said, and R.J. knew when she looked at her friend at that moment, that Francie was picturing herself as Ingrid Bergman in *Indiscreet*, so in love that she couldn't control herself. She also knew that though Francie was hurting, she loved herself in that grown-up role so much that she would play it out. But for Francie, unlike Ingrid, the ending would be real bad.

\*    \*    \*

Mona Feldstein Friedman was a travel agent who wanted to be a stand-up comic, and the truth of the matter was that she was very funny at parties when she told stories about crazy things that happened to her clients. But she knew that if she wanted to be serious about being funny onstage, she had to do more than just tell stories about people she knew. She needed ideas. She needed jokes. She needed songs. Pearl Goldman, Francie's mother, who had booked the New York trip and several of her trips to Florida through Mona's travel agency, suggested that Mona make an appointment with "my genius daughter Francie, who when she graduates will follow in her brother's footsteps to Juilliard, and her girlfriend from the grocery store." So she did. And when the two sixteen-year-old girls arrived at her apartment and she saw how nervous they were, Mona Feldstein Friedman had to hold back her look of disappointment.

"I'll tell you right now, I have very little money," Mona Feldstein Friedman said as the two girls sat down on the orange crushed-velvet sofa in her living room. "So I'll pay you what I think the material is worth."

Neither Francie nor R.J. had any idea what that meant, so they both nodded. Then they told her about the songs they had written for the Follies. R.J. described some sketches, and when they finished, Mona Feldstein Friedman was giddy with excitement because these girls were good, but she tried to conceal it because she didn't want them to get too pushy.

They wrote her a parody to the tune of "Dancing in the Dark," called "Pittsburgh After Dark." They wrote her a monologue about a Jewish immigrant who tries to hide the fact by becoming a nightclub singer, only her cover is blown when she sings the song "Getting to Know You," because when she gets to the line in the song where she's supposed to sing "you are precisely my cup of tea," she sings, "you are precisely my *glass* of tea."

Most nights at nine, when R.J. came up from working in the grocery store, Francie would come over and stay until midnight. Every Sunday, Francie would get there very early in the morning and they would work all day on the words. Some days when the songs were ready they would go to Francie's and try them out on Steinberg. On those days Pearl Goldman would come in and listen and beam at her daughter.

"I'm kvelling," she would say, meaning that she was very proud.

When Mona Feldstein Friedman's show opened at Weinstein's Back Room, Pearl and Sam Goldman and Rifke and Louie Rabinowitz were invited to sit at a front table free. The show was a hit. And while the audience was still applauding, backstage—which in this case meant behind a screen at the rear of the platform—Mona Feldstein Friedman handed Francie an envelope containing fifty dollars, and another one to R.J. Cash. R.J. was flying. After packing grocery bags and carrying them out to people's cars, and unpacking merchandise and dusting shelves, and sweeping the sidewalk outside the grocery store in the warm seasons and shoveling the snow in the cold seasons, she couldn't believe that this could be called *working*. Laughing with Francie, her best friend, making up songs, something they both loved to do together, and they were getting paid to do it.

"Thank you, Mona," R.J. said, grinning.

"This will help," Francie said mysteriously and put the envelope in her purse. R.J. held hers in her hand, elated. Especially when Mona, heady from the cries of *bravo* (though they were from her brother-in-law Harvey, who sat in the back row), said, "This is only the beginning." And it was. Mona got great reviews. R.J. and Francie were mentioned by name in the *Pittsburgh Press* and the *Pittsburgh Post Gazette*. Mona called the girls constantly, needing new ideas for her show, and she paid them in cash each time. The Weinsteins had plans to remodel the restaurant so the back room could accommodate a larger audience, and R.J. was making enough money to stop working in Uncle Shulke's grocery store.

One Saturday night just before she went to sleep she was making some notes for herself about things she wanted to tell Francie, when she heard the telephone ringing in the hallway. It was late. Her parents were both asleep. Who could be calling at this hour?

"Hello, Rosie Jane." It was Pearl Goldman, and R.J. knew immediately from the tone in Francie's mother's voice that the trouble she'd anticipated about Francie and Avery was starting now. "Is my daughter there?"

"You mean Francie?" R.J. asked, stalling for time to think, knowing that was a stupid thing to say because Francie was Mrs. Goldman's only daughter. "Uh, no, she's not."

"She's not," Mrs. Goldman said, repeating R.J.'s words, and she didn't sound surprised, just as if she was repeating what R.J. said so that Mr. Goldman could hear. "Well, you see, I thought she might be there, since she sleeps at your house every Saturday night to work on Mona's show. Isn't that right?"

R.J.'s heart was pounding. It had started pounding when the phone rang, but now she could feel it against her rib cage. Francie may have slept at her house once or twice in the last several months, but certainly not every Saturday night. Why did her mother think so? Should she lie? Where was Francie? R.J. loved Francie. Wherever she was, she would have to protect her. She would lie.

"Don't lie, Rosie Jane," Mrs. Goldman said before Rosie could open her mouth. "Don't lie or I'll tell your parents and your school and everyone who knows you." Mrs. Goldman's voice had gotten higher and higher and was now verging on hysteria.

"Where is my Francie, goddammit? Is she with that *sheygets*, my daughter? Is she in a motel someplace with that goyishe son of a bitch? Where is she? I'll kill her. I'll kill her. I'll die." And then big heaving sobs came.

"I don't know," R.J. said, sure that Mrs. Goldman didn't even hear her. She was afraid that her parents had heard the phone or would hear her talking and come out to see what was wrong.

"*Oy*, God," Mrs. Goldman cried. Then R.J. heard her say, away from the phone, "Sam, she's not there. Call the police." And then there was a click and R.J. stood holding the dead phone.

R.J. went back into her room and sat on her bed. She never turned the light off. Just sat waiting and dreading what would happen next. All night. She remembered the times she'd sat on the floor of Francie's bedroom, laughing and playing Scrabble and smoking Parliaments, which Francie called "my brand" even though she had the same pack in her purse for two months because both she and R.J. only smoked when they played Scrabble together. Francie. The day they each took five dollars of the money they'd earned from Mona's show, caught the bus downtown, and bought friendship rings. The rings were a circle of gold-plated hearts. Francie bought a size four for R.J., and R.J. bought a size six for Francie, and over a cheeseburger in the Sun Drugstore, they exchanged them.

"Who's your best?" Francie asked.

"You are. Who's yours?" R.J. wanted to know.

"You are," Francie said as she licked some ketchup from her fingers. Francie.

At nine o'clock in the morning, R.J.'s eyes were stinging and bloated, and she was shaking with exhaustion when she heard Francie's familiar knock, and she ran downstairs to the door and threw it open. Francie stood grinning in the doorway.

"I got a great idea called 'Mona in Miami.' We use the 'Miami Beach Rhumba,' and Mona comes out wearing this outfit—"

"Francie, your mother knows," R.J. said. "She called last night. She knows you haven't been—"

"Sleeping here." Francie finished the sentence, and grabbed on to the door jamb, as though if she didn't hold it tightly she would collapse.

"She thinks you were with Avery," R.J. said, hoping, praying Francie would laugh at that and have some explanation of where she'd been that would make everything okay. Take away the picture that had been in R.J.'s mind all night of Francie and Avery.

"Avery and I are getting married, Arj. I've saved every penny of Mona's money, and Avery's gonna marry me. I mean, see the thing is . . . we'll never starve, because if Mona quits needing you and me, I can always play cocktail piano somewhere." When she said that last part, R.J. knew it was something Francie had probably repeated over and over to reassure Avery, so she didn't mention that sixteen was too young to get a job playing cocktail piano. "Anyway, let's get to work," Francie said, moving forward so R.J. would have to walk back up the stairs. "I'm gonna need the money."

That night when Francie got home from R.J.'s, Pearl and Sam Goldman had a suitcase packed with her clothes in it. After screaming at her and calling her a liar and a prostitute they made her leave, and she moved in with Avery's married sister to wait until the wedding. After that,

Avery would work in the gas station full time and they would get a small apartment in Hazelwood. R.J. knew all the details because Francie, elated but edgy, still came to work in the evenings with her. Sometimes it made R.J. uncomfortable to think that Francie, her best friend, went home and slept with a man. Maybe naked. And had sex. There were times when she wanted to stop in the middle of their writing and ask, "What does sex feel like? Does it hurt? Is it wonderful?" But she never did. Never asked questions. Just let Francie give her whatever information she felt like giving.

"They'll take me back some day, Arj," she said about her parents one night while she and R.J. were working on a song for Mona about how she wished she looked like Jackie Kennedy. "They'll miss me and they'll take me back no matter what I do."

Two weeks later, on a Saturday night, when Mona Feldstein Friedman tried out the "Mona in Miami" number, Francie and Avery drove to Maryland to get married. R.J. sat alone at a table in the back of Weinstein's Back Room. The audience was laughing at Mona, who was complaining that all the men in Miami Beach were so old that it should be called God's waiting room. R.J. took a sip of the Coca-Cola one of the waiters regularly brought her while she watched Mona. She imagined Francie and Avery driving on the turnpike in Avery's Nash Rambler with the radio on. Francie with her arm around Avery, who was telling her how much he loved her. For a moment R.J. wished she were in Francie's place. Except for the part about her parents.

Francie had tried over and over to call Sam and Pearl Goldman, but she'd only get as far as saying, "Ma, please," or "Daddy, listen," and when they heard her voice they would hang up. She put letters in their mailbox, and she got no response from them. She stood outside the beauty parlor where her mother went every Tuesday, and when her mother came out she ran to her and tried to get her to talk to her. But her mother kept walking and got into her car and drove away, even when Francie stood there and begged.

R.J. could hear Mona saying words, and the audience laughing, but now it was all just loud noises to her. She had tears in her eyes that made Mona a blurry picture on the stage. Before Mona got to the part about all the women wearing mink stoles even though the temperature was in the nineties, R.J. stood and walked out the door to the bus stop. A light rain had started to fall, but R.J. didn't bother to stand under the bus-stop shelter. She stood at the edge of the curb, watching the street become slick and wet until it reflected the purplish glow of the streetlights. When the Murray Avenue bus came she got on it and stayed on it past her own stop, to Lilac Street, and got off. But now the rain was coming down hard, and she quickened her pace as she headed up the hill to the duplex where the Goldmans lived, up the steps to their porch, and knocked on the door.

After a few minutes Francie's brother Marshall opened the door. Marshall was very handsome. R.J. was surprised to see him home from New York, but Marshall, on the other hand, only said, "Wet out there, Rosie Jane?" as if he'd been expecting her, and when she walked into the living room she realized why. Pearl and Sam Goldman, and Francie's aunt Blossom and her uncle Marvin Fishmann, and Hy and Bessie Heft from the hardware store, and Francie's grandfather, the one who called the piano Steinberg, were all sitting there, on the same kind of wooden folding chairs Rifke had rented so relatives and friends could sit shiva when Bubbe died. The chairs were all in a kind of circle around the closed baby grand piano, as if it were a coffin. As if Francie was in it.

"Mrs. Goldman," R.J. said. For the first time, in the heat of the living room, she could feel how wet her clothes were. She was surprised by the loudness of her own voice, and the others must have been, too, because the conversations they'd been having when she walked in all stopped while they looked at her. Pearl Goldman didn't have any look of recognition on her face.

"I came here to tell you that Francie loves you and I thought that maybe if you heard it coming from me, you would understand that—"

Pearl Goldman never let R.J. finish. She jumped to her feet and screamed, "Francie's dead. There is no Francie, and you get out of here."

"She's your daughter," R.J. said, "and she loves you and you have to—"

"No. Dead. She's goddamned dead," Pearl Goldman screamed.

Francie's brother Marshall walked over to R.J. now and took her arm.

"Rosie Jane, you'd better go," he said.

"But I can't go. Someday they'll be sorry they did this," R.J. said, reaching out a hand to Mrs. Goldman, who turned away from her. Mr. Goldman stood now, too, his hands in his pockets.

"Someday you'll wish you could be with her. Someday there'll be grandchildren."

Mrs. Goldman turned, eyes wide, to her husband.

"What did I tell you? She's pregnant by that goyishe dog!"

"She's not," R.J. said. "But one day after they're married she will be and you'll want to be there."

"For goyishe grandchildren?" Pearl Goldman said, horrified, and then she said, "Ptooey," as if she were spitting on the ground.

"You better go," Francie's brother Marshall said again, his grip on R.J.'s arm tightening. But R.J. didn't move. She stood tall and looked at both Goldmans and begged them.

"Don't do this. She isn't dead."

There was no response.

"Don't, please. She isn't dead."

Marshall moved her slowly but firmly toward the door, and as if to say a polite goodbye, the other guests stood.

"Do you want to borrow an umbrella?" Marshall asked as he opened the door and R.J. found herself standing on their porch.

"No," R.J. said. "Marshall, Francie is—" And then the door was quietly closed in her face. A crackle of lightning across the sky lit up the night for a moment, and R.J., her wet clothes sticking to her, walked down to the street and home.

Her parents were sitting at the kitchen table, and while Rifke warmed up some soup, R.J. told them the whole story about Francie. Her mother *tsk*ed and looked down at the table and commented with the Yiddish expression of anguish: "*A zochen vey.*" What a pity. And her father grunted and at one point pushed the spoon so hard into his matzo ball that when it broke apart, the noodles spilled out of the bowl onto the table. When she had finished telling the part about how Marshall had closed the door on her, her mother nodded, as if to say she wasn't surprised, and then added inexplicably, "Well, at least we have our health."

"Ma," R.J. asked. "How can they sit shiva for her? I mean, it's crazy. She isn't even dead. She isn't." And she put her head down on the kitchen table and said it again. "She's not dead."

But R.J. was wrong, because only minutes before, Avery Willis's Nash Rambler, on its way back from Cumberland, Maryland, skidded on the wet turnpike and had a head-on collision with a gasoline truck, and the newly married couple was killed instantly.

At the Follies during the curtain call, Mrs. Joseph, the drama teacher, asked the audience to "please observe one minute of silence for our departed friends Avery Willis and Francie Goldman." She said it that way—Avery Willis and Francie Goldman—because Francie's parents had telephoned the school and requested that she not be referred to as Francie Willis, even though that was legally her name when she died.

*A*fter five years of traveling all over the world with his father, Davey had had enough. Enough of sitting at endless dinner parties with some general's wife on his left and some senator's wife on his right. Enough of waking up in the morning and not knowing in which company apartment he'd fallen asleep the night before. He would look out the window of the flat in Belgrave Square to the street below and see a group of boys his own age running and shouting to one another in play and he would envy them.

Once he got on the elevator to go upstairs to the penthouse on Park Avenue and two boys were already on the elevator waiting for the doors to close. Though Davey faced the front, he could tell that the boys were sniffing and snorting and poking one another behind his back. Probably because they could tell that he was the eleven-year-old freak who sometimes lived here, other times in London or Paris or Los Angeles, and who had never once been to school.

"Best goddamned education there is," his father always said. "Learns history while it's happening. From men who make it."

It was true. Rulers of nations, giants of industry, men who were only faces in the news to most of the world taught Davey how to play golf, how to tie his tie, how to grill a steak to perfection. Made him laugh with funny stories about their own boyhoods. Entertained him and his father with backgammon and sumptuous meals and conversations about world problems. Problems these men not only knew a great deal about, but had the power to control. Davey listened and asked questions and was never patronized. Instead he was always answered thoughtfully and carefully, as if to make certain that when the answer was complete, the boy understood even the fine points.

"School would bore him silly," his father said. Davey wasn't so sure. He sensed that the real reason his father was keeping him out of school had nothing to do with the education he was or wasn't getting and everything to do with their shared loneliness over Lily's death. Even the passing of five years hadn't helped decrease the pain for either of them. And with every passing year, Davey noticed his father becoming quieter, more closed off from the world. Never once in all those years had Davey seen him laugh the way he had when Lily was around.

Davey hungered for stories about Lily and would listen gratefully to any old friend of the family's who had a memory of her to share.

"I fell in love with your mother," Roland Spencer said to Davey one night at a dinner party at the house in Hancock Park. Yona had just removed the dinner plates and Rico was pouring the last glass of champagne. "Just about the time she met your father," the handsome actor said, then smiled and added almost to himself: "How's that for a case of bad timing?" Davey remembered how Mr. and Mrs. Spencer used to come for screenings all the time when Lily was alive. Now, the few times Davey and Mal were in Los Angeles, Mal would see to it that they were invited over for dinner. Mr. Spencer was retired, which meant that what he did most of the time was play golf and talk about going into politics.

"I was always too shy to tell her, though, so as it turned out, we were only friends, even though she was so beautiful she made my heart race every time she walked into the room."

Davey glanced protectively over at nice Mrs. Spencer, who was waving away Yona's offer of coffee or tea, and chatting animatedly with his father. Now Mr. Spencer looked meaningfully into Davey's eyes. "I was a big star then," Mr. Spencer said. "And I harbored the secret hope that if I got brave enough to ask her, she'd want to marry me because we had so much in common. One day just before she left the studio, I stopped by her dressing room. She hadn't told the studio boss, Julian Raymond, that she was leaving yet, but she was packing up her things. She told me how much she loved your father and showed me a letter your father had written to her earlier that day. He wanted her to carry the letter with her to remind her how much he would miss her during those few hours."

As Davey listened to Roland Spencer talk, he noticed how the actor would pause for a moment to search for the right word, the way he had when he played Abraham Lincoln in *Good Evening, Mister Lincoln*. And also the way he tried to hold back a smile when he remembered something pleasant, the way he had in *All My Darling Daughters*.

"The letter said"—Mr. Spencer looked into space now, as if the letter were there for him to read, and then went on—" 'There isn't a moment while we're apart that I don't long for you. You are everything I prayed my love would be.' "

Davey looked away and moved his finger back and forth on the white linen tablecloth, making a pile of the crumbs he had spilled there during dinner.

"I knew then," Roland Spencer said, "that up against Rand Malcolm, I didn't have a snowball's chance in hell." Then he laughed a hearty laugh and said, " 'Cause if it was me, I'd have had to hire writers to be able to say those things."

Davey smiled at Mr. Spencer's joke on himself, then looked over at his father, who now, although he was nodding and murmuring an occasional *mmm-hmm* to Mrs. Cornell on his left, wasn't really listening to her at all. It was funny to think of his father as a man who was more romantic than Mr. Spencer, a movie star women fans cried over and stood in line to see again and again. Davey remembered now hearing a story about a woman fan who killed herself the day it was announced on the news that Mr. Spencer had married Mrs. Spencer, because now he was no longer "an available dream." People behaved in crazy ways sometimes. Or maybe just grown-ups did, and children, as Yona once told him, were just meant "to love life."

But Davey could never remember feeling like a child. Maybe because for the last five years he had been living a man's life. At eleven he knew more about limousines than he did about bicycles and infinitely more about mixing martinis than making milkshakes. He had never been to McDonald's, but he was acquainted with Mr. Kroc, and the one time he'd gone to Disneyland, he and his father had been shown around the park by Mr. Disney.

"I want to go to school," he said to his father. He had practiced saying it aloud again and again, but now it came out so softly that his father didn't even look up from *Le Monde,* the newspaper he was reading at the table. They were in the apartment in Paris, on the Avenue Foch right near the Arc de Triomphe. It was the morning after another long late dinner party, where Davey had sat between Mrs. Niarchos, the wife of the Greek shipper, and Eleanor Benning, a friend of his father's. Mrs. Benning must have had a lot of business to do all over the world, too, Davey thought. She was in Paris now, and she was also in London last week when he and his father were there. And a few weeks before, when he and his father were in New York and Davey had the stomach flu, his father said, "Having supper with Mrs. B.," and was out the door. In black tie. Mrs. Benning called Davey "honey," and called his father "Mal, darling."

"My son Douglas, who's a bit older than you are, goes to the Hollingsworth School in Pennsylvania," Mrs. Benning had told Davey more than once. The Hollingsworth School was very tough, but everyone knew that Douglas Benning had been admitted because the estate of his late father, Keaton Benning, had financed the Benning Gymnasium. "The boys and girls have a glorious time there," she said, smiling a big smile. Mrs. Benning always wore glasses, and the chandelier, which hung low over the dining room table, was reflected in them so Davey couldn't see her eyes at all.

"They have fishing and hunting and ski trips," she said. "They also have summer athletic programs. And they have a reputation for having the prettiest girls. It seems my Douglas never wants to come home." And then she'd laughed and said, "Oh, yes. I know everything there is to know about young boys."

"I want to go to school," Davey was about to say again, but before he could, he heard his father's voice come from behind the newspaper.

"It's a mistake," Rand Malcolm said.

"No, sir, it's not," Davey answered.

"Let me look into it," his father said, and kept the newspaper in front of his face until the boy finished his breakfast and left the table.

In the last five years they hadn't spent one day apart. By now, Davey knew his father very well. He knew that a certain faraway look in the eyes meant that though his father might be looking right at him while Davey was describing a model airplane or a comic-book character, he wasn't really listening. Or that a certain twinkle in his eye meant that though he sounded very serious about a subject, the truth of the matter was that he was only kidding. This morning, despite the fact that Davey hadn't seen his father's face, he could tell by the sound of his voice from behind the newspaper when he said *It's a mistake* that he was very hurt.

School was already in session and Davey would have to start late but he didn't care. The plan was to visit at least three schools before he made a decision. As it turned out, Davey liked Hollingsworth so much that they didn't bother to look at any others. By prearrangement, their tour of the campus was given by Douglas Benning, a lumpy-looking gravelly-voiced boy who said, by way of explaining why the gymnasium bore his family's name, "That's how my mom bought me in here."

Davey was going to laugh at that, but his father's tight-jawed reaction made him reconsider. Douglas Benning was not too bad; neither were the bay-windowed, hardwood-floored, high-ceilinged dormitory rooms. The food in the cafeteria, the gold-buttoned navy blazer uniforms, or the short-skirted navy plaid uniforms worn by the girls. The girls. With flashing eyes and squeals they bumped and pushed one another and hugged—even hugged one another in the cafeteria line. One whispered a secret into another one's ear which made the second one's eyes grow wide, and she yelped with excitement. And then both girls jumped up and down. One girl braided another's hair while they talked. Another girl was so overwhelmed by the pile of books she was carrying that when she tried to move them onto her hip, her loose-leaf notebook fell to the ground, and when the papers flew all around, two of the other girls rushed to help her pick them up.

Davey's eyes couldn't get enough of the girls. Girls.

Watching them was like watching creatures in the zoo. For him. That was how unique they looked and how amazingly they behaved. Girls. They were funny. And pretty. And not a little bit frightening. Like that one with the silver-blond hair. She had the most beautiful hair, and the most beautiful hand to push it away from her face, and the most beautiful face.

"Casey," someone screamed, and the girl looked across the cafeteria and waved a vigorous wave and smiled. Casey. Casey. Davey sat at the table eating his roast beef, mashed potatoes, and gravy, answering the questions the eager admissions director was asking him. Favorite sports, favorite athletes, favorite books, favorite authors, and every now and then he would take one quick look at Casey. She was leaving her roast beef on the plate. Too busy to eat because she was laughing with her friends. At things that must be really funny because she didn't stop laughing all through lunch. Casey.

Two weeks later Davey stood in what was now his room in the dormitory. The suitcase containing the clothes in which Yona had carefully sewn the DAVID MALCOLM labels sat on the bed. His father, who had a plane to catch for Switzerland, stood at the door looking at his son. Their years together had been good for the man. They had taught him the patience to pause in the corridor of the White House to tie a little saddle oxford. To wait at the bottom of the embassy stairs while a banister was being tried out for sliding, to postpone a meeting so he could stop at the Louvre and take the boy on his own personal tour.

"See you Easter," Davey said.

"Easter, hell," his father said. "Next weekend."

Davey just shook his head no, and watched his father try not to react. Then Rand Malcolm turned and walked from the room, down the corridor to the stairwell and out of the building. The bright sun reflecting on the snow-covered lawn of the dormitory made his eyes water. He could see his breath in puffs in front of him as he walked the long path toward the parking lot where his car and driver were waiting. A group of boys were throwing snowballs at one another, and a large one came speeding by, just missing Mal's ear.

Goddamned kids, goddamned institutions. He was just a few feet away from his car when he heard Davey's voice.

"Dad," the boy said. Of course, thought Rand Malcolm, he's changed his mind. Strong-willed, bullheaded, just like his mother. Makes a decision, then regrets it and comes around. He had the world by the balls living with me, so no wonder he's changing his . . .

"Yes, fella?" he said, turning to see Davey red-cheeked and coatless in the snow behind him.

"You forgot something," the boy told him and handed him the plaid muffler he'd left behind on a chair in the dormitory.

Rand Malcolm took the muffler silently, and when he had, his son turned to go.

"See you at Easter, fella," his father said.

Davey's hot tears fell on the cold snow. "Okay, Dad," he said, but he didn't turn around to look back.

The schoolwork was easy for Davey. He was so far ahead of himself in every seventh-grade class that he was working on some eighth-grade subjects. The hard part was getting used to being a child. He had never played Wiffle ball or thrown a Frisbee. Never had to take P.E. or wait in line for a meal or the bathroom. Never known anything about razzing. But he loved the parties. Throwing popcorn, roasting marshmallows. Chubby Checker and the Twist. And all the girls squealed when they heard "Johnny Angel." The girls. No one at these parties danced the way he had seen his father dance with Lily at the country club parties, or on her birthday when the band came to the house and played her favorite song, "Always." The girls mostly stayed on one side of the room and the boys on the other. But there was a real disc jockey who played records, and Casey was there.

"Casey Baylor, Baylor Steel, that's who she is, Talcum Powder," Douglas Benning said, catching Davey's gaze. Davey looked away quickly, but it was too late. "Talcum Powder's in love." Malcolm had become Talcum, which had devolved to Talcum Powder.

"Malcolm Paper loves Baylor Steel," Benning said, his fat face grinning. He looked as if he'd gotten even fatter since they met. "What a merger."

Davey looked around, hoping no one had heard. No one had. "Forget it, Talcum. She likes Charlie Keats. He's a jock. Money can't buy that for you. Even the kind your dad has."

Charlie Keats. In the ninth grade. No shot. And why was Benning giving him static about money? When Keaton Benning died, everyone knew he left a fortune to his wife and this bulk of a drip who was probably richer than any ten adults Davey knew. As Douglas Benning moved into the crowd to bother someone else, Davey looked over again at Casey Baylor, who just happened to look back at him. And—this had to be his imagination, but—he thought she was smiling. Then she was walking over to him. Gliding, floating like a character in a dream.

"I think my parents know your dad. Are you David Malcolm?"

Davey nodded.

"Maybe you've even met them. They're friends with the Cornells in Los Angeles. And the Allburns."

"I know," Davey said. "I mean I know the people you just mentioned. And I've probably met your parents. I mean, I've traveled everywhere with my father."

Casey grinned. "I've heard. My parents told me about you. That you've never had to go to school. Lu-cky." She dragged the word out. "Mine never take me anyplace good. Hardly ever. I just come here and go to camp."

Davey looked at her pretty pink face and hoped that Douglas Benning was watching. Casey. Boy, he could show her the world.

"Yes," he said. "My dad wanted me to go to Switzerland with him, but I thought it was kind of time for me to settle down." He thought for a moment when he said that that he sounded like Roland Spencer in the movie *Bachelor Days.*

"Lu-cky," Casey Baylor said again.

"You in seventh?" she asked. Davey nodded.

"*Moi aussi,*" she said. "You in French One?"

He shook his head. "Four."

"Boy, you're smart. Probably learned in France or something."

"Yep," Davey said, then wished he'd said *oui.*

"Lu-cky," Casey Baylor said, and then turned and walked back over to where her girlfriends were standing. Davey loved her so much it made his stomach hurt.

From then on she said hi to him every time she passed him in the halls or on the campus, which was a lot. Once she stopped and said, "I talked to my parents last night.

They told me they met you when you were very little. When your mother was . . ." She looked uncomfortable.

"Alive," Davey said.

"I didn't know you didn't have a mother," she said, and touched his arm tenderly. "I'm sorry." And then she walked on.

She had talked about him with her parents. She was thinking about him. He barely thought about anything but her. There were some boys who had girlfriends. They sat with them at auditorium programs. Or walked them back to their dormitories at night after the dances. Davey wanted Casey Baylor to be his girlfriend. How did that work? What did girls want you to do? Expect you to say? Then he remembered the letter. His father had written his mother a letter that was so good even Roland Spencer couldn't steal her away. What did it say? He had to think of it. *There isn't a moment while we're apart that I don't long for you. You are everything I prayed my love would be.* Davey got out of bed, opened his notebook, took a pen, and began writing.

"Concentrate. Do your best. Empty your minds of everything but *The Mill on the Floss*," Dr. Becker said as he passed out the blue test-books. "Answer the first five questions on the board with a one-paragraph answer. Number six is an essay question. Good luck."

Davey had put the letter in Casey's mail slot this morning, and *The Mill on the Floss* was the furthest thing from his mind, but he jotted down the first answers he thought of, and after each one looked up at the clock, knowing he would see her when English was over and she came out of History, and she would have read it by then. Casey. She reminded him of Lily a little bit. Probably because she was so beautiful. And she would certainly be thrilled by his letter the way Lily was by his father's. She would agree to be his girlfriend and . . . The bell rang just as Davey finished his essay answer, and Dr. Becker waited until each student had passed in the completed notebook before he said, "Dismissed," and the relieved boys and girls all jumped to their feet and clamored for the door. Casey.

The door to the History room was still closed and Davey stood nervously outside. Then with a burst and a slam against the wall it opened, and the class poured out. Casey. Maybe when she saw him standing there she would run and put her arms around him. But she didn't. She was walking with Terry Loring and Ellen Spence on either side of her, and both of them were reading over her shoulder. The letter. They were squealing, and when they looked up and saw Davey they squealed even more.

"There he is," Ellen Spence said. "He longs for her. He wants her and loves her. Aggh. My God."

Some of the people who had started to walk away to other classes stopped.

"Ugggh, he spent his life praying," Terry Loring said. "How dorky."

Casey's eyes met Davey's for only a second. Her face was bright-red. "Oh, David, this is a joke. Right? I mean, it's so yucky," she said, rhyming it with lucky.

"What is?" Chip Dennis asked. No, Davey thought. No.

"This love letter," Casey said.

Davey flushed as Chip Dennis took the letter. A ninth-grade boy. Reading the letter he had written and rewritten at least five times last night. Not finishing until close to midnight. He turned to walk away and hadn't gotten very far when he heard Chip Dennis laugh and say, "Her silver hair glimmers like the moon shining on the snow. That could really make you blow your lunch. And wait till you hear the P.S."

At dinner in the cafeteria no one sat near him. He was at a table all alone. He couldn't eat. From across the room he thought he heard various phrases from the letter he'd written Casey being repeated amid a great deal of laughter. He had to get out of here. He would never live this down. He would call his father and tell him that he was right. That going to school had been a mistake and that he wanted to go back on the road and forget about schools forever. Or maybe just until college. But he had to get out of here fast.

He took a fistful of change and his personal phone book and went to the pay phone in the hall near his room. He tried New York, Los Angeles, London, and Paris. His father's offices and homes. It was late at night in London and Paris and no one answered. Yona in Los Angeles wasn't sure where to find his father, and in New York the line at the apartment was busy and both his father's secretary and Mr. Samuels had left the office for the day. He left messages. Any minute his father would call him back, and tomorrow he would rush from wherever he was and come and get him. Still wearing all his clothes, Davey fell asleep on top of his bed.

In the morning he decided that he wouldn't go to classes that day. Why should he? By tonight he wouldn't be going to this school anymore. Or any school. He hadn't had one bite of his dinner the night before, and he was hungry. He would go to breakfast. He washed his face, and still wearing rumpled clothes, he walked through the cafeteria line, loading his plate with eggs, bacon, corned beef hash, and toast. His last meal here. That was certain. Someone would come today and get him. In the meantime he would stay in his room and read.

He was opening his paper milk carton, and without looking up he could feel Douglas Benning sit next to him. More razzing. By now Benning would have heard all about the letter to Casey. Benning slapped him on the back.

"Talcum Powder." Davey held his breath for the onslaught of insults. "You are the luckiest guy in the world," he said, "because you and I are going to be seeing a lot of each other."

"No, we're not," Davey said, "because I'm leaving this school today."

"Me too," Benning said. "And for the same reason."

The same reason? Because his life had been destroyed by a girl he loved? And still loved, even though she did this to him? What could Benning—who picked a piece of bacon from Davey's plate with his fat fingers and stuck it in his mouth—possibly mean?

"Leaving to go to the wedding," Benning said.

"Wedding?"

"My mom and your dad," Benning said, wiping his mouth on the sleeve of his blazer. "They called last night. They tried to reach you, but the line on the pay phone on your floor was busy for a really long time. So whaddya say, old bru-ther dear? You and I are going to New York together for the wedding. Maybe they'll give us some champagne and we can get drunk. Ever been drunk, Talco?"

Davey stood, leaving his uneaten breakfast to be thrown away, and went upstairs to pack.

## R.J.'S STORY

### 1962

$T$he Hoberman brothers sat on either side of Yossie Hoberman's desk in the cluttered office they shared above the bustling HoBros department store.

"This, as far as I'm concerned, gets my vote," Tubby Hoberman said. "It's the best use of color, the most imagination, the most pizazz. For me. I mean it's a real subjective thing—don't you think so?"

"Hey," Yossie said. "Let's not take ourselves too seriously here. We're judging a coloring contest for Christ's sake. Fill in the friggin' Easter Bunny with your Crayolas and don't go out of line."

Tubby Hoberman's cheeks flamed red. "Goddamn right this is serious, putzo. I mean, are we or are we not givin' the little bastard who wins the contest fifteen hundred simoleons? Therefore, it's a big responsibility. Whether you think so or not."

"Arright," Yossie Hoberman said and took a sip from a bottle of Coca-Cola that had been sitting on his desk all day, then made a face.

"The farkakter Coke is warm and it's so hot in this office I'm shvitzing like a pig. So let's make a decision and put the winning picture up in the window and phone up the goddamned winner and go home."

And with that he took a handful of the coloring contest entries, threw them in the air, and watched them shower down all over everything. When the pictures had scattered and landed, Yossie looked all around, then pointed and said, "I pick the one that landed on the radiator."

"You got good taste," Tubby said, moving to pick up the various Easter Bunny pictures from where they lay. "Tomorrow morning we'll call and break the good news to some extremely lucky individual."

Louie Rabinowitz was dying in the intensive care unit at Montefiore Hospital, and his wife, Rifke, and daughter, Rosie Jane, sat on a green plastic sofa in the waiting room playing gin rummy because all the television stations had signed off for the night, hours before.

"Oh, God, don't let him die," Rifke murmured softly, and discarded an eight of hearts because she was holding only picture cards. This time it was a severe heart attack, not a scare or a warning or too much creamed herring like the other times. There was no doubt in the minds of the doctors who admitted him that Louie was going to die very soon.

As R.J. shifted uncomfortably, the plastic sofa squeaked under her, and even though she wasn't sure she needed it, she picked up the discarded eight and inserted it into her hand next to the five and six of hearts, just in case a seven should come along. The sound of the ambulance's screaming siren was still vibrating in her head. The ambulance that had come flying down Murray Avenue while R.J. was on the telephone taking a grocery order from Mrs. Pritzker, who lived at the Morrowfield apartments.

R.J. hated having to work in Uncle Shulke's grocery store again, but she had no choice. It had been a year and a half since Mona Feldstein Friedman, who had continued to buy R.J.'s ideas for a while after Francie died, divorced her husband and moved to New York, hoping to break her act in at the Upstairs At The Downstairs. And R.J., unable to find another comedy writing job in Pittsburgh, needed desperately to earn money. As always, there was barely enough for her parents to pay the telephone and the light bill or the rent to Uncle Shulke. So there she was again, working every day after school and on the weekends, waiting on customers, carrying groceries to their cars, unpacking orders, marking the cans and the boxes, and sweeping the sidewalk in front of Uncle Shulke's store, which she jokingly called "the downstairs from my upstairs."

The ambulance was so loud that R.J. had to put a finger on the ear that wasn't against the phone to block out the howling siren. But worse than the piercing sound was her sudden realization that it had stopped. With a screech. Outside the store. She was sure there must be some mistake, until she looked out the window and saw the two men leap out of the front seat, open the back door, and rush with the stretcher up the outside steps that led to the apartment. The apartment. My God. That was where her mother had gone only two minutes earlier to get herself a sweater because she felt chilly after cleaning out the refrigerator case.

"*Oy, Gott, mayn Louie,*" she heard her mother wailing now from upstairs. Then she cried out in Yiddish, "*Loz im nit shtarbn.*" Don't let him die. And by the time R.J. rushed up into the apartment, the two men were on their way down, carrying the blanketed stretcher with only the chalky face of her father showing. Louie's eyes were closed and R.J. was afraid he was already dead. Dead. No.

The men moved swiftly past her and eased Louie into the back of the ambulance. A crowd had already begun to gather near the front of the store. R.J. could barely make out the familiar faces of the neighborhood merchants and customers as they pushed in closer to get a look. *Louie, Pop, Mr. Rabinowitz*—she heard their voices assure one another as she stood helplessly by. She could hear her heart pounding in her ears, and feel it pounding all the way down to her fingertips. It was so strange to see her mother, who clutched her gray cardigan sweater in her red worn hands, wait until her husband was safely aboard, then scramble into the back of the ambulance with no one helping her, as if she'd done it dozens of times.

Maybe, R.J. thought, she'd seen someone do that on television.

The white-coated driver was about to slam the doors shut.

"Wait," R.J. said and ran forward. *Rosie Jane,* she heard people say. *Poor thing, tsk tsk,* and the driver helped her climb in next to her mother, who was making a moaning sound from deep in her chest.

Then the doors closed. The siren's scream pierced the

air again, and the wild ride began, tossing R.J. against her mother, and then her mother against R.J. as it lurched and stopped and careened around corners. R.J. thought of the lightning bugs she and Bubbe used to catch and put into a Rokeach beet borscht jar. Bubbe would punch holes into the lid so the lightning bugs could breathe. And when R.J. decided they had enough bugs captured, she would close the lid, shake the jar, and the two of them would watch the lights blink on and off the way the lights did at night on the buildings in downtown Pittsburgh. Then R.J. would always open the lid and set the lightning bugs free. She knew that when the ambulance doors opened at the hospital, she and Rifke would feel the way the lightning bugs did when the lid of the jar was opened.

The skin on her father's bald head was dry, and his mouth was open. There was a tube in his nose and an intravenous tube in his arm. R.J. looked away at the white-coated medic who sat across from her instead. The man was holding her father's wrist and checking his pulse with the watch on his own wrist. He wore a white coat and a plastic tag with his name on it. Hugo Dunlop. Please, Hugo, R.J. wanted to beg him, don't let my father die. She could feel the ambulance go around corners on two wheels, and she was very afraid that she would throw up and be embarrassed in front of Hugo Dunlop. Probably he was used to people throwing up. A man with a job like that. Please, Hugo Dunlop, don't let my father . . .

I.C.U. I.C.U. Peek-a-boo, I.C.U. That's where Hugo Dunlop and the other man rushed Louie, ran with him down the hall when they arrived at Montefiore Hospital. To I.C.U. And then a doctor came out and told R.J. and her mother that it didn't look good, which struck R.J. as so funny she had to hold in a macabre giggle. To stop herself from saying "No kidding, doctor, when they found my father clutching his chest and retching and then carried him out of our house on the stretcher, we thought that it looked sensational, and now you're telling us that it doesn't look good? How *could* you?" But she didn't say a word.

"Gin," Rifke said, and for a moment, as if she'd forgotten where she was, thinking only of her triumph over her daughter's usually expert card game, she laughed out loud. Then she regained her deathwatch composure and said, in Yiddish, *"Lomech sheyn lachen."* I should only be allowed to laugh under such terrible circumstances—which is what she had said earlier when she and R.J. watched Myron Cohen perform on the Ed Sullivan show on the waiting-room television set.

R.J. looked up at the clock. It was five minutes before four in the morning. The hospital rules said that one member of the immediate family could visit Louie in the ward at five minutes before each hour.

*"Mama, du vilst arayngeyn?"* R.J. asked her mother. Do you want to go in?

Her mother shook her head no in a way that didn't just say *No, I don't want to,* but rather *No, I couldn't stand it,* and then she gestured for R.J. to go. R.J. patted her mother on the arm, stood, and walked out into the corridor, down to the ward and pushed open the door. She parted the curtain that separated her father from the other patients and walked close to the bed.

"Daddy," she said to him. Her jaw quivered in her effort to talk quietly and hold her screams inside. Screams that started at the bottom of her feet and forced their way up into her chest and throat, fighting her to let them out. Her father's breathing sounded bubbly. Maybe the tube in his nose had been put in wrong. Maybe there was blood in it and she should go and find a doctor.

"Daddy," she said, "Mama and I watched the Ed Sullivan show tonight in the waiting room, and guess who was on. Myron Cohen. He was so funny that after it was over, even Ed Sullivan was laughing. First he told the one about the lady in Florida who tells her friend that she feels sorry for her husband because while she's lying there in the sun, he's back in New York, working like a horse. And the friend asks her, 'So vy you didn't bring him along?' And the woman says, 'Who needs a horse in Florida?' " That was the place in which her father would have chuckled. R.J. hoped he was hearing her and laughing inside. Maybe, please, God, this would make him feel better, hearing about Myron Cohen, and he would come around. "And then he did the one about the woman who told her son if he fools around with girls he'll go blind, and the son says, 'Maybe I'll just do it until I need glasses.' " Then she laughed a little burst of a laugh which she had to catch as it turned into a cry. And when she felt as if she had pulled it back inside, she spoke again.

"Daddy, it won't be long until I find out if I'm accepted to the drama department at Carnegie Tech," she said.

Her father had been so worried about the money for her college tuition. He had sat with her at the kitchen table, filling out endless financial aid applications, but so far she hadn't heard back from any of the lenders. Probably it was worrying about how to get the money that had done this to him. That and his anger at Uncle Shulke, "that capitalist bastard," as her father always called him. He wouldn't lend R.J. a penny. In fact, he had not only turned down her request for the loan, but while he did he laughed at her—that big Uncle Shulke laugh, where he threw his head back so you could see all of his back teeth. And every one of them was gold.

"My Rosele Jane," he had said. "If you want to be a teacher I say okay. You want to be a medical secretary I say okay. But you wouldn't get one ruble from me for no goddamned school of drama." When he said *drama*, it sounded a lot like the way he pronounced the city in Florida which he was on his way to, for his annual vacation. "My Yama."

"Uncle Shulke," R.J. had tried, hoping her quavering voice wouldn't give away the fact that she wanted to do anything in the world rather than have this conversation. She could hear both of her parents moving around outside the swinging kitchen door, shushing one another so they could take turns listening in. "I want to major in writing."

"Writing, shmiting," Shulke said, and dipped a piece of kichel into his cup of tea, held it there until the end was as soggy as he liked it to be, then took a big bite out of it.

"A woman gets one degree," he said with a mouth full of kichel. "The one with the letters M.R.S. Meantime she becomes a teacher—in case, God forbid, she has to fall back on it. You want my money, kiddo, that's the only way you'll get it."

R.J. had looked down at the orange-and-brown linoleum floor. An ant carrying a crumb was passing under her chair. She watched it move forward and disappear behind the Frigidaire.

"I got rules, honey girl," Uncle Shulke told her. "And one of the rules is no drama." He popped the rest of the kichel in his mouth, then took another big swig of tea.

R.J. wanted to pour the tea over his head. She wanted

to let the tears come, but if she did, her eyes would be red
and today was her interview. So she shook her head and
left the kitchen through the swinging door, which just missed
her mother, who stood on the other side of it clucking her
tongue in disappointment. R.J. went into her room to sit on
her bed and collect her thoughts. She could hear Uncle
Shulke in the kitchen talking to her mother. He was talking
loudly, but the only words she could make out from the
conversation were "I ain't paying for no goddamned drama,"
and then she heard her mother repeating again and again to
the older brother she not only idolized but who, according
to family history, had carried her out of Russia on his back:
"I don't blame you. I don't blame you."

R.J. touched her father's hand now. Over and over
tonight her mother had said that he started to die the day
he walked out of the Settlement House. Painting the signs
the last few years for Shulke's store was his only means of
income. The one thing that excited him, besides his Labor
Zionist meetings, were the drawing classes he taught to the
little children at the Hebrew Institute. For free. Finally using
the drawing talent he had hoped to use in architecture
school, though he'd never gotten there. That kind of thing
would never happen to her. Nothing, especially Uncle Shulke,
could ever change her mind about writing. Even after
Francie's death, R.J. continued to write the school Follies.
Late at night, after working in the store and doing her
homework, she sat on her bed and wrote down funny
sketches and songs that made her giggle out loud. When
she turned them in to Mrs. Joseph and the drama group,
they loved them too, so in a rush of confidence she decided
to mail in her work with an application to the drama
department at Carnegie Tech.

The minute she heard the letter drop in the mailbox
across the street from the store, she wished she could find a
big can opener to open the box and pull it out. Why would
they ever take her into that school? Because she'd written
stupid songs for a former travel agent to sing in the back of
a delicatessen? Or dumb sketches for a bunch of high school
kids who were in the school show just to get out of going to
classes?

When the call came from the drama department that
they wanted to see her, she was sure they'd made a clerical
error. On the morning of the interview she was so sick with

nerves that she threw up and was going to cancel the appointment, because she was sure she'd never get through it.

Still shaky from her sick stomach, she went to the telephone that sat on her father's cluttered desk and called Information to get the telephone number of Carnegie Tech.

"One moment," the operator said, and while R.J. waited, she opened the desk drawer absently to find a pencil and paper so she could write the number down. The paper she pulled out had the blank side up, but when she turned it over, she realized it was a draft of a letter her father had written to Mr. Katzman, his former boss at the Settlement House. Writing in the English that was still stilted after all these years in America, Louie had tried to state all the ways in which the Settlement House had been unfair to him. The letter made R.J. ache with sadness. One of the grievances her father had listed was the Settlement's failure to reimburse Louie's bus fare to a social workers' convention in Philadelphia which they'd asked him to attend. And to tell them that he needed the money very badly to pay bills. The amount of the bus ticket was $3.55. R.J. closed her eyes and held tightly to the telephone receiver. The Information operator came back on the line. "Would you like Fine Arts? Administration? Technical offices? Or the department of Architecture . . ."

"Never mind," R.J. had said. "I don't want the number anymore." Ten minutes later she sat on the bus, on the way to her interview.

"Daddy," she said now, holding his lifeless hand. "I love you so much." Surely she had overstayed her five-minute visit. She wanted to put her head down on his chest and beg him to stay alive, and to tell him she would somehow find a way to make up for all the disappointments he'd had, but instead she said, "I'll be back," and walked to the waiting room, where someone had covered the now sound-asleep Rifke with a yellow blanket and had left another for R.J. She took the blanket, curled up on another plastic sofa across the room, and fell asleep.

She was awakened by a powerful breeze of Old Spice that wafted into the waiting room, followed by Uncle Shulke, looking tan and harassed at having to return early from "My Yama." Rifke let out a wail and fell into his arms.

"Don't let him die," she cried. But this was not a cry to

God. This was a cry to someone who, if not quite as powerful, was certainly a lot more accessible and far more reliable. Someone who could not only fix a parking ticket for anyone in the family, but someone who personally knew a pharmacist who would give him paregoric without a prescription when Aunt Malke was sick; someone whose name alone would provide discounts in most of Squirrel Hill's stores.

"No one's dying so fast," Shulke assured her with as much confidence as if he really had the final say, and Rifke sighed a comforted sigh, as if to prove that she believed he did.

Now that Shulke was here to take over, R.J. excused herself and walked into the little bathroom next to the waiting room. She turned on the water and waited for it to get warm, splashed her face, and dried it with a scratchy paper towel from the metal holder on the wall. Then she rinsed out her mouth and ran a comb through her long straight black hair and pinched her cheeks to put some color in her olive skin. She looked into her eyes in the mirror, and shook her head sadly. I'm too young to have a father die, she thought. And then nodded at her reflection in sad agreement.

When she turned off the water she could hear her mother's screams from the waiting room. And when she opened the door from the bathroom she could see her mother tearing at the lapels of Shulke's coat as the screams ripped at her throat, then beating at his chest, then pulling again at him, railing against the news she'd just received from the poor young doctor who stood nervously by.

"Dead, dead, dead," her mother screamed, pounding harder and harder on Shulke's chest. And Uncle Shulke, who had once been beaten nearly to death by the men with bayonets who broke into his family's home in Russia, didn't move, just stood stoically and let his sister react to her loss. Unlike the doctor, who looked as if he was just an intern or a resident, and was flushed and nervous and clearly unequipped to handle the display of raw emotion he was seeing. "I'm sorry," R.J. heard the young man repeat over and over softly. "Gee, I mean I'm sorry."

R.J. wasn't crying. Couldn't cry. It was as if her mother's screams, which finally began to decrease in volume as her voice gave out, were pained enough for both of them.

Her father, dead.

The door to the waiting room opened and a nurse came in carrying a pill in a little cup which she gave to Rifke with another cup of water. The pill must have been a tranquilizer because Rifke took it, and after a few minutes she was very quiet. Standing, still hanging on to her brother. Her mouth was limp, her eyelids bloated into puffy red awnings that half concealed her bloodshot dark-brown eyes. Then she turned to R.J.

"He loved you," she said.

"I know, Ma," R.J. said, and when she walked to her mother and held her, she could still smell Shulke's Old Spice on her.

"Let's go home," Shulke said, and moved the two distraught women toward the door.

"I'm sorry"—R.J. thought she heard the young doctor say it again as they walked into the corridor to collect her father's belongings and go home.

Rifke had forgotten to close the apartment door, and it was still open when Shulke pulled up outside the store. Even from outside they could hear the telephone ringing, but R.J. didn't rush to answer it. Instead, she helped her mother out of Shulke's Cadillac, put an arm around her, and walked her slowly upstairs. The phone rang again and again while she walked with her into the familiar front bedroom and helped her off with her shoes, and to lie down, and covered her with the afghan Bubbe had crocheted for the double bed where Rifke had slept for more than thirty-five years with her beloved Louie. The tranquilizer she had swallowed at the hospital was taking over completely now, and Rifke was asleep before R.J. got to the bedroom door and closed it behind her.

"Hello?" she said into the phone. R.J. wanted just to shout into the receiver to whoever it was: "How can you call here today? My father is dead."

"Is this Lois Rabinowitz?" a man's voice asked. "Because if you *are*, today is your lucky day."

"Who is this?" R.J. said.

"If Lois is there, it's time to tell her that today, she's a lucky winner."

This was a joke. Had to be some kind of a joke. Some crackpot calling.

"There is nobody here by the name of Lois," R.J. said

carefully, and already had the phone away from her ear and about to hang up in the cradle, when she heard the man on the phone shout, "Maybe it's Louis. That's it. Louie. Louis. That's it. Sorry."

R.J. put the phone back to her ear.

"It doesn't say Lois at all. It says Louis. Is he there? Is he?"

"He's dead," R.J. yelled into the phone, not believing it was true and not believing that now, finally, she was crying, and it was to some stranger on the telephone.

"No," the voice said. "Dead? Hey, I'm sorry. I'm Yossie Hoberman over at HoBros department store and he just won our contest, and if it'll make you feel better, lady—and I mean this with all due respect—he just won fifteen hundred dollars."

R.J. didn't say anything, just cried a quiet little cry.

"Geez, geez, I'm really sorry." The man on the phone said in a very quiet voice. "I mean, this is really a sad set of circumstances here. Would you mind very much if I asked you how he died?"

"A heart attack," R.J. sniffed.

"Izzat right? Boy, I never heard of that before. You're tellin' me your kid had a heart attack?"

"He wasn't a kid. He was my father. He was sixty-four years old."

"No. What? Oh, wait a second. Oh boy, this is funny. I mean the Louis Rabinowitz I'm lookin' for is a kid. I mean . . . I think he's a kid. Oh, shit, Tubby," R.J. heard him call out. "Didn't it say in the friggin' rules that the people who colored the friggin' Easter Bunnies had to be kids? Lemme see the rules. They're sittin' right on your desk, you fat shmuck. Oh, Christ. Some good publicity in the neighborhood. Not only is the guy who won the contest sixty-four . . . but he also happens to be dead. Hey," the man said to R.J. "Um, I got to hang up and call you back."

R.J. was still sitting by the phone when, having parked the car, Uncle Shulke came upstairs to make sure that Rifke was all right and to tell R.J. he was going over to Burton Hirsch's Funeral Home to make the arrangements for Louie.

"Uncle Shulke, wait," R.J. said, and then she told him every word of the phone call from Mr. Hoberman.

"Yossie Hoberman, that *shmendrick*," Uncle Shulke said. Then, smiling a jaunty little smile, he picked up the phone and dialed. R.J. went to her room, but she heard him on the phone for a very long time. Talking quietly but firmly.

By the next morning, R.J. had enough money to pay for her tuition, and two weeks later she was accepted to the drama department at Carnegie Tech.

# BOOK THREE

# R.J.

*B*eth Berger had hair that was so blue-black that behind her back some people referred to her as Elvis. And she dressed like a man. Not just tailored blazers and pleated pants and shirts with cuff links. She also wore ties every day. And to dressy parties she wore a tuxedo. More than anything she wanted to be thought of as eccentric, to be thought of as unique, just to be thought of, because for years she had lived in the shadow of her handsome film director husband, Larry Wayne. Finally, after job after low-level job at the studios and networks, she had made her way to her current position at Meteor Productions. And now, at least in her mind, she had a little bit of power.

R.J. sat in the chair across from Beth Berger's desk, to which Beth Berger's secretary had shown her ten minutes earlier. Beth Berger sat behind the desk. Her chair was tipped against the wall, and her feet, clad in black boots, were propped on the desk at a diagonal from her body. Her right hand was holding the telephone and her left hand was fiddling with the knot in her tie. R.J. had been waiting for ten minutes and Beth Berger hadn't looked at her once.

"Yes, me too," Beth Berger said into the phone, and there was something about the way she said it that made R.J. certain that the person on the other end of the phone was saying something sexy to her. R.J. looked down at the blank note pad on her lap, took a pencil she'd been using to doodle and wrote what she was thinking: HELP GET ME OUT OF

HERE. Oh, God, if she didn't need this job so badly she would have stood indignantly and marched out of there at least seven minutes ago.

"I do too," Beth Berger whispered into the mouthpiece of the phone, "I swear I do, but someone's in my office so I have to ... Yes, me too." She hung up the phone and finally turned her eyes in R.J.'s direction, but R.J. could tell that she wasn't really seeing her.

"I'm R.J. Misner," R.J. said, as if to an amnesiac.

"I know who you are," Beth Berger said, and then just sat there with the glow of the phone call still in her eyes.

"I'm here to discuss the pilot about the nurses," R.J. tried.

"Nurses," Beth Berger said, jogging her mind back into place. "Oh, that's such a great idea, if I have to say so myself. It was my idea, and Jake loves it."

Jake must mean Jake Howard. Her boss. "A bunch of nurses live together in an apartment. One is a psychiatric nurse, one is a surgical nurse, and one is whatever else kind of nurse there is. And we get to know them at the hospital and at home. It's funny. Don't you think?"

Before R.J. could say that there wasn't even enough of an idea even to call it an idea yet, let alone to know if it was funny, the buzzer buzzed and Beth Berger swung her feet down from the desk and grabbed the phone nervously.

"Who is it?" she said to the person who had buzzed her. Then she turned to R.J. "I have to take this call," she said and pushed a button on the phone. "Hi, babe," she said into the mouthpiece. She picked up a pen and tapped it on the desk repeatedly as she spoke. "I've got a huge meeting with Jake at the network tonight—you should probably not wait for me. Just have a bite with the kids and I'll get there when I get there. Okay? Yeah. Love you. Bye." She hung up the phone, took a deep breath, and instead of looking at R.J., she put her face down on her desk, wrapped her arms around the back of her head as if she were protecting herself from something about to fall on her, and after a minute she said, "Oh God, oh God, oh God." Then she looked up at R.J. and sighed.

"I am so in love," she said. "So madly in love I can't see straight, can't think, can't work, don't care about anyone or anything but this man. It's just unbelievable."

"Isn't that nice?" R.J. said, hoping she could change

the subject back to the nurses as soon as possible. She wanted to talk about the project. Comment intelligently. Get the job. Start working and make a few dollars. She did not want to hear this woman's personal story.

"He is so sexy and beautiful I can't stand it," Beth Berger said, wriggling girlishly in her big leather chair.

It was true. Beth's husband, Larry Wayne, was a very attractive man, R.J. thought. She had seen his picture in the *L.A. Times* just a few weeks before.

"But, oh, God. It's so insane. I don't know how much longer I can go on lying to my husband."

*Oy vey*, R.J. thought. No. She'd now known this woman less than five minutes and suddenly she was becoming her confidante. Spare me, she thought. Beth Berger could obviously tell what R.J. was thinking because she raised a hand as if asking R.J. to indulge her and said, "Please. It's just that in my twelve years of marriage to Larry, and you're not going to believe this, I've never had an orgasm."

The nurses, R.J. thought. I want to talk about the nurses. One is psychiatric. One is surgical, and one is . . .

"But this man—and mind you, he's very ordinary looking, not gorgeous like Larry—but he makes me so crazy that I can't stop screaming and begging for more."

"Uh, Beth," R.J. said, "I think that's great, but . . ."

"He's staying at an apartment in North Hollywood. A little tiny nothing apartment, and I tell my husband I have network meetings, and I go to North Hollywood every night and we get into bed the minute I walk in and it is so incredible. Last night I made him dinner . . ."

"Great. Look, I really don't think that I . . ." R.J. picked up her purse. This was too much.

"Hey, I know you want to talk about the nurses," Beth Berger said, "but just let me tell you this one thing. Woman to woman. I mean, only another woman would get a kick out of this. I was going to make a romantic little dinner for him. You know? The best way to a man's heart and all that? So I went to the Italian butcher to get some veal so I could make him veal piccata, and of course I couldn't put the veal on my charge account in case Larry looked at the bill and remembered that we didn't have veal at home that night. So I paid for the veal with cash, and when the butcher was ringing up the sale he said to me: 'You know, you look just like my customer Mrs. Larry Wayne. Only I know you're not, because Mrs. Wayne always puts the meat on her charge account.' " Beth Berger let out a hoot. "Can you believe it? My heart was pounding like I was a criminal." She slapped at her desk and laughed a laugh that made her face bright red.

R.J. bit the inside of her cheek. Unless she said something now to stop her, this woman would go on and on. This was not right. The red of Beth Berger's face was paling a little and was now only a bright pink.

"Always puts the meat on her charge account," she said, still amused at her own story, but the seriousness of R.J.'s face was definitely having a sobering effect on her.

"Beth," R.J. said, "I have a real instinct that this isn't such a good way for us to start doing business." Now Beth Berger's face was pale pink. "I mean, probably if you think about it, you'll agree that the kind of personal information you're giving me could be stuff that next week you'll wish you hadn't told me. Maybe you'll even wish that in an hour," R.J. said. "So why don't we just proceed here? Okay?"

Beth Berger shuffled some papers on her desk. She was obviously embarrassed.

"You're right," she said, hurriedly now, and glanced at her watch. "Anyway, about the nurses. Listen, I know your work, I always watch Patsy's show, the network likes you, so why don't I just call your agent today and we'll make a deal, and we'll meet again next week and we'll talk story?"

The buzzer buzzed. Twice this time.

R.J. was taken aback, but thrilled with the turn of events. She was glad she had stopped the conversation where she had. "Great," she said. Beth Berger grabbed the phone. "Yes?" she said nervously into the receiver. Then she listened for a moment and looked at R.J., who stood. She wasn't going to sit through another phone call. Beth Berger held her hand up like a traffic cop to tell R.J. to wait a second, then held the phone against her navy blazer.

"We'll talk more next week. Okay?" and she smiled.

"You bet," R.J. said as Beth Berger pushed a button on the phone. R.J. was nearly out the door when she heard her say into the telephone: "Sweetie, Daddy will be home for dinner, but I have a meeting, so ask *him* to help you with the map of Italy, all right?"

A job. She had a job. Thank God. A pilot. Nurses. One

was psychiatric. One was surgical. Talk about having nothing to go on. But so what? She'd make it work. She'd get home and try to come up with good solid funny characters, and at the end of the day she'd call her agent and see what the offer was. Whatever it was she'd take it. Pay her bills. Put a few dollars away for Jeffie's bar mitzvah. Beth Berger. So crazy. Imagine telling a total stranger about her illicit sex life. Her affair. And this was a woman R.J. would be working with for the next however long it took to write the pilot. The cost of doing business. That's what Arthur would have called having to deal with a person like Beth Berger.

At home at the card table, R.J. made some preliminary notes, thinking about what the emotional makeup of the nurses could be. How their lives at the hospital affected their interactions with one another. Who else lived in their building. What kind of men they'd be involved with. What were the doctors like whom they worked for? She stopped for a few minutes to make a meat loaf for Jeffie and put it into the oven. Then back at the card table she made a note to call a friend of Dinah's who was a nurse at Valley Presbyterian Hospital and interview her. Then she wrote some more notes about the characters, and when she finally looked up it was six o'clock. She would call her agent and see if the negotiations had begun.

"Hiya babes." Her agent, Stanley, answered her call, and before she could ask he said, "Hey, sorry, but it's no go on the nurses pilot. She says you're not right for it."

"What? Who does?"

"Berger at Meteor. Says she thought it over after the meeting with you. You're just wrong for the project. Go figure. Huh?"

"Stanley, she told me I had it."

"Hey! I'm just the messenger. She hired Karen Ambler off a M*A*S*H spec script. Don't worry," he said. "Maybe you'll sell *Laugh a Minute* tomorrow."

"Thanks, Stanley," R.J. said. She hung up the phone, stood, and walked downstairs to check on Jeffie's dinner. The meat loaf was raw. She was furious at herself for forgetting to turn on the oven, until she reached for the knob and realized she hadn't forgotten at all. She had turned it on but there was no heat. Maybe the pilot was out. She struck a match and lit the pilot but it wouldn't stay lit. The oven was broken. She made the meat loaf into hamburgers that she cooked in a frying pan on the top of the stove, and called Jeffie down for dinner. After dinner she would go over her notes for *Laugh a Minute* for tomorrow's meeting.

"It's about a woman comedy writer," R.J. said to Kip Walters, who smiled and said encouragingly, "That's great." Thank heaven, R.J. thought. "And she works on the staff of a TV variety show," she went on.

"Like on *The Dick Van Dyke Show*," Walters said. He was still smiling.

"And all of the bizarre people she has to deal with when she's working. She's the only woman on the staff."

"Funny," Kip Walters said. "Funny. Like who are they?"

"One is a chauvinistic head writer who calls her 'the broad,' and then there's a bunch of really neurotic guys and she mothers them as if she was Snow White and they were the seven dwarfs."

"I love it. This is great. Go on."

"And she's always wisecracking to everyone, because she has a hard time turning it off."

"But inside she's vulnerable as hell," Kip Walters added, nodding.

"And her conflict," R.J. said, feeling confident now, "is that on top of working day and night on this show, she's raising a son and she has to be at home, too, so we get to see the real problems of the working mother."

In an instant, the smile disappeared from Kip Walters's face, and he opened his mouth, inserted his index finger, and pretended to gag.

"Yecchh," he said. "Major turnoff. Real problems. I'm not interested in real problems. Next."

"Pardon?"

"What else have you got? Something sans real problems. This network needs an eight o'clock show. A fairy tale world. Nothing real. Got anything like that?"

"I don't. I really don't."

"Too bad. Let us know when you do."

*    *    *

"This oven is shot, lady. I'm amazed it lasted this long. It's at least thirty years old. And ovens are like women. After a certain age, they just don't get hot no more."

R.J. had waited ovenless for this repairman for two weeks or she would have thrown him out the door for that. Instead, she watched him as he laughed at his own joke. And while he was laughing he said, "It'll run you about two hundred and fifty bucks."

An oven. How could she do without an oven? Two hundred and fifty dollars. Christ. "Go ahead and fix it," she said. While the man was fixing the oven she went back upstairs to work, and the phone rang. It was her agent, Stanley.

"Good news," he said. "Not great news, but good news. You know your story about the chicken?" He'd obviously never read "Chicken in a Pot."

"Yes."

"I sold it to *Women at Work* magazine."

"Stanley! That is great news. I'm thrilled. How much?"

"Two hundred and fifty dollars."

The oven, R.J. thought.

"Before my commission, of course," Stanley said.

Almost the oven, R.J. realized, amending her thought. But most of all it was a sale, in a new form. She had tried something new and it had worked. She sat at the card table for a few minutes after she put the phone down, smiling. Imagining herself going to the newsstand to buy the copy of *Women at Work* that had her story in it and how much fun that would be. Short stories. She was now a writer and seller of short stories. And she would write more of them, too, as soon as she could make some money to support herself and her son so she could afford to.


"Stanley sent you over because he said you're my writer," Dick Crawford said. Above the sofa where he sat was a poster of a bikinied woman's groin. "Just the girl to write this idea I have, so I'm going to pitch it to you. It's real simple. A guy, his wife, and her kid sister. The wife and the guy are in their early thirties, see? And the kid sister is twenty-one and gorgeous and she lives with them. And what we have to believe, even though it's never stated, is that the guy is slipping it to the sister on the side. What do you think?" The successful television producer gave R.J. a boyish grin.

"I think Stanley was wrong," she said, standing. "I'm not your writer." Then she left.



The green blanket had holes in it. It was a wedding gift from Arthur's aunt Louise, but since Aunt Louise sent a blanket that was double-bed size and not king size, which was the size of the bed, and Aunt Louise lived in Canada, they couldn't return it, so they used the blanket to sit on at picnics. And this was sort of a picnic. An outing with Jeffie's class to the Los Angeles County Art Museum, and afterward a brown-bag lunch on the grounds. Jeffie had invited R.J. to be a driver and a chaperone in that same kind of way her mother used to invite poor people in the neighborhood over for Passover dinner. Pitying. Anticipating gratitude. And when R.J. wavered, not sure that under her unemployed circumstances she ought to give up a writing day, he said, patting her arm, "You really should, Mom. It'll be good for you."

That sold her. Obviously her son had noticed the edge of panic she was feeling because of being out of work, and the way she hardly left the house anymore, and he was hoping to be able to keep her happily occupied, at least for a few hours. And the truth was she was having a great time. Every one of the boys in Jeffie's class was taller than R.J. was, and so was almost every one of the girls. They were all so darling.

"I see your name on the Patsy Dugan show, Mrs. Misner. Is it fun working for her?" one of the girls asked.

"It *was* fun. I'm not working there anymore. Those are reruns you've been seeing."

"My mom said Patsy Dugan had silicone in her breasts or implants. Is that true?" Natalie, a girl with frizzy blond hair, asked seriously. Then, as if to emphasize the question, she blew a big pink bubble with the gum she'd been chewing.

"I don't know," R.J. answered. It was a warm clear California day. Jennifer, a girl who had a turned-up nose and wore big tortoise-shell glasses, poked the bubble, which splattered all around Natalie's mouth.

"Have you ever seen them in person?" Matt Wallace, Jeffie's friend asked. He was foraging in R.J.'s basket. Probably for more cookies.

"Seen who in person?" R.J. asked.

"Her breasts," Matt answered.

"Aghhh," the kids screamed. "In person."

"Can't say that I have," R.J. replied, trying not to laugh.

"I mean, you could tell if you'd seen them because they're much harder when they're fake."

"Ugh, how do you know that, Matt?" Natalie shrieked.

"They look like footballs," the boy said.

"Footballs, agghh." That sent the group into screams of laughter. Infectious laughter that made R.J. laugh. And soon they weren't laughing about footballs anymore. They were just laughing at one another's laughter, and at Natalie's trying to remove the bubble gum from her face, and every now and then someone in the group would say *footballs*, and they'd all fall apart all over again. Including R.J., who was glad she'd worn her overalls and not any decent clothes, because somehow she'd managed to get mustard all over one leg and Hawaiian Punch all over the other. Oh, God, these kids were so cute. If anyone on the faculty heard what they were laughing about. Her eyes were wet from laughing so hard and she said, "Agh, I need a Kleenex." As she reached into her purse to pull out a tissue, she noticed that a handkerchief was being handed to her, and when she looked up at the handkerchief bearer, she saw David Malcolm. Oh, God. She wasn't wearing a drop of makeup. She was covered with food. She was dressed in a pair of overalls and an old T-shirt.

"Hi," he said, smiling.

R.J. smiled at the sight of him, but she wanted to disappear under the green blanket. He was so wonderful to look at in a suit and tie. And he had such a sweet smile on his face. Her heart was pounding and her face was hot with the excitement of being near him.

"Hey, look who's here," Jeffie said.

"How are you, Jeff?" David asked with a big smile, and offered his hand to Jeffie to shake.

"I was on my way out of a meeting at the museum and heard the laughter over here, so I looked over, and I might have known you'd be in the middle of it," he said, grinning at R.J. "What was so funny?"

His question sent the whole group into hysterics again, except for R.J., who was trying not to laugh. Oh sure. Tell proper David Malcolm that she'd been discussing Patsy Dugan's breasts with a bunch of twelve-year-olds.

"Football," she answered, and all the kids squealed again.

"Yeah, football," Matt Wallace said.

"I had no idea you were a fan," David said to R.J.

She couldn't answer. Just stood and straightened her wrinkled overalls, certain that she looked horrible and dumpy and askew.

"God, you look adorable," David said. "When I spotted you in the middle of that group of kids, for a minute I thought I was mistaken and that you were one of them."

She smiled. He was a charmer. There was no doubt about that.

"I've got to hurry back to my office," he said. "Why not walk me back to my car?"

R.J. hesitated.

"Go ahead, Mrs. Misner," Natalie said. "He looks like Robert Redford."

Oh, God, R.J. thought, realizing that all the kids had been taking this in.

David smiled at the girl and then winked and said, "Only infinitely more attractive."

"This is Mr. Malcolm, everyone," R.J. said.

"And you're gonna walk him to his car," Matt said.

"Yeah."

David offered his arm and R.J. took it and they walked toward Wilshire Boulevard. It had been nearly a month since Big Sur, and R.J. had thought about him, dreamed about him, had fantasies about him. Never even imagining that in a spread-out place like Los Angeles she could ever hope to bump into him again. Once at the movie studio had been outrageous luck. This was too good.

"Why does the license plate on your car spell out the word *rainbow*?" she asked quietly. She'd thought about asking him that over and over.

"Because Rainbow Paper is the name of the company where I work," he told her.

It was silly. It wasn't an omen. It was a coincidence. They were nearly at the corner.

"You don't really have to walk me all the way to the parking lot," he said. "It was just such a treat to run into you having so much fun with all the kids, and I wanted to ask you how you were doing. You seemed to be under a lot of pressure when we were together. Have you found a job yet?"

"No job yet, but I sold a short story to *Women at Work* magazine."

"That's great. I'm proud of you. What was it about?"

"About ten pages."

"Still doing those one-liners," he said.

"It's about a failed romance," she said, serious now.

"Ahh," he said, knowingly. "I'll wait until they make it into a movie."

"From your mouth to God's ears," she said.

They arrived at the corner and stopped, both of them knowing she should go back and attend to the kids.

"Why don't we have dinner tonight?" he asked.

Dinner. It would feel so good to put on something pretty, to leave her Blue Chip-stamp card table for a while and go to a restaurant and look across a dinner table at that gorgeous face. If that's all the date would be. But inevitably after dinner there would be tension about whether or not they should spend the night together, and that would lead to wondering if there should be a relationship, and of course it could never be what she wanted, because she was so wrong for him and vice versa and . . . No, a dinner date would be nice, but she didn't feel as if she had the strength for the aftermath.

"Nothing's changed, David," she said. "We still don't have a chance and—"

"And you know what you want and it's not me," he said with a little smile, and then he ruffled her hair and walked away across the street.

All the way back to where the kids were waiting, as her sandals scuffed along the sidewalk they sounded as if they were saying *shmuck shmuck shmuck*. How could she have let him go again?

"He's gorgeous," one of the girls said when R.J. returned to the blanket, where all the kids were lying sprawled on their stomachs.

."Yeah," R.J. replied. Then she ate one more cookie and started packing up the picnic supplies. When everything was packed she said, "All aboard the Yellow Mustang," and the kids jumped up to join her.

Manuela made a chili casserole, and R.J. poked at it, barely tasting it as she ate. Jeffie kicked the table base with his sneakered foot in a regular rhythm as he wolfed his down.

David. So often after the time they'd spent together in Big Sur, R.J. had wanted to call him. To tell him he was terrific. To tell him she had appreciated his grace despite her lousy behavior. She'd certainly never tell him the dumb thing about the rainbow and how she felt it was a sign from her dead husband. And wasn't it a coincidence that Rainbow was the name of the company he worked for? It would have sounded so crazy. Surely he already thought she was bananas to want marrige so badly that she wouldn't, couldn't continue to see him, a man who was an obvious impossibility, so clearly not a candidate.

After dinner she helped Jeffie work on an English paper about Sydney Carton. She had been reading *A Tale of Two Cities* every night before she fell asleep so she could keep up with what her son was doing in school. Jeffie made some notes. R.J. thought about David.

"C'mon, Mom," Jeffie said, bringing her back. "We only got a B on the one you helped me with about Madame Defarge. We gotta do better this time."

"You never told me we only got a B. What didn't the teacher like?"

"I think it was the part you said I should put in about Madame Defarge being like a spider knitting her evil web. That was a tip-off to Miss Flood that you were in on it. She underlined it in red and wrote 'Get off it, Jeffie' in the corner."

"You mean because she suspected that your mother was a writer who helped you?"

"No, I mean because it was dumb."

"I'm going to sleep," R.J. said.

"It is a far, far better thing that you do," Jeffie teased. R.J. grinned and yawned and stood.

"Mom, what are we gonna do about my bar mitzvah?" he asked before she got to the door. "I mean, I don't care if it isn't fancy, but I'd like to have a party and maybe have music or, I don't know. Just something neat," he said. He looked so much like Arthur when he said that. The way he held his head to the side, cast his eyes downward as if he was embarrassed to ask her for something for himself. Afraid that it might be too much bother. R.J. felt a rush of love for him. In a world where she heard so many parents complaining about problems with their children, this was a great kid. A funny warm boy who was always helpful and cheerful, even after the tragedy of his father's murder, which could have left him a cynic.

"We'll figure out something great for your bar mitzvah," she promised, and then wondered how she could pull it off. "You sure I shouldn't stay and work some more on Sydney?" she asked as she stood in the doorway.

"I'm sure," he said, and stood and kissed her, and the phone rang.

"I'll get it in my room," R.J. told him.

By the time she got to her room the phone had rung four times, and she snatched the receiver from its cradle.

"H'lo."

"R.J., long time no see. This is the long-lost Michael Rappaport."

The temptation simply to put the receiver down was enormous. What in the hell did he want? She was amazed at how her breathing changed and she felt shaky just hearing his voice.

"Hello, Michael," she said.

"R.J.," he said, "I know this is really out of left field, but I had to talk to you tonight. I've felt for a long time that I owed you this call."

"Believe me, you don't owe me anything. I don't—"

"I know. You don't care. And I don't blame you for not caring. But I needed to make this call because I wanted you to know that I'm in major therapy."

*Major.* Major was a big Hollywood word. Anything that was important or serious was major. There was always some word like that going around. When people used it, you knew they were trying to sound "in on it" and you should stay away from them. Now Michael Rappaport calling to confess that he was in major therapy was clearly supposed to have some profound effect on her.

"Good for you, Michael."

"R.J., you're being cold and I don't blame you. I suspected you would be, but despite your feelings, see if you can hear what I need you to acknowledge." The lingo. He had the lingo down pat. He was in therapy all right. "You embodied my worst fears. That is to say that everything you needed and wanted in a relationship was everything I was afraid to give. I'm learning that I'm incapable of intimacy, and marriage speaks to a kind of intimacy I couldn't handle. Well, my shrink thinks that I should have married you anyway and worked my problems out within the marriage with your help. But of course, I told him that—"

"Michael, let me stop you," R.J. said, "and may I just say the following to you. . . ." She paused and took a deep breath. "Bye bye."

She sat with her hand on the receiver for a very long time. Then she opened her night table drawer, shuffled through some slips of paper, found the one she wanted with the telephone numbers on it, and dialed. After a few rings, David Malcolm's answering machine clicked on, and his sweet pleasant voice said, "Please leave your name, telephone number, and a message. Thank you."

Then there was the beep. This was it. Put up or shut up, as her friend Francie used to say when she challenged R.J. to do something that she feared. She knew that she could hang up. David would never be the wiser. Or she could tell him she'd changed her mind, hoped that he hadn't changed his, and have another chance to be with this sensational younger man, who, aside from all his other obvious charms, had mental health. Mental goddamn health. No whining. No apparent fears. No locking himself indoors. Straightforward mental health. What was it he'd said to her about Norman Vincent Peale? Positive thinking. And she had laughed.

No, he was not the package she had ever imagined, and vice versa. There would never be the kind of future with him she felt she required. But there could be fun and joy with him, like their time together in Big Sur. And lust and heat. There was no denying the siren call of lust and heat. She had to let herself enjoy him and not be afraid. Because if she stayed afraid, she was as bad as Barry Litmann and Hobart Fineburg and Michael Rappaport and all the others.

"This is R.J.," she said to the waiting message tape, "and I really would like to see you," and then she put the receiver down.

She took a shower, reread the last few chapters of *A Tale of Two Cities*, which never failed to put her to sleep, and just as she started to doze, the phone rang.

"H'lo."

"Last eligible gentile man before the freeway," David said.

R.J. smiled. "I changed my mind and I'd like to see you," she said quietly.

"I'm glad," he said. "Tell you what. I've got some black-tie event to go to on Saturday night. A friend's party. Why don't we go there, then duck out early and have a late supper alone?"

"I'd love that," she said.

"Pick you up at eight."

R.J. hung up the phone and fell asleep with a smile on her face.

*I*t was the end of May, and the fallen blossoms of the jacarandas spread like lavender fans on the street beneath each tree. R.J. drove down Valley Vista Boulevard on her way home from Fashion Square, where she'd browsed in every shop. Black tie. There wasn't one article of clothing in her closet that qualified as something to wear to a black-tie party. Well, maybe one. The dress she had bought for the Emmy awards, five years ago—or was it six?—when Patsy's show and the writers were nominated, but it was blatantly out of style and even though she hated to admit it, it was a little too tight. But after a morning of looking everywhere, it was obvious a new dress was out of the question. Formal dresses cost a fortune, and the money she had left had to be stretched until heaven knew when.

The drugstore. She had to stop at the drugstore to pick up a few odds and ends for the house. The truth was that the drugstore could wait and she was just trying to avoid what was becoming the hateful moment of sitting down at the card table and trying to work. Trying to invent work in her head. What a bizarre profession writing was. Putting words down on paper to amuse other people? Putting words down on paper to expel the words from your soul? She would go to the drugstore. She was about to turn into the Thrifty parking lot when she saw the sign on the storefront across the street and it made her laugh. USED STAR'S CLOTHES. She added her own thought: Stars who haven't been used need not apply. Surely they had meant the sign to say STARS' USED CLOTHES, and then she shook her head as she parked the car.

"It's come to this, Misner," she said out loud. "Now you're so desperate for work, you're rewriting signs on stores." CHEAP it said on another sign underneath. Well, maybe before she went into the Thrifty she'd stop in and take a look at the clothes.

A little bell jingled as she opened the door and was confronted by the clusters of racks and more racks of ladies' clothes which were crowded into the tiny space.

"Be right with ya, hon," came a voice, and from behind a rack emerged a woman with salt-and-pepper gray hair cut into a style that had been called a "pixie" when R.J. was in school. Bright-blue eyes shone from the woman's very wrinkled face, and on her tiny body she wore a perfectly tailored suit.

"Just browsing," R.J. told her.

"Browse away. I'm Frieda Seltzer. This is my store. So if I can help ya, gimme a holler," she said in a voice and accent that sounded to R.J. just like Ruth Gordon's. "I got recent arrivals; I got some not so recent; I even got vintage. I buy outright, buy on consignment, even buy at estate sales. So look around. You want to try on, be my guest. My prices are very fair and if you're serious, I'll negotiate."

"Thank you," R.J. said, and began moving clothes along a rack just to get Frieda Seltzer to go away, but Frieda stood her ground. If R.J. stopped for more than a second to look at something, Frieda Seltzer would immediately wax historic about it. "Ann-Margret, poor darling, fell from a stage in Las Vegas and came back looking more gorgeous than ever. So brave. Imagine. Ahh, Eva Gabor. A stunning human being, and she only wore that once. Can't you picture her in it? That one, the one you're looking at. With the beads? Cher. When she did that special. So many have tried it on, but who else is built like that, if you know what I'm saying. If a toothpick gets invited to a fancy dress ball, maybe I can sell it." She smiled. She had lipstick on her teeth.

R.J. shuffled through the rack a little more quickly. The clothes had a mothball smell that reminded her of her mother's closet in the apartment in Pittsburgh. Maybe if she didn't stop and look closely at the dresses, Frieda Seltzer would understand that she wasn't interested in the history of each one; but as fast as she went, Frieda had a story—Debbie Reynolds on consignment; Jo Anne Worley, an angel on this earth; Ethel Merman, the greatest talent of our day. R.J. paused to examine a long green-and-black silk dress that looked as if it was a small size.

"Cindy Williams," the woman said. "She's your size and your coloring," and then she added hastily, "and I'll let you have it for forty-five dollars if ya like the way it looks on you. It's a stunning item."

R.J. held the dress up in front of herself. Forty-five dollars. To have something new, albeit used, to wear on her date with David. Maybe she should try it on. It was either that or go back to her writing table.

"I'll try it."

Frieda Seltzer stood outside the tiny dressing room talking nonstop. It was obvious that today was not one of her busier days and she was lonely for the company. R.J. stopped listening to most of it, trying to decide, when she finally got her sweat pants and sweat shirt off and slid into what Frieda alleged was Cindy Williams's dress, if she looked okay, nine gray hairs notwithstanding. Of course with the right makeup and . . .

"Picture it with makeup and hair and the right shoes," Frieda Seltzer said from outside the dressing room, as if she'd been reading R.J.'s thoughts. "Come out, I'll take a look."

R.J. took some lipstick out of her purse and applied it just to give her a better idea, and when she came out of the dressing room to look in the three-way mirror, she stood on her toes to see what effect high heels would have on the length.

"I don't carry no shoes. People are funny about wearin' one another's shoes. Especially the shoes of someone dead. Did I mention that I do a lot of estates? That can be spooky. People get weird in those situations. I been in this business a long time. I seen a lot. I had Vilma Banky; I had Mary Pickford; I had Lily Daniels."

"Not bad." R.J. thought about the dress. Cindy Williams had a bigger bust than she did, but maybe if she just shortened the straps.

"All of 'em of course were long before your time," Frieda said.

"I remember Lily Daniels," R.J. said, just to be polite, as she turned to catch a glimpse of how the back of the dress looked. "I loved her."

"Oh, honey, my absolute favorite in the world, so you can imagine when I got the call how I ran. And the call didn't come from the husband, mind you. Quite the contrary. The call was from the other wife, who he married after years of being a widower. And you want to know what? All those years later, Lily's clothes were still sitting in the closet like he wished she would come home. And I guarantee you he did wish that. Everyone knew that she made a life for him, and when she died he closed up like an oyster. Well, the new wife went crazy when she saw them clothes. She picked up the phone and called me and said, in so many words, get this garbage outa here. Of course to the husband's face, she made it look like she was doin' him a favor, movin' out the sad memories. Hey, you're a smart girl, you get my meaning, but the husband, I forget his name, some rich guy, not in show business, do *you* remember?"

R.J. said she didn't, and twirled a little in Cindy Williams's dress to see how it would look when she and David were dancing.

"You can imagine his loving Lily so much he wouldn't even throw away her clothes. And you should have seen the items. All soft and beautiful and feminine the way she always was. And Mrs. Number Two, if you'll excuse me, a bitch of the first order. Making snide comments about the clothes being cheesy and Lily having no taste, and making nasty remarks about her being an actress. Even after her death this horrible woman was jealous of her memory. Well, of course I didn't argue with her—it wasn't my place—but she wasn't fit to kiss Lily Daniels' hem."

"Forty dollars," R.J. tried. She had never negotiated for anything in her life.

"Sold," Frieda Seltzer said. "You won't be sorry." R.J. went into the dressing room to change, and Frieda Seltzer kept talking about Lily Daniels's clothes and how the second wife insisted on cash that minute, which she swore she was going to give to charity, but Frieda had been positive it was a lie and that the woman was keeping the money for herself. She was still rambling when R.J. handed her the dress and a check, and emerged a few minutes later in her sweat clothes, hoping she'd made the right choice about the dress and that David would think she looked good in it.

"Enjoy it, honey, in the best of health," Frieda Seltzer said, and handed her a bag containing the dress and the receipt.

"Thank you very much," R.J. said, and headed for the door. She had already opened it and the bell had jingled when she could have sworn she heard Frieda say "Malcolm from Rainbow Paper."

R.J. turned back in surprise.

"That's the name of Lily Daniels' husband. I just remembered. Rand Malcolm. A zillionaire. The man from the Rainbow Company. You know. That's the name on every paper plate and cup you use. Even toilet paper, pardon me. That's the kind of money we're talkin' about, and the second wife sells the clothes to me for cash."

Oh, God, R.J. thought. Oh, God.

"Don't you think she shoulda given 'em to the Good Will or the Salvation Army? Some charity. Not that I'm complaining. I made a fortune from sellin' them, but still . . ."

"Thanks again," R.J. said, and pulled the door shut behind her with a loud jingle. Of course. Lily Daniels. David's mother. That's who he looked like, with those big expressive eyes. My mother worked at this studio for a few years, he said. Rainbow. The name of the company I work for. This was too much. From the beginning she could tell he was refined, raised in luxury—he'd told her a little about it—but Rainbow Paper. Really rich. From another world. And she was trying to look good for him by buying Cindy Williams's old dress. People in the Thrifty drugstore who passed the shampoo section must have wondered why R.J., putting all the pieces together in her head, stood there for a long time, laughing out loud.

"So who do you think was responsible for your first date to begin with?" Dinah said, lifting her suitcase onto the bed. "I hate unpacking, I hate packing, I hate traveling, and believe me this trip was not pleasure. My mother is falling apart at the seams. Anyway, when I was leaving for the airport that day, I'm halfway out the door and Jason Flagg calls me. He says his friend met my friend the writer and wants to call you. I didn't even ask who his friend was. I was so thrilled that if you had a good time, maybe you'd forget about Tom Thumb."

"Forgotten, believe me," R.J. said. She was sitting in front of a mirror with a trayful of Dinah's earrings, trying to decide which pair to borrow to wear with the green-and-black silk dress.

"The pearls," Dinah said, not even looking at her, moving back and forth between her suitcase and her clothes hamper.

"Di, I'm worried."

"What's to worry? This kid's a friggin' prince on horseback," Dinah told her. "Take it for what it's worth. Use him up, honey. Use him up, because the romance is certainly not going to go anywhere, and don't kid yourself that it could or might or should. There's no such animal. To begin with, that father—and I know because I've read a lot of articles on him—is one tough customer. And the kid is probably his big hope. The old man probably has political ambitions for him. The kind of stuff that requires a perfect wife. Not some older left-leaning Jew with a kid who wrote tit jokes for Patsy Dugan."

"Jesus, Dinah, is that who I am to you?" R.J. flared.

"Not to me, honey," Dinah said, smelling a blouse she had just taken out of the suitcase, then tossing it into the open hamper, which was now heaped with dirty clothes. "To me you're the greatest girl on earth. But I can guarantee you, the old boy probably already has your phone tapped."

"That's nuts," R.J. said, standing. She didn't need Dinah's earrings. She would go home. She'd done her duty. Picked Dinah up at the airport, after a call early this morning that she'd hoped, as the ringing awakened her, would be from David.

"Arj," Dinah said now, lifting the empty suitcase and putting it on the top shelf of a closet, "all I'm telling you is don't be naïve. Tonight you're going to be a guest at a club that won't let you be a member. Well, Rand Malcolm may let you be a guest in his son's life . . . but he sure as hell ain't gonna let you be a member there either. So don't make it a big deal. Have some fun. I met David at the same party you did. He's gorgeous. Looks like Robert Redford. Go have a good time, and when he stops seeing you because he's marrying the latest twenty-two-year-old debutante, you know what? Wish him well, wish the debutante well, and keep moving."

"I don't want that, Dinah."

"Make yourself want it. Believe me, it's all that's available," she snapped. Something was wrong.

"You seeing Robert tonight?" R.J. tried.

"No," Dinah said, turning quickly to pick up the clothes hamper.

"I guess I figured since you hadn't seen him in so long, you'd—"

"Yeah, well, why would I want to see Robert, who only called me once the whole time I was in Florida?"

"One time?"

"That was plenty," she said, carrying the hamper toward the bedroom door. "Since what he called for was to tell me he's going back with his wife."

"Oh, Di," R.J. said, able to tell just from her friend's walk how bad she felt. "Are you okay?"

"Shit, no," Dinah said, turning and putting the basket down. "I'm dying. I'm out of my mind and dying. And I hurt and I ache and I sat on the plane coming back, wishing it would crash so that maybe Robert would read the list of crash victims in the paper and feel bad. Can you imagine? After all the things he said about her, the furry-fingered asshole goes back with her." Dinah was blinking furiously, trying to hold back the tears. R.J. put out her arms, and though her friend was seven inches taller and a lot wider, she fell into the needed hug and put her face down on the top of R.J.'s head.

"I loved that schmucko, Arj. I loved him so berry mush. That's what we used to say to each other, because I once told him that one of my twins said that when she was a baby. And then he started saying it to me. I love you berry mush, he always said to me when we hung up the phone. And now he's got the nerve to love his wife more berry mush than he loves me."

"Oh, Di, he couldn't. Believe me, he couldn't. I'll bet he just went back with her because of the kids or because he felt guilty. But how could he love anyone better than you? You're the greatest and the most fun and the most darling, and you're so special, and I know he loved you. I could see it every time he looked at you."

"Yeah?"

"Absolutely."

Dinah loosened her grip on R.J. and walked toward the mirror.

"I wouldn't blame him if he didn't love me. I'm a big pain in the ass."

"But he did."

"Sometimes I caught sight of his face when I was yelling at my kids, and I would have sworn he was thinking: 'What in the hell am I doing with this bitch?'"

"Di, don't."

"So he waited until I was on the other side of the country with my very sick mother, because he was too chickenshit to tell me the truth. Just like my ex-husband. They're all like that, you know," she said, staring at herself in the mirror. Then she looked at R.J. in the mirror and said, "Except maybe David Malcolm. I mean, wouldn't that be nice, if he turned out to be the exception? It would be nice for you and for me."

R.J. didn't say a word, and Dinah turned.

"For you, because it's enough already," she said. "I'd like to see you have some real joy in your life. And for me because I don't even care if I'm not the one it happens to. I just want to know that somebody can find a love that works. So go get him, Arj."

The two friends hugged a long sad hug.

*I*f David Malcolm knew how-good he looked in black tie, he could rent himself out as a lethal weapon. To die, as Dinah would have said if she had seen him walk into R.J.'s living room. To die. And now R.J. could see how strong his resemblance was to Lily Daniels.

"You look very pretty tonight," he said to her, and she was reminded of Barbra Streisand in *Funny Girl* looking at Omar Sharif and being unable to say anything in her infatuation but "Hello, gorgeous." That thought made her smile. David smiled back.

"Ready?" he asked.

She took one last look at herself in the mirror. Cindy Williams's alleged dress had a nice little bounce to it as she moved, and the colors looked very good with her hair. "Ready," she told him. Jeffie was spending the night at a friend's. She locked the front door of the house and slid into the leathery smell of the front seat of the Jaguar. David held her hand as he drove.

"Why do you suppose," he asked her as they drove down Sunset toward the beach, "that you're so tough?"

There it was again.

"I've been thinking about that a lot, and wondering why my experience of you continues to be that your dukes are always up and you're ready for combat. I'm enormously curious to know why that is."

She thought for a moment, then answered. "I guess because at bottom I believe that the world is a very difficult place. I've had to put up a fight often enough that I'm conditioned to expect that there are more to come. So I'm in a state of readiness."

"But doesn't that sometimes make you jump the gun? Stand ready for a fight when there isn't one forthcoming?"

She smiled. "Maybe. But I guess I believe that there will inevitably be one forthcoming."

"Hey," he said, in a mock tough voice. "Whatsa mattah? You forgot about Dr. Peale?"

She laughed and he slipped a tape into the tape deck. Frank Sinatra. The same one he'd taken to Big Sur.

"You mean we're not going to stop and dance?" she said when Sinatra sang. "The bloom must be off the rose."

"I promise you we'll trip the light fantastic when we get there." That struck her funny. He was only twenty-nine years old and his dialogue was sometimes straight out of a Fred Astaire musical. He asked her about Jeffie and her work and told her this party was an annual one that a friend of his gave just to get an old gang of friends together. At Surfside, a beach club near Trancas. She felt different with him now. Not only because she'd just found out that his mother had been one of her favorite movie stars, but all the information Dinah had spewed out about his father and the money and the debutantes and clubs that didn't allow Jews—it was all racing through her brain. Not to mention the fact that David never offered any information about himself. Did he assume she knew all those things from Dinah or Jason Flagg, or did he want to keep them from her?

"Two reasons you tell everything and he doesn't," Dinah had told her. "A) is because he doesn't want to get deeply involved, and B) is because he's a WASP. We're not used to people like that who don't show their feelings. I dated this guy in college. My parents were sick about it. His name was J. Pembroke Bently. Do you love it? Anyway, one Saturday night he didn't show up for our date. Well, you know me. When he came by on Sunday, I read him the riot act. And when I finished he told me very calmly that the reason he hadn't been there was because he had to go home to wherever in Connecticut and say goodbye to daddy. So I said, 'Oh, yeah? Where'd your dad go?' And he said, 'Oh, you know, he passed on.' The guy's father died, and he took one day out and came back like nothing was wrong. I mean, R.J., when my father died I threw myself down on the grave screaming 'Take me with you.' Of course at the time I had twin baby girls and a cheating husband, and dying seemed like a better idea than another day with any of them, but . . . My point is that WASPs are cold fish. They hold everything inside."

It doesn't matter, R.J. thought. Tonight I'll dance in his arms and look up at that face, and make him laugh—which is what she knew he liked best about her—and just enjoy everything about him and his friends and this beautiful beach club.

"Dave, boy!" Malco!" Lots of people greeted him. The women were all fair-haired and pretty and well-groomed and perfectly coiffed and made up. The men in their tuxes were lean, tall, and handsome, apple-cheeked prep school boys grown up. David introduced R.J. all around. She'd never known people had names like the ones she was hearing. Oh, some real ones, Janes or Lindas, but then there was Buffy, Tookie, Bobo, Binky, and even one named Tee-Tee.

As they were walking toward the dance floor R.J. said quietly to David: "Sounds like a list of nicknames for genitals."

He laughed an outraged laugh, then took her hand and led her onto the dance floor. The brief moment they'd danced above the ocean in Big Sur hadn't prepared her for this. Thank God, she thought, for all those high school parties where she'd learned to follow. The funny old-fashioned band dressed in white tie played "Our Love Is Here to Stay," and David moved against her and with her and near her and made funny comments about the band and the other dancers in her ear. And he held her so close that she could sense every move before he made it, so that after just a few minutes it felt as if they'd been dancing together for years. And she was letting it happen. For the first time in years she wasn't thinking *no*. She was feeling *yes*. And there was a joyous giggle in her throat that bubbled out from time to time. The band segued into "They All Laughed," and R.J. thought the words: "They laughed at me wanting you, said I was reaching for the moon. But oh, you came through. Now they'll have to change their tune." Whirling, moving. David Malcolm, you are too delicious. Divine. Another segue into "Always."

"This was my mother's favorite song," David said.

"My mother's too," R.J. said. Lily Daniels Malcolm and Rifke Kaminsky Rabinowitz had a favorite love song in common. For at least a minute or two after the music ended, David kept holding her close. Then a few friends stopped to talk to him and R.J. excused herself to go to the powder room and check to see if her makeup looked all right.

She couldn't stop smiling. This felt good. All of it. She smiled at a busboy who was putting salads on the tables. She smiled at a couple who had just walked in through the front door. She smiled at the black woman washroom attendant who sat reading a magazine in the lounge, and she breezed by into the bathroom area and looked at herself in the mirror. Rosie Jane Misner, she thought, taking her blusher out of her purse. You are having fun. You're having the time of your life with this beautiful man in this beautiful place, and boy, are you surprised. You're learning to let go of all your wimpy neurotic fears and you're looking pretty goddamned good in Cindy's dress, if I have to say so myself. And even though you're unemployed, everything will be okay because . . .

There were two women talking to each other from cubicle to cubicle, but R.J. was preoccupied with her own thoughts as she added a tiny bit of blusher to her already flushed cheeks, put that away, and took out her lipstick.

"He could have any woman he wants. Why would he want her?" *That* she heard. Catty, she thought. She opened the tube and put on some lipstick. Maybe she would get her hair cut next week. The bangs were beginning to droop.

"Oh, you know. For the shock value."

She closed the tube, replaced it in her purse, and took out her little round hairbrush. Both women laughed.

"Besides, variety *is* the spice of life," one of them said, and they laughed again.

"Did you catch the dress?"

"The worst."

"I heard the old man hasn't been well. He was hospitalized for a while and they had to put in a pacemaker."

"Maybe dating her is how his son is planning to finish him off."

Laughter. A flush.

"It's a good thing his ex-wife isn't here to see this. She'd laugh her sides off."

"I'll say."

The latch on one of the doors was jiggling. About to open.

"Oh, pooh. I snagged my darn stocking. I hate when that happens. What should I do?"

R.J. never heard the answer. She moved quickly out of the ladies' room and into the crowd. She didn't see David anywhere and she didn't know anyone else in the room. Shock value. Any woman he wants. When she realized she was walking frantically around the big room, she stopped to catch her breath. Hey whatsa matter? she tried to ask herself. You forgot about Dr. Peale? R.J., listen, she said to herself, the way she always did when she was trying to calm herself down. Those women could have been talking about any man in this room, not necessarily David. And the horrible woman they were laughing about didn't necessarily have to be her. David had never mentioned being married before. Surely he would have mentioned it. *They hold it all inside,* Dinah said.

And those women didn't have to be talking about David's father. Probably most of the men at this party had rich fathers who would be picky about the women their sons dated. She was just paranoid because of all the things Dinah had told her. *With her dukes up* was how David described it. Certain that something bad had to happen. It was a lousy way to be.

Ah, she spotted David who was waving to catch her eye from where he stood with two other people. She hurried to him.

"Missed you," he said when she got there.

"Missed you too," she said, but she still felt shaken. He put an arm around her.

"R.J.," he said, "I'd like you to meet Helen Ashton. Helen is my former sister-in-law. And this is Dr. Peter Acklin." The woman and the man both nodded and said, "Nice to meet you." Former sister-in-law. Not the ex-wife of a brother—David was an only child. Had to be the sister of . . .

"Peter is the doctor who installed my father's pacemaker."

"Nice meeting you," R.J. said, and in the spots where Cindy Williams's dress clung to her body, she felt decidedly sweaty.

"Missiz?"

R.J. heard Manuela's voice at her bedroom door. It was just daylight, and she had been in that half-sleeping, half-awake place, remembering last night. The way David had eased her out of the Surfside Club and into the car, and back into town to Trader Vic's for mai tais topped with floating gardenias, and it wasn't clear which intoxicated her more, the drinks or the flowers with their heady scent. And then the delicious dinner.

"We rushed things," he said. "I did. That weekend. Going away was a mistake. Too fast. But now we'll take our time. We have lots of time."

"Oh, yeah," she said, smiling, spinning from the mai tais, "*you* may have time, but I'm an ancient thirty-seven."

"True," he said. "You're definitely on your last legs—which, by the way, despite their years, aren't too bad."

"Too bad?" She bristled. "Those are the best legs in Pittsburgh. Unfortunately, I happen to be in Los Angeles at the moment."

He laughed and their eyes searched each other's.

"You're still not too sure," he said. "You look like you're about to make your speech again about how we can't work." Now they were both very serious.

"You never told me you'd been married," she said.

"Irrelevant," he said. "It lasted only two months, for reasons too boring to tell you."

"You're a foreign quantity to me, David, and I don't know how to behave. You might as well be from another planet. You're the man my grandmother and my parents told me not to date. Now I don't have a grandmother or parents, and I'm scared. The combination of things that you are—I don't understand them."

"But from what you've told me, you haven't done so well with the men who *do* fit the standard, so maybe breaking the mold is what you should be doing," he said. Then he took her two hands in his.

"Missiz?" Manuela said again. R.J. sighed.

"Yes, Manuela?"

Manuela came softly into the room.

"What's wrong?" R.J. asked.

Manuela began to cry, and somehow let R.J. know that her husband in El Salvador was in trouble and she had to go back and help him. But she would need money. As much of her back wages as R.J. could provide.

R.J. sat up and held the trembling woman in her arms. She would take a loan, get cash some way immediately.

"I'll get it right away," she told Manuela. "I promise. You've been such a good friend."

She got out of bed and dressed, and had breakfast waiting for Jeffie when he woke, and when it was nine-thirty and time for the bank to open, she went out to the garage, got into her car, and it wouldn't start. She called the auto club and they sent a truck to tow her to a service station, where she waited for two hours for the mechanic to tell her it would cost fifteen hundred dollars to get the Mustang running, which was more than she'd paid for the car when she'd bought it used.

She told the mechanic she'd think about it, took a bus home, walked up the hill to her house, and just as she pushed the door open she heard the phone ringing. She walked to the phone with a sigh. No more bad news.

"H'lo?"

"Is that you, R.J., honey?" a woman's unmistakable voice asked. It was nobody if it wasn't Patsy Dugan.

"Patsy?"

"Well, how you been, girl?" Patsy asked.

All the possible answers flew through R.J.'s mind so quickly that she didn't know what to say. Patsy took her silence as an opportunity to go on.

"You know, I've been thinkin' about you for weeks, and finally this mornin' I said to Freddy, 'I have to call that girl up and see how she is.' Now I know you prob'ly think it's strange that I'd be sayin' anything to Freddy at all, except for maybe *fuck off*, but the truth of the matter is he's been beggin' me to git back together with him, and I been sayin *no way*, and finally what really kind of swayed me was the numbers."

"What numbers, Pats?" R.J. said, knowing Patsy wanted her to ask.

"Them Nielsens. I mean, think of what a kick in the ass

my Nielsens are gonna get if me and Freddy go back together on TV."

All those months of unreturned calls, and now here Patsy was, calling her as if nothing had happened. All gossipy and chatty. This was a business call. Patsy Dugan was not calling to invite her for a cup of tea.

"R.J., honey. Are you there?"

"I'm here, Pats," R.J. said.

"Whatcha been workin' on?"

Working on? An unsellable pilot idea. Trying to get my life in order. "Oh, I just sold a short story to a magazine."

"Well, ain't that great?" Patsy said. "I cain't wait to read it."

Or to have someone read it to you, R.J. thought to herself, but said, "Well, it ought to be on the stands in a few months." Why didn't Patsy just come out and say what she wanted?

"You know," Patsy began. Here it comes R.J. thought. "When that little ass-wipe Harry Elfand fired you, I was mad as a snake. But I was havin' enough trouble with that lowlife son of a bitch so I couldn't start fightin' with him about the writin' staff. He was such a goddamn woman-hater anyhow, he probably couldn't stand havin' a funny gal like you around all the time. Anyhow, that don't matter anymore on accounta I just fired him. Fired 'em all. And I'm startin' a whole new show. With Freddy again, like the old days. From scratch this time. And I want you aboard, girl. What do you think?"

A job. A new show. Back with Freddy. Patsy was right. The ratings would go through the roof. And all of it sweetened with a lie that it was Harry Elfand who had fired R.J. Or maybe *that* was the truth and Harry had lied. R.J. would never be sure. Going back to the insanity of a variety show. It was a horrible thought. Chaos. All-consuming. A job. She would take it, and thank God.

"Have your business people call my agent, Stanley Hoffman," R.J. said to Patsy.

"Welcome back, honeybunch," Patsy told her.

Stanley called her late in the day to say that Patsy was offering her the job of head writer. The pay was substantial. The work would be killing. But she would handle it. R.J. remembered a time when she went with Dinah to see a play. They had seats close to the back of the theater, and

R.J., who had recently suspected that she was becoming a little nearsighted, noticed that all the actors looked blurry to her. Dinah was wearing a pair of glasses and R.J., just out of curiosity, had reached over and removed them from Dinah's face, put them on her own, and looked at the stage, which suddenly moved into sharp focus. Now, in one day, here she was—employed, and mad about a man. Funny how the world looked better to her. In much sharper focus.

Working draft: possible opening dialogue for Patsy and Freddy Reunion show.

FREDDY

Well, darlin'. Here we are. Together again at last. America's sweethearts. And I for one would like to say right out in front of everybody that I'm thrilled to be back here with my baby, because frankly, honey, when you had your own show, I was worried about you. I mean, without ol' Freddy and that special way I have of deliverin' them straight lines, to tell you the truth, sweet thing, you were dyin' on the vine.

PATSY

I knew you'd come crawlin' back.

FREDDY

And I am sure that the whole country is out there lookin' in, happy that Patsy and Freddy are back together. Provin' one thing.

PATSY

That they know a good joke when they see one?

FREDDY

That you and me belong together, Pats. That we're America's favorite couple. Why, when I walk down

the street with you, no matter where we are, I always
hear someone sayin', "My God, would you get a look
at the two of *them*."

PATSY

Honey, I hear people say that when I walk down the
street *alone*.

FREDDY

Boy, you are tough. I don't get it. Why would a pretty
little gal like you think she has to be tough?

PATSY

Oh, I guess on accounta I think the world is a pretty
tough place. There's war and bombs and homicides,
not to mention the worst of it. Eighteen-year-old girls.

FREDDY

Ahh, sugar. I told you I'm through philanderin'. Are
you still bein' hard on that gal?

PATSY

It ain't *my* bein' hard on her that we're worried about.

*(Forget it . . . network censor will cancel taping if this is even in
the first draft.)*

*I*t was as if neither of them had ever had a romance before. As if they had invented the idea. Every time they were together, hope raced through R.J. Hope she had been certain she no longer had. In spite of her new job with Patsy and Freddy and all her responsibilities with Jeffie, and Manuela's absence, and David's demanding schedule, every day held the charged excitement that David compared to Christmas morning.

"I'll have to take your word for it—Chanuka was never that exciting for me," R.J. said.

Sometimes they would send sweet love notes back and forth between their offices. And even when she came home after what could sometimes be a fourteen-hour workday, he would cook a wonderful meal for her at her house or his apartment. They spent many Sundays picnicking at the beach with Jeffie, and came exhausted back to R.J.'s to make barbecued burgers in the backyard. David took Jeffie to play golf at his club, and Jeffie took David to play Donkey Kong and Pole Position at the arcade, and one Sunday they all went soaring in gliders near the desert. And one afternoon, David took Jeffie to the Planes of Fame Museum at Chino airport. Dear God, R.J. prayed, please don't let all the goodness just be part of love's first blush. Don't let it go away or turn bad, the way the others did.

She tried to get herself to enjoy each day and not worry. *And when he stops seeing you because he's marrying the latest twenty-two-year-old debutante*—Dinah's words were never far from her mind. Sometimes she would look in the mirror at a few more gray hairs or another line that appeared under one of her eyes, and have to look away because the fear would start to rise that something could happen to take David away from her. As if he'd turn to her and say, "You're *how* old? Oh, I'm sorry. I didn't hear that part. I've got to be going now."

Sometimes the difference between their ages was the subject that could send them into gales of laughter. One night he came over and was telling her about a meeting he'd had that day with a man who worked for the company. The man's name was Bob Smith.

"Was Howdy there too?" she asked, joking.

"Pardon?"

"Howdy Doody. Buffalo Bob Smith and Howdy Doody," she said.

He looked at her blankly. He had no idea in the world who Howdy Doody was.

"Who is he?"

"Never mind."

"Who *is* he?" he asked, coming closer, about to pounce and tickle her into telling.

"Never," she squealed, laughing.

"Who?" He held her close and chewed on her neck.

"He's a guy I used to know who had red hair and freckles just like you, but it's okay—I like you better."

"Oldies but goodies," he said one day when they were on their way to the beach and he was turning the radio dial. "Not unlike yourself, my love."

Frankie Valli singing, "You're just too good to be true, can't take my eyes off of you."

"I was getting married that year."

"I wasn't even shaving yet."

"Many a tear has to fall, but it's all in the game."

"Ooh, this is old. I had my first kiss," R.J. said, remembering.

"I'm only sorry it wasn't from me," David said, "but I was busy learning to tie my shoes."

"No!" she squealed.

"Okay, so I'll admit I was a little slow for my age."

"Isn't it amazing that I saw your mother before you did?" she asked. "I mean on the screen, before you were even born. She was so beautiful."

"Lily," he said. "I still dream about her sometimes. I'm not sure if it's because I remember her or because I've seen her movies so often over the years."

"I loved *Woman on the Run.*"

"That used to be my favorite," he said, "but some of the others are even better." Then he scowled. "I've been trying to get them together. Make a reel of them, and for various reasons I haven't been able to. Goddamned movie studios these days change executives so often, by the time I get a guy to clear it, he's out."

They both laughed.

"Doesn't it bother you that every time you go to the polls to vote, I do, too, and my vote cancels yours out?" she asked him one night. It worried her a lot. "I mean, our ideas about things are so different. And people break up over ideas."

"Nah, they break up over money and sex," he said, a teasing glint in his eye. "When it comes to those, we're doing just fine."

She laughed.

"Besides," he added, "I think the fact that your politics need some work will be a great challenge to my gifts as an educator." He grinned.

"There is no way you are changing *my* mind or my politics," she said.

"How about this way?" he asked, pulling her close and chomping on her ear until she shrieked.

"David!"

"Admit that you voted for Nixon," he teased.

"Never," she laughed, jumping out of bed. He got up and chased after her. "No."

Finally they collapsed together on the living room floor.

One night after he'd made dinner for her at his apartment and then made love to her in front of the fireplace, she told him: "You know, when you grow up on Sandra Dee, no matter what happens in your life to tell you different, and no matter how often you tell your friends you think love doesn't exist, and no matter how often you read *The Cinderella Complex*, somewhere in the back of your mind and heart you always believe a love like this will come along. And when you're thirty-two, you live on stories about women who met the man of their dreams at thirty-five. And when you're thirty-five, you weep over articles about women who finally found a soulmate at forty."

"And when you're an over-the-hill old bag of nearly thirty-eight?" David asked, nuzzling her cheek.

"You meet David and say, 'Sandra Dee, eat your heart out,'" she said. Then she looked at him. Sometimes his beautiful face was so filled with unabashed appreciation for her, it made her want to throw her arms around his neck and say, "Let's freeze time. Let's never lose these feelings. Never let the disappointments make us bitter, or the sameness make us bored. We have to always remember the way we feel now—which is lonesome when the other one leaves the room."

It thrilled her when he laughed at her dumb jokes and her stories about her childhood, and the self-jabbing remarks she made about how if they stayed together he'd soon be wheeling her into the sun at the old folks' home. And he loved to see her shake her head in amazement when he told her the stories about his own childhood. The tragic death of Lily, and the way he ran away after her death, and the years he spent traveling all over the world with his father. He had never once yet invited her to meet his father. And it wasn't because Rand Malcolm wasn't around. Many nights when she had to work, or had the instinct that she and Jeffie needed a night alone, David would say, "I'll miss you, but I'll get a bite at the club with Dad."

One weekend Jeffie asked if he could spend the night at Matt Wallace's. R.J. said yes, and after she told David, he showed up with an overnight bag.

"Why should Jeffie be the only one who gets to stay overnight with a friend?"

R.J. threw her arms around him. It was their first chance to linger in bed since their trip to Big Sur.

In the morning she awakened wrapped in his arms.

"You stay right there while I get the paper," David said.

The minute he was out of the room R.J. rushed into the bathroom, brushed her teeth, brushed her hair, and slapped on a little blusher. By the time she got back to the bedroom, David was reclining there engrossed in an article in the paper. She opened the *Calendar* section, turned a page, and heard him say, half to himself, half-aloud: "How about this?" When she looked over his shoulder she saw a picture of a handsome older man. RAINBOW PAPER CHIEF RAND MALCOLM NOT RUN-OF-THE-MILL GUY. Every now and then David would chuckle over something he read.

R.J. read along with him. She knew very little about his father. Just the gossipy things people had said about him. Now she read his irascible point of view about politics and social issues and shook her head. My God. Everything Rand Malcolm believed was the opposite of everything she believed, had been brought up to believe. Knew was right. He loathed environmentalists. He thought the ERA was unimportant. He believed gun control, a cause to which Jeffie had donated part of his allowance every week since Arthur's death, was "a stupid little issue." R.J. was aghast. She was about to say something when the phone rang. She answered it.

"Don't read this morning's paper," said a voice. It was Dinah.

"Too late," R.J. told her.

"Didn't I tell you? If that man finds out about you, it's going to be—"

"Dinah," R.J. said, trying to sound jovial, "David's here and we're about to have—"

"Sex?" Dinah asked. "Sorry."

"Breakfast," R.J. said, "but I accept your apology."

"Hi, Dinah," David said to the air, still reading the article as R.J. hung up. "What'd she say?" he asked.

"Based on her reading of the article, that I'm not the first on your father's list of women best suited for you."

"True," he said, not looking up.

She stood there and looked at his intense, beautiful face as he read.

"And what about Pop Rabinowitz?" he asked. "If he were still around, would he and Rifke be bragging to the family about your finding me? A Republican and a goy?"

She smiled and moved close to him on the bed. Her bed. It was fun to have him there.

"Absolutely not," she confessed. "They would have . . ." Francie and Avery. It had been a long time since she'd thought about them, but now they stood hand in hand in her mind's eye, and the memory of the hysteria that surrounded their marriage so long ago did too. "They would have been very upset," she told him.

"I'll make breakfast," he said.

While he was in the kitchen cooking, she reread the entire article. This can't work, she thought. We're from two different planets and— She interrupted her own thought. Dr. Peale, she thought, Dr. Peale. In spite of all the negatives . . . Dr. Peale.

The night Manuela came back they all had a special celebration. Manuela made a big home-cooked late supper for them, because R.J. didn't get home from work until nearly ten. Later, when Jeffie went off to sleep and R.J. and David sat outside hand in hand looking at the lights of the Valley, she said to him: "Even if you wake up one day and ask yourself *What am I doing with that old bag?*—these have been the best months of my life."

And David said, "Even if *you* wake up and say *How am I going to get rid of this kid?*—me too." And they kissed. David stood to go, and R.J. put her hand on his sleeve.

It was their policy for him not to spend the night when Jeffie was at home. Not to have Jeffie find him there in the morning. Too confusing for the boy, they both agreed. Now R.J. wished they'd never made that policy. She needed to have him next to her all night. To have him tell her how much he cared. The word *love* had never been spoken. As if they both knew that saying it had the power to change everything. Make it too serious. Serious could hurt.

He ruffled her hair and was gone. R.J. sat watching the lights of the Valley for a little while longer, then stood, and on her way to her room she stopped to peek in at Jeffie.

"I like him, Mom," Jeffie said, not asleep after all.

"Honey, we need to talk about this. I'm glad you like him, but I've made a mistake with you in the past about men I've dated, and I don't want to repeat it with David. And the mistake is about expectations. I've looked at a lot of men as husbands for me and fathers for you, and that's why you looked at them that way too. And then, when the relationship was over, you and I were much more disappointed than if we had just said that this person is a nice friend for now and we're glad to have had his company. That's what we have to do with David. Because of everyone I've dated, he's the least-likely candidate to be husband and father, and I don't want you or me to kid ourselves."

"Baloney, Mom."

"Not baloney."

"How come? What's wrong with him?" Jeffie asked, not looking at her.

"Nothing's wrong with him. He's just younger. Much younger. And he isn't Jewish, and I was raised very Jewish. And I want . . . wanted to be with someone who is . . . and . . ." Now she found her mind racing for answers. "The main thing is, you know how I was raised—living upstairs from a grocery store and working to survive. He's lived a life of servants and grand houses all over the world, and the best schools and camps and . . ."

"So?" Jeffie said.

"What do you mean, *so*? That makes a big difference. And it creates dramatically different people who—"

"Who what?" he asked.

"Are crazy about each other," she answered quietly.

"Yeah, so where's the problem?"

"I don't know," she said.

It was midnight, and R.J. sat in the last row of the bleachers of the ice-cold sound stage. Patsy and Freddy were bickering hotly between takes of the last few pickup shots for the Fred Astaire and Ginger Rogers sketch. The good old world of series television.

"This sucker ain't funny no more to me," Freddy said. R.J. stiffened. Happily, David sat next to her, holding her hand in one of his and patting it with the other.

"It's working great, Arj," he whispered to her. "He's heard the jokes five hundred times, so he can't tell . . . but believe me, they're funny. Honest."

"Let's take your close-up here, Patsy," the director said.

R.J. smiled at David. He loved to tease her by telling her she was "the luckiest woman in the world," but she knew it was very true.

Now the fight was escalating and this time Don Jarvis, the producer, was involved.

"Shit. I ain't givin' up no million-buck deal. That's fer goddamned sure," Freddy hollered.

R.J. was picking up only bits and pieces of it, but it sounded as if now it was about Patsy and Freddy being offered a job in Las Vegas and the two of them wanting to take a hiatus from the show to go and do it, and Jarvis not wanting them to take the time off.

"Christ, we've already taped sixteen shows, you mother-fuckin'-slave driver," Freddy yelled at the top of his voice, and Don Jarvis, a small man, backed away, as if the power of Freddy's voice could knock him over. Freddy was an obnoxious, mean man. He was back with Patsy for business reasons but still seeing the poor little teenaged girl, who occasionally showed up at rehearsals, driving Patsy mad. R.J. put on her jacket. This fight had nothing to do with her. She and David were heading for the door when Don Jarvis called out, "R.J.?"

She turned.

"Can you get your writers to take a few weeks' hiatus and stay with the show?" R.J. had no idea what her staff had in mind, or even if the Writers' Guild would allow that. She hesitated.

Then David said softly, so only she could hear, "Say yes, I can and I will, because my lambie and I will have time to go to Paris for a few days." Paris. David was offering to take her to Paris.

"I'll try, Don," she said.


R.J. had never been to Europe. For some of her life she couldn't afford to travel, and when the time came that she could, it was because she was working so hard there wasn't any time. She had told that to David when they first met. Now she sat in the back of a taxi next to him, and when she saw the Eiffel Tower come into view, her eyes filled with tears. She was embarrassed by how choked up she felt.

"I know," David said. "It's gorgeous, isn't it? I've been here many times, but every time I'm still staggered by its beauty."

"This is my first time," R.J. said, telling him something he already knew. She was so overwhelmed with emotion she couldn't look at him.

"Well, it's really my first time, too, because I'm here with you," he said.

"Smooth talker." She kissed him.

"Speaking," he said.

Beautiful. So beautiful. The beauty of the city as it

passed by the taxi window left her breathless, and combined with all she was feeling for David, she was afraid that anything she said would set off an outburst of feelings that would embarrass both of them. When they had checked into the Plaza-Athénée and the bellman had closed the door behind him, leaving them alone, R.J. excused herself and went into the bathroom to be alone because she felt so silly about the tears of joy that wiggled down her face, carrying little pieces of black mascara. She looked into the bathroom mirror and laughed through a trembling lower lip at how stupid she was for crying. Then there was a tap on the door.

"May I come in?" David asked.

She dabbed her eyes and opened the door, and he stood in the doorway, holding a full champagne glass in each hand. He walked into the bathroom, looked around, and then handed her one of the glasses, touched his glass to hers, and they both sipped.

"Well, this isn't exactly the specific environment I had in mind in which to say this," he said, gesturing with his glass around the bathroom. "Although, as bathrooms go—or in this case, *salles de bain*—this *is* a lovely one. But . . . I love you very much." It was the first time he'd ever said those words to her.

R.J. sniffed a big sniff and her lower lip trembled, and she took a very long swig of champagne, then put her glass down on the floor and her arms around David's neck and felt the softness of his cashmere sweater next to her cheek.

"And I love you," she told him. "Thank God I found you to love and to . . ." She couldn't go on.

"To soften up your act?" he asked.

She grinned through her tears.

"Boy, you cry a lot. Why is that?" he asked, and then kissed her. "Is there a reason why you cry so much? I mean, why would you? You're the luckiest woman in the world." And then he kissed her again. And again. And soon she was carrying their champagne glasses into the bedroom, which was where David, who was now saying "I love you" to her for the second time and the third time and the fourth, was carrying her.

They spent three days touring the city and its environs, and R.J. floated blissfully beside David, hearing only half of what he read to her from the guidebooks, because all she really wanted to do was touch his face or hold his hand, or

tease him about his French accent like a lovesick teenager.
Sometimes he would catch the look on her face and say,
"Oh, Sandra? Miss Dee? Here we are at Versailles," and
they would laugh.

"The approach is everything," he would say with his
hands over her eyes. Before he would let her look at anything remarkable—the "Mona Lisa," the "Winged Victory,"
any Monet, Notre Dame Cathedral—he would cover her
eyes with his hands and make sure she was standing in
exactly the right place to get the most perfect view of it, and
then he would take away his hands making sure she could
appreciate each work completely.

One day they just walked. Everywhere. Hand in hand.
Stopping to peek into store windows. To watch other peo-
ple talking, other lovers walking. Down to the Faubourg St.
Honoré, past Hermés and Dior, past the Palais de l'Élysée.
In and out of antique shops and past perfumeries. Down
tiny back streets to the Place des Ternes, looking up at the
Arc de Triomphe. Sometimes stopping just to look at each
other and smile a smile of shared joy.

"Ahh," David said, suddenly taking her hand and pulling her into a store called Maison du Chocolat.

"Oh, God," she said, looking at the goodies in the glass
cases.

David spoke in French to the saleswoman, who filled a
small brown box with his choices. As they walked, he and
R.J. tried each one, oohing and ahhing over them, feeding
them to each other.

That night he held her, and just before they fell asleep
he said, "I didn't even know that this was an option."

"That what was an option?"

"Loving this way. This much." Then he pulled her
even closer and he was asleep.

"Some old friends are in town tonight, close friends of
my father," he told her the next morning as they were
eating breakfast in the hotel courtyard. It was their last day
in Paris. "Apparently they heard from my office that I was
here and left a message that they'd like to meet for drinks
tonight at the bar at the George Cinq. Would you mind?"

The mention of his old friends always caused a little
discomfort in her stomach, wondering what they would
think of her. Until now, she'd met only one couple. Daphy
and Charlie Woods. It was in Westwood, one night after a

movie when she and David had bumped into them, and after standing outside the Bruin Theater talking, the four of them had decided to go out for coffee together.

"We love David," Daphy Woods, who never stopped talking, told R.J. "Anyone he picks is all right with us. No matter how old or what religion." So if she'd ever doubted it, R.J. knew that the word about her was out in David's crowd.

"I don't mind at all," she told David now.

The others had already arrived at the George Cinq and were seated around a large table when R.J. and David arrived. One couple was R.J.'s age; another was a couple in their early fifties. The third was an English couple about David's age. The wife was pregnant. They were all dressed beautifully and the conversation was very lively.

"Bellinis all around," the young husband said, "except for my wife, who will have the peach juice plain." R.J. had no idea what a Bellini was. The pregnant wife had a pronounced British accent. She was pretty and bubbly and excited about the nursery she was planning for the child she hoped would be Nicky Junior.

"Can you just imagine Nicky as a father?" someone said.

"God, no," said a few of the others.

"What about you, Dave boy? When are you going to bite the bullet and contribute to the gene pool?" someone asked.

"Probably not ever," David said.

"Does J.R. know that?" one of the women asked.

"It's R.J.," R.J. corrected her. The woman didn't even hear her.

"If J.R. hears that, she may want to find herself someone more eligible," the woman said, smiling.

"R.J. has a son," David told her.

"Oh, really? How old?" the woman in her fifties asked.

"Twelve," R.J. answered.

"No? Really?" the pregnant woman said. "You hardly look old enough."

R.J. forced a smile. She was very uncomfortable.

"Are you longing to have another?" the pregnant woman

asked. R.J. didn't have a chance to answer when the pregnant woman went on.

"It's silly really, but now that I'm pregnant, I find myself looking at couples and wondering how their babies will turn out. Strikes me you and David would produce a lovely baby."

"You know," the older woman said, looking at David and then at R.J. and then back at David again, as if assessing the way their features would combine to make a baby, "when they breed dogs for red, they always breed in a little black."

R.J. looked at the woman. Dogs.

"Which means the baby *could* have red hair."

"Quite right," said the English husband.

Dogs. Was that some slur against R.J.'s lack of breeding or was it just the way people like this thought about things? After all, she did include David in the comparison but . . . R.J., stop it, she told herself. Just stop it. You take your own terror about not being right for David and you listen for other people to tell you that it's true. Stop.

The conversation had moved on to something else, and now it broke into small conversations, and the man—the gray-haired fifty-year-old man—turned to talk to R.J. Probably, she thought, because he was sitting next to her and that was what he was supposed to do. And just as the Bellinis were arriving—champagne and peach juice—and everyone was oohing over them, he asked, "You and David serious?"

"Yes," she said, "we are."

"His father will never accept you," the man said.

"To us," someone said, as they all held their glasses up, "because good folks are scarce." But R.J. didn't hear the toast. She only heard the man's words. This wasn't Dinah reading articles about Rand Malcolm. This was a friend. Practically family. The horse's mouth.

"And not only because you're older than Davey—by how much?"

"Seven and a half years." She felt as if she were on trial and had to answer the questions honestly, though she wanted to scream "None of your goddamned business" and pour her drink on him. Instead, she sipped the Bellini.

"But because you're a Jew. It's that simple. He will do

everything and anything he can to end it. You met him yet?"

"No."

The man smiled a knowing smile. David was on the other side of the table talking to the pregnant woman, laughing now at something she was saying.

"Of course not," the man said. "Because David knows just what he'll say about you."

R.J. steeled herself. "David and I have so much to work through, before we even get to what his father will think, that I really can't get myself to worry about it right now," she said, trying to keep some semblance of a smile on her face. But with that she was lying on the stand, and she and the man both knew it. She finished the Bellini in two swallows. When she looked at David, he was looking at his watch and then at her.

"R.J. and I have got to run," he told the others. "We're going to be late for our dinner reservation."

"Where're you two off to?" someone asked.

"Wouldn't you like to know," David said, holding R.J.'s chair so she could emerge. "I'm going to have a quiet dinner with a beautiful woman. So, happily, my friends, I bid you all a fond adieu."

"Nice meeting you," R.J. made herself say, catching a bemused look on the older man's face just before she and David turned to walk away.

Too much Bellini too fast, she thought, as the Paris twilight blurred past her, with David guiding her by the elbow.

"Nice folks," he said, "aren't they?"

She didn't answer. He didn't notice.

"Now this place we're going for dinner is really corny, but it'll be good fun and romantic and ... R.J., what's wrong?"

"Is there a reason why you haven't introduced me to your father?" she blurted out and was immediately sorry that she had.

"Yes, there is," he said. "Because up until now it didn't apply."

"Huh?"

"It wasn't appropriate. It didn't matter. I don't bring women I'm seeing by to meet him."

"Women you're seeing?" Oh, R.J., stop. This is Paris.

This is perfect. Don't become a nagging shrew because of something some other person said.

"That's who you were," he said, and took her in his arms. And when he felt her resist he said, "It's good luck to kiss in sight of the Eiffel Tower." He was changing the subject.

"David."

"As soon as we get back to town," he said, now kissing her forehead, "I'll take you to have dinner with Dad."

Ah, so he wasn't keeping them apart. Not worried about bringing her home to his father after all. And she was going to get what she wanted. What she asked for. Now she really had something to worry about.

"*H*ow was Vegas, Pats?" R.J. asked as Patsy plopped her rhinestoned purse down at the end of the writers' conference table. It was the first time Patsy had ever been on time for a read-through. She and R.J. were alone in the room.

"Well, it woulda been fun if ol' suckhole Freddy woulda stayed home."

"You two crazy kids fighting again?" R.J. hated to think of the havoc the fight between Patsy and Freddy would wreak on this week's script. The writing staff she had now was hard-working and inspired. A lot of new writers with good ideas who were making the long days seem easier.

"When ain't we? What did *you* do while we were gone?"

"I went to Paris," R.J. said.

"Paris, France?"

"Yep."

"With that good-looking redheaded dude who's always hangin' around?"

"Uh-huh."

"See? What'd I tell ya? You met somebody. Well isn't that great? 'Cept for one thing. It ain't gonna last. Nothin' personal . . . but men are such a buncha dogs. All they do is walk all over us and we let 'em. And the truth of the matter is if we didn't have a cunt they wouldn't walk across the street to talk to us. Well, fuck 'em all. Especially Freddy

Gaines. And none of 'em are any different. This guy of yours is good now, but the minute he's through with you, honey, all you'll see is dust where that boy was standin'."

"I don't think so, Patsy," R.J. said. "This man isn't like that. I think he's really special and loving and there for me." God, it felt good to be able to say that. To believe it. Even for now.

Patsy laughed a bitter laugh that made R.J. feel bad for her. But these days she felt bad for everyone who didn't know the joys of the kind of love she had. That sweetness. Tomorrow night was the dinner with David's father. She felt like a character in a fairy tale who had to get through the big test, like climbing the glass mountain or slaying the dragon, before she could truly win her love.

"It's early yet, honeybunch. Talk to me in six months," Patsy said as the rest of the writers came pouring in the door for the read-through.

She had bought a white silk skirt and a white lace blouse for the trip to Paris, and decided she would wear them with pearls to dinner with his father.

"Dinah," she said into the telephone. She was ready an hour before David was scheduled to pick her up. "I have terrible stage fright. I'm more nervous than I ever was for anything in my life, and all I'm doing is going to have dinner."

"Will there be any other people there?"

"A man named Fred Samuels, who works for Mr. Malcolm, and I think a few other friends. Di, tell me something I can take with me. Some thought I can hold on to, to calm down." God, she must be desperate to be asking Dinah, who would probably say, "You might as well be calm because he'll hate you, no matter what you do."

"Well," Dinah said, and R.J. knew she was stalling, trying to come up with some straw for R.J. to grasp. "Think of it this way," Dinah said, vamping until ready. "The reason you should be calm is that you and the old boy have a lot in common."

That made R.J. laugh. "Thanks, Di. I knew I could count on you."

"No, now wait," Dinah said. "I mean it. Don't laugh.

You really do. I told you, I've read lots of articles about him, and what you have in common is that you're both examples of the American Dream.''

R.J. could tell by the lilt in Dinah's voice that she was getting caught up in her own improvisation now. "You see, he worked his way up and so did you. He was an orphan, Arj. In that Rainbow orphanage in Chicago. 'Til he was a teenager. It's why he named his company Rainbow Paper. No parents and no money and he worked his way up. So did you. Only he used business and you used jokes.''

R.J. was twisting her long pearls into a knot and then out of the knot and then into the knot again.

"So I'll just walk right in there and say: 'Hi there, Mr. Malcolm. I'd like you to know that we have the American Dream in common,' '' R.J. said, twisting the pearls again.

"I can guarantee you won't have to tell him that," Dinah said.

"You mean because it's written all over my face?" R.J. laughed.

"No. I mean because he's tapping this call," Dinah said.

At least that brought a smile to R.J.'s face. She was still wearing it when she opened the door for David.

"Your pearls are all twisted."

"Just nervous," she told him, hoping he'd say "That's ridiculous—why would you be nervous? My father will love you." But he didn't say a word, all the way to Hancock Park, and R.J. untwisted the pearls and then twisted them again, and David moved the radio dial from station to station. They pulled up to a gate and David pushed a button somewhere in his car and the gate opened. The house was big and brick and grand, and R.J. was glad to see several cars parked outside. Maybe it was a big party and . . .

A man wearing a short white jacket answered the door, greeted David, smiled at R.J., and led them into a high-ceilinged living room that seemed to R.J. the size of a hotel lobby. R.J. spotted Rand Malcolm immediately in the group of three men and two women who were sitting and talking at the far end of the room. There was no mistaking the man's relationship to his son. Despite his age, he was chisel-jawed and handsome, and though the once-strawberry blond hair was now white, it was still thick and wavy. But there was something else that was immediately obvious, and that was the way the focus of everyone in the room was on him. Every person's body was positioned to face him.

"How're you doing there, fella?" he called out in a deep resonant voice, spotting them now, and R.J. was conscious of the tapping sound her high heels made as they moved across the hardwood floor toward the group.

The men all stood. R.J. noticed that David's father stood a little more slowly than the rest and held on to the arm of the sofa when he did.

"David," one of the women said and kissed him, then turned to R.J.

"This is Mrs. Spencer," David said, "and this is my stepmother, Eleanor, and this is Senator Spencer, and our good friend Fred Samuels, and my father. This is R.J. Misner."

"Pleasure," Rand Malcolm boomed, or maybe he didn't boom but it sounded like a boom to R.J., whose mouth was dry and who hoped this wasn't the whole party. Eleanor Malcolm was a bony woman in her late fifties. She wore a black suit, and she smiled a smile that was only on her mouth, not in her eyes. R.J. remembered the story the woman in the used-clothing store told about Lily Daniels's clothes.

"Would you like some shampoo?" Mr. Malcolm asked R.J., who stood frozen, staring at him. He couldn't have said that. Shampoo?

"Pardon?" she said. Then she realized he was gesturing over her shoulder where the man in the white coat was standing holding a tray of filled champagne classes, offering one to R.J. Ahhh. Shampoo. Instead of champagne. Hah. A joke. God knows, she hadn't expected him to open with a joke.

"Thank you," she said, and took a glass from the tray. The men were all still standing. Why didn't they sit down? Oh, God, they must be standing because *she* was standing. She'd better sit. So she sat, and when she did, they did. *Oy vey,* she thought, then had to stop a laugh at how funny blurting that out would have sounded. Like the joke about the Jew who was trying to pass, and when he said *oy vey,* he always followed it with "whatever that means."

"Well," came a voice. It was Mrs. Spencer. She was trim and neatly dressed. R.J. remembered seeing her picture in the *Los Angeles Times*. "Mal, how was Japan?" R.J. didn't hear the answer. She was trying to take in this man. Rand

Malcolm held a red swizzle stick, shaped like a golf club, between his thumb and forefinger, and answered in gruff short bursts of sentences. David was talking quietly to Senator Spencer, and Fred Samuels, a bright-eyed man with a big toothy smile, sat himself down next to R.J.

"So, David tells us you're a writer. What do you write?"

Uh-oh, R.J. thought. She remembered David mentioning this man. His father's right hand. Maybe he'd been given the assignment to check her out.

"Mostly television," she said.

"Which shows?" he asked.

"I write for Freddy Gaines and Patsy Dugan," she said. Perfect, she thought. Evoke the image of Patsy and her sex-queen reputation and her well-known foul mouth and now they know you work for her. Not to mention Freddy the child molester.

"I love Patsy Dugan," Fred Samuels said, grinning a real grin now. "Isn't she back with her ex these days? She's so funny. Only I guess you're the one who's really funny, because you write the things she says. Now I think that's terrific."

"What is?" Rand Malcolm asked.

"R.J. writes for Patsy Dugan," Fred Samuels said.

"Who in the hell is that?" Malcolm asked.

"Oh, you know, Mal," Eleanor Malcolm said. "The one Johnny Carson always makes fun of because she's so well endowed."

"I watch three things on television. Football, the news, and that show on opposite the news . . . I switch over when the news gets too stupid. The one about the bar and the fat guy who runs it."

"*Joey's Place*," R.J. said.

"Funniest goddamned show in the world," Rand Malcolm declared. "About people who hang out at this seedy restaurant, and one of them's an investment banker who's always losing money—I love it. What do *you* write?" he asked, looking directly at R.J.

"I'm the head writer for Patsy Dugan and Freddy Gaines' variety show. I write and supervise the comedy sketches." Compared to his big voice, hers sounded like the squeak of a mouse.

"Any money in that?" he boomed. She felt like Dorothy talking to the Wizard of Oz.

"Quite a bit," she answered. Maybe that was a trick question. From the corner of her eye she could see smiles on the faces of the Spencers and Fred Samuels. David was out of her line of vision, but she could feel his eyes on her. How was she doing?

"David," Eleanor Malcolm said, standing and coming to David's side. "While everyone's chatting, why don't I show you those chairs I have for you that were your mother's? They're perfect for your apartment."

David excused himself and he and Eleanor left the room. R.J. felt very alone.

"Like what kind of money?" Rand Malcolm wanted to know. She had just said *quite a bit*. But what was quite a bit to her, what seemed like a fortune because it was getting her bills paid and letting her finally have some savings, was probably a joke to these people. Besides, he couldn't possibly mean for her to tell him exactly . . .

"Well, I'm the head writer. I worked my way up to that and—" The American Dream. "So I get more than all the other writers on the show." There. That ought to satisfy him. He couldn't possibly want her to tell him exactly . . .

"How much money is that?" Yes, he certainly did want her to tell him. Exactly.

She couldn't believe the conversation had taken this turn. What could she say? Her mind raced and she blurted out, "Enough to give me a tax problem this year."

The others laughed. Rand Malcolm didn't.

"And what do you do with it?"

"With . . . ?"

"The money? Do you own a car? A house?"

"Yes. A car and a house."

"What kind of mortgage?"

"No mortgage. It's paid off. So's the car."

"Smart girl," he said.

She breathed for what felt like the first time since she'd walked in. She didn't mention that her husband's death had meant mortgage insurance, which was why the house was paid off, and the car was so old when she got it, it had been paid off for years. This was really the third degree. She managed to take a big swig of champagne and then another, and then realized that that was a stupid thing to do. Clearly she needed to be on her toes with this man. This was worse than she'd imagined.

"Do you have any savings?" came the next question.

"Yes," R.J. said. This was getting to be a little bit funny. Maybe because of the champagne.

"What are you saving for?" he asked.

"My son's bar mitzvah," she answered, and then there was a big long pause during which she almost burst out laughing. Well, she thought, now the beans are on the table. I write jokes for Patsy the sex queen, I'm a Jew, I've got a kid. The only thing we haven't covered yet is politics.

"What does your father do?"

"My father died about twenty years ago. He was an immigrant, and he became a social worker in a settlement house."

"Commie?"

"Socialist." That did it. Every last bean. *And*, she wanted to add, he wouldn't have liked *your* politics either.

The man in the white coat came into the room. "Dinner is served," he said. Mrs. Spencer stood, so R.J. did too. Then the men rose and the whole group walked into the dining room. The smell of the food was exquisite but R.J. knew she wouldn't touch a bite. David and his stepmother met them in the dining room.

Dinner was served by two women, and the man in the white coat came to each place and poured white wine in one glass and red wine in another, and R.J. looked down at her left at the forks and remembered that for years, when she first started going out to restaurants, she had thought that the reason the restaurant put all those forks next to your plate was to give you a choice of which size you preferred to use. The elegance of the china and the crystal and the tablecloth and the dining room itself was more than she'd ever seen in anyone's home. And when she looked at David sitting across the table talking to Mrs. Spencer, she tried to picture him when he was a child, in this house, eating meals at this table with his parents, or just with his father. She remembered David telling her recently that until he went to prep school, he had never eaten a meal that wasn't served to him by a servant.

"Where are you from, dear?" Mrs. Malcolm asked her.

"I'm from Pittsburgh," R.J. answered. Sometimes when people asked her that, since the Pirates and the Steelers were doing so well, she'd add "City of Champions" when

she told people she was from Pittsburgh. But this time she
didn't because she didn't think anyone would laugh.

"Well, surely you must know my dear friends," Eleanor said, "the Mellons."

The Mellons. R.J. heard David expel some air from his
nose, as if he was trying to hold in a giggle but part of it had
escaped in spite of him.

"Um . . . I don't. No," she said. "I mean, I know of the
family but . . ."

"Where did you go to school? In Pittsburgh?" Mrs.
Malcolm asked her. R.J. couldn't see her eyes because she
wore glasses, and the light of the chandelier above the table
was reflected in them. All this time, she thought, I've been
worrying about the father. I forgot all about the stepmother.

"Carnegie Tech," she answered.

"Well, I know all about that school, because it merged
with the Mellon Institute and became—"

"Carnegie-Mellon." R.J. nodded. "But that was after I
graduated."

"You graduated before 1967?" Eleanor Malcolm asked,
though she already knew the answer. The part of her face
that R.J. *could* see was her pinched mouth, which now
looked as if she was trying not to smile the triumphant
smile of someone who had caught her prey. There was an
uncomfortable pause until she said, "How old *are* you?"

R.J. didn't even give herself the advantage of the truth,
which was that she was thirty-seven. "I'll be thirty-eight
next month," she said.

"Ahh" was all Mrs. Malcolm said. No one said anything else to her until R.J. and David were leaving.

"Good talking to you, dear," Rand Malcolm said, and
shook her hand, then went back to talk to the Spencers.

"Yes," was all Mrs. Malcolm said.

David walked her out of the house to the car and she
slid into the front seat of the Jaguar. The ride home was too
quiet. She needed David to say something, but there was
nothing to say. My parents liked you? It would be a lie. At
best his father was indifferent to her, and those questions
were just his way of being social. At worst Rand Malcolm
would call his son tomorrow, maybe even late tonight, and
tell him to stay away from her.

David. Why wasn't he saying anything? She was filled
with relief as he pulled the Jaguar into her driveway. Safety.

David looked very distracted and very pale. She loved him, and something was very wrong. He was obviously sorry he'd taken her to be with his father. Maybe answering the questions, which she'd thought was the honest thing to do, was dumb. Maybe David had wanted her to tell his father that the answers to those questions were none of his business. Whatever it was . . . something was wrong.

"Coming in?" she asked. Keep it light, R.J., she thought.

"No," he said. "I'm going to get on home if you don't mind."

There was something about the way he said it that made her feel panicky. It was cold. Worried. Nothing loving or playful about it.

"I love you," she said.

"I know you do," he said, with no intonation, and walked her to the door, leaving after a quick kiss.

He usually called her just before lunch, but today he didn't, and then again at four o'clock he sometimes called to discuss what time she'd get out of work, but he didn't do that, and when he hadn't called by seven she was feeling distracted and jangled as if she'd had several cups of coffee. She had to go into a rewrite meeting and tell all the other writers how to make the script funnier, and all she wanted to do was curl up by the phone and wait until he called, so she could hear his voice—that voice—say, I miss you. The writers were all assembled at the table. R.J. stopped at the receptionist's desk. It was a new receptionist, as of this morning.

"Uh . . . if this person calls"—R.J. wrote David's name on a piece of paper, stopped herself from drawing a heart around it, and gave it to the girl— "could you, uh . . . come and get me?"

The receptionist, who never looked up from the makeup mirror and the lip liner she was using to outline her lips, answered with an open mouth.

"Not me. I'm going home," she said. "I was told by the producer that I didn't have to stay any later than seven."

"Right," R.J. said. Then she peeked into the conference room and said, "Be right back," to the writers, who were gabbing away, then ran into her own office, where she closed the door and dialed David's number.

"Please leave your name, telephone number, and a message."

"Hi. I'm at the office 'til ten or eleven. But it's okay to call me after that at home. Miss you. Bye."

It was nearly impossible to concentrate in the meeting, but the writers were cheerful and funny and had lots of good ideas, so they finished earlier than she expected and she dialed David's number again just before she left the office at nine-fifteen. Trying to sound calm on the tape.

"Me again. Going home early. Hope you're okay. Love you."

Luckily, the exhaustion from her day took over so she somehow managed to fall asleep, but at four o'clock in the morning she was suddenly wide-awake. Terror. Where was he? How badly could she have behaved to make him stop calling her? Stop loving her? Stop, R.J., please, she said to herself. Why does it have to be something *you* did? Maybe something's really wrong. Maybe something's happened to him that's completely unrelated to you. Maybe he was electrocuted by an electric razor in his apartment or beaten up in an alley someplace. It was pitch-dark in her room and R.J. sat up in bed, heart pounding furiously, laughing at herself because she was rooting for the possibility that the man she loved desperately and passionately had been electrocuted or mugged, rather than that he had ended the relationship with her. She dozed and woke and dozed and woke until she dove for the phone when it rang at seven A.M.

"Mrs. Misner, this is Lefty. I'm sick, so don't pick me up for car pool."

"Okay, Lefty. Get better. Bye."

Her stomach ached and her chest felt as if an elephant were sitting on it. No. What she was thinking was crazy. There had to be some kind of an explanation. Before she left for work, she called his office. Something she'd never done.

"Rainbow Paper."

"David Malcolm, please."

"Thank you."

"David Malcolm's office.

"Is Mr. Malcolm in, please?"

"Who's calling?"

"R.J. Misner."

"I'm sorry, he's not. May I take a message?"

Did that mean he was only not in to *her*? What if she'd lied and said it was someone else. Would he be in for . . . ?

"Can I reach him anywhere? It's important," she said.

"I should be hearing from him. May I tell him you called?" the secretary asked.

"Yes, please, and—"

"Will he know what it's regarding?"

That I'm dying, she wanted to say. That I can't get through a day without his face near mine, his kisses on my neck, the way his freckles bounce up and down when I tell him a joke.

"Yes," she answered.

"And does he have your number?"

He has my number and he has my heart and my soul. Please. You're a woman. You must know how it feels to love a man so much that your entire being sings when he walks into the room. Please, if you've ever loved anyone like that, make him call me.

"Yes" was what she said.

"Thank you."

"Thank *you*."

That night at eleven-thirty she was certain she'd never fall asleep, so she called Dinah because she knew Dinah was an insomniac.

"Di," she said, "don't ask questions. Just talk to me. Okay? Say anything, but talk."

"About what, R.J.? You okay?"

"Anything. It doesn't matter."

"Talk about anything," Dinah said, thinking. "Okay, here goes. I was in Neiman-Marcus today and there was a woman at a counter who didn't have a nose. Buying eye makeup. I almost died. So after she walked away I said to Carmen the salesgirl: 'What happened to her?' so Carmen tells me that the woman's husband used to be a prize-fighter, and he practiced on *her*. Isn't that horrible?"

R.J. put her head on the pillow, not really listening to Dinah's words, just the sound of her voice.

"And then Carmen said to me: 'She's my biggest customer, because she figures what she doesn't have in a nose, she'll make up for with eyes.' Can you imagine? We were both plotzing. Two holes in her face, above her lip. It gives her a serious disadvantage in a horse race." Dinah laughed. "And then after that I met the girls in the Valley at Jôna. Marcy bought the cutest white T-shirt with big green parrots on it, and Marge got it in black, and . . ." By the time Dinah had finished describing all the clothes she and her daughters had bought on their shopping spree, R.J. was asleep. When she awakened, this time at six, with the receiver in her hand, she wept. David, she thought. Not you. Before she left for work she called his apartment again and got the machine. Then the office.

"Is he out of town?" she asked, hoping the secretary wouldn't hear the begging in her voice.

"I gave him your message" was the reply. "I'll tell him that you called again."

"So, Mom, did another one bite the dust?" Jeffie asked. He was still awake when she arrived home late from work.

"What's that supposed to mean?" R.J. flared. Then she realized she was talking to her son, someone who had been hurt more than she had by her crazy, unruly life. She knew she couldn't get away with telling him that David had been very busy lately and hope that would be enough. She could see by his expression that he was deeply concerned.

"I don't know," she said. "I think our differences finally caught up with us. I think they became very apparent to David, because he seems to have . . ." The next word seemed so dramatic she could hardly get herself to say it: "disappeared."

"Forever?" Jeffie asked.

"It's starting to look that way," she said.

Jeffie thought about it, then sighed.

"I'm sorry," she said.

"Me too," he said.

Every day there seemed to be a navy Jaguar not too far ahead of her at a traffic light, but with cars in between, so she couldn't see the driver or if the license plate was RAIN-BOW. Goddamn rainbow. That was the red herring that had made her think David would be different. The one. After she'd made fun of Dinah for being of the "Someday My Prince Will Come" school of thought. Oh, God. There was a navy Jaguar now, pulling into the parking lot at the network. Why would it be David at the network building? Well, *maybe* it could be. Maybe he was back from wherever he'd gone and he was coming over to her office to see her to tell her why he'd stayed away. Instead of calling, he wanted to tell her face to face. How did she look? She pulled the rearview mirror toward herself to check. Fine. Not enough sleep, but fine. And he would get out of his car, and she would get out of her car, and they would walk toward one another and . . . She put her foot on the gas, raced around the corner, and just missed colliding with a red Mercedes that was coming around the other way.

"You asshole," the blond woman who was driving the Mercedes hollered, and screeched out of the way, then kept driving. R.J., nerve ends screaming, put her hand up to cover her mouth. "David," she said out loud. "Don't do this."

She could see the navy Jaguar in the distance. It had parked and now its driver emerged. It was Selma from program practices. R.J. remembered now that Selma's husband had bought her the car for Christmas.

It was tape day, and there were a few last-minute changes that had to be given to Patsy, so after R.J. put her purse in her office and checked for messages, she went down to the stage to Patsy's dressing room. The makeup man was taking a few last passes at Patsy's false black lashes with his mascara wand when she walked in. I'll make this fast, R.J. thought. She wanted to stay out of any conversations with Patsy except for the necessary ones about the show.

Patsy waved into the mirror at R.J.

"Hiya, darlin'," she said.

"Pats, we're taking out the joke about Freddy's mother, so when we come back from the commercial, instead of saying—"

"Oooh, honey," Patsy interrupted, elbowing the makeup man out of the way and craning her neck to look back at R.J., "if I was to guess, I'd have to say that Mister Loving-and-there-for-you might be givin' you a hard time. You look like garbage."

"Thanks, Pats. Anyway, Freddy doesn't like the joke about his mother, so if it's all right with you—"

"Well, I guess I know what I'm talkin' about after all. They're all a buncha pig shit. Only the pig shit comes wrapped in different packages. Cowboys. Good-lookin' red-heads. But they're all the same."

R.J. left the room in tears.

\* \* \*

Dinah and the twins were over for an early dinner—"Like the old days" Dinah said—and after the meal, while the kids played Atari games, she and R.J. sat in the living room.

"So it was what it was," Dinah said. "Be glad. Some people never get that much. It doesn't even matter what turned it around. Because you can't dwell on it. You have to move on."

Move on? This was David. Her love. Where could she go after loving and being loved like that in return? After finally letting her guard down. Why had she believed him? And why hadn't he just called and said, "I can't do it," instead of avoiding her, ignoring her, not telling her to her face? What was once her terror was becoming anger.

"Ma, I have homework," one of the twins whined.

"I know. We're leaving in a minute," Dinah said. When the phone rang, both Dinah and R.J. froze.

"It's him," Dinah said. "I just have a feeling that it's him. Go get it."

"It's not him," R.J. said. "He hasn't called me in three weeks. Why should he call now?" But she hurried to the phone anyway and grabbed it.

"H'lo."

"Hiya, babes. Are you sitting down?" It was Stanley, her agent.

"No, but go ahead anyway," she said.

"Kip Walters wants to do your pilot."

"That's impossible. He hated it. I didn't even pitch the whole thing to him. He wanted an eight o'clock show."

"Yeah. Well, evidently he tried it out on the brass and they liked it. Also, it doesn't hurt the salability of it that you're Patsy's head writer. The question is, with your schedule, when in the hell are you gonna have time to write a pilot?"

"I'll have time," R.J. told him. "I foresee having a lot of extra time in my life."

"Hey," he said, "if you want to do it, I'm delighted. I'll call and make a deal with those guys. Huh? Isn't that great? You're doing great there, kiddo. Doesn't that make you deliriously happy?"

"Mmm. Deliriously happy," R.J. said, and put the phone down.

# BOOK FOUR

# DAVEY AND ROSIE JANE

## 1966–1976

## *DAVID'S STORY*

### *1966*

$R$and Malcolm and Eleanor Benning (David always thought of his stepmother as Eleanor Benning, even after she'd been Eleanor Malcolm for five years) slept in separate bedrooms. And for some reason—the most likely being that before a certain age matters like that don't interest one—David never noticed until he came home from Hollingsworth that summer. He was fifteen, nearly six feet tall, having kissed and been kissed more times than he had his wits about him to count, and filled with a deep and abiding interest in who was sleeping in the same bed with whom. Probably in the case of his father and Eleanor, he might not even have noticed if it hadn't been for Eleanor's frequent complaint that the family's very grand Hancock Park house, which had four huge bedroom suites, was inadequate because it had no guest bedroom. Let's see, David thought. There's my room and one for Douglas, and one for . . . Ahhh, he realized. There were two others. One for Eleanor and one for his father.

"Night-night," Eleanor would say when a dinner party was over, not even making a pretense of going to her husband's room first and then slipping, via some secret entrance, into her own, the way she would in a Restoration comedy. No, in a Restoration comedy, David remembered now from literature class, she would have slipped *out* of her own chambers and *in*to his father's. At any rate, it was clear to David Malcolm that his father and his stepmother were not "getting it on"—which is how they referred to sex at Hollingsworth, but only when they were being very polite.

On the other hand, Yona, who was the head house-keeper and laundress, and Rico, her husband of nine years who was the family chauffeur and sometime houseman, couldn't conceal the passion they still had for each other. Rico would tickle his wife provocatively as they passed each other in the hallway of the Malcolms' Hancock Park home. And she would pinch him lustily as he bent over to check the various mousetraps he had set everywhere since the mice had decided, as the Malcolms had, that this year they would summer in Los Angeles.

And David watched it all, the passion and the dispas-sion, through the screen of adolescence—to which one's lifetime judgments too frequently stick. And it made him feel so lonely that, for the first few nights after his arrival, he spent the endless dark hours longing for the girls at school. The teasing writhing of Cathy Kirk, or even the steely mouth-full-of-braces kisses of Linda Martin, which weren't much but at least had filled his time.

Of course he needn't have given it another thought, for as F. Scott Fitzgerald tells us, a young man with a large income lives the life of a hunted partridge. After David had been home for only a few weeks that summer, he could sense that the hunt for him had begun in earnest. His first clue was when the mother of a fifteen-year-old girl he knew only vaguely invited him out to the club to caddy. When he agreed and arrived for the early-morning tee-off, there was the woman's daughter, her makeup perfect, her hair pulled back under her headband, her long tanned legs nearly as brown as her Bass Weejuns, as she perched on the back seat of the golf cart. She had decided—at the last minute, she told him, although her appearance spoke to endless preparation—to join him and her mother for the ride. At six-thirty A.M.

And there were a few brothers of girls who dutifully made overtures of friendship. One in particular invited him over to the house to hit tennis balls. Coincidentally, in the adjacent pool was Sis, doing the stroke that had won her kudos and medals at Westlake. What a surprise when she emerged from the water, wearing her brand-new bikini, to find David Malcolm, back from the East and staying around for the summer. And not nearly as subtle, but certainly worth notice, was the carful of girls who drove by the Malcolms' house on their way to and from the Marlborough summer school and yelled "Dayveee" every time they did, frequently waking him from his hot adolescent dreams, which despite their extraordinary cast of characters were becoming less interesting than his hot adolescent reality.

The phone rang relentlessly in the Hancock Park house, and Yona, answering it with a knowing grin on her face, always reported in her deep husky voice as she handed David the phone: "It's a woman."

David, who had learned above all else to be a gentleman, did what he thought was right, which was to take each girl who presented herself as available at her word, and pursue her. As numbers would have it, many of them turned out to be less interested in him than their mothers thought they should be. Many others were less interesting to him than their mothers wished they would be. Finally, after careful thought and consideration David culled out the one who was the obvious choice to be his summer love.

Her name was Alison, and she was very beautiful. In fact, she looked like him, with thick red hair and blue eyes. She played a great game of bridge and sometimes she would be his partner in beating Eleanor and his father. She was on the varsity tennis team at Westlake and she was older. Sixteen and a half. And she had her own car. She seemed to be very aroused by his kisses, and always made him believe it was with enormous effort and terrible regret—and because of the restraints placed on her chastity by her fiercely overprotective parents—that she didn't submit to him completely. And best of all, she let him know that in a moment of rebelliousness, which could strike at any time, she might one night let him have his way no matter what her parents said. So for all of those reasons, even before the end of July had arrived, she owned him. Eleanor Benning hated her.

Eleanor hated every girl he had brought home. And always with good reason. Big legs, too short, brainless, she had said when the girl had barely closed the door behind herself. As if anyone had asked her opinion. But Ali stopped Eleanor cold, because there was nothing she could find about the girl that didn't work. Ali had perfect manners, wrote prompt and lovely thank-you notes, dressed appropriately, spoke when spoken to. So all David's father's wife could do was pick on David's preoccupation with the girl, which she did every day.

"My word, aren't we wasting away our summer?" she said as David emerged from his blackout-curtained bedroom one day at eleven after a late evening with Alison. "If there's one thing I know about, it's boys," Eleanor said, an absurd statement, since she knew nothing at all about boys and yet that was what she loved to say about herself. "At least my Douglas has found an outlet for his adolescent energy. Not necessarily one of which I approve but . . ."

Her Douglas. Everyone at school thought Douglas Benning was the biggest dork alive, and unfortunately everyone knew, because "her Douglas" never left it alone, that he and David were brothers. "Stepbrothers," David would always tell them hastily, clearing it up, so no one would think that fat turkey was a part of his natural family.

"Stepbrothers," Douglas would always repeat, and then as his perverse idea of a joke, and undoubtedly insulted by David's renunciation of their kinship, would step hard on David's foot and laugh. God, was it great that Douglas wasn't at home this summer! David wouldn't have to see his nasty pimply face every day, the way he had at school, or last summer on the Orient Express, or the summer before when they sailed around the Caribbean on the *Sea Cloud.* Stuck with him on a family vacation in a compartment of a train or a cabin of a boat. It was torture. This year, oh blessing of blessings, "her Douglas" was at school where he was learning how (and every time David thought about it he laughed at the picture that came into his mind) to race high-performance cars.

Imagine Benning—"Gutterball Benning" at the bowling alley, "The Tilt" Benning on the pinball machine, Benning, who couldn't even hold onto his fork in the cafeteria—having the reaction time necessary to race those cars. But he had whined to his mother so loud and so long, she had finally sent him the money and agreed to let him go there. An outlet for his adolescent energy.

"Why does Mrs. Malcolm hate me?" As the icing on the cake to all of her other virtues, Ali was very observant.

"Why do you care?" David asked. He was unbuttoning her blouse in the back seat of her GTO convertible, while a movie neither of them had any intention of watching played on the drive-in screen.

"Because I admire her." The answer so startled him that, before he regained his presence of mind, he almost rebuttoned the hard-earned buttons he had opened.

"Ali" was all he could say, but for a moment he was sure he might be spending the rest of the evening actually watching the movie.

"I mean, she was a very successful socialite when she was married to Keaton Benning, and then she was a great patron of the arts while she was a widow, and then she married your father, and everyone says she's just right for him and . . ."

Ali went on, but David had stopped listening. There was something about her having all that information that he didn't like, because it spoke to research into his family of a kind that he was hoping she hadn't done. In fact, the reason he had finally chosen her over all the others was that she seemed very blasé about who he was, and seemed sincerely interested in who he *really* was.

After that night he noticed her cozying up to Eleanor whenever she could, a feat which, if she could accomplish it, would be nothing short of a miracle, considering nobody else ever had, could, or wanted to. Yet somehow, Mrs. Malcolm, as Ali always called her, seemed to be falling for it. Eleanor seemed to like the girl so much that once David was certain he overheard a conversation in which she was actually trying to sell her Douglas to Ali. "Thoughtful, dependable, a perfect boy," she said. "And I miss him so much this summer." She hadn't telephoned him once, and vice versa.

No. Eleanor didn't like Ali. She was a phony. One of the great phonies of the world. She'd call everyone "my love," as in "It's so grand to see you, my love," and they'd leave and she'd criticize everything about them down to their shoelaces.

She'd give formal dinner parties in honor of this one and that. Lambaste the servants until the dinner, the flowers, and the musical ensemble were just perfect. Then insist that his father stand up and offer a toast, which she reacted to as if she hadn't heard it a dozen times while she was rehearsing him. And when everyone was gone she would go around the long rectangular table in her mind, and one by one annihilate each person's virtue, taste, intellect. Whichever trait she decided he or she didn't have. And every time he saw her do it, David, who thanked heaven for boarding school, watched his father retreat into his newspaper or some work he'd brought home from the office, and a vague memory of Lily would flash through him. Her laugh, or the way she and his father had sung duets or looked together at a particular event. Pulling each other close as they danced.

"I totally despise P.D.A.," is what it sounded as if Alison said softly as she eased her body away from his hold that night at the club. It was the first time they had ever danced.

"Despise what?" he asked, loving the way her hair smelled and wondering what time they could elude the chaperones, sneak away to the parking lot, climb into the back of her car, and make out. The thought of that made him pull her against him again, and now he realized something was wrong. She strained to pull away, and this time she stopped dancing, even though the band was still playing. Now she stood with her hands on her hips, looking hard at his face. Ali, my God. What was wrong?

"Public display of affection," she said. David looked quickly around the floor at the seven or eight other couples who were dancing, to make certain none of them had heard her. None of them seemed to.

"It's not right," she said, looking at him as if to say "If you don't agree, I'll walk right off this dance floor."

"All right," he said to get her to start dancing again, for God's sake. What did she mean? He hadn't kissed her hair or, instead of holding her hand in his in the classic dance position they'd both learned at Miss Beckworth's Cotillion, put his arms around her waist so she would put her arms around his neck. Nothing like that. And two of the other couples were dancing that way. He guessed that just pulling her tight, feeling her breasts pressed against him, was P.D.A., and he hadn't known. God. He never imagined it would upset her this much. When they were alone she always let him undo her bra.

"What we do when we're alone is no one's business, David," she said, knowing exactly what he was thinking.

"You're right," he said. Lying. Lying to get her to dance again before everyone saw they were having what looked like a fight. But the music ended and Ali turned coolly and walked to the buffet table with David following. After dinner, when he asked her to dance again, she said no, she didn't feel like it.

Later, in the driveway of his house with the rain pouring all around them, an unseasonable time for rain, she let him go a little further than last time, and the windows of her GTO were steamy, and he told her: "I'm crazy about you," because he wanted to save saying *I love you* for a little longer. But all she said was, "Oh, yikes, it's eleven. My father will kill me." Then she sat up, hooked her bra, adjusted her dress, gave him a quick kiss, and kind of nudged him out into the rainy night, where he stood for a long time without going inside, because he needed the pounding wet rain to cool himself off.

"Oh, my God. Oh, no, please. I can't stand it. No." He heard the cries coming from the kitchen when he unlocked the front door. "Ohhh, God." It was Yona. Moaning. Maybe she and Rico were fighting and he should stay out of it and go upstairs, but it wasn't a fight, because now Rico's voice came gently. "Don't cry, *mi amore*. It is the way things must be." And then Yona sobbing again, so he went to the door that separated the kitchen from the dining room and looked through the glass square that the servants used to make sure they didn't collide with one another when they served and cleared the table. He was about to push it open when he realized he was barging in on an intimacy. Yona was kneeling on the kitchen floor weeping, and Rico sat on the floor next to her, a loving arm moving up and down on her back. David could see wet spots on the floor where Yona's tears had fallen, and another and another as they continued to fall. As Yona took a deep breath in between sobs, Rico put his face next to her neck.

"*Cara*, it wasn't so important," Rico said gently.

"No," Yona protested. "It was a life, like you and me. A creature of God and now it's gone. Maybe it was a mother or a daddy of a baby, and the baby will look for it and long for it."

David followed Yona's gaze, and realized now she was talking about the tiny mouse lying pinioned to one of Rico's traps. Dead.

He pushed the door open. Yona looked up at him with wide tear-filled eyes.

"Davey, see," she said. "Isn't there a way? There must be a way to catch them and send them away someplace instead of doing this to them. Without killing the poor little things." Then she looked down sadly again at the tiny brown field mouse pinned to the wood trap. "Isn't there?"

She looked so beautiful, sitting there so sad-eyed and trembling.

"I don't know," he said, then turned to Rico. "There might be more humane traps. I mean, traps that don't kill them."

"Mrs. Eleanor," Rico said. David noticed that neither of them could bring themselves to call Eleanor "Mrs. Malcolm." "She wants them killed."

Yona began to sniffle as if she was going to cry again, and Rico promised to think of a way, to find some way of not having to kill any more of the little mice. David said goodnight, and as he closed the door and walked back into the dining room he took one glance back through the glass panel and saw Yona, still seated on the floor, and Rico, who was on his knees next to her, his arms around her, rocking her back and forth while she wept some more.

"I may just decide to keep this," Ali said, grinning at David and then looking down again at his Hollingsworth ring. Although it was much too big for her, she slid it up and down on the ring finger of her left hand. They had just been to the polo match in Montecito to watch Ali's cousin Robin play, and now they were having lunch at a restaurant in Santa Barbara. "And I don't just mean for the summer," she said, her eyes dancing. She was so pretty and the only real girlfriend he'd ever had. And this wasn't the first time she'd taken his hand, held it for a while, then licked his finger and wriggled his ring off the way she had a few minutes ago in the car, before the valet-parking boy had walked up and opened the car door and welcomed them to the restaurant. She "borrowed" it a lot, and he knew she wanted him to give it to her. To ask her to go steady with him. Come to Hollingsworth to visit next year. Be waiting for him at home when he arrived for school vacations. And he didn't know what to do.

To begin with, it was rare for him to be in Los Angeles

during any given school vacation, and his presence always depended on his father's plans. Probably he couldn't even promise her that he'd be here for Thanksgiving, and that was in a few months. He thought he'd heard Eleanor say that they'd all be in London in November, and New York for Christmas. Or maybe it was the other way around. He had stopped thinking about those logistics a long time ago. Always a week or two before the vacation he would get a call from Fred Samuels, who would laugh and say, "Guess where you get to spend this lovely holiday, David!" Like the announcer on a game show. If it was Gstaad, someone would make certain that his skis, poles, and clothes were in his room when he arrived. If it was the Caribbean, his snorkel mask, fins, and wet suit were waiting. The sameness of school had made travel exciting to him again, and now he arrived at each place eager for adventure.

"You could spend Thanksgiving with my family," Ali offered. "Christmas too."

"That's a nice thought," he said. But there was something wrong. Cloying. Too eager, and he wasn't sure how nice it was. But still he was with her every day and night, and another time when she took the ring he let her keep it overnight. The next day she said, "Um, listen, I'll tell you what about the ring—I'll just keep it until it's time to go back to school. Okay?" And he said okay. But he was glad she had asked him that on the telephone and not in person, because if it had been in person she might have been able to tell that he was confused.

He knew the summer was over when he actually started missing Hollingsworth. God, he *must* be bored if he was missing *that* rat's nest. Not the classes, and certainly not the disgusto food, but his room and the friends he'd made in the dorm, and the football games. He was finally thriving among his peers for the first time in his life and he loved it.

Late one night—he remembered it was very late, because Johnny Carson had been over for a few hours—he lay in bed in the silence of the big old house, thinking about how much he wanted to get back there, when the phone rang. He sat up, trying to imagine who it would be. Ali. Neither of them had their own phone numbers, and once in the heat of a kiss they had made a pact that at exactly two A.M. the next morning he would call her, and she would grab the phone quickly and they would talk all night. It had been hot to be under the covers and to taunt each other from far away. Maybe this was . . . It rang again, and then somewhere in the house, someone else answered it.

In the darkness he felt around until he found the phone on his night stand and he grabbed the receiver. A man's voice was talking very seriously, but it wasn't his father, and it wasn't Rico. "Don't know if it was a change in track conditions because of the weather or a tire problem or exactly what, but we're investigating all the possibilities, and in the meantime I extend my deepest sympathies and if there's anything any of us can do, please know that we will. . . ." Benning. A *brain fade* is what David once heard race-car drivers call it when their concentration broke just long enough for them to lose it, get reckless, and crash. Benning was always in a state of brain fade. And now he was dead. David heard Eleanor Benning Malcolm's voice say thank you, and he hung up the phone. Now he could hear Eleanor and his father talking, and by the way the lights were lighting up under the phone lines, he could see that phone calls were being made. Probably to the pilots to let them know they had to get the plane ready to take his father and Eleanor to pick up Douglas's body.

Body. Dead. God. When somebody died, even if it was someone like Benning whom you couldn't stand, it hit you like a train running over your chest, because you had to think about all the things that person was going to miss out on by not being alive. Like graduation and having your own place at college. It made you glad it wasn't you who died, and guilty for being glad.

After a while he heard his father's heavy footsteps walk downstairs, then Eleanor's high heels. They would probably wake up Rico to take them out to Clover Field Aviation. David realized now that the day was breaking, so he got up and put on his navy terry-cloth robe and walked to the top of the steps. Afraid to see Eleanor's face and yet with a feeling he would not admit until years later was fascination to see her pain and grief. What could he say to her?

In the living room, he could see his father offering Eleanor a tiny snifter with brandy in it, but she gestured it away. She was completely dressed in a fashionable black suit he had seen her wear before. His father was wearing a suit too. He was holding his wife's hand, in the consoling way a doctor does a patient's. After a few silent moments she opened the black purse she had placed on the table next to her, looked at herself in a little mirror she had inside, and then closed it. His father held the brandy up to her lips again and offered it to her. This time she took a tiny sip. The two of them were silent for a long time, and instead of announcing that he was standing on the landing, David just watched them. He could hear Rico in the servants' quarters hurrying around getting dressed.

"Well," Eleanor said to his father, putting the glass of brandy down on the table. Then she sighed, shook her head, and said, "At least now we have a guest room."

And David turned, walked quietly into his bedroom, and went back to sleep, until noon. When he woke up he called Ali and asked her to come over.

"And if you wouldn't mind, I'd like you to bring my ring with you, please," he said. "Because I really would like to have it back."

# ROSIE'S STORY

## 1966

*R*osie Jane Rabinowitz's mother had an ailment as yet undiagnosed by doctors but diagnosed by herself as "a nerve pressing." It created a ringing in her ears that made her answer the doorbell when no one was there, and to say "huh" to people after they'd asked her a question, making them have to ask the question again in a much louder voice.

"Ma?" R.J. asked. "Don't you think I ought to take you to see a doctor about your hearing problem?"

"Huh?" Rifke answered, and R.J. repeated the question.

"Don't be ridiculous," Rifke said this time, lighting an L&M and inhaling deeply, a habit she'd taken up four years before, when her husband, Louie, died. "It's nothing but a nerve pressing."

But when the headaches began, R.J. insisted they make an appointment at the University of Pittsburgh Hearing Center. It was November, but the first appointment they could get was for January 8, because that was the first time the hearing clinic had available. Twice Rifke had to call Pitt and cancel. The first time was because R.J. needed to attend the first rehearsal of the senior play she'd written, and Rifke, who didn't want to go to the doctor's appointment alone, said, "Please, Rosele, go to your rehearsal. We'll change the doctor for another time. It's only a nerve pressing."

The second time they canceled the appointment it was because Uncle Shulke was having a hernia operation and Rifke insisted on staying by the telephone in the store all day to make sure her brother was "out from the knife," as she called it.

"Rifke, you'll call me at the hospital from the Hearing Center," her brother Shulke told her, flattered by her concern for him and returning the favor.

"I'll cancel," Rifke insisted. "It's a nerve pressing."

The appointment was moved, this time to the fourteenth of February. Valentine's Day. R.J. sat watching her mother, who was wearing headphones which were attached to a machine with dials, raising a finger for the nurse every time she heard a tone, then again every time she heard the sound of a tuning fork. After that, the mother and daughter were ushered into a small examining room to wait for the doctor, and Rifke nervously smoked L&M after L&M, filling the tiny room with smoke.

When the door opened and the doctor entered, R.J. was surprised at how young he looked. Maybe he was in his early thirties, not much more, with dark wavy hair and dark-brown eyes behind horn-rimmed glasses. His face was very serious.

"Mrs. Rabinowitz?" he said to Rifke.

"Huh?" Rifke answered.

The doctor, who was used to people who had hearing problems, moved closer to Rifke and knelt near her chair so his face was just below hers and he could look up into her eyes.

"I'm Doctor Feld," he said, and R.J. had to stifle a laugh when Rifke, who had a mouthful of smoke and didn't know what to do with it, let it go right in his face.

The doctor didn't flinch. "I've looked at the results of your tests," he went on. "I'm going to examine you now. All right?" Rifke nodded. "So," he said, "perhaps you should put out your cigarette."

Rifke held the cigarette up above her head as if she were the Statue of Liberty and it was her torch, and R.J. took it from her. The young doctor busied himself with his equipment. Something that looked like a flashlight with a small inside-out funnel at the end of it.

There was no ashtray, so R.J. ran some water from the faucet into the stainless-steel counter sink, then threw the soggy remainder of the L&M into a nearby step-on can while the doctor put the pointed end of the funnel in Rifke's ear, turned on the light, and said, "Hmm?" with a question mark at the end of it in a way that worried R.J. Then he looked in Rifke's left ear and said nothing. Then he turned off the light and knelt again in the same way he had before and looked deeply into Rifke's eyes.

"Mrs. Rabinowitz," he said. "Your stapes, which is a bone that's responsible for transmitting sound, has had a new growth of bone, so it no longer vibrates the way it should, causing you to need amplification of sound intensity. There are two ways to better the situation. One is to surgically remove the stapes bone and replace it with a small wire. The alternative, and what I'd like to suggest, is something that may improve your hearing somewhat, and that's the use of a hearing aid. Nowadays they no longer have to be unattractive or cumbersome, as I'm sure you're aware. For example, I see that you wear eyeglasses. Well, in that case, a tiny mechanism can simply be affixed to the stem of those glasses, allowing the appliance to go completely unnoticed and yet enhancing your ability to detect sound."

Rifke's face was expressionless as she listened, but she was nodding almost imperceptibly in that way R.J. knew so well, which meant: "Yeah, yeah, yeah. Get to the point already."

"So," the doctor said, standing—and R.J. noticed now that he wasn't very tall, maybe only five seven or five eight—"I'm going to suggest the following. What I think you should do is talk this over at home and make a decision about whether or not you'd like to purchase a hearing aid. And if your decision is affirmative"—a little stuffy, R.J. thought—"please let my office know and I'll arrange to have you fitted for one. Do you have any questions?"

"Yeah," Rifke said. "I got one very important question."

"Fine," the doctor said, assuming a posture that indicated he was ready to listen. "What is it?"

"My question is . . ." Rifke said, pausing as if to give herself time to decide whether or not to ask it, "are you single?"

R.J. looked down at the floor. No, Ma. For God's sake, don't do this. The doctor drew himself up for a moment, as if he wasn't sure he'd heard her correctly. Then every possible grain of stuffiness fell away, and he shook his head and laughed a laugh that moved his whole body. After a few seconds Rifke laughed, and R.J. laughed too. With relief. My God, she was embarrassed.

"Yes," he said, "I am."

"So is my daughter, who likes to be called R.J. because it's more modern than Rosie Jane," Rifke said. Doctor Feld turned to look at Rosie, really look at her this time. After a moment, his eyes held hers, and for some reason there was such a curiously strong connection between them that years later she jokingly described it as Tony and Maria's meeting at the dance at the gym in *West Side Story*.

"Isn't she a doll?" she heard her mother's voice ask from somewhere.

"I'd say so," the doctor answered.

"I'll be sure to bring her back for a hearing aid if you think that's what's called for," R.J. said, trying to change the subject and hoping the doctor couldn't tell how humiliated she felt, and wondering in a panic how she looked. She had run home from a rehearsal in her jeans and black sweater to get Rifke here and home again so she could rush back to school and do some more work on her play.

"Wonderful," the doctor said—about what she wasn't sure. "I'll tell my nurse that you'll call to set a time." He turned to go, but turned back again, took Rifke's hand and patted it. "Nice meeting you, Mrs. Rabinowitz. And thank you for the introduction to your daughter."

"It was her pleasure," Rifke said.

When he was gone, Rifke lit another L&M, held it thoughtfully, after the first puff, between her stained index and third finger, and said to her daughter: "How you gonna find out if you don't ask?"

R.J., thrilled to have her mother's diagnosis be less than severe, and still shaking a little from embarrassment and a little from the doctor's long look, helped her mother on with her coat, took her arm, and walked her to the bus stop.

When they got back to the grocery store, Uncle Shulke was standing by the counter eating an apple.

"*Nu*, Rifkele? What did the doctor say?" Juice spurted out of the sides of his mouth.

"He said he was single," Rifke answered with a smile.

"I mean, what did he say about your ear?" Shulke asked.

"About my ear," Rifke told him as she put on her apron to get back to work, "he said it was a nerve pressing."

The next day R.J. couldn't get Doctor Feld's face out of her mind. Alvin Feld. That's what it said on the bill he'd given her, which she'd presented to Uncle Shulke. A doctor. That look he'd given her. Older. How old? Maybe even thirty-two. Ten years older. Old. Her senior play was being rehearsed in the studio theater. She would sit quietly in the back row of the cinder-block building, making notes on her script in the darkness. Sometimes she hated the readings the actors gave her words, wondered how they could be so stupid as not to understand how she'd heard them in her head. Other times she heard meanings in what they said that even she hadn't realized were there, and it thrilled her. Once in a while, for a few minutes she would try to dissociate herself from it, to pretend that it wasn't a rehearsal but a performance, and she was hearing the words, seeing the actors for the first time. Was it boring? Did it work? Was it funny? Alvin Feld. Wouldn't it be nice to be in love with someone and have him come to the play with her when it opened, and when it was over, hold her close and say, "It was wonderful and I love you"?

"He called!" Rifke said before R.J. was halfway up the stairs that night.

Rifke stood at the top of the stairs, wearing a babushka around her recently washed and pincurled hair. She looked more and more like Bubbe every day.

He called. R.J. felt a rush of *please, please, please, let her mean.* . . .

"The ear doctor." Hooray.

"But he wasn't talking ears. And such a gentleman. How are *you*, Mrs. Rabinowitz? And how's your ringing? And is your single daughter by any chance at home? I said no. He said when? I said eleven. He said, Is that too late for me to call? I said don't be silly, call anytime. He said thank you. It's two minutes before eleven. You better get ready."

R.J. laughed. "What ready? I should get dressed up?"

Rifke laughed. The phone rang. Rifke raised an eyebrow and looked at her daughter as if to say *go get him.*

Before the second hearing-clinic appointment, Alvin Feld was R.J.'s big romance. He courted her with flowers and romantic dinners in restaurants, and called her every night. And she loved that he was so grown up. A man. A

Doctor. Whose word was important. People respected him. She respected him, and he loved her. They were in love.

Every week now he bought the groceries for his tiny apartment in Shulke's store. He showed up every Sunday morning, after a visit to the deli, with lox and bagels. He took both mother and daughter to the movies once a week. And when the day came a few weeks later, after he and R.J. had convinced Rifke that wearing a hearing aid didn't mean you were "an old kocker," and the now-trusted Dr. Feld turned up the volume on the newly installed appliance, the first words Rifke heard him say were "I want to marry your daughter."

Needless to say, Rifke's delight in being able to hear so well for the first time in years couldn't compare to the ecstasy she felt in having landed this boy for Rosie. She blurted out the first words she could think of: "Oy, thank God."

Alvin Feld loved telling their friends that story. The night of the dress rehearsal, R.J. told it to her girlfriends in the drama department, and they all laughed, because to them it was a joke about how a Jewish mother already thinks that her twenty-two-year-old daughter is an old maid. Which they all knew was ridiculous, because they were all going on to New York to be actresses, or to rep companies in Minneapolis and Washington, D.C., to be apprentices to set designers, or costume designers, and marriage wasn't even a consideration.

R.J. didn't tell them that she laughed at "Oy, thank God," because those words expressed her feelings too. Because the truth was, she was afraid to try to be a writer for a living. She still harbored a deep fear that her admission to the drama department had been a clerical error—that they'd meant to stuff a regrets letter into her envelope and had enclosed an acceptance by mistake. Writing, shmiting. Maybe Uncle Shulke knew the answers after all, and she should have a teaching degree.

On the opening night of her play, she felt feverish. It was that same weak sick feeling she got when she had the flu. Her face was flushed with heat, and she was shivering at the same time. Maybe she shouldn't sit in the third row between her mother and Alvin. What if she had to vomit? What if something in the play didn't work and she let out an involuntary "no"? Maybe she should stay in the back of

the theater and pace the way she envisioned Broadway
playwrights doing? But now Alvin was moving her along,
into the third row behind her mother, toward their seats,
and she was stuck. Trapped in her feverish panic. The lights
were dimming. Thank God. At least the lights were dimming, so she wouldn't have long to wait for the torture to
begin.

It felt like an interminably long time before the curtain
went up, and she held on to the sleeve of Alvin's seersucker
jacket. Dr. Feld. Dr. and Mrs. Alvin Feld. God, if she said
yes, they could be that as soon after graduation as she
chose. Married. The curtain—thank God the curtain was
going up. There was some polite applause for the set, and
suddenly the play was moving along. Her own words
bounced around in her head. Already it was the second
scene and it was starting to be funny. The audience was
getting it. With some laughs bigger than she'd expected.
Bigger than at any of the rehearsals, when only a few
people from the drama department watched. Jaded. Those
people were jaded. But these people tonight, these people
were a real audience, and they were loving it.

There was no act break. It was a ninety-minute piece,
and she was afraid the audience would get restless. Her
back was stiff as she arched to listen, tried to hear if anyone
in the audience was whispering or shuffling uncomfortably.
But no one seemed to be. Her mother, now a new woman
with a hearing aid, smiled constantly at the stage and nodded. R.J. was relieved, since she'd feared that the subject
matter might be too sexy for Rifke's old-world ideas. The
play was about girls in a dormitory. They spent a lot of time
talking about losing their virginity. Rifke seemed amused
through it all. But Alvin! Alvin was another story. He never
once changed his position in his seat. Never once looked at
R.J. as if to say he was enjoying it. The play was nearly
halfway over and he'd never laughed once.

The fever rose again when that realization hit her, and
her stomach ached. He hated it. Obviously. Probably thought
she'd been lying to him when she'd told him all those many
weeks ago, embarrassed because she felt as if she were too
old, that she was a virgin and wasn't ready to give up her
virginity. How could she know so much about diaphragms
and sexual situations? Now, when she looked and saw the
frown on his face, she wanted to stop the play for a few

minutes, just long enough to tell him how she'd listened night after night when she was studying in the living room at the dorm, to story after story, and heard the various approaches of the various girls to their own questions about sex and promiscuity, and found it so funny and so moving that she'd had to write about it. Alvin. He coughed. A big cough. She'd known him for nearly two months and she'd never heard him cough like that. Maybe he was coughing to drown out the words that were coming out of the actors' mouths, because he knew they were R.J.'s words and he didn't approve. When the lights came up and she looked into his eyes, she would know.

The last few scenes went quickly, with even bigger laughs. But instead of enjoying them, R.J. noticed only that Alvin never even cracked a smile.

"I'm amazed a girl like you lasted this long," he had said to her after their third date, when she had told him about her virginity. "How is it you've never had sexual intercourse?" It sounded very doctorly when he said it that way.

"I was too poor," she joked.

"I don't think it costs any money," he laughed, holding her.

"I guess I mean, I already felt self-conscious about being that girl from the other side of the tracks. I didn't want to take the chance of being that tramp from the other side of the tracks. People talk and exaggerate, and it's too important."

"I won't pressure you," he said, but when on a few dates his kisses got urgent, he murmured, "Please, honey, please change your mind." But she didn't. Didn't think she should. What if she didn't marry him after all? Marry him. A man who didn't like her play. Maybe, she hoped, this was his way. Not to laugh, but to listen very carefully to the rest of the audience, and to be objective, and at the end when the curtain went down, to put his arms around her and whisper "fabulous" in her ear. He coughed again. That same big cough, and a few minutes later the curtain went down. It shot up immediately for the curtain call, and the applause was loud. The actors flew onto the stage with elated faces, and R.J. felt a swift wave of envy as she imagined them all when the curtain came down, squealing with excitement, then rushing down to The Greek's to have a beer and talk over every beat of the play with the director and the stage manager. But not the playwright, because she was with her mother and Alvin Feld. Dr. Alvin Feld, who wanted to marry her. A man who was what the girls in high school called a J.M.D.—A Jewish Mother's Dream.

"So, Ma," R.J. said, putting an arm around her mother's shoulder as they stepped out of the theater into the warm spring night. "What did you think?"

Rifke looked all around at the young people emerging from the theater. She smiled and nodded as she did, as if she was glad to be among them, absorbing their excitement. Then she opened her purse and took out an L&M and some matches.

"Ma?" Rosie asked, avoiding at all costs looking at Alvin, who was standing behind her. Her mother opened the pack of matches and was about to light her cigarette when she looked at R.J.

"*Oy*, one second," Rifke said suddenly, realization filling her face. Then she reached up to her eyeglasses and made an adjustment on the volume of the hearing aid. When she was satisfied with the volume level she said, "It was so loud in the beginning, I turned it all the way down."

Her smiles. They were for a play she only saw. Never heard. R.J. wanted to cry and she knew she still had Alvin to deal with. She was about to turn to him when Evie Bingham, her mentor, her severest critic, her playwriting teacher for the last four years, burst from the doors of the theater, spotted her, moved purposefully toward her, and squeezed her arm.

"In my office tomorrow, girl," she said, in a way that made R.J. know she liked the work, and before she could be introduced to Rifke and Alvin, Evie had disappeared into the crowd.

It was time to look at Alvin. R.J. turned. He was standing, hands folded at his waist, looking around at the crowd, and R.J. thought he turned his head too quickly to get a better look at the miniskirted, white-booted freshman girl who walked by.

"So, Doc," R.J. said quietly, wishing he would never have to look around or answer her so she wouldn't have to hear him say what she already knew, which was that he hated it. Disapproved. Of her play. Of her, after all. Because even though she'd been inspired by other people's conver-

sations, the play really contained her point of view. Her
sensibilities. He turned.

"Fine, Rose," he said. The liar. "The audience really ate
it up."

But you, Alvin, she wanted to say. What did you
think? Was there anything about it you thought was funny?
Had insight? Instead she said, "Do you think so?"

"Oh, sure," he said, and took her arm. "They were
very amused." Then he took her mother's arm too, and
walked them toward the parking lot in silence.

"If," Evie Bingham said, and she paused, a momentous
pause, "anyone in this department that sanctifies Ibsen and
Chekhov ever comes back to me and reports that you said
we had the following conversation, please be advised, Miss
R.J. Rabinowitz, that I will deny ever having had it. So do
you—as your people would say—*farshtey*?"

R.J. nodded. This woman. Evie Bingham. Two plays
produced off Broadway, one on Broadway, two novels, and
a volume of short stories. This woman was her idol. She
had the best sense of humor, the warmest way about her.
In R.J.'s worst moments of self-doubt in her four chaotic
years in the drama department, she had always been able to
go to Evie for counsel. It had started when the money for
R.J.'s freshman tuition was used up and her ability to stay
in the school for the next three years looked very iffy. Evie
had spoken on her behalf to get her the yearly academic
scholarship which had made it possible for R.J. to stay in
school.

"Not a word," R.J. promised.

"I have friends in Hollywood," Evie said, and then
winced and covered her eyes. "Oh, my God, what a sordid
admission." Then she uncovered her eyes and got serious.
Her gray hair was cut in straight bangs across her forehead.
She had a long nose and olive skin with very large pores.

"Honey, you are the most commercial writer of any
I've ever taught," she said, "which around here is probably
a huge insult. But it's true. I mean, you're a cream puff. In
the best sense. You see silliness around you everywhere you
go, and I love that. And you know where else they love it?
In the world of tel-tel-tel . . ." It was a fake stutter and she

and R.J. both laughed at the joke. "God, I can't even say it."

"Television," R.J. said.

"As I said, despite the sordidness of the admission, the truth is, even living in Pittsburgh, I do have a friend or two in that world. You know—alumni and all that. So, if you want my opinion, and after having suitably dazzled you for four years I'm certain that you can't live without it, you ought to make it through the commencement exercises and hightail it out to Los Angeles."

Los Angeles. The only thing R.J. knew about Los Angeles was what she'd seen on *77 Sunset Strip*. Television. Evie Bingham was praising her work. Or was she? Maybe this was a huge insult.

"It's rare what you have," Evie said, now very seriously. "A point of view that sees jokes in pain. Don't waste it. I mean, what were you going to do after you graduated? Did you have any plans? I mean anything crucial that couldn't wait?"

"No," R.J. said, very serious now too. "I was just going to get married."

"See what I mean?" Evie Bingam said, pointing in R.J.'s face and laughing. "That's funny. Go to Hollywood. Next, please," she said, as if she were a waitress at a bakery counter. "Please speak up. Who's next?" Then she slapped her desk and laughed some more.

Actually, Alvin had never officially asked R.J. to marry him. What he had done was to talk about their future together as if it were a *fait accompli*, even after the taboo play. Though they were together constantly for the days following it, the play was never talked about. Los Angeles. Uncle Munish's son Maxie had moved there years ago, and he was probably the only person R.J. even vaguely knew who lived in that strange exotic place. Kookie, Kookie, lend me your comb.

Alvin and Rifke were playing gin at the kitchen table and R.J. was lying on the living room couch, staring at the television. Bill Burns and the eleven o'clock news. It was just ending. "Good night, good luck, and good news tomorrow," Bill Burns said.

"Amen," R.J. heard Rifke say from the dining room table. Bill Burns said the same thing to the TV audience every night, and every night Rifke said the same thing back to him.

R.J. got to her feet and walked to the kitchen. Alvin's jacket and tie hung over the back of his chair. His shirt collar was open, and his lower lip was extended in a pout, as he looked with a furrowed brow at his hand of cards. For a second he reminded her of her father.

"I'm going to Los Angeles after graduation," R.J. said, to her mother and Alvin. Neither of them looked up. Alvin discarded a king.

"Gin," Rifke said, grabbing the king, shoving it into her hand, and slapping another card face down on the table.

"No," Alvin said, sincerely distressed.

"What do you mean, no?" Rifke asked, fanning her cards face up on the table. "Give a look here, sonny boy. Is that gin or not?"

"God," Alvin said, shaking his head in disbelief, holding his as-yet-unmatched cards out to show Rifke. "You got me with my pants down. I don't know who dealt these lousy cards." And they both laughed.

R.J. couldn't believe it. They were ignoring her completely. Rifke pulled an L&M from her pack on the table. Alvin lit it for her.

"How many points?" Rifke asked, and R.J. had to fight off a feeling that she was the other woman.

"Let's see," Alvin said.

"Los Angeles," R.J. said louder. "Right after graduation. I have a few dollars and I want to go there."

"Where?" Rifke asked. *"Vi geystu?"*

"Fourteen," Alvin said.

"Hooray," Rifke said.

R.J. walked into her room, got undressed for bed, and went to sleep.

The money was some she'd managed to save over the last year, in a box in her sock drawer. It was enough, she figured, after a phone call to Mona Feldstein Friedman's ex-husband Jerry, who still ran the travel agency, to get her to and from Los Angeles and keep her there for a month. By then she would have met all of Evie Bingham's "contacts," as Evie called them that morning when she telephoned R.J. to give her their addresses and phone numbers. R.J. had it all figured out. She could have the television people tell her what they wanted her to write, and she could come back to Pittsburgh, write it, and mail it to them. Alvin would go to the hospital every day, and she would stay home and write. Then, after the people she was writing for knew her well and knew her work, they could call her anytime they needed more, and she would send it to them. It sounded like a perfect plan to her.

The morning she told it to Alvin he patted her hand and shook his head, then raised a finger to tell the waitress he wanted more coffee. R.J. looked down at her bagel and cream cheese, wishing she were hungry, wishing she didn't feel like crying. Wishing they weren't sitting in Weinstein's, so in case she did start to cry she wouldn't have to be seen running to the ladies' room by half of Pittsburgh.

"It's my fault," Alvin said. "I should have realized that eventually your age would be a problem."

"What does my age have to do with it?"

The waitress came and poured some more coffee into Alvin's cup. He waited for her to finish and get a good distance from the table before he answered.

"It makes you naïve," he said. "Foolish. You believe in fairy tales, Rose. Have fantasies about things that won't ever come true. And it's not because you're dumb. You're not. If you were dumb I wouldn't want to marry you."

"Thank you," R.J. said, then wondered what in heaven's name she was thanking him for.

"It's because you're a little girl of twenty-two, and instead of having real values and a real understanding of what's worthwhile, you have delusions about the way things might be. And I understand. So here's what I think you should do." His voice changed into the one he used when he was being a doctor. She'd heard him use it with her mother that first day and with patients on the telephone. "Proceed with your plans. Go wherever you have to, to get a firsthand sense of what's real. And after you've made the distinction and you're sanguine that you simply can't have both—being married and having your absurd notion about a career as a Hollywood writer—you can decide. I only hope for your sake that I'll still be here."

"Alvin," she said, tearing a strip of her paper napkin, and then another. "If the television people won't give me assignments that I can write in Pittsburgh after we're married, what *will* I do?"

"Do?" Alvin said, but he was stalling, stuck for an

answer, and R.J. noticed for the first time that he had a few gray hairs above his ears. "What does my mother do? She makes the house nice for my father." R.J. had met Alvin's parents. His father, a salesman, seemed dark and moody and brooding. His mother was birdlike and weary. "Or *your* mother?" he added, and then realized that Rifke was not a good example, so he moved on. "My aunt Sheila," he said, pleased with himself for striking gold. "That's who you'll be like. You never met my aunt Sheila, but she is really a great person. Kind of offbeat, like you." He meant that as a compliment. "In fact, I don't know why I never introduced you. She does the shows for the Hadassah. They're wonderful shows. Last April she wrote the President's Day luncheon for my mother's best girlfriend, Helen Baum. My mother raved about it."

The minute she got home from brunch, R.J. called Jerry Friedman the travel agent to firm up her plans to go to California.

Graduation day was hot and muggy, and the black commencement gown stuck to R.J.'s street clothes underneath it, and the band inside the mortarboard made her head sweat. The a cappella choir sang "The Battle Hymn of the Republic," and when she looked out into the bleachers she spotted Rifke and Alvin together in the twelfth row. They were laughing and talking animatedly to each other. In the years since Louie's death Rifke had changed a lot. Come out of herself. Lately she was even flirting with some of the men who came into the store. Happy with the new world of being able to hear.

Two of the men—Silverberg the produce man, and a customer named Solly Blywas—had asked her for a date.

"I think they've been asking me for years," she confided to her daughter. "I just never heard them before." R.J. laughed. She loved her mother and would miss her. She had a passing thought, which she quickly shook off, about her being successful in California and sending for Rifke to come and live with her there, and both of them loving the sunny climate, away from the bleak gray winters of Pittsburgh forever. But no. There was Alvin. Here. And she would come back and marry him. The graduation ceremony droned on, and when it was finally at an end, R.J. stood, and when they called her name, walked to the podium and collected her diploma. When she looked at the twelfth row, Rifke was waving a congratulatory wave.

When she came out of the gym, where she'd turned in her cap and gown and said tearful goodbyes to some friends whose parents were taking them home right away, Alvin was standing waiting by the gym door. Alone.

"Let's get her home," he said, gesturing to Rifke, who sat on a bench under a tree a few yards away. R.J. was alarmed. She didn't like the look on Alvin's face.

"What's wrong?"

"Just a headache," he said.

R.J. hurried to her mother. "Ma," she said. "You okay?"

Rifke was smoking a cigarette.

"Yeahsure," Rifke said, as if it were one word. "I got a nerve pressing."


R.J. would have thought it beyond the call of duty for Cousin Maxie, whom she didn't even remember, to pick her up at the airport, if she didn't know that it was because Uncle Shulke had called in some chit from the past to get him to do it.

"How is that son of a bitch?" Maxie, who was open-shirted, fuzzy-chested, and sweaty, asked as he threw R.J.'s bags into the back of his station wagon. He got into the driver's seat, moved a baby car-seat out of the passenger seat into the back, and leaned over to pull up the door-lock button so R.J. could get in.

"The same," she answered as she slid onto the hot plastic seat. There were six or seven McDonald's wrappers on the floor by her feet.

"Yeah, I'm sure, the lousy *gonif*," Maxie said. "You know what a *gonif* is?"

"Yes," R.J. told him as he pulled away from the curb, looking at her instead of into his rearview mirror. They were almost hit by a bus.

"You *shvartze* jungle bunny," Maxie yelled—at the driver of the bus, R.J. assumed. Now they were safely in the lane that was moving out of the airport.

"Yeah, Shulke always hated your father, and you know why? Because your father was a Commie. He believed people should pull for one another. Shulke, if it was a few years ago in the South, woulda been a slave owner. And he made your mother work very hard all those years. For no money. Everyone in the family knew what a *momzer* he was. A no-goodnik. You're too young to remember how he treated Bubbe.''

"I remember, all right," R.J. said, watching the Los Angeles landscape go by. This was the farthest she'd ever been from home. The West Coast. She'd survived her first airplane flight. Look at that. Those were oil wells. Right in the middle of the city. Oil wells.

"Shulke never wanted his own mother to live in his house. So that *feygele* son of his, Barry, sees Bubbe's teeth in the glass and gets so scared that Bubbe has to move out."

"And move in with my parents," R.J. said.

"That's right. Your mother, who is an absolute angel, takes in Bubbe, and still Shulke charges her rent. The bastard.'' Maxie was quiet for a while. Then he spoke up again in a voice so loud it was as if he thought R.J. were in another car instead of a foot away from him. "So you're comin' here from Pittsburgh to do what? To be in show business, don't make me laugh. I know all about show business because I'm in the coffee business so I service a lot of the networks and studios. Let me tell you somethin'. You know how many girls get off the bus, the train, the plane every day who are a hell of a lot prettier than you are and want to be actresses just like you do? And I don't know about you, but those girls? They'll do anything to get a job and—''

"I want to be a writer," R.J. said quietly. Maxie's car radio was on with the volume turned very low. The Beatles were singing "Michelle."

"What kind of writer?"

"Comedy mostly."

"No chance. They don't let girls be comedy writers. It's always guys. A buncha guys. Like on *Your Show of Shows.* Ever watch *Show of Shows*? All guys wrote that show. Red Skelton? All guys."

"Are we far from the hotel?" R.J. asked.

"Ten minutes." For the rest of the ride, neither he nor R.J. said anything. In fact, Maxie didn't say a word until he had given her bags and hair dryer to the bellman at the apartment hotel where he was dropping her, and was about to get back into the car.

"By the way, the station wagon here is my wife's car. I drive a Mercedes. Next time you talk to your Uncle Shulke, tell him that. You can also tell him that last year, Kaminsky Coffee grossed a million five." And he got into the station wagon.

"Thanks for the ride," R.J. said, but she suspected he didn't hear her.

After the bellman left, R.J. stood in the middle of her hotel room and looked at the one big and one small suitcase, and the green plastic dome-shaped hair dryer. Everything she owned in the world. This room with a kitchenette was cozy, bigger than any she'd ever stayed in before, except maybe the one she'd shared with Francie the time Francie's parents took them to New York.

Los Angeles. She was in Los Angeles. Alone. From her window she could see the swimming pool below. There were four or five people lying oiled on lounge chairs, and three of them had telephones next to them. The telephones were on long cords that were pulled out the open doors of what must be the people's respective apartments. It looked as though they were all expecting important phone calls.

She would unpack and start making her own important calls.

She arrived on Wednesday, and before the weekend she had meetings set up for every day of the following week with Evie Bingham's contacts, and she had made friends with two of the people in her building. One was Dinah Goldsmith, a bleached-blond, curly-haired casting director from New York who was casting a movie in Los Angeles, and hoped to move west permanently. The other was Arthur Misner.

R.J. wasn't sure what he did exactly, but it was something in the music business called A and R. He was one of the people she'd seen with the telephone on the long cord pulled outside. He had very curly brown hair and green eyes and a toothy smile and he was funny, but in a kind of shy way. Not obvious or loud. He told R.J. he had a girlfriend in Detroit who would probably be coming out soon to live in Los Angeles. She told him she had a boyfriend back in Pittsburgh, and that within a matter of weeks she'd be going back to marry him.

By the end of the third week she knew she'd never felt closer to any male in her life than she did to Arthur Misner.

At the end of each afternoon she would rush home from her meetings with the producers and script supervisors and bombard him with stories about her day. The one with the comedy writing team of Bernie Weinberg and Arnie Breno-witz. Bernie, the tall one, had gone to Carnegie Tech. Arnie, the short one, sat at a desk across from Bernie's desk. He ate sunflower seeds and then spit the shells a few feet away into a wastebasket.

"So Evie sent you?" Bernie asked with a big grin. "Evie was my teacher, what was it . . . fifteen years ago? I don't know why she thinks I have jobs here for writers. She doesn't get that *we're* the writers here and we don't need any other writers. Besides, you want to have a life like this? Some nights we're here past midnight. Be smart. You're a fairly attractive person. Meet a guy, preferably out of the business, and marry his ass, honey. Don't kid yourself. There's no glamour here. See this office? What's missing? How about a window? Writers don't get windows. We get *gornisht*. You understand *gornisht*?"

She nodded. She wanted to be able to say something funny but she couldn't think of a thing, she told Arthur later.

"*Oy*, she's going to cry," Bernie said. Arnie crunched another sunflower seed.

"No," R.J. said. "I . . . I . . ." She wished he hadn't said she was going to cry because that made her feel like crying and . . .

"Sweetheart," Bernie said, and now he walked over and reached a hand into Arnie's sunflower seeds, stuck one in his mouth, and sucked on it while he talked. "You want to be a writer? Write. Pick a show you like. It doesn't have to be *our* show. It can be *Beverly Hillbillies*. It can be *Gilligan's Island*, *I Dream of Jeannie*, but sit down and try to write one. Then show it around." His teeth crunched down on the shell; then he chewed and swallowed the whole thing. "Then get back to us."

Speculative scripts. In essence, that's what everyone told her she should write. Pick one television show you love. Watch it again and again. Get to know the characters; then write an episode and use it as a writing sample. Take a month or two and then get back to them. Yes, her play was fine. Nicely done. Showed great promise. Write a spec script. Then there was Karl Berman, the froggy-looking producer friend of Evie's who had met R.J. at the door of his house dressed in a bathrobe with yellowy egg stains on the lapel.

"I'm *looking* for a young writer," he said, putting his big fat feet up on the coffee table. "I got a movie project that's about high school kids and every writer I know is too jaded to handle it. I already have a deal to do it at Columbia."

A black Doberman pinscher was outside, pawing at the glass door from the pool.

"I've been having a real hard time finding anybody. What do you think?"

A job. To write a movie. She didn't even know how to write a movie.

"I think it sounds interesting" was all she could think of to say.

"I mean, if Evie likes you—shit, she was a bridesmaid in my wedding to my ... let's see ... third wife? No. Second. I love Evie. You know?"

R.J. nodded. She couldn't wait to tell Arthur the part about Karl Berman not knowing if Evie was a friend of his second or third wife.

"Want to try to take a pass at it?"

"Sure," R.J. had said, not believing that here she was, making a deal to write a movie, and how quickly she was conquering Hollywood.

"Tonight after dinner we'll talk more about it," he said, and now he was leering. No.

"I have plans for dinner," she said.

"Break 'em," he ordered.

"I can't." She stood.

"No dinner, no job," he announced, standing. His robe was opening.

"Fine," she said. And, queasy, she headed quickly for what she hoped she remembered correctly was the front door, because if it wasn't, she'd run into the Doberman. The last words she heard were "What did you think? I was gonna just give you a job? Are you crazy? Do you know who I am?"

The most recent meeting had taken place at a hot-dog stand, where the story editor insisted she have a chili dog with him. While he was telling her his own success story, she'd had to run to the gas station next door and be sick.

Arthur laughed at all of them, and in turn he told her

about all the Hollywood characters he met up with in a day. Eventually, Dinah would join them, and dinner would be take-out for the three of them by the pool.

"Maybe it would be good," Dinah said knowingly one night, as she scraped the sweet-and-sour sauce from a piece of sweet-and-sour chicken because she was on a diet, "if we introduced the girlfriend in Detroit to the doctor boy-friend in Pittsburgh, because that way we could save her a ticket out here and you a ticket home, and everyone would live happily ever after."

Neither R.J. nor Arthur looked up from the food on their plates. "Or maybe I should keep my big mouth shut."

"Maybe," Arthur said shyly, "the three of us should drive down to Palm Springs this weekend. I can get a room, and you two girls can share one cheaply, and R.J. would probably love to see Palm Springs. It's a lot like Pittsburgh."

"Ma," R.J. said into the phone that night. She called Rifke three times a week. "How's by you?"

"Huh?" Rifke said, then added: "Oy, I took off my glasses so I can't hear. Wait a second. Is it you, Rosele? Now I got 'em on."

"Yeah, Ma. How do you feel?"

"Me? The same. Tonight I worked in the store, I had a sandwich and some soup at Polonsky's with Mort Silverberg, I watched Bill Burns, now I'm watching Johnny. What about you?"

"I'm fine. I'll be home in about ten days."

"My son-in-law the doctor came by today," Rifke said, and R.J. felt a heavy feeling. Guilty and sad. "Does he call you?"

"A lot," R.J. said.

"Good," Rifke said, reassured.

"I miss you, Ma."

"*Meyn kleine meydele,*" Rifke said, sounding so much like Bubbe that R.J.'s eyes filled with tears. "*Du bist meyn velt.*" You are my world.

After they hung up, R.J. remembered that she'd forgotten to tell Rifke that she was leaving on Friday for Palm Springs and wouldn't be back until Monday morning. It didn't matter. She would call her mother from there.

Their first dinner in Palm Springs was at Bob's Big Boy, which Arthur called *Robaire's.* Their second was at Denny's, which he called *Chez Denis.* The three of them got too burned at the pool of the Motel Six, and stayed up talking until dawn all three nights about everything any of them had ever felt. Dinah read R.J.'s play and said it was like Broadway. Arthur said he loved it and added, "If Neil Simon knew you were lurking out here, he would be a wreck."

When they were packing to leave Palm Springs, Dinah asked her: "How can you be so crazy about Arthur and go back to some guy who sounds from your description like a big-headed shmuck doctor who's going to stifle you for the rest of your life?"

R.J. didn't know what to answer.

"I have to get back to Pittsburgh. I miss my mother, and she really needs me. I'll send all the producers my speculative scripts from there, as soon as I've written them, and then . . ."

"And then, what?"

"We'll see."

The desk at the apartment hotel was very busy when they got back. People were checking in and out, so R.J. didn't stop for messages. But when she got to her room the red light on her telephone was blinking, so before she even opened her overnight bag she dialed the message operator. The phone rang for a long time, and finally he picked up.

"Oh. You've had a lot of calls," he said.

"From?" she asked.

"Let's see. One from Maxie . . ."

"My cousin." What could he have possibly wanted? Maybe he felt bad about the way he'd acted the day she arrived. Or maybe he knew she'd be leaving in a week or so, and Shulke's deal with him included his taking her back to the airport as well.

"Someone named . . . God, I can't read this. It looks like S-H-U-L-something-something."

"Shulke, my uncle," R.J. said.

"Yeah, well, he called a million times at least. Then someone named Dr. Feld called a lot of times, and then . . ."

R.J. was cold. Icy-cold in the hot apartment in the hot California day. Why these calls?

"My mother?" she said in a panic. "Were any of the calls from my mother?" She had been so caught up in Palm Springs she hadn't once called Rifke. Friday, Saturday, and Sunday. And here it was Monday morning and . . .

"Nope, just the ones I told you about, hon."

"Thank you," R.J. said, and hung up the phone. Oh, God, what was—

The phone rang almost immediately.

"Hello?"

"Well, my God. I don't believe it. You're finally there. Where in the hell have you been? Where could you possibly go for so many goddamn days? Who do you think you are not to call your family back and let them know where you are and if you're safe? Were you off for the weekend with some Hollywood movie star or what?"

"Alvin, my God. I was in Palm Springs with two friends, and I had no idea anyone was trying to reach me. What's the problem?"

"The problem, Little Miss Hollywood, is that your mother died of a cerebral hemorrhage early Saturday morning and no one's been able to reach you. The funeral is tomorrow morning. Why don't you make some airline reservations and let me know when you're coming home." He didn't even say goodbye. Just hung up.

R.J. put the receiver down and began to cry out loud. The lonely, plaintive cry of the orphan she now was. Rifke, gone. Mama. No. *Du bist meyn velt.* My world. Now she was no one's world. Why had she left Pittsburgh? *Just a nerve pressing.* It had been a warning all along. She lay on the bed, just looking at the ceiling for a long time. Then finally she picked up the phone and called to make a reservation on a flight to Pittsburgh.

*"Yiskadal v'yis Kadosh."* R.J. sat between Uncle Shulke and Alvin in the front row at the Burton Hirsch Funeral Home, tearing absently at the edges of the card someone had given her earlier with the transliteration of the mourner's Kaddish. She didn't look behind her, but she could feel that the room where the service was being held was filled with people who had come to say goodbye to Rifke. Many of them were customers from Uncle Shulke's store. Over the years she had worked there, Rifke had befriended everyone: the old orthodox Jews who walked by every Friday evening on their way to services; the black cleaning ladies who waited at the bus stop outside the store for the bus to

take them home to the Hill District; the neighborhood children who, though they never had quite enough money for a Fudgsicle, somehow managed to negotiate with Rifke and to leave the grocery store with one anyway.

R.J.'s ride with Alvin from the airport to her mother's empty apartment the night before had been strained. He had greeted her at the gate with a perfunctory embrace, waited for her bags without even a word, and then escorted her to what he pointed out was his brand-new car. A beige Cadillac. It smelled good inside. Leathery and rich. They were almost all the way to Squirrel Hill when he said, "Both your parents are dead now, Rose. So I guess I'll be your roots now. Marry me and we'll be a family." It sounded like lines from a bad play, recited by a terrible actor. But the message was one she'd thought about in the few hours after she got the news of her mother's death. A family. Now she would never be a part of one until she got married. Now she was alone in the world. Alvin had said something else, too, last night. Something about R.J. forgetting "that Hollywood nonsense," and about how she "belonged in Pittsburgh." R.J. thought about what it would be like to be Mrs. Alvin Feld. To live in Pittsburgh and go everywhere in a beige Cadillac.

The tall, thin, bearded rabbi, who was a friend of Uncle Shulke's and had never once met Rifke, was giving what was obviously a standard speech about how in life Rifke had been a beloved mother, sister, friend. R.J. knew it was the same thing he said about every woman who died. And then he began to recite a last prayer. Soon the service would be over. No. That bland speech. Those over-the-counter words were the last words anyone would say about her mother before they lowered her into the ground, R.J. thought. And then, almost as a surprise to even herself, she was standing and walking toward the bema, where the rabbi stood in front of Rifke's coffin. One foot in front of the other she moved, not even certain what she would do when she got up there. She could hear the comments from her aunts and uncles. *"Zeynor! Rosenu geyt tsu tsim bema."* Look at Rosie going to the bema.

The rabbi looked curiously at her at first, but the determined look on her tearstained face made him step aside and leave room for her at the podium. Though it was the proper height for the tall rabbi, R.J. had to stand on her toes to make sure she could be seen over it.

"My mother," she said, but it came out so softly, even with the microphone, that she began again: "My mother, Rifke Kaminsky Rabinowitz, never had a bad word to say about anyone. She called me her *velt*. Her world. And I won't ever forget the things she taught me. She came—" Just then the P.A. system emitted a piercing high-pitched sound that filled the whole room, and R.J. bit her lip, trying to hold back the tears. Someone must have adjusted it after a moment, because the room became still again and R.J. went on.

"She came to a new world that was strange and not a little bit frightening to her, but she worked hard and made a life for herself and for my father and never complained. In fact she laughed at people who did. If she was here with us now she would say *'Forvos veynstu? Siz besser tsu lachen.'* Why do you cry when it is better to laugh? *'Ich bin tsuzamen mit meyn Louie in Ganayden.'* Because I'm with my Louie in heaven.'" R.J. took a deep breath to try to gain some control, then spoke again. "I miss her" was all she could get out this time, knowing if she said one more word she would break down.

Instead, she focused on the faces of the friends and family who looked up at her. They filled the tiny chapel all the way to the last row. Aunt Chana, Aunt Malke, Uncle Benny, Aunt Sasha, Mr. and Mrs. Heft, Mr. and Mrs. Fishmann, Mr. Katz from the fish market, Arthur Misner. My God. R.J. couldn't believe her eyes. It was Arthur. In a coat and tie. In the next-to-the-last row. He nodded ever so slightly when their eyes met and R.J. nodded back, then she glanced nervously over at Alvin to see if he had noticed. He hadn't. He was looking down at a prayer book that he was leafing through with a kind of pout on his face.

The rabbi said, "Thank you," then nudged R.J. gently away from the podium and she stood next to him, not knowing what to do while he advised the congregation to rise and exit toward the back of the chapel, and asked for the pallbearers to come forward and carry the coffin to the hearse which would transport it to the cemetery. Alvin was a pallbearer, and when he and R.J. brushed past one another as he moved toward the coffin, and she moved into the crowd, he said nothing about her speech. R.J. made her way toward Arthur, who stood waiting at the back of the synagogue.

"Arthur, how did you know?" she asked quietly when she finally stood next to him. A *mensch*. A fine person. A good citizen. Arthur Misner was a *mensch*. That's what Rifke would have called him. Rifke would have liked him, R.J. found herself thinking. Okay, so he's not a doctor, but Ma, a man flies all the way from Los Angeles for a funeral? That's already a *mensch*.

"They told me at the front desk that you rushed off to the airport by taxi last night. So I called your home and spoke to some uncle of yours who told me about your mother. Dinah drove me to the airport and I took a red-eye to Chicago and an early-morning flight here. I'm sorry about your mother, R.J.," he said. "It was very brave of you to be able to get up and say a few words. Even though I didn't know your mother, I'm sure she would have been proud."

A *mensch*. "Thank you, Arthur," R.J. said. She put her hand on his arm and watched as one of her tears fell, making a darker-navy spot on his navy linen blazer. She could feel the group of people pushing forward, some of whom probably weren't coming to the cemetery and would want to express their condolences to her now.

"R.J.," Arthur said, "I came all this way to pay my respects to your mother, but mostly what I came to do was to ask you to please come home with me. To Los Angeles."

"I'm glad, Arthur," she said. "Very glad."

"*Oy*, poor little Rosele Jane," Uncle Shulke said, coming up now and throwing his arms around R.J. "They took my sister—how could they take my Rifke? She was the best one of all of us and they took her. *Oy*, God. Why?"

As R.J. held and comforted her Uncle Shulke, walking with him to the front of the funeral home and helping him into the first black limousine behind the hearse, then sliding in beside him, she wondered exactly how she would tell Alvin Feld that she was going back to Los Angeles with Arthur Misner.

# DAVID'S STORY

## 1973

*T*here was a student at the Wharton School named Farley Coburn, who was as ill-behaved as his father was rich, and judging by the net worth of this particular father, it would have left no one surprised to find Farley behind bars before his forthcoming graduation from business school. The windshield wiper of Farley's turquoise Dino Ferrari always had a parking ticket stuffed in it; he was currently being sued by a young lady he swore he'd never met, for the paternity of an impending heir; the owner of a nightclub in downtown Philadelphia was looking for him in connection with something related to drugs. And David Malcolm, who was his roommate, thought that Farley was one of the greatest guys he'd ever met.

"A classic," David said when Farley told him he'd just given the Ferrari, pink slip and all, to a poor black family he'd chosen at random in the Philadelphia ghetto. Farley was lying on the sofa in their Walnut Street apartment that morning when he confessed the story of his generosity to David, who was sitting in a nearby chair, the fingers of his two hands touching to make a steeple, his head shaking in disbelief.

"Do you honest-to-God think it's a classic?" Farley asked. For the two years during which their friendship had flourished, Farley had always put a lot of stock in David's approval.

"A classic," David said again, "because you're a fruitcake. You're trying to pretend you don't care about your old man or anything he stands for, or anything he gives you, so you're pissing it away, and that's a crock."

"I'm not pretending," Farley said, and he rolled over on his stomach, buried his face in the sofa pillow, and remained in that position for a while. Then he picked up his face and looked at David and said, "He's an ostentatious nouveau riche prick, and I wish he'd stop understanding me so well and forgiving me all the time so I could have a reason never to talk to him again, because I hate him."

"A classic," David said. "Fars, you're a cliché. Next thing you'll be telling him that inherited wealth corrupts and you want to be out of the will."

"I did that already," Farley said, sitting up and rubbing his hand again and again over his scruffy face, which he hadn't shaved in days. "*You* met him, Malcolm. *You* tell *me*. What did *you* think of him?" Farley yawned. He'd had a big night the night before, trying to decide to which black family exactly he should give his Ferrari. Philanthropy could sometimes be exhausting.

David had met Farley's father many times on the man's numerous visits to Philadelphia to rescue his son from one crisis or another. Once, Bill Coburn and David had talked a drunken Farley down from jumping off the balcony over the quad, where Farley had gone when he'd learned his father was on his way through Philadelphia for a meeting with Walter Annenberg and wanted to stop by the apartment to say hello while he was in town. Many times David had been left with a frustrated Bill Coburn across a dinner table at a restaurant, after Farley had stormed out because of something his father said to him that Farley had described as "cutting my balls off."

"I think," David said to Farley, "that he's rich, and that he loves you, and that you can stand on a corner wearing a propeller hat and reading *The Communist Manifesto* aloud, or poison his tankful of tropical fish, and you know what? It ain't gonna change."

"He embarrasses me," Farley said.

"Then you're a jackass," David told him.

"Fuck you," Farley said.

"Fuck him. Fuck everybody," he said again as they sat aboard the Coburns' private 727, which Farley's father had sent to bring him home to Dallas for a weekend a few weeks before graduation. David was invited to be a house-guest.

"Want to puke?" Farley asked David. Farley's fondest wish was that just once, someone would mistake him for coming from the Lower East Side of New York, and he spent as much time as he possibly could trying to behave and sound as if it were true.

David, certain that Farley's was a rhetorical question, watched amazed while a waiter dressed in white tie served him an artichoke stuffed with chicken salad. Amazed, because if someone had read his mind only minutes before, he would have known that that was exactly what David was longing to have for lunch. When Farley, the man of the people, was served a rare cheeseburger, he sent it back because it needed "a little more fire."

"I mean, this'll really make you puke," Farley said. "He's buying a fucking movie studio."

"Who is?" David asked. He was waiting to begin his salad until Farley's burger returned, but he could already tell, merely by looking at the chopped chicken peeking out of the artichoke, that it contained too much mayonnaise.

"Billy," Farley said—which was his rebellious way of referring to his father, whom he always called "father" when he was present. "For seven hundred million bucks. And a lot of it is going to be his own money, the asshole. That's the perfect business for him to get into. Full of phony bullshitters just like him. I mean why do people go into show business? To get their name in the paper? He already has that every day. To get laid? He swears that he's madly in love with my mother."

"How about to make more money?" David asked, and ran his teeth over an outside leaf of the artichoke, then discarded it into the bowl at his right hand which had been placed there for that purpose.

"How much more money does the asshole need? You see, that's what I mean about him." Farley's burger arrived and he lifted the bread and examined it with a discerning eye. Then he made a paste of some Dijon mustard and a little bit of ketchup, smeared it generously on the back of the bun, picked up the burger, took a bite, which he chewed and swallowed, and then said to David with a twinkle in his eye: "Don't you just hate airplane food?"

\*     \*     \*

Kate Coburn walked across the tarmac toward them with a leggy stride that held so much self-confidence, it was hard to believe she was Farley's sister.

"Look at the gazongas on this broad," Farley said to David, who remembered how the last time he'd visited the Coburn family, Kate, then seventeen, had rubbed her bare foot over his loafered one all during dinner. At nearly twenty, what had been her pent-up little-girlness was in full bloom.

"Class," she said. "My brother's got real class."

"At least he has enough to bring *me* home with him," David joked.

"True." Kate grinned, and gave David a hug that offered him higher hopes for the weekend than he'd had on the airplane.

"No bags?" Kate asked her brother, who carried only a small shaving kit, compared to David's fine leather carry-on.

"No clothes," Farley answered.

"Tonight's black tie," she told him.

"Thank God I got six of 'em in my closet," Farley said, "and that I don't wear underwear."

"You're gross. Billy's having this party for you, you know. In honor of your graduation."

"Ahh, fuck Billy."

Farley nodded to the chauffeur as the three of them climbed into the back of Bill Coburn's long white limousine.

"Freud notwithstanding," Kate said, "I have no interest in fucking Billy. Let's watch *Days of Our Lives*." She turned on the television in the back seat of the car. "I love *Days of Our Lives*," she said. "When Billy buys the movie studio, I want him to invite the whole cast to the first party he has, so I can meet them."

David sat between the two siblings. As the car sped toward the Coburns' estate, he was amused.

To call the party a *party* was an understatement. It was an extravaganza, with too much food and too many flowers and women who wore too much jewelry, and David was having the time of his life, dancing with Kate Coburn, who wore a pale pink strapless dress and no jewelry, and was so exquisite that if he hadn't felt her warm body close to his, he would have thought she was a vision.

"I'd like to raise a congratulatory toast to my son," Bill Coburn said from the bandstand, raising a glass of champagne. Everyone tried to pretend not to notice that Farley wasn't anywhere to be seen in the huge party tent that had been built over the outdoor tennis court. Instead, they all raised their glasses, too, as Coburn went on: "Who will be graduating from the Wharton School of Finance in two weeks, if I pay his library fines." Everyone laughed. "And to his best friend, a fine young man who will also be graduating and who honors us with his presence, David Malcolm."

"Fars is in his room smoking a joint," Kate said between her teeth to David as she squeezed his arm, and the guests all raised their glasses and drank the toast. The music started again.

"We'll probably be moving to Los Angeles," she told him, as they spun back onto the floor. She brushed a chestnut-brown curl away from her eyes, where it had fallen when they twirled. David remembered thinking how stupid strapless dresses were when some of the girls at school wore them. On Kate, a strapless dress was a work of art.

"Will you show me around when we do?"

"Gladly," David told her.

"I hate the thought of making all new friends. . . ."

"You'll do it easily," he assured her.

"And dating . . ." She looked into his eyes.

"Some very lucky man will probably fill your dance card the first day you arrive," he said.

"I want it to be you, David," she told him.

"That's very sweet," he said.

"Not sweet. I do," she said. "My brother loves you and my father thinks the world of you, and . . . do you like me at all?"

Oh boy, what a question, with the love songs playing and that pale pink dress. Strapless.

"Kate . . ."

"Come for a walk," she said. In a moment they were on their way out of the party tent. A walk. He let her lead him across the floor to the exit. Just before they stepped out through the flap of the tent, David was sure he caught a glance exchanged between Kate and her father, who was on the far side of the crowd but managed to catch her eye nevertheless. There was something about the exchange that unnerved him, though not enough to make him let go of Kate's hand, which pulled him toward the swimming cabana and the dressing room, where dressing was not what she had in mind.

The bubbling wall-to-wall tank of darting, diving tropical fish created a strange backdrop to the man as he sat on the white sofa in his den across from David. David sat on an identical white sofa. The Giacometti coffee table between them held the recently brought-in tea service, but neither of the men had any interest in the tea.

"David, one of the reasons I'm having this discussion with you at all is because experience has taught me that you speak the truth, not to mention that your own relationship with your father seems to be exemplary. Now, would you like me to tell you about my relationship with *my* father?" David said nothing. His mind wandered to his own father and how different Bill Coburn was from Rand Malcolm in every way.

"Believe me, I made Farley look like a model child. I began carousing with prostitutes when I was eleven. Once, in anger, I set fire to a building my father not only owned but was inhabiting at the time. Happily, my father's will to change me and his unerring patience prevailed and turned me around. When I was nineteen, I was in the South of France, about to marry a French girl of fifteen, when he called to say he was making me a partner in his oil business. I left the girl and came home, having no idea what that meant, but confronted with so much responsibility, I decided that maybe I ought to take it on. And by the time I was twenty-one and my father died I was able to take over the business completely. The rest is history." He stopped speaking and looked at David as if to let him know it was his turn to say something.

"Sir," David said, obliging. "I have this terrible suspicion that what you're about to tell me is that you're going to try that method of instilling responsibility in Farley, and that's why you're buying a movie studio."

"David, you're a very smart young man. Smart enough to know that the reason I'm planning to buy the Hemisphere Corporation is because it's a good deal. I'll make a fortune, no matter what happens to the movies we make. That said, we both know that my relationship with my son could use some shoring up, to say the least. And if the lengths to which he goes to alienate me are any indication of the scope of his imagination, he has enormous potential as a creative force in the film industry."

"You're making a big mistake," David said, and then paused before going on, because he was stopped by how much he had just sounded like his father when he said that.

"Mr. Coburn, forgive me. I appreciate your love for your son and your desire to do for him the kind of thing your father did for you, but my experience of your son speaks to that effort's being a colossal waste of time."

"So does mine, David, so does mine." Coburn sighed and stared thoughtfully, lower lip protruding, the way David had seen him do on the nights Farley had run angrily from the restaurants in Philadelphia.

"My plan," he said after a while, "would be to start him right at the top. Make him head of production. Darryl Zanuck did that for his son, you know."

"And then fired him," David said. "Not to mention the fact that by the time his father hired him, Richard Zanuck had already produced a few movies. Farley never even *goes* to the movies. If you give him that job, the studio will go under in a matter of months. Besides, I think it's a moot point. Farley won't say yes to it. He just won't show up."

An intercom buzzed. Coburn ignored it.

"Maybe," he said after a while. "But you could be wrong, David. Because I believe I have something going for me that Père Zanuck didn't."

"I'm sure that's true, sir," David said, smiling. He liked this "crazy bastard," which is what his father would have called Bill Coburn. Rand Malcolm's advice to the man about how to handle Farley would have certainly been in his traditional five words or less: Kick him in the ass.

"But specifically to what do you refer?" David asked.

"You."

"Pardon? I was asking about your advantage over Darryl Zanuck."

"And that was my answer. You. What I mean by that is that despite my son's frequent rude behavior, I truly believe that the reason he hasn't overdosed or been institutionalized or murdered in the last two years he's spent in Philadelphia is largely because of his friendship with you."

"You give me entirely too much credit," David said, but he remembered how more than once during those two years he'd thought to himself that having Farley as a roommate, all the time he required, all the attention he insisted on, was like having a full-time job.

"Maybe," Coburn said, "but you see, I believe if *you're* there . . ."

"If I'm where?"

"At the studio as well. Let's say as head of marketing? I have no qualms about that, David, mind you. I have a copy of your stellar transcript in my desk drawer, not to mention the lessons you've certainly learned just by virtue of being your father's son."

"I'm flattered," David said, "but I—"

"Don't be," Coburn said, "it's purely selfish."

"Mr. Coburn—"

"Bill."

"I thank you for your confidence in me, but your son and I, albeit clever, are two young punks right out of business school."

"What makes you think you know any less about it than the geniuses who are running it now? In that business the only thing that's for certain is that nobody knows a goddamned thing." Then his eyes lit up. "You know, the more I think about it, I kind of like the idea of it. You kids take over and show those guys what-for."

David smiled at the pictures that were running through his head. He and Fars in some plush office at a movie studio. Running the place. The same studio where his mother had starred so many years ago. Wouldn't that be an irony? The only thing Coburn had said that made any sense was that the movie business, for the most part, was a roll of the dice. Guesswork. No one had ever been right all the time, or even most of the time. But the rest . . . putting him and Farley at the helm. Preposterous. If he even tried telling the story of this offer to his father, Mal would stop him after the first sentence and refuse to listen to the rest. "The guy's a horse's ass," he would say.

David was searching his mind for a way to get out of all this gracefully, when Bill Coburn stood.

"You don't have to answer now," he said. "Let's go hit some tennis balls."

Great, David thought. A little more time to formulate his polite no. As they walked across the lawn toward the tennis court, which had been converted in the early morning from the candlelit, flower-filled ballroom of the night before, Coburn said his last word on the subject. "I think it would be great to see you two kids beat the hell out of the faggots and kikes who are running that town."

David killed him on the tennis court. A few hours later he stood in the huge Mexican-tiled shower with his eyes closed, feeling the jets from all four sides beat against him, when he heard the shower door open.

"I hope like hell it's Kate," he said.

"Well then, I guess it ain't your day, asshole," Farley answered.

"I've lived with you for two years," David said, wiping the water out of his eyes with his fingers. "I can't believe it took you this long to get friendly. But then, you've always been a little slow."

"Don't fall in love with my sister, shit-heel, because once we're running Hemisphere Studios, we'll get all the pussy we can eat, and then you'll regret it."

David turned off the faucets, reached for the thick white towel that was hanging on the door, and dried off while Farley lifted himself up onto the counter between the sinks and perched there.

"Fars, I distinctly recall you telling me not twenty-four hours ago that the movie business was full of lowlifes, publicity hounds, and whoremongers," he said, noticing in the mirror that he probably should get a haircut as soon as he got back to Philadelphia.

"You rang?" Farley said, grinning. A grin that had nothing to do with happiness. A grin David had seen him assume to mask his pain when his father was around.

"Hey, Malcolm, how long've you known me? You think I'm gonna get a job this good anytime anyplace from anybody else as long as I live? And my old man is right. Nobody knows what they're doing in show business, so I've got as good a chance as anybody else." David wrapped the towel around his waist now and combed his hair. Farley watched for a while, then said, "Davey, we could have the time of our lives. Imagine it, the family business. You could even be *in* the family. Kate is bananas over you. Say the word and you could probably be my brother.''

Kate. The look she'd shared with her father. The old man figured the only way he could pull this off with Farley was if David came along for the ride.

"Fars, it's an impossible game. You can't win. If your father wants to buy the studio, that's one thing, but you have to take a lesser job, a learning job, and see how it's done first. Then, when you know something, you move up. Or work somewhere else for a while. Learn all you can. Then reevaluate. Both you and Billy are setting you up to fail. Don't do it.''

"I guess that means you won't be joining me?" Farley said, the forced grin still on his face.

"I'll be at Rainbow Paper," David said.

"Starting at the bottom?" Farley asked. David heard the sneer in his voice.

"Pretty damn near," he answered.

That night Bill Coburn had dinner brought to him in his room, and never emerged to say good-night. At about seven-thirty, after a loud blast from a honking horn outside the front gate, a perfumed and flushed Kate, whom David hadn't seen since the night before, came flying down the front steps and rushed out the door, shouting back, "Got a hot date," and was gone. And Farley was drunk and asleep by eight. David, who was served his dinner alone by the pool, read a few magazines and retired early. On Sunday a quiet Farley drove him to the airport to put him on the commercial flight he was taking back to Philadelphia.

"So I'll see you at the graduation, my friend," was all he said, punching David on the arm when the flight was called. Then he turned on his heel, and David watched him walk a round-shouldered walk out of the airport. He never came to graduation.

"Name's on your office door," Rand Malcolm told his son, by way of congratulating him after the commencement exercises.

"Thanks, Dad," David said. They were walking toward the waiting car, on their way to lunch.

"You start work on Monday. Want to know which department?"

David shook his head no. "I'll let you surprise me," he said.

A few weeks later, one July day, David read in *The New York Times* that Kate Coburn, twenty, had married Roger Hunt, forty-two, to whom she'd been engaged for a year. In August he read in *The Wall Street Journal* that, due to an inability to come to terms, negotiations between William Coburn and the Hemisphere Corporation had broken off.

# R.J.'S STORY

## 1973

When R.J. got back from the newsstand she parked the car, then looked at little Jeffie, who was sound asleep in the back seat. Eyes tightly closed. Breathing evenly. He clutched his yellow thermal blanket in his tiny fist and, in his sleep, rolled the tattered satin edging between his thumb and forefinger. Instead of waking him, R.J. lifted him carefully out of the car, hoping he would stay asleep just a little while longer so she could look through the stack of magazines she'd just bought to try to find a place to sell some of her poetry.

Arthur was in New York for a few days—no, maybe it was Nashville. Anyway, he would call her tonight and tell her he missed her and where he was staying, and what time she could pick him up at the airport on Sunday. Meanwhile, she had plenty to do. The shower drain was stopped up; the refrigerator bulb was out; the garage was a mess. She turned the key in the front door and pushed it open with her shoulder, then stood in the foyer of their rented house looking into the ugly ornate gold-framed mirror their landlady had pointed out to them as one of the "fine antiques" with which the house had been decorated.

Her face was flushed from the Valley heat *and*, she noticed, very round. Probably because, though three and a half years had gone by, she had never lost all of the weight she'd gained during her pregnancy. Some of it showed around her cheeks and what used to be her waist. Maybe she was eating too much from frustration, which was something she had read in several articles that women did who weren't happy in their lives.

She frowned at herself, then smiled what wasn't really a smile, just lips moving back so she could examine her teeth. That rule of frustration definitely didn't apply to her. She was ecstatic. To begin with, she had her wonderful husband, Arthur, who worked hard and adored her and their son. Her parents would have loved Arthur. His parents were crazy about her. And he respected and supported her writing career.

At first she and Arthur had been romantically poor. Struggling to get ahead. Arthur working in the record business and R.J. working during the day, sometimes at three different jobs to help keep the household afloat. Answering the telephone at a beauty parlor in Beverly Hills, showing prospective tenants through the models at a condominium complex in Hollywood, wrapping gifts at a children's shop in the Valley. There were times when she sat across from Arthur at Steak 'n Stein, sawing away at the tough slab of meat that came with salad and a baked potato for under three dollars, and thought about Rifke. How much her mother had wanted her to marry Alvin Feld and be a doctor's wife. The ultimate.

She grinned when she remembered two of her mother's homilies and the way Rifke shook her nicotine-stained finger when she offered them. "Ven poverty valks in the door, love flies out the vindow," and the ever-popular "It's just as easy to love a rich man as it is to love a poor man."

Rifke. She hadn't practiced what she preached. She loved Louie Rabinowitz with blind devotion, and he was a man so worried about money that he never bought a new pair of shoes until Atillo, the shoemaker on Murray Avenue, looked at the old pair he'd already remade twenty times and said, "I'ma can't save you sole no more." It was an announcement that always sent both her parents into shrieks of laughter. Her parents' marriage had convinced R.J. that struggling with someone you loved was okay. The way it was supposed to be.

Late at night, when Arthur slept, she crept into the closet-sized kitchen of their tiny apartment, made a cup of tea, then sat on the living room floor and worked on a speculative script. It was cold and lonely and not easy to be funny when she knew she had to be awake soon to hurry to her morning job, but she moved ahead slowly, one page a night, sometimes just a few thoughts, reading them at breakfast to Arthur, who always loved her ideas, laughed at her jokes.

Then Arthur got a new job, at A&M Records, and he started making a nice living. They rented a small house in the hills and bought some furniture. They went to concerts and to evenings at the Troubador and met exciting new people. One night at an A&M party, R.J. met a man who told her he managed musical performers. The manager said that his performers needed what they called "special material" for their acts.

Special material. That meant funny songs and jokes to tell in between the songs. Exactly the kind of thing R.J. had written in Pittsburgh for Mona Feldstein Friedman. The day after the party R.J. had sent the manager a copy of the material she'd done for Mona and the first act of her unfinished speculative script, and crossed her fingers. A week later he'd called her and said he loved them. Since then she'd sold two songs to John Davidson and one to Charo for their nightclub acts, and next week she was going to have a meeting with a man who was producing a nightclub act for Telly Savalas. It wasn't playwriting, or screenwriting, or television writing yet. But it was work as a professional writer, and it was comedy, and that was a beginning. And Arthur was proud of her. Without a doubt her life being married to him was so much better than anything she'd ever had before.

This cute little house. This angelic little boy. She rubbed her nose against Jeffie's soft cheek, then carefully placed him and his yellow blanket down on the living room sofa, ran out to the car and brought in the magazines, put those on the living room floor, and plopped herself down there to read. The only noise breaking the silence of her Hollywood Hills nest was the sound of the automatic pool sweep, clicking and swooshing out there, like a plastic octopus rubbing against the tile. Jeffie might stay asleep for another hour. It was her chance to get work done.

Work. It was hard to think of writing as work. Especially the jokes and special lyrics. It felt like just a grown-up version of what she'd done in Pittsburgh. Only now she was making really really good money for it. Money Arthur would ooh and ahhh over as his wife's "private little income." Already, from the few songs and sketches she'd sold, she earned more than she had during the first few years of their marriage in all of her jobs combined. And Arthur was doing great at A&M. "On the way up." Destined to be a big success in the music business.

Thank God, R.J. thought again and again, that she hadn't married Alvin Feld, that she had listened to her instinct to move to Los Angeles, and not stayed in Pittsburgh to get lost in the role of being the wife of a man who thought her wanting to write was a dumb fantasy.

With Arthur she could be a wife and a mother and work too. As long as everything in the house was taken care of and Jeffie was happy, she could do anything she wanted. Of course, entertaining was important, too, and she was learning how to be very good at that. So when Arthur wanted to have anybody over from A&M, he could really be proud of the dinners she served. She had taken a vegetable class at Design Research and an all-around cooking class at Beverly Hills High School when she was pregnant.

It was fun for her to be able to do those things. For the first time in her life she didn't have to appear at a job all day every day. And she was able to write. Sometimes. When there weren't a million other things to do. But of course, pretty soon Jeffie would be in school. Well, not pretty soon—in a year and a half he'd be in school, and then she'd really get some writing done.

*Cosmopolitan*. Maybe she'd try to write something and submit it to *Cosmopolitan*. She really had to psych these magazines out and determine what kind of material they wanted. Sexy. Articles in *Cosmopolitan* were sexy and mostly for single girls. "How to Tell if a Man Who Won't Show His Emotions Really Loves You." Who cares, she thought, stopping to look at a lingerie ad, and realizing that, since Jeffie's birth, she hadn't bought one piece of new underwear. Horoscopes. Pisces. Always the romantic dreamer, this month brings Neptune's Nymphet a new love. Thanks anyway. Maybe *Mademoiselle*. She was about to open it when Jeffie awakened with a start and began to cry.

"No, my love. No, Mummy's sweet boy. Don't cry," she said, going to the sofa and sitting next to him. He put his sleepy face down on her shoulder and hummed the little baby song he always hummed when he first woke up. God, she loved him so much. More every minute. She would give him lunch, then take him to the park and play. She could look at the magazines tonight when he was asleep.

That night, the phone jangling on the bedside table next to her jarred her awake.

"Arj?"

"Hmm?"

"Did I wake you? It's only nine o'clock there, isn't it?"

"Hi, honey," she said sleepily. She was lying on her bed surrounded by all the magazines, which she still hadn't read. Between lunch and dinner there had been too many things to do around the house and Jeffie needed her to play and . . .

"How come you're asleep so early? What'd you do all day?"

She didn't remember.

"How's Nashville?" she asked, instead of answering.

"It's great," he said. "Remember I told you about that Bluegrass group here that I'm courting? Well, the lead singer is this girl who is so dynamic I've never seen anything like it. She's going to be a huge star. The group is ordinary, but the only way I'm going to get to her is to take them all. Eventually she'll get the picture and dump them but . . ."

He was rattling on, but R.J. could tell he really didn't care about the information he was giving her. He was just trying out on her the pitch he was going to give his boss tomorrow about the group he'd discovered.

"So what do you think?" he asked when he'd finished his spiel.

"Sounds great," she said.

"How's my son?" he asked.

"Wonderful."

"Does he miss me?"

"Of course," she said.

"Do you?"

"A lot," she said.

"Me too, baby. See you Sunday at American at five," he said. "Oh, and I've been eating like a horse, so make dinner something really light. Okay?"

"Okay."

"Love you."

"Love you."

Arthur. She loved his sweetness. The way he called her

*baby*. The way he was working so hard to build a future for them.

On Sunday night, after Jeffie was asleep, they had lemon chicken and carrot salads and sourdough bread and white wine, and when she unpacked his suitcase, at the bottom in a paper bag was a Grand Ol' Opry T-shirt he'd brought back for her, and he grinned when she wore it to bed.

"What does our week look like?" he asked her after he'd turned off the light and was curling his body against hers.

"We're going to the Grammys on Tuesday, and the Kalishes are coming for dinner on Wednesday, and on Thursday, Dinah wants me to go to some C.R. group with her. It doesn't meet until eight, so I'd still be here for dinner, and if you wouldn't mind putting Jeffie to bed, that would really be great." She lay there in the dark, wondering if Arthur's silence was because he didn't want her to go to a C.R. meeting. If he thought it was stupid. If he was about to say "C.R. group? Get serious, baby. Everyone knows that your C. is already plenty R.'d," or some other Arthur comment like that. Then she realized that the reason he wasn't saying anything was because he was sound asleep.

"I'm here because I hated getting my legs and armpits and crotch waxed so I wouldn't offend Herbie."

Some of the women cheered and some laughed, and Jessica Norman, who was wearing a sleeveless blouse, held up her arms and proudly revealed her bushy armpits. "I'm never removing another hair from my body again," she said, and there was another cheer.

"Next," someone said.

"I'm Ellen Calter, and I'm here because my husband always gave me papers and said, 'Sign these, honey,' and I did, and honey left me for his secretary and I had signed away everything to him without realizing it."

Ellen Calter sat down, but this time there wasn't any cheering, just the clicking of tongues.

The meeting was at Joanna Pollack's house. Joanna was a painter who lived with Ryan Adler, a sculptor, and the white-walled modern house was a gallery for their art.

Dinah and Joanna had gone to Bard College together in New York. The large assortment of women sat on every available surface in the living room. Sofas, pillows, hearth, floor. If one more woman walked in the front door, there wouldn't be a place to put her.

"By the way"—Joanna Pollack spoke up—"as we're going around the room, when we get to you, if the real reason you're here is not because of some burning desire to raise your consciousness but because somebody dragged you here, you can say that too. Next."

"My name is R.J. Misner," R.J. said, "and I'm here because Dinah Goldsmith Weinberg dragged me here."

She saw two women exchange looks, as if to say "Isn't she naïve," and suddenly Dinah stood and spoke in a voice that surprised R.J.

"Bullshit," she said. "Next to me you're the most oppressed woman I know. It doesn't count if you have a career because your husband lets you. That's a privilege, not a right. You married Arthur for the same reason I married Ted. Because they said it was okay with them if we worked. Why did we *ask* them? Did Arthur ask you if he should quit his job and stay home to take care of the house and the baby?"

Christ, R.J. thought. Look at Dinah. She is really bugged. Veins forming a V were bulging out on her forehead.

"Isn't it true?" Dinah asked her.

R.J. was embarrassed. All the women were looking at her now. She never would have agreed to come to a C.R. meeting, which was all Dinah ever talked about anymore, if she'd known she was going to be attacked this way by her best friend.

"I don't . . ."

"It's insidious," Joanna Pollack offered, in a much nicer voice than Dinah's.

"But I'm happy," R.J. said.

"So were some of the slaves in the South," someone across the room said.

She was about to say "I don't feel like a slave. I love my life," when she looked around the room at the faces looking at her. Many of them wore smiles. Knowing smiles.

"Let's go on," Joanna Pollack said.

The woman next to R.J. stood.

"I'm Reva Weingarten. I put my husband through medical school, internship, and residency. Now he has a thriving practice and I want to go back and get my associate arts degree and he laughs at me.''

R.J. felt a tap on her arm from Dinah, who offered her a piece of chewing gum with a look that asked *Are we still friends?* R.J. nodded and took the gum, which she slid out of the silver wrapping paper. Then she put the paper in her purse because she didn't see anywhere to throw it. Someone was hissing and booing about Reva Weingarten's husband. R.J. looked at her watch. It was only eight-thirty. She would never make it through this whole meeting.

She thought about Arthur putting Jeffie to bed right now and how adorable the two of them had looked, just before she left tonight to pick up Dinah. They were both naked in the bathtub. Jeffie standing. Arthur making a waterfall for him from a yellow paper cup. Jeffie's little fist stopping the stream of water as he squealed with glee.

"Say bye to Mommy," Arthur said. Jeffie had been too intrigued by the water to look up.

"Ted gave me so much shit I couldn't believe it," Dinah had said when she got into R.J.'s car. "He's so threatened when I go to these meetings, it's a joke. What did Arthur say?"

"Nothing." She didn't mention that when she told Arthur where she was going he had been sound asleep.

"Oh, c'mon. Arthur? He didn't make some joke?"

"No joke."

"Amazing," Dinah said.

It had occurred to R.J. as she had walked out the door earlier, that Arthur thought she was on her way to have a "girls' dinner," which is what he called it when she and Dinah made plans every now and then to get together without their husbands. And chat. It wasn't that she was afraid to tell him where she was going, which is what Dinah thought. It was that when she *did* tell him, he'd been sleeping, and then she'd just never bothered to . . .

"Arthur always says that every time I go into an unfamiliar experience I should pretend that I'm an anthropologist," R.J. said.

"Meaning what?" Dinah asked, pulling down the visor in front of her so she could look into the mirror behind it and fluff her freshly permed hair. "That you're not a part of it? Just an observer?"

"Well, it gives me an objectivity about things," R.J. answered. They had been driving down Ventura Boulevard. R.J. loved Ventura Boulevard. Dozens and dozens of little shops. It seemed as if there were new ones every week. Each with a story to go with it, like charms on a charm bracelet.

"Yeah, that's just his way of making sure that you set yourself apart and don't take it seriously," Dinah told her, and put the visor back up.

I'm *not* involved, R.J. thought now, looking around the room. I understand what these women are saying, but I'm not involved. Joanna Pollack was reading an article by Robin Morgan, and R.J. remembered when Robin Morgan was a little pigtailed actress who played Dagmar on *I Remember Mama*. She had watched it a few times on a Friday night, at Uncle Shulke's house after *Shabbes* dinner.

When the meeting was over, a blond woman with long straight hair stood and said, "I thank God that I found you people. I thought I was losing my mind." A few of the others stood and embraced her, and many of the other women were wiping their eyes from the emotion. Women were talking animatedly to one another and R.J. felt as out of it as she had in grade school. Inadequate. In the car on the way home she felt a distance from Dinah, who opened the car door to get out the second R.J. pulled up outside her apartment building, as if she couldn't wait to get out of the car. Then she turned and said, "Sorry if I was too tough on you," and was gone.

"You see, what you have to remember about Dinah," Arthur said in bed that night, after doing all the jokes he would have done on Sunday night if he'd heard her tell him where she was going, "is that she'll jump with both feet into whatever's happening." He was flipping channels on the television as he talked. "I mean, she was one of those people who dropped acid seven or eight years ago. Do you get my point?"

R.J. was making a grocery list.

"Baby?"

"Mmm," she said. But she wasn't sure what one thing had to do with the other.

\*　　\*　　\*

Harvey Lembeck's comedy workshop met every other Monday night in a drafty old room, upstairs from the editing department at Columbia Pictures, and from the minute she walked in the door at seven, when it began, until past midnight when it was over, R.J. was afraid. Afraid she wouldn't be called on to get up and work, afraid she *would* be called on to get up and work, afraid when she got up she wouldn't be funny. Afraid, afraid, afraid. Why was she doing this? She didn't want to be a performer. But it was a way for her to try out new material, to meet other writers, to hear what was funny out loud instead of just in her head, so every other Monday night she forced herself out the door. If Arthur was home on those nights he put Jeffie to bed. If he wasn't, R.J. hired Cindy, a teenager from the neighborhood whom Jeffie liked.

Comedy workshop. She had to be funny if she wanted to continue to stay in it. Already she had seen a few people drop out, discouraged by their own performances in the group. And worse yet, a few had been asked to leave when Harvey didn't think their work was up to par. It was a thrill for R.J. to walk into the lobby at Columbia and see the big black-and-white photos by the guard's desk of Katharine Hepburn and Spencer Tracy and Gregory Peck and know that those people had walked right in those same doors, nodded to the guard, who buzzed the door open for them and let them pass, just as he did for R.J. Rabinowitz Misner. From Pittsburgh.

"You're up, peanut," Harvey Lembeck would say. It was a nickname he had given her the first night she'd attended the group. "You get up and work with Billy. You're in a movie house and the couple behind you are having a fight and won't shut up." Or "You're robbing a bank and the bank teller won't take you seriously, no matter what you do. Frank, you're the teller." Or "You walk into what you are certain is your apartment and there is a guy there you've never seen who swears it's his apartment." Subjects for the improvisation.

Her mind would race almost as fast as her pulse was speeding, and the improvisation would start. Sometimes it was deadly. She could feel it flopping from the first line, dying, falling dead from the moment she opened her mouth. Other times, what she said and did would come out so funny that it was all she could do not to start laughing herself when the rest of the group laughed. On those nights she would fly home to Arthur the way she had when they'd first met at the apartment hotel, and pray while she drove that he was still awake, so she could relive her excitement by telling him everything she remembered about how the jokes and sketches had worked. Arthur would laugh and tell her he was proud of her for being what he was certain was "the best one in the class."

Sometimes celebrity guests came to watch the work. Harvey Lembeck knew everyone. Garry Marshall, Harvey Korman, Elaine May, Jerry Lewis. Then the pressure was really on. Having to get up in front of those people. After class they would answer questions, and R.J. was always too tongue-tied even to ask any.

She had been in the workshop for only three months when Harvey Lembeck called her at home. "Peanut?" he said when she answered. Why was he calling her? Even though she was home, in the safety of her kitchen, it made her nervous to hear his voice. He was the teacher. The arbiter of humor. His approval meant so much to her, in that barnlike poorly lit room at Columbia, that her mind went into full alert now, wondering if she had to be funny over the telephone with him. All she could think of was hello, and she stuttered saying that.

"You interested in a writing job?" he asked.

All the silly answers people in the group gave to obvious questions raced through her mind. Is the Pope Catholic? Does a bear shit in the woods? Or, as one of the guys had said a few weeks before, Does the Pope shit in the woods? A writing job. "Yeah," was all she could say.

"It's over at Dick Clark's company," he said. "I recommended you already but I figured I ought to ask you before I had them call you. I think it's for some special about the fifties."

"Yeah?" she said again. Great wit is my specialty, she would tell Dinah later when she reported the conversation and the news that Harvey Lembeck had called her at home because he'd recommended her for a writing job. Arthur. After she thanked Harvey Lembeck at least twenty times, she got off the phone and tried Arthur at the Warwick Hotel in New York. He had left this morning and should be there by now. He wasn't and she left a message that she'd called. Someone from Dick Clark's office was supposed to call her this afternoon to schedule a meeting sometime later in the week. A meeting for a television special. She couldn't wait to tell Arthur.

He called her at ten that night. "I'm going to have to stay here all week," he said. He sounded tired and irritated. "There are three different acts I have to see, and they have gigs every other day, so I might as well just hang out and get them all over with at once. How are you doing, baby?" he asked.

A long time later, when she thought back on this telephone conversation, she remembered that what she wanted to answer was "I'm fabulous. I'm thrilled. I'm so excited I can't stand it. Tomorrow I have an interview to write a television special." But she didn't. She didn't mention a word about it to him in that phone call or in any of the phone calls with him every night that week. On Thursday night when he called, instead of telling him how she had wowed Bill Lee, the producer of the Dick Clark special, with some of her material, and instead of telling him that, wonder of wonders, she actually had gotten the job, her first television job, hooray, she talked to him about Jeffie, and the Tiny Tots group she went to with him at West Hollywood Park, and that she'd had the front doorbell fixed. And she decided that the reason she wasn't saying anything to Arthur on the phone about it was because it would be so much better to tell him in person and see how excited he was for her.

Several times over the few years they'd been married, especially since Jeffie was born, they had talked about getting help in the house. A combination house-cleaner/babysitter. If she could continue to get television jobs, they could really afford it. On Friday she had gone to an agency that specialized in domestic help and found a woman who would come in every morning and straighten up the house and be with Jeffie. In addition, R.J. would pay Cindy the babysitter to come by for a few hours after school to be with him too. When Arthur got back from New York, she would dazzle him with the way she had pulled everything together so she could be ready to start work in two weeks. For seven weeks. Five of the weeks, the writers would be working in offices at NBC, and two of the weeks would be in Philadelphia at the original studio from which *American Bandstand* had been televised in the fifties.

There was always something sexy about Arthur's return. They both knew it and felt it. And R.J. would prepare for it by piling cookbooks on the breakfast table that morning and ploughing through them until she found something special to make. Then she would plop Jeffie into the car and, eager with anticipation, hurry to the market and the flower shop, and sometimes, like today, she'd even have Cindy come after school to be with Jeffie and then go and have her hair done.

"Wow," Arthur said, walking out to the curb at American Airlines where they always picked him up, and putting his arms around both R.J. and Jeffie, who stood waiting. "Look at my glamorous wife and my handsome kid." He got into the driver's seat while R.J. put Jeffie into the back, then slid into the passenger seat. "What's happening, you two?" he asked. Still R.J. didn't tell him. She would wait until he'd had a chance to relax and they were at dinner.

He was quiet the entire time, except to say that the sauce was a little too spicy. Finally, with dessert—fresh berries and cream—she told him. About the call from Harvey Lembeck, about how nervous she'd been at the interview at first, but then began to roll once she could tell that the producer really liked her material.

Arthur's eyes danced with pride when she told him how Harvey Lembeck's agent had offered to make the deal for her. Negotiate. And how much money he had managed to get her per week. All of this handled on her own. Not to mention how she'd hired the housekeeper, Manuela, who seemed really eager to have the job and who would start a week from now, to get oriented before R.J. started work.

"My wife," Arthur said grinning. There was a television commercial for some vitamin, maybe it was Geritol, where the husband listed all the things his wife accomplished in a day, then looked at the wife with pride and said the part that Arthur was about to say now. It was a little joke he and R.J. had. "I think I'll keep her."

"Now here's the part I'm not real sure about," she said, poking her spoon into a strawberry to cut it in half. "Two of the weeks are in Philadelphia, so shall I take Manuela and Jeffie with me, or shall I fly back on the weekends to be with him? I can do it either way, but I think taking him would probably be the best thing for him because . . ." She spooned the strawberry into her mouth and bit into it, tasting the tart red juice as it filled her mouth. Then she looked at Arthur's face. The pride was gone from his eyes and she wasn't sure what was replacing it. Fear? Anger?

"No," he said.

"Huh?"

"You're going to have to tell them you can't take the job."

Oh, a joke. R.J. smiled. He had to be kidding.

"Right," she said.

"I don't mind you working, but not out of town. I don't want my son staying in some hotel in Philadelphia. I want him here and you here when I get home." Not kidding.

"Arthur," R.J. said. This was impossible. This wasn't Arthur. "You can't be serious. You travel all over the country every week in service of your work. I'm talking about two tiny weeks. Don't be ridiculous."

"I want you to call them tomorrow and tell them you'll be glad to work on the show here in Los Angeles, but you have a small child and you can't go to Philadelphia. If they want you on those terms . . . fine."

"Arthur, I won't do that. I'm going to take the job, and go to Philadelphia too."

He was quiet. She looked down at her strawberries. Finally he spoke, in a voice that didn't even sound familiar. Didn't sound as if it came from him. Her husband. The man she thought she knew.

"This marriage won't survive it."

She didn't believe that. It was an empty threat. This wasn't something that destroyed a marriage. Where two people loved each other. Had everything going. Had a child they both adored. He was testing her. Without looking at him she got up from the table and took her dirty dishes to the kitchen. As she was putting them into the sink, she heard him say in that same voice, "I mean it."

Neither of them said another word that whole night. She bathed; he stared at the television. She did a crossword puzzle; he showered. He read; she turned off her light. He turned off his light; she got out of bed, went into the living room, and read the magazines she'd bought nearly a month before.

In the morning Jeffie's cries awakened her and she realized she'd slept on the sofa all night. Arthur had left for work. She dressed Jeffie, made him breakfast, took him for a long walk, washed the breakfast dishes, cleaned her room, did some laundry, and gave Jeffie lunch. At two-thirty, when she figured executives were back in their offices after lunch, she gave Jeffie a big stack of blocks to play with and called Bill Lee. While she waited for him to pick up the phone and take her call, she felt queasy. When he got on the telephone she told him that she couldn't go to Philadelphia, hoping he would say she could work on the show for the other five weeks.

He was sweet, but he sounded very busy, with the telephone ringing a lot in the background, and twice he apologized for having to put her on hold while he took other calls. But when he finally got back on the phone he said he was sorry and that one of these days he would use her on some other show. And then he had to rush off to go into a meeting.

Jeffie had fallen asleep, so R.J. went outside and sat at the pool for a long time, listening to the pool sweeper clicking and swooshing as it made its way around, sucking the algae from the tile.

The phone had probably rung six or seven times before she actually heard it, and when she did she got up and walked slowly toward the house, as if she were hoping the ringing would stop before she got there so she wouldn't have to speak to anyone. She picked it up in the kitchen.

" 'Lo?" she said softly.

"Hello?" A woman's voice said.

"Yes."

"R.J. Misner?"

"Yes."

"This is Reva Weingarten."

R.J. had no idea who that was.

"I'm calling because I'm trying to get some kind of head count for this Thursday. Do you know if you'll be coming to the C.R. meeting?"

Jeffie was waking. She could hear him calling her from the living room. The front doorbell rang. It was probably the plumber. She had called him this morning to come and look at the drain in the kitchen sink that was on the fritz. At least now she'd be able to do the lunch dishes that were sitting in a messy pile on the counter.

"Yes," R.J. said into the telephone. "I'll be there."

$A$s David Malcolm made a hard right and pulled his navy Jaguar sedan up the driveway toward the stately old house on Bellagio Road, the two women seated in the back of the car said, "Oh yes," in unison. The women were Babs, David's wife of two months, and Helen, his sister-in-law of same.

"Didn't I tell you?" said Daphy Woods, who was sitting in the front passenger seat so she would be more easily able to direct David to all the houses they were seeing that day. Daphy was a close friend's wife and had been a residential real estate broker for ten days. It was a career she'd decided on in order to keep herself from, as she put it, "going absitively bonkers" now that all the kids were in school. "But the inside is even more divine," she said. "With a kitchen that was in the Homes section of the *Times*, and when the Copeleys lived here it was in *Architectural Digest*."

David helped the ladies out of the car, and for a long moment even Daphy was quiet as they all stood looking at the house. Then, with Daphy in the lead, key in hand, they made their way across the lawn to the house. This is a mistake, David thought, and when Daphy, who stepped aside to let the clients enter the house first, as she'd been taught, turned back after she'd opened the door and saw the look on his face, she laughed nervously.

"Oh, c'mon, David," she said. "This is just for fun, you duck. I *know* you liked the one on Mandeville, but this one is my newest listing and I have to show it off."

Daphne Waverly Woods was a piece of work. She'd been married to David's close college friend Charlie since their freshman year in college. She talked endlessly, called everyone a duck, and admitted that all she knew about real estate was how to get from one house to the next. But when it came to the math and the money, she admittedly would rush home to Charlie and have him do all the paperwork for her. David and Babs were using Daphy as a broker for the same reason that the Marsdens were listing their Trousdale estate with her, and the Perrys had listed this big old barn, because she was Charlie's lovable wife.

Babs and her sister were already in the kitchen. David could hear their voices echoing back to the entry hall of the huge empty place. He walked in to see them admiring the woodwork on the cabinets. Babs was running her hand with the short shiny-buffed fingernails over the wood. What was she feeling for? She knew nothing about wood. Less about kitchens.

"Hon-bun, look at this amazing kitchen," Babs said.

David and Babs had been together for two years and she'd never cooked one meal. Either they went out, sent out, or he cooked.

"It's a kitchen all right," he said.

"Oh, Barbara, you know men don't give a good gosh darn about kitchens," said Babs's sister, with a conspiratorial glance at Daphy, who giggled in agreement. Babs's sister—who looked, sadly, like a much less attractive version of Babs but who wore the same hairdo and the same style of clothes in an unsuccessful effort to be the same type—linked arms with Babs, and with Daphne following behind them they walked out of the kitchen, through the crystal-chandeliered foyer, into the roller-skating-rink-size living room. David leaned against the kitchen counter staring blankly through the French doors to the forest behind the house. He was worrying about all the work he should be doing at the office. When Babsy called this morning and pleaded with him to come to lunch at the club and then house-hunting, just for a few hours, God knows why he didn't tell her it would have to wait until Saturday. Now he could hear his wife and his sister-in-law heading up the wide marble staircase.

"Daph," David said, walking into the living room, where Daphne was opening the drapes to reveal a glen of stunning lilac trees, "not that there's a chance in the world that I'm your customer, but how much is this place?"

"Two five," she said, "but confidentially, I think you could get it for two million. The seller is anxious. What do you think?"

"I think if I had a house·worth that much sitting unsold, 'anxious' wouldn't begin to describe me."

"David?" he heard Babs calling from upstairs. "You *have* to see the tile in the bathroom."

David and Daphy walked up the stairs. Babs stood at the top, eyes huge with excitement. Babsy. He loved her. She was beautiful and brilliant and she would have had her law degree by now if she hadn't dropped out of school "just to vegetate" for a while. Her perfect blond bob bounced around her neck—that adorable neck, the back of which he loved to kiss—and she walked ahead of all of them now into the master suite, which opened onto a porch that sat nestled in the luscious lilac trees.

"I am passionate for this house," she said, looking first at David and then at her sister, who said, "I love it too. It's perfect." And then at Daphy, who agreed. "Oh, yes. Perfect."

David took a deep breath. There was a frantic edge in Babs's voice when she said to Daphy: "Tell us all the statistics. I think it's us."

Before Daphy could say a word, David spoke, going to Babsy's side and putting an arm around her. Sometimes she was such a little girl. With all her education and sophistication, she still didn't have any sense about . . .

"Darling, this house is selling for two and a half million dollars," he said, certain that fact would make her gasp and they would be in the car in a minute on their way back to take a look at the perfect house in Mandeville Canyon for which the asking price was $850,000.

"So?" she said instead, extending her lower lip in that way David had, in the past, told her he loved. "I mean, I am Mrs. Malcolm now." David could see that even Babs's sister was embarrassed by that one.

"And that means?" David asked.

"That I can afford it," Babs said, with a little laugh he'd heard her use to mean *I'm only joking*. But she wasn't.

"It's wrong for us, Barbara," David said. Now he realized that she was very serious.

"Why?" Babs asked, face tense and looking as if she

might cry. He had never ever seen her cry. Daphne and his sister-in-law left the room so quickly that they nearly collided getting to the door.

"It's too big, it's too much to maintain, but most of all, it gives us nothing to look forward to. Where do you go if you have a house like this at our age?"

"You sound like your father."

"Goddamned right."

"Don't swear at me, David."

"Let's go," he said.

"No," she said. "I want to see the wine cellar."

"Fine," he said. "I'll be in the car."

"I hate Mandeville Canyon," she said. Her face looked mean now, as if she were talking about some vile enemy. "If there's a fire, you can't get out of the canyon at the top. I won't live there."

"Then we'll keep looking."

"Why won't you even . . ."

"Babs, you're acting like people you say you can't stand when *they* act like this."

"I'm going to see the wine cellar," she said, and breezed by him.

This will pass, he said to himself, and walked down the marble staircase. From somewhere in the house he could hear Daphy pointing out the features in what was probably the same voice she'd used when she was a docent at the Art Museum. He walked outside and got into his car to wait. Babsy would recover. She was probably just going through the adjustment that all new brides do. Not sure how to behave or what he expected of her. She was so young and all she knew about the world was the way she had seen her parents live, and her friends' parents.

The three women emerged from the house and got back into the car, and when he dropped them at their own cars at the parking lot at the club he got a kiss on each cheek and an invitation to dinner from Daphy, a pat on the hand from his sister-in-law that seemed almost sympathetic, and a curt goodbye from his wife.

His desk at the office was piled high with messages: the foreman of the mill in Mississippi, one of the corporate officers in New York. His father had left a message at nine and another at noon, and he had to return a call to the pilots and let them know he needed to fly to Canada on Monday and . . . His private line rang. Babs.

"Yes?"

"Why do you always sound angry when you answer? Honestly, David."

She was calling to apologize. She was a good person and she knew she had behaved badly, so now she would say "I'm sorry, Davey," and he'd say "Don't even think about it" and hope he could get her off the phone quickly so he could get back to work.

"My sister and I both agree that we should make an offer on the house on Bellagio," she said.

"No, Babs," he said.

"David, don't say no until you hear Helen's idea. It's brilliant." He could picture her, his bride: She was probably sitting outside their apartment on the little tiny balcony in her bathing suit. She'd been patient to put up with living in his too-small bachelor apartment with him.

"What's the brilliant idea?" he asked, shuffling the messages on his desk.

"We'll make a very low offer," she said, emphasizing each word as if she were telling him something profound. If her naïveté wasn't such a royal pain, it would almost be cute. Babsy. She was fixated on that goddamned barn of a house.

"I agree," he teased. "Let's offer them a measly two million two ninety-nine. Now *there's* a bargain if I've ever heard one."

"No," she said. "You heard Daphy say the seller was anxious. So we Jew them down. And maybe we could get it for under two million."

"Babsy," he said, as if to a child. "Let's forget the money. All right? We're talking about something else here."

His secretary walked in and put a note on the desk in front of him. A union boss from the Chatsworth, Georgia mill was on the phone. The workers were on strike and David needed to talk to this guy. Now.

"I have to go," he told her.

"Why? Finish what you were saying. Of course we're talking about money. I mean that house is perfect for us, David. Let's look at it again. Say that you will. I'm not saying we have to buy it, but just tell me that you'll look at it again."

"No."

"If I get pregnant right away, can we . . ."

"No."

Barbara Ashton Malcolm slammed the phone down on David Malcolm and he laughed to himself as he changed lines, realizing that after talking to his wife, talking to the union boss of his striking workers would be a relief.

The next two days and nights were filled with a Babsy he'd never seen and couldn't understand. She wanted to talk only about the house on Bellagio Road.

"The tile," she would rhapsodize, "the stairway, the porch off the bedroom."

"No," he said, penciling some changes into the draft of the annual report: "Regarding the aggressive development of the computer forms department . . ." By the time his workday was over at eight-thirty, he didn't want to go to the club for dinner, but Babsy had promised they would meet the Woodses there.

"Buying a place in Bel-Air, Malco?" Charlie Woods asked, boxing David on the arm. David could see, from the corner of his eye, that Daphy was elbowing Babs, and he knew that both of them were listening carefully for his answer.

"Not a chance," David said, and quickly changed the subject to Charlie's new law offices. Babs was sullen for the entire meal, in spite of Daphy's funny stories and giddy attempts to pull her out of it. All the way back to the apartment she was silent. In the morning, David woke with an aching neck and rolled over on his pen and the rough draft of the annual report he'd worked on until midnight, when the pouting Babs had fallen asleep wearing a black sleep mask that matched the black nightie he'd loved so much on their honeymoon.

It was seven-thirty. He was unusually late for his morning start. He had to get moving or he'd miss the timing on his East Coast calls. Babsy must be in the kitchen starting the coffee. It was the only thing she knew how to make. Naked and bleary-eyed, he walked into the bathroom, brushed his teeth, and turned on the shower. A three-by-five note card was scotch-taped to the mirror of the medicine cabinet. An apology, surely. He let the water run and walked closer to read Babs's flowery handwriting.

*I am moving in with my mother until you stop acting like such a Scrooge. I hate this cold awful side of you that doesn't even take my feelings into consideration. I hope I haven't made a mistake loving you and believing in you the way I have.*

*B.*

Impossible. He had known she was like a little girl in so many ways. But all the good ways. Her dependence on him, her need for his approval, and she was so goddamned bright. Top of her class at Harvard. He'd sat glowing at her graduation, in the back of Dunster House, watching her walk to the podium time and again to accept her awards. He had glowed with pride in her, the same way her parents had. And now this? It made no sense. He turned off the water and dialed his in-laws' number. Delia, the Ashton's black housekeeper, answered.

"She here, Mr. David, but she say to tell you she ain't talkin'."

"Deeeeee-liaaaa," he said in that way he did that always made the woman giggle.

"I'll go see what I c'n do," she said.

While he waited he put on a robe, went into the kitchen, where he picked up the wall phone and started some coffee. Finally Babs's icy voice spoke into the phone.

"Yes, David?" she said.

"This is preposterous," he said.

She didn't say a word.

"I can't believe you're going to behave this way. Sacrifice our happiness over some goddamned house."

"It seems to me that you're the one who's doing that. You're so immovable you won't even discuss it with me. All you do is say no to me as if I'm some child. Well, I'm not a child, David, I'm your wife."

His patience was flagging. "The first part of that sentence is obviously not true, and the second part won't be either unless you stop this and come home."

"Don't you threaten me."

"Barbara," he said. "This is getting dangerous. So I'm going to forget it ever happened and go to work now, and let's just proceed. I'll see you when I get home from work and we'll forget you ever acted this way. But I can't waste any more time on it. Goodbye." Then he hung up the phone, burned his hand on the coffee maker, took a fast shower, and went to work.

Once, in prep school, David, fearing his fate at sixteen might turn out to be driving the utilitarian beat-up family Chevy station wagon, wrote an essay entitled "Why I Should Have a Porsche." With the aid of friends he listed all the safety features of the car, with statistics from *Car and Driver* and Porsche advertising. He even cut out a picture of the car and pasted it on the front page. When he handed it to his father, Rand Malcolm put on his glasses, leafed through it, then threw the manuscript across the room and said to his son: "The goddamned thing's too long."

At lunch, when David told his father, with some embarrassment, about Babs's bad behavior, the older man scowled, took another bite of his sandwich and, when he'd chewed it and swallowed, said, "You have to educate her." Rand Malcolm knew Babsy's parents well and liked them. He admired the girl's intellect and her academic accomplishments. He approved the marriage, but also let David know as soon as he announced his plans that he himself had waited to marry until the sensible age of thirty-eight. And what if Babsy wouldn't change? David wanted to ask, but didn't. Clearly the expectation was that it was his job to get his wife to stop acting like a brat.

Two weeks went by. There were endless problems at the company to occupy his mind, not to mention his worry about what seemed to be his father's failing health since the previous week, when Mal's doctor had called David at home.

"You must urge your father to slow down," the doctor said. "He's killing himself."

So much to worry about that by the time he got home each evening and heated up the dinner that Berta, his father's cook, had sent over, David was ready to collapse, and the silent Babs-less apartment was almost a pleasure. Sometimes he would turn on the television set and just stare mindlessly as the shows went by. Carol Burnett, Patsy Dugan. Silly jokes, splashy colors, no thinking. Just what he needed.

Babs hadn't called once. He knew she was waiting for him to capitulate. You have to educate her, his father had said, obviously meaning *Don't acknowledge this kind of behavior*. He felt as if he were the parent of a spoiled child. One night

Daphy Woods called him under the guise of inviting him to her younger son's soccer game, but the call was obviously at Babsy's bidding.

"Don't you miss her?" Daphy pried.

"Daph," he said, "let's not discuss it."

At the end of three weeks he felt a great sadness. Despite her parents' objections, he and Babs had lived together for a year before the wedding. He really was lonely for her and missed the good times they'd had. Their trips together. The parties they'd given for their friends. The night they'd won the dance contest at the club. It was at the beginning of the fourth week, when he got out of the elevator in his garage on his way to work, that he was served with the divorce papers. He looked at them and then made a sound that was something between a gasp and a shocked laugh.

"Boy," he said aloud. "Some judge is going to get a real hoot out of this one." But when he got into his Jaguar and drove out into the morning to go to work, for a minute he sat at the stop sign, not sure if he should turn left or right to get to his office.

# BOOK FIVE

# R.J. and David

$T$he prison cells were filled with hollow-eyed wretched convicts. They leaned heavily against the bars, harassing the guards and taunting one another with catcalls and hoots. But in one tiny cell, far at the end of the row, one prisoner was oblivious to their cries. Thinking only of himself. Because that prisoner was having a conjugal visit with his wife after not having been with her in five years.

"Oh, baby," he said, "you sure look good to me. Bring yourself over here, and let's get together."

"Not tonight, darlin'," said the wife. "I got me one real bad headache."

The camera crew laughed. Patsy took a compact out of her purse and powdered her nose, and Freddy stood and walked toward her. The black-and-white striped prisoner's costume made him look even sillier than usual.

"A headache?" he growled. "On the first night we been together in five years?"

"Stop the tape," Patsy said, looking at the director. "That dumb pea-brain did it again." Then she turned to Freddy. "Don't you remember that you ain't supposed ta walk over to me on that line, ya big mess of turkey poop? I swear to God, you are the dumbest white man alive."

R.J., who had been sitting on a metal folding chair in the back row since seven in the evening, looked at her watch. It was one in the morning. This was the latest she'd been at the studio in weeks. The writing staff was doing well under her guidance and the material was working.

"*Meydele*," Eddie Levy had said to her yesterday when he called. "It kills me that you're working for that *meshugene* broad. No offense. But I hate to see it. At least Elfand, no-good bastard that he was, gave Patsy back some of the same kind of shit she dishes out. But you? She'll eat you for breakfast."

"You're sweet to worry about me, Eddie, but so far it's working out okay. And it sure pays the bills. How's by you?"

"By me I got bad news, and I got good news."

R.J. grinned. Never a straight answer.

"Which do you want first?" he asked.

"The bad news," she said.

"I got fired from *Three's Company*."

"Now the good news?"

"I got fired from *Three's Company*."

They both laughed.

"So big deal, so I don't have a steady gig anymore. But you know what? I already got a job on a special. It's one of those trips-down-memory-lane shows. The sixtieth anniversary of Hemisphere Studios. Every day I sit and work with a film editor culling out old clips. It's fun. Then we transfer everything to tape and I write the commentaries and the intros for the people who are hosting. It's gonna be great. Carson, Hope, George Burns. All of 'em doing my intros. Not bad, huh? Better than Artie Zaven. He's writing Saturday morning cartoons for Hanna-Barbera."

"Better than Sherm Himmelblau," R.J. said. "He goes from one show to the next, writing episodes."

"Hey, listen," Eddie Levy said. "A hell of a lot better than Nussbaum. He's dead."

"Is he *still* dead?" R.J. asked. A dumb old joke but they both laughed again.

"So you'll call me one day and we'll meet at Canter's for a pickle. Yes?" Eddie said. "My office is right around the corner."

"I promise," she said.

"It'll be nice. We'll sit, we'll eat. I'll complain about my job. You'll complain about your job. That's what I call a good time."

She wouldn't complain. It was a tough job, but she was

doing it well. And more important, it kept her busy. Very busy. Which was what she needed more than anything. David. It was exactly a month today since she had last seen him, and still her chest felt heavy with longing every time she thought of him. Still she looked at the message pad by the kitchen telephone every night when she got home from work, wishing each night when she walked in the door that once she would come in and see a note in Jeffie's deliberate hand saying *David Malcolm called*.

Sometimes she would get home and play a game with herself, trying not to look at the message pad right away. Making deals with herself that maybe if she sat down and paid some bills first, or maybe if she did a little homework on tomorrow's assignment for the writers, that when she went into the kitchen after that, a message from David would be there.

Dinah, who hated animals, had been fixed up with a veterinarian, and they had had several dates.

"Hey," Dinah said, "my mother wanted me to find a nice surgeon. So what if he operates on canaries? I like him, and it proves that there is life after assholes walk out on you." As if that would be of great reassurance to R.J., that she too could eventually let go of the past and move on to greener pastures.

Tonight she put on her yellow robe and walked into the kitchen. She was wide-awake. It was two-fifteen in the morning. She had to be back in the office in six hours. She poured herself a glass of milk and stood in the dark room, leaning against the counter, drinking it from what she realized now was a McDonald's glass with a picture of the Hamburglar on it. The only sound was the hum of the refrigerator. The kitchen was spotless. All that was sitting on the counter were a few Hershey's Kisses. *Silver tops* was what her mother used to call them when she sold them to the children who came into Uncle Shulke's grocery store. Jeffie must have left them there. R.J. remembered when she was a little girl that she used to think a silver top was the best bite of chocolate there was. Maybe she would eat one with her milk. After all, she hardly ever treated herself to sweets. And besides, both she and the Hershey's Kiss were from Pennsylvania, she thought to herself, and smiled.

"The Keystone State," she said out loud as she unwrapped the candy, pulling at the paper strip that said

HERSHEY on it, which in turn released the thin foil wrapping. Then she put the tiny brown acorn-shaped candy into her mouth. Stale, she thought as she bit into it. Or something. Not the taste she remembered as the best bite of chocolate she'd ever had. Probably left over from last Halloween. She walked back to her bathroom and brushed her teeth. David. She remembered their long walks together through the streets of Paris. Holding hands. Stopping sometimes just to look in each other's eyes, filled with the wonder of their love for each other. Their visit to the Maison du Chocolat. How they'd fed one another the exquisite bites of chocolate. Chocolate. Kisses. That's what it was. That's what was wrong with the candy tonight. She had gone too far ever to come back to Hershey's Kisses. She had tasted the most delicious, and there was no turning back. David Malcolm was the Maison du Chocolat of men, and no one else would ever do.

She was pulling back the comforter and about to slip into bed when she realized that for the first time in a month she had forgotten to look at the telephone message pad by the kitchen phone. Healing, she said to herself. I'm healing. She sat down on the bed and reached to turn off the light. Didn't look at the message pad, she thought. Maybe someone important called. Maybe her agent or . . . Probably she should go and look.

R.J., she said to herself, you really *are* pitiful. A man dumps you. Never tells you why. Never even returns the calls you make to ask him why. And you live your life, reduced to rushing home and suffering because you still believe he'll come around. That any minute he'll act like the white knight you made him out to be. But it doesn't work that way. He's gone. Goodbye, and . . . Maybe you could have just a little bit more milk, she thought. Then she stood and walked slowly to the kitchen, carrying her empty glass. When she got there she didn't even turn on the light, just opened the refrigerator door and, using the refrigerator light, read the message pad, on which there was a note saying MOM, DAVID MALCOLM CALLED.

Oh, God. She left the refrigerator door open and walked closer to the message pad. Yes, that's what it said. MOM, DAVID MALCOLM CALLED. Her feet did a little dance as she turned on the kitchen light to look at it again, just to make sure she wasn't imagining things. There it was. DAVID MAL-

COLM CALLED. But when? Where was he? No number with it. Did he want her to call him back? Would he call *her* back? Oh, how she longed to rush into Jeffie's bedroom, wake him up, and make him tell her every word, every syllable David had said to him. She closed the refrigerator, leaned against it, picked up the message pad and ran her hand back and forth over the page where Jeffie had written David's name. What did he want? What could he possibly say to explain the disappearing act?

She lay awake for another hour, trying out pieces of conversation in her head that she would use if he called back. Goddamn you for walking out like that, whatever the reason. It's diabolical behavior. Not the behavior of a man who says he's in love. I can't think of anything, any reason that makes your disappearing the way you did legitimate.

If only she could be strong. If only she could be calm and controlled and not weep when she heard his voice, and not forget all the rational things she had thought about saying to him night after night when she lay alone in her bed, unable to sleep. David.

Finally she drifted off, and after a few hours she sat up, awakened suddenly by the sounds of Jeffie in the kitchen. It was daylight. Seven. The clock said seven. She put her robe on and was still tying the belt when she got to the kitchen. Jeffie had a mouthful of Wheat Chex, and when he saw her face, he swallowed fast. He knew what she wanted him to tell her.

"He said he's out of town. And that he'll call you back. That's all."

"Thanks, honey."

She had coffee. A piece of wheat toast with peanut butter on it. And then she showered with the shower door open because Manuela was off and Jeffie had left for school and she wanted to be able to hear the phone. And she decided just to towel-dry her hair instead of blowing it dry, because the sound of the dryer might drown out the sound of the phone. She hated that he was still doing this to her. But no. She was still doing it to herself. He would call back when he called back and she had better get dressed and get . . . The phone rang. She wanted to let it ring a few times, but she couldn't.

"Hello?"

"It's David," he said. He sounded bad. A poor connection. But that wasn't what was making him sound bad.

"Hello, David."

"I called to see how you are," he said quietly.

R.J. recognized the hiss of long distance on the connection.

"Where are you?" she asked.

"Out of town," he said. Out of town. Vague. He wanted to be vague.

"I'm fine," she lied. She wanted to sound detached. To make him think he hadn't hurt her, but her anger forced its way up, and she heard it in her voice and hated it. "Except for the fact that for the last month I've lived in the mystery of why a man, who told me he'd never known love like ours, suddenly disappeared from the face of the earth without so much as a goodbye, which is the lowest way to end something I've ever heard of, and believe me, I've heard of a few. To just run away? And then to call me from some place referred to as 'out of town.' Yeah. Other than that . . . I'm fine."

"I didn't run away," he snapped. It was the first time she'd ever heard anger in his voice. "I came to Houston. I'm with my father. At the Medical Center here. He's not well, R.J. Probably dying."

Oh, God. "I'm sorry," she said.

"But you're right," he said. "I should have called you. And I'm sorry that I didn't. For the first few days I didn't because all my energy was focused on my father and his needs. And then, when I realized that a few days had already gone by and I hadn't called, I consciously chose to take a few more days. And then I guess it became weeks and . . ."

For a long time there was nothing to be heard on the line between them but the hush of the long distance from Houston to Los Angeles. It hurt R.J. to breathe while she waited to hear where all of this was leading.

"I feel so helpless," David said finally, "because there's nothing I can do for him. And I know I should just thank heaven he and I had all those years together but . . ." More silence. R.J. knew just how he felt. She had felt it time and time again. And again. Recently, when she was cleaning out her closet, she realized that hidden away in the zipper pocket of the black clutch purse Mona Feldstein Friedman had given her as a Chanukah present and which she still carried when she dressed in black, were four copies of the Hebrew transliteration of the mourner's prayer. The now yellowed ones from Francie's funeral and her father's funeral, the one from Rifke's funeral with the ragged edges R.J. had nervously torn during the service, and the crumpled one from Arthur's funeral.

"I understand," she said.

"I've had plenty of time to think," he told her. "Sitting in my room at The Warwick. To take a long look at my own life, and I know it's time . . . time"—she could hear the struggle in his voice not to let go—"for me to make some decisions about how I want to spend the rest of it. And R.J.," he said, "I'm really not . . . in good shape."

There was the shrill sporadic noise of what sounded like a hospital paging system in the background.

"How's Jeff?" he asked after a while.

"Fine."

"Manuela?"

"Fine."

"Give them my best, and I'd better go," he said to her. No. He was disconnecting again. Slipping away.

"David . . ."

"R.J., take good care," he said, and then there was a click and he was gone. Again. She continued to sit holding the receiver next to her face until a pulsing beep tone reminded her that the phone was off the hook. As she dressed, she heard his voice over and over—how he had to "make some decisions" about how he was going to spend the rest of his life. David. Losing his father. The remaining parent. The man whose unique position had created for his only child a magical, heady, untouchable place in the world, and now he was dying. Poor David.

She turned on the *Today* show as an attempt to shut out her thoughts. He was thinking about how to live the rest of his life. Clearly the plans didn't include her. That was the message of the call. If they did, if he wanted her, needed her, thought she could give him any comfort, he would have asked her to come to Houston. Even just to be there waiting for him at the hotel in the evenings when he came back. No.

He was evaluating his future, and as she'd feared long ago, she didn't fit. On the *Today* show some actress was plugging a TV movie, and R.J. listened while she got dressed for work. Then, while she put her makeup on, Norman Cousins was the guest, talking about his new book, and she stopped to listen. Sat down on the bed to pay more attention. When the interview was over and they cut to a commercial, she dialed the phone.

"Hemisphere's Sixtieth," someone answered.

"Eddie Levy, please."

"Thank you."

"Eddie Levy's office."

"Is he in? This is R.J. Misner."

"I'll ask him."

"*Meydele?*"

"Eddie, the editors you're working with. The film expert and the one who edits it to tape. Could I get them to do me an enormous favor if I pay them for their time?"

"I don't know why not. I'll go find out and give you a call right back."

"Thank you."

Then she dialed again.

"This is Harry Elfand. I'm either in the shower or in Europe, whichever comes first. Leave a beep after you hear the message. Nice talkin' to ya."

"Harry, it's R.J. Misner. It's important. Call me back right away."

Then she dialed one more time.

"R.J. Misner's office."

"Janet, I won't be in for a day or two. Tell Don Jarvis that I'm sick, and the writers know what to do without me. Okay?"

"Sure. Anything I can do?"

"Yeah. Pray that what I'm about to do is the right thing."

Harry Elfand sat by the pool of his Encino house. It was eleven in the morning and he was drinking a beer.

"Don't tell me," he said as R.J. walked toward him. She'd been shown out there by Josie, his round white-haired wife who was as polite and sweet as Harry was cantankerous.

"You need help kicking Patsy's ass and you came to me

for advice," he guessed. "Well, here it is. You shouldn't have gone back to her show. See? And I'm not even talking sour grapes here, because that bitch has to pay me off for the next three years, so I'm in fat city. And I wasn't exactly starving before."

"Nice to see you too, Harry," R.J. said, and she sat on the edge of the diving board. "This isn't about Patsy."

Harry looked at her closely now and saw how serious she was.

"You in trouble, kid?" he asked, quietly now.

"No, in need. For something you've got and I want you to lend me."

"Not money?"

"Nope."

"Sock it to me," he said.

When R.J. left Harry Elfand's house with what she came for, for the first time in the long years since she had known him, he hugged her. A long hug. Then wished her luck.

$D$avid sat on a hard chair that he'd pulled very close to the hospital bed. Sometimes five or even ten minutes would go by when neither he nor his father would speak. Then the old man would remember something about the past, or have an idea about business, and with what it hurt David to see was a great deal of effort, he would say a few words to his son.

"Thanks for being here, fella," he said this time. He had said that repeatedly over the last four weeks.

"You're welcome, Dad," David answered. The first time his father had thanked him for staying by his hospital bed every day and night, David had blurted out, "Well where else *would* I be?". And thought to himself how much that sounded like something R.J. would say. Oh, God. R.J. He had to do something about R.J. Had to call her back, and instead of fumbling around, this time he would tell her . . .

"You're welcome, Dad," David said now.

Rand Malcolm winced suddenly from what was clearly a burst of severe pain.

"Why don't I ask them to give you some medication?" David asked.

"Don't need any goddamned medication," his father said, and closed his eyes.

David looked long at his father's face, noticing what a toll the devastating illness had taken on his once-handsome features.

"Maybe some water though, boy," Mal said, and David

held the glass to his mouth while he sipped, then watched him lie back exhausted on the pillow, as though just the act of lifting his head to take the water had been too much for him.

"Think I'll nap for a while," he said softly, and after a few minutes David could tell by his father's breathing that he had slipped away into sleep.

"Treat you to lunch?" came a soft voice from behind David.

"Hi, Case," David said, without turning, and when he felt Casey's pretty hand on his shoulder he touched it, then held it tightly.

"Looks like he's out for a while," Casey said. "We can just grab something in the hospital if you like."

David turned to look at her. Casey Baylor. No matter how much time he spent with her—and in the last weeks it had been considerable—his first look at her each day, that perfect face, that amazing long lean body dressed in another smashing outfit, always took his breath away. It had from the minute he'd bumped into her in the hotel lobby the day he arrived. He'd been so goddamned exhausted from staying awake the whole night before, persuading his father to make the trip to Houston.

Maximum deterioration, Eleanor had told David when she took him away from the dinner party that night. Four weeks ago. Could it really have been that long? Primary disease of his heart muscle, Mal's cardiologist, Peter Acklin, had told Eleanor and Mal when Mal had gone grudgingly for a checkup. He must be hospitalized immediately and he was refusing to cooperate. Saying he had too much business to take care of. Had no time for any goddamned hospital. David must intervene.

David's mind had raced during the whole dinner with Senator Spencer and Mrs. Spencer and R.J., though the circumstances demanded that he sit there trying to behave as if he were enjoying himself. He remembered hurrying R.J. out the door and home, and as soon as he'd dropped her off at home he'd rushed back to his father's house, where he sat up all night urging Mal to go to Houston.

"There are doctors there who can relieve your symptoms, prolong your life," he'd said, praying that it was true. And when the early morning light dawned and Mal finally agreed to the trip, a relieved David had grabbed the phone to alert the doctors, awaken the pilots and warn them to ready the plane, secure hotel accommodations near Houston Medical Center, and rush home to pack a few of his own things.

Getting a hospital room at the Houston Medical Center had been easier than finding the appropriate hotel accommodation for Eleanor, who had, she said, "to maintain certain standards, even during a crisis." And David, containing himself, told her that if the reservations he'd made at a hotel across from the hospital didn't suit her, she could make her own. So she telephoned some "dear old friends" in Houston, and told David and Mal, who seemed relieved, that she would follow along in a day or two when her life was more organized.

David had spent the first day checking Mal into the Medical Center, staying with him through dozens of tests, and finally getting him settled quietly into his room on the seventh floor. It was a fine place to be if you had Mal's problem, David told himself over and over. But he was trembling when he finally made his way to the hotel to check in for the first time, carrying the hanging bag he had run home to pack hastily the night before. He was unshaven, weak with exhaustion, with the smell and feel and taste of hospital all over him.

"Checking in," was all he'd been able to get out to the desk clerk. "Name's David Malcolm."

"Is it David Malcolm from Los Angeles?" he heard a voice ask, and he turned to see who had spoken.

The blond woman couldn't have been talking to him. He had no idea who she . . .

"Casey Baylor," she said, extending her hand. He took it. Her eyes never left his. "We went to prep school together. Hollingsworth. I transferred in the eighth grade to a school in Europe. You can't possibly remember."

Sweet heaven. Remember? Was she joking? No wonder he'd written that humiliating love letter to her all those years ago. He remembered the first moment he'd laid eyes on her in the Hollingsworth cafeteria. Even then he'd had great taste. "I do," he said. "I remember."

Casey's gorgeous face had become serious then.

"My father's in the Medical Center," she told him. "For bypass surgery. I hope you're not in Houston because of medical problems."

"Unfortunately, that *is* why," he told her. "My father has cardiomyopathy." That's what the doctors had told him after they'd spent a few hours with Mal, confirming Acklin's diagnosis. Primary disease of the heart muscle.

"I'm sorry," Casey said. "Maybe we can offer each other some solace."

In his exhaustion David had looked into Casey's eyes to see if there was some deep meaning behind those words, and when there didn't seem to be, he was relieved. Not only because of R.J. and the confusion he was feeling about her, but because here, now, with Mal so ill, he had no energy, nothing left to have to feel anything for anyone else. Think about anyone else. He had intended to go to his room, take a shower, and call R.J. that first night.

But he didn't. Instead, after his long hot shower, he had turned on the television set and watched, he wasn't sure what, hoping to block out the news the doctors had given him earlier.

"The function of his left pumping chamber couldn't get any worse. Because of his age, he's not a candidate for a heart transplant. There are several things we can do to improve his condition and reduce his symptoms. Most patients who have reached this stage of his illness will not live more than six to twelve months."

David had stayed awake that night just long enough after the eleven o'clock news to leave a wake-up call for six A.M., so he could be with his father for the next series of tests that would begin that morning.

Then a week had gone by. The kind of week which, when it's over, it's difficult to recall what happened on which day. Was it the day the cardiac catheter was inserted in Mal's heart, and maybe that was Wednesday, or was Wednesday the day the doctors decided to change all of the medication because Mal was dangerously retaining too much fluid? David knew it was a Sunday night when he'd mentioned R.J. to Mal, because they'd had the television on, watching *60 Minutes*, and all of a sudden it ended and there was Patsy Dugan in full sequined regalia, and Freddy Gaines picking at his guitar, the two of them singing into one another's faces.

"This is the show that R.J. writes for, Dad," David had said.

"Who the hell is R.J.?"

"R.J. Misner, the girl who was at dinner the night we left for Houston."

"Don't remember who that was," Mal said, and turned off the television.

And then there was that other night in the hospital when it felt to David as if it must be very late because there wasn't a sound anywhere on the seventh floor. Eleanor had long since gone back to her friend's house to sleep, and a restless Mal began to reminisce about the past. His training as a pilot. The great old planes he had flown. David thought of Jeffie and the boy's passion for airplanes. His excitement when David had taken him to the Planes of Fame Museum at the Chino Airport a few weeks before.

"Got models of every one," Mal said. David remembered the collection of model planes Mal used to keep in a glass case at the Rainbow Building.

"I know a twelve-year-old boy who would love to see those planes," he had said. "R.J.'s son. He's a fine—"

Mal interrupted. "Eleanor says Frank Baylor's here, and the real pretty daughter."

It was such an obvious choice for a subject change. The point was clear. I disapprove, so I drop the subject. David didn't mention R.J. again.

"Casey. I went to Hollingsworth with her. Her name is Casey."

Some nights when Mal slept, David would pace the carpeted hallway of the luxurious hospital wing. Trying to imagine life without his father. Many nights he would stand leaning against the wall outside the room, grinning, as a memory from his childhood flickered by. Like the tour his hurried father had given him of the Louvre. "Now there's 'Winged Victory,' fella. Over there's the 'Venus de Milo.' That one's called 'Mona Lisa.' That's about it . . . let's go." Now and then a memory of his times with Mal moved David to tears, and as he pulled a handkerchief from his pocket one night, he received a sympathetic nod from a young nurse who passed silently on her way to the nurse's station, which was somewhere outside the corridor, making the plush-carpeted seventh floor feel more as if it were in a hotel than a hospital.

Frank Baylor's room was on the opposite end of the floor from Mal's. From time to time David would bump into Casey, who was either pacing or leaning against the wall outside of her father's room, probably having her own recollections. Sometimes she would stop to talk. Briefly at first, exchanging polite inquiries with him about the progress of their fathers. Then exchanging medical information each had acquired. More than either of them had ever wanted to know about an ailing heart. Then there were longer conversations about business.

Over the years since her father's health had begun to deteriorate, Casey had been running Baylor Steel. It was a job for which she was eminently qualified, having received her M.B.A. from Harvard and having been groomed for it by Frank Baylor, who, though he had four business-school-educated sons, knew that Casey, the baby in the family, was the only one capable of filling his shoes.

And now, as their father faced a medical crisis, Casey's brothers—who had bargained that eventually she would marry, have children, and lose interest in the business—were afraid of being shut out completely, and were gunning for her. The story about the brothers' jealousy was one that Eleanor told David one night as he drove her from the hospital to her friend's home. Casey would never have revealed a family disharmony like that to an outsider.

She was always remarkably poised. Even after her father's surgery, when he developed a lung infection, a serious complication. Late one afternoon of the third week, when Mal was asleep, David and Eleanor were about to get on the elevator to go for a cup of coffee. It had been a tense day, with Mal insisting that they take him home as soon as possible. The elevator door was closing when he heard Casey's voice from down the hall. "Wait," she said, rushing up. David stopped the door with his hand and pulled it open.

"I hope neither of you thinks this is inappropriate," Casey said, "but Daddy's feeling a little better today, and when I told Dr. Markson that the only way I fight tension at home is to play golf, he offered me the use of his country club course. Will you join me?" she asked them both.

David held on to the elevator door, which was trying to close, and looked at Eleanor, whose face was as pinched and tense as if it could crack.

"We can get clubs and shoes at the pro shop," Casey urged.

"A fine idea," Eleanor said.

There was no one else on the rolling green golf course but the three of them. At first they all walked from hole to hole without talking to or looking at one another. Each lost in private thoughts, breathing in the clean warm smell of the day, trying to shake off for just a moment what was going on at the hospital. After a while, Eleanor moved closer to Casey and began to keep up with the younger woman's leggy stride. It couldn't have been easy. Casey was very athletic and strong. She could hit a golf ball a long way with perfect form.

"Smart girl never to have married," David heard Eleanor say. Casey didn't reply.

"I've been married twice," Eleanor said as they reached the fourteenth tee. David stood on the men's tee, Eleanor and Casey below, on the women's. "To two of the best men this country has to offer, and you know what? They're all self-involved, narcissistic, and demanding."

David was teeing up and lining up his shot.

Casey answered Eleanor softly. "I've always believed that you get back what you give," she said, in a voice so absent of cynicism or sarcasm or malice that Eleanor couldn't take it personally, and David, who was impressed again with Casey's dauntless poise, hit the ball farther than he had in years.

On one of his father's good days David brought Casey into Mal's hospital room and introduced them. Mal was not too sick to be impressed by the woman's extraordinary beauty, her polite conversation, combined with what he already knew about her business acumen from the mutual friends he and Frank Baylor shared.

"Monty Allburn sings your praises," Mal told her. Casey seemed pleased to hear that news, since Allburn was the chairman of the board of Baylor Steel. "Says you're one smart cookie." It was the most animated David had seen his father since their arrival in Houston.

"Thank you, sir," she said. "That's very high praise and I appreciate it."

Casey and Mal had exchanged small talk, and when he seemed to be tiring but too polite to say so, she excused herself and was barely out the door when Mal said to David: "Now, that's the right woman."

The right woman. Lily had been the right woman for Mal, even though it looked at first as if he'd picked her because she was a young beauty. As it turned out, her youth had been what had enabled him to mold her, shape her, "educate her," as he had suggested David do with the impossible Babsy. Despite his own intense dislike for Eleanor, David understood why in his late years Mal had no doubt convinced himself that she was now the right woman for him. Knew a lot about business, had the same political beliefs, was sophisticated, made a good traveling companion, was a perfect hostess, and didn't demand much.

According to those standards, R.J. Misner was hardly the right woman. Not even in the ballpark. Nobody was going to mold her into anything other than what she was. She didn't understand a goddamned thing about business, could barely keep her household accounts straight, had never even known a Republican before she met David, and though they'd never entertained together, he knew she couldn't care less about the social graces and had no interest in food or wine. The only dish she'd ever cooked for him was something she called "chicken in a pot," and it was godawful. Not to mention that since he'd known her she'd had the same two bottles of Blue Nun in the lettuce drawer of her refrigerator. "Letting them age," she had joked when she'd seen him look at them and then at her, as if to say "You must be joking." R.J. was not what Rand Malcolm would call the right woman.

In the long silent times he had spent in what he now realized, since his call to R.J., was four weeks, and in the hours he'd spent with Casey, David knew there was no getting around that. When it came to the way things were supposed to be, he and R.J. couldn't be more ill-suited: As R.J. once put it, "Unless I was Tina Turner," and then she'd added, "Okay, maybe it would be worse if I was Ike Turner."

"Yes, you can treat me to lunch," David said quietly now to Casey, though he knew that when his father fell into that deep drugged sleep he was oblivious to the sounds in the room. Casey took his arm as they left Mal's room, and as they walked down the hall to the elevator they passed a group of nurses who, David noticed, looked at the two of them together and smiled knowingly, as if the story of a match made at the bedside of two seriously ill fathers was one they were looking forward to gossiping about.

The right woman. His father's message was clear and very easy to understand. Once, at a dinner party, David remembered hearing a man say, "I'm certain this is horribly narcissistic, but I think the reason I love Julia so much is because if I were a woman, she's the woman I would be." As they walked into the hospital restaurant, David looked again at Casey and thought that if he were a woman, he would probably be Casey Baylor.

There is something very soothing about the familiar. When two people share a common vocabulary of gestures and timing and behavior. When nothing about the other comes as unexpected or jarring. When most words become unnecessary. A kind of wonderful shorthand between two people whose upbringing has been unswervingly alike. Who seemed to have had, as Casey liked to say, "the same trainer." The two of them talked about it again and again. How they'd been taught the same lessons at home. Stand up straight. Sit up straight. Have a firm handshake. Speak up. Say what you mean. Make your point. Rise when an older person comes into the room.

"I remembered another one," Casey said over lunch today. "I sit behind my father's desk at Baylor Steel, running the whole shooting match when Dad is out, and when one of my father's friends calls, I still get on the telephone and say, 'Sorry, but Dad's out of town, Mr. Warren.' Mister! Can you imagine? I'm a thirty-one-year-old woman."

David laughed a laugh of recognition. "I do that too," he said. "And then I ask, 'And how is *Mrs.* Warren?' "

"Always," Casey said, laughing for the first time since she'd been in Houston. The laugh lit up her beautiful face.

"It feels good to laugh," she said, but couldn't look at David when she did, because she was struggling to keep down the emotion. "This has been a grueling vigil," she said. "You've made it easier for me." The doctors would tell her today if she could take her father home the following morning.

"Likewise, Case," he said.

David reached for the handkerchief he always carried in the pocket of his blazer, to offer it to Casey, at the same time that she reached into the pocket of her blazer for a tissue, and as she did, the sadness on her face turned into a grin.

"I can't believe what I nearly forgot to tell you," she said. "I'm a terrible pack rat, and the other day I called my secretary and asked her to go back and look through some old memento boxes I have, to see if she could find this."

And from the pocket where she'd also located a tissue she pulled a folded piece of what looked like the kind of notebook paper David remembered from Hollingsworth, and handed it to him.

"If this is what I think it is . . ." David said in disbelief, opening the paper and then shaking his head as he saw the note he'd written nearly twenty years before in the perfect penmanship he'd learned from his early tutors: *There isn't a moment while we're apart that I don't long for you. You are everything I prayed my love would be.* Even now, so many light-years later, David felt a flush of humiliation for the boy who had written that letter. A sadness for the overwhelming need he must have felt to write those words. And the P.S. Sweet heaven. He had completely forgotten about writing that. *P.S. Someday, Casey, you will be my wife.*

He looked at Casey, who looked flushed now too.

"You do know," she said, "that I have a law degree, and I believe this will hold up in court if there should be a breach-of-promise suit."

"Is that right?" David said, smiling. This woman was something special. There was no doubt about that.

"I'll tell you what," she said, standing. "You finish your salad and think about your defense. In the meantime, I'm going to run up and be with my father. His doctor's coming by any minute to give us news about going home." She started to walk away.

"Casey," he said. She turned. "Why don't we have a late supper tonight after our fathers are asleep and talk some more?"

Casey took a deep breath, nodded, and was gone, the sweet scent of her perfume still in the air.

Two of Mal's doctors and Eleanor were in the hospital room with Mal when David got back.

"I want to go home," Mal announced by way of explaining their presence. His angry eyes flashed in his pale, drawn face. "Die in my own bed," Mal said. "Not in some goddamned hospital."

David looked first at the doctors, then at Eleanor. She was nodding in agreement with Mal.

"Really, David," she said. "He's right. It's time to go back. We do have doctors there. It's not as if—"

"We want to try one more drug," one of the doctors interrupted. He spoke directly to David.

"What in the hell for?" Mal asked.

"To improve the derangement in his liver and kidney function which has resulted from the heart failure."

"Dad, a few more days. That's all it would be. Right, doctor?" He looked at both white-coated men. The one who had already spoken didn't respond; the other one made a gesture that looked like a combination nod and shrug. Eleanor sighed and looked appraisingly down at her fingernails, as if, David was sure, she was worried that she might never again see her Beverly Hills manicurist.

"A few more days," David said, and the doctors, who sensed that the only way Mal might consent was if they left him alone with David, walked out the door. Eleanor walked out after them. David moved closer to the bed. Where there's life there's hope. Where there's life there's hope. He remembered R.J. telling him that's what she had repeated over and over to herself when she stood at her own father's bedside. He remembered how she described that intensive care ward in the hospital in Pittsburgh where her father lay dying, with only a curtain surrounding him so that R.J., at his side, could hear the pain of the other dying fathers and mothers and their children. She had wept in David's arms the night she told him about it. Remembering how she'd stood there trying to keep her father alive by telling him jokes. Jokes. Only R.J.

"Dad," David said, "let's give it a few more days, and then we'll go home."

His father nodded, a tired nod, and David sat close to the bed for the rest of the day. There was a baseball game on television that both of them looked at, but neither of them had any idea who was playing. After Mal's dinner, when he had taken some medication to sleep, David walked out of the hospital and across the street to the hotel. When he got to his room he sat on the bed, picked up the phone, and dialed R.J.'s number. He couldn't let this be like the call he had made the other day. Fumbling for words. Not saying what he had to tell her. This was going to be the hardest call he'd ever had to make. Somewhere in the deepest part of R.J. she would have to understand. His father was dying and he didn't have much time. He had to do the right thing.

Ring after ring, he counted them. Nine, ten, eleven. No one home. He put the receiver down and breathed a little easier. Tomorrow morning would be soon enough to tell her. Then he took a long shower and got dressed for his dinner with Casey.

*R.J.* 's eyes were heavy with exhaustion.

"... Why did you have to let this happen? I thought we were going to have our whole lives ahead of us. I love you more than anything, and now it looks like you're leaving me."

"*Do* you love me, Red? Do you really? Well then, maybe my life was worth something after all."

"I think this cut should be the last. It's by far the best," Burt Cohen said.

R.J. nodded in agreement. Cohen was the tape editor, an associate of Eddie Levy's who had been sitting at the editing computer at Teletronics between R.J. and Eddie for the last two days and nights. He had transferred reel after reel of Lily Daniels's films to tape. As many of them as they could get their hands on, and for hour after hour he had pored over every one of them with R.J., finding just the right dialogue, expressions, moments at which to cut away, to create a perfect reel for her to take with her to Houston.

Sometimes R.J. would look at Lily in a scene and be amazed at how much David was like her. A certain turn of the head, the way she wrinkled her nose when she smiled. Watching the old films on the monitor had made her remember the nights she'd sat in the Manor Theater with Bubbe, and the recollections warmed her in the cold, hollow editing studio.

"You're right. This is our finale," R.J. said, and then couldn't hold back a yawn.

"Looks to me like two A.M. is past your bedtime," Burt Cohen said, smiling at R.J. He was a darling guy. Early forties, straight dark hair, green eyes, sweet sense of humor. R.J. could tell that, despite her haggard face, tired eyes, and disheveled unwashed hair, he was interested in her.

"Are you kidding?" Eddie Levy said. "When we were working for Harry Elfand we didn't start *warming up* until two A.M."

"Burt, this reel is wonderful," R.J. said, "but I don't want to leave until I have *it* and a backup copy of it in my hands."

"Why don't you go home and get some sleep," Cohen said, and helped R.J. to her feet. "And trust me to finish this. We've got it all down, and all it will take now is a little refining. I'll bring the original and the backup cassettes to you first thing in the morning."

R.J. was reluctant to leave.

"He's right," Eddie said. "You'll feel better if you catch a few winks before your flight."

R.J. picked up her purse. "I'll come by on my way to the airport," she told Burt.

"I pass your neighborhood on my way home," he insisted, and took her arm to walk her out to her car. But first she gave a quick hug to Eddie Levy, who was pouring a last cup of muddy studio coffee into a white Styrofoam cup.

"Good luck, *meydele*," he said, patting her back tenderly.

"Thank you both for everything," she said. "This means so much to me."

The parking lot behind Teletronics was lit by a bare light bulb above the back door. R.J. unlocked the door to the Mustang, Burt Cohen opened the door for her, and she slid into the driver's seat.

"This must be some special guy," Burt Cohen said.

"He is," R.J. told him.

"If you ever find out otherwise," Cohen said softly, "look me up." Then he closed the door to the Mustang, and R.J. backed up and drove into the Hollywood night.

The airport in Houston was busy, but R.J. had no bags to worry about. Only a small overnight case and the enve-

lope of precious cargo she had carried on and tucked carefully under the seat. Every now and then during the flight
she had reached for it with her foot, relieved to feel that it
was still safely in place. David needed her. That was clear.
Needed someone to help him through this. So what if he
hadn't asked her to come there? Probably he hadn't been
able to say it. Afraid she couldn't leave her job. Afraid after
her little tirade that she was so angry with him about the
month he had stayed away that she would never consider
coming to Houston to comfort him.

She was tired. In the few days that had passed since his
mysterious call she had hardly slept. Working nonstop to
assemble the tapes.

"The Warwick Hotel," she told the cab driver. And as
the cab sped along she sat looking out the window, into the
passing cars, wondering about the people in them. Where
they were going. What they were thinking, and if any of
them felt as shaky as she did now. She held the large
envelope on her lap. David. Suddenly a surge of panic filled
her. Maybe this was wrong. Not just wrong. Idiotic. Ridiculous. His father was dying. She didn't even know the man.
Met him one time. And now, without even announcing
herself, she was showing up in Houston, Texas? *Turn around,*
she wanted to tell the cabby. She should turn around and
get on the next plane back to Los Angeles.

Why had this stupid idea made sense to her for the last
few feverish, sleepless days and nights? Like a crazy person
she had worked, knowing she was racing against a clock.
And now, finally, stopping to be rational, she was sure the
whole idea was embarrassing, dumb, pushy, wrong. She
was tired, very tired. Maybe she would feel better after she
got to the hotel and had a bite of food. Maybe . . .

"This is it, lady," the cab driver said.

After she'd checked in and tipped the bellman—even
though she had carried the bag to the room herself and he
had simply opened the door for her—she looked around the
hotel room, thinking about the first day she'd arrived in Los
Angeles from Pittsburgh, fifteen years before. So wide-eyed.
So young. She washed her face and dried it, then sat on the
bed and picked up the phone, and when the hotel operator
answered, she asked to be connected with David's room. He
wouldn't be there. He'd be at the hospital. But maybe. It
rang many times. She counted them. After eleven rings she

put the receiver down. Then she walked over and opened the glass doors, went out onto the balcony, and looked down at the fountains below in the front of the hotel. Maybe she'd go downstairs and have something to eat before she delivered her package.

The lobby was empty and R.J. walked from the elevator to the front desk. She would leave a message for David, letting him know she was here.

"May I help you?"

"David Malcolm," she said. "I'd like to—"

"Oh, yes," the desk clerk said. "He left something for you."

That's impossible, R.J. thought as the man handed her a note, which she opened. David couldn't have any idea that she was there. He couldn't have . . . It was David's handwriting.

C.

    I wanted to tell you that last night was very special for me. It's easy to see why I proposed to you. How lucky for the rest of my life that you turned up in Houston. I'm breaking the news to my father this morning.

                             David.

Oh, God. R.J. closed her eyes. This note was meant for some other woman. A woman David proposed to. And the desk clerk had assumed that if a woman was looking for Mr. Malcolm, he should give the note to her. Breaking the news to his father. Dear God. Blurry with despair she made her way to the elevator. The ride to her floor seemed endless. She rushed down the hall to her room, pushed the door open, let it slam closed behind her, and sat on the bed, wondering what to do next. God, what a fool. The real reason he hadn't called her. *Another woman* was the reason. Still holding the envelope containing the cassettes, she moved to the tiny desk near the bed, pulled a piece of stationery from the hotel folder, and with a white plastic hotel pen, she began several times and tore up several versions of what she wanted to say to him. Finally she finished one that said:

David,

    I made the mistake of coming here and realized when it was too late how dumb that was. Enclosed please find two cassettes. Norman Cousins writes about the healing power of laughter. I remembered your father saying how much he loved a show called "Joey's Place." A writer I know worked on that show and had these tapes. If you can get a VCR into your father's room, maybe they would help him.

Another friend of mine is working on a television special for the anniversary of Hemisphere Studios. Through him I was able to assemble some clips of highlights of Lily Daniels's films. She was more wonderful than I remembered.

The man at the hotel desk gave me a note you left for someone else. I guess it was a truly lucky mistake. The worst part for me was to find out that instead of being too tough all along, I just wasn't tough enough.

R.J.M.

She reread it a few times. Fine. It was fine. Not too emotional. To the point. Reasonably polite—verging on the WASP, Dinah would have told her. She felt nauseated and sad and stupid and angry, and thought for a minute that maybe she should go and find the son of a bitch and slap him and kick him and scream every vile thing she could think of. But instead she called the airlines. The next flight to Los Angeles wasn't for a few hours. She would get out of this place and wait at the airport. Back in the lobby she stopped at the desk. The man who had given her the note was laughing with someone on the telephone. R.J. waited until he hung up and asked her: "What can I do for you?" She left the package of tapes and the note for David, explained to the registration clerk that she'd had a change of plans, and she checked out. The doorman gestured for a waiting taxi, and R.J. climbed in. "Airport, please," she said, and the taxi pulled into the traffic of the hot Texas day.

David stood in the hospital room looking out the window at the taxis and cars passing below. The new drugs seemed to be having a positive effect. Where there's life, there's hope. Mal had been sitting up this morning, eating a light breakfast when David gave him the news. Now he napped fitfully, but his face had more color in it than David had seen in a long time.

"Knock knock, everybody," came the sweet voice of Casey, who breezed into the room. She made an apologetic gesture when she saw that Mal was asleep. Then she put an arm around David's waist and gave him a kiss on the cheek.

"Well?" she asked expectantly.

"I told him," David said, grinning.

"And?" she asked.

"He blessed it," David said. "I knew he would."

Casey emitted a joyous sound and threw her arms around David in a hug. "I didn't have a moment's doubt either," she said, hugging him. "Oh, I stopped at the desk and there was a package there for you, so I took the liberty of bringing it over." From her tote bag she removed the large manila envelope. It had his name on it in what looked curiously like R.J.'s handwriting. R.J. He had tried her twice at home this morning and no one was there. Then at her office, but her secretary said that she hadn't been there for a few days. The envelope was open now and David looked at the contents. Two video cassettes and a smaller envelope.

"I can't imagine," David said, opening the envelope. "I wasn't expecting anything and I . . ." He held the cassettes on his lap and read the accompanying note. When he finished, he stood, and as he did, the videotapes clattered from his lap to the floor. "Casey," he said, "I'm going to leave the hospital—just for a little while, but it has to be now, so forgive me for rushing off." He looked at his watch and was out the door. "I'll explain it all when I get back," he called over his shoulder.

R.J. stood in line at the airport gift shop with a handful of magazines. *Cosmopolitan, Redbook, McCall's, Harper's Bazaar, Vogue*. Patsy and Freddy were on the cover of *People*, so she didn't buy that. She would look at the fashions, read the articles, recipes, horoscopes, fill the hours until her flight left and she could be out of here. At the counter she added a box of raisins and a bag of cashews to the pile, in case she got hungry.

David. A man in the front of the line had red hair and

freckles and she looked long at him, actually wishing for a moment that he would turn into David, see her in line, and say to her ... Stop! *Oy vey,* R.J., please stop, she told herself. Fairy tales. That's where things like that happened. In fairy tales. How many people have to die, have to disappoint you, to make you stop believing in fairy tales? Isn't it enough of a fairy tale that you started out in life not knowing which words were English and which were Yiddish, in a household where there weren't two cents to rub together, and now you have a remarkable son, and you're living in a beautiful home, with someone to help you take care of your life so that you can work? And you're making a career in the most competitive business there is. Why do you beat yourself over the head because you've met another man who can't cut it? Can't be what you want. A man who tells you how much he loves you and a month later is about to marry another woman? Read. Read the magazines. Get lost in other people's stories. Letters to the Editor. A column called "Can This Marriage Be Saved?"

Finally at two-thirty they announced that her flight was boarding, and she stood with all the others and moved into the line which began edging forward to the gate. Now there were three people ahead of her, then two, and ...

"R.J."

The strong hand on her arm. She looked at it first. Pale. Freckled. Then into David's eyes.

"Wait," he said.

The milling airport travelers were a fast-moving colorful background behind him. His eyes were bloodshot and he looked washed-out and tired. She loved him so much and hated herself for ever thinking that coming to Houston was the thing to do.

"Thank you for bringing those tapes," he said. "I'll try them tonight. It's a wonderful idea, and I know you worked hard on them. He seems better today, but they don't give him too long. I mean, the tapes may be too late."

She couldn't speak. There was nothing to say. She loved him. She hated him. She loved him.

"R.J., listen to me. The note you got was meant for Casey Baylor. R.J., do you remember who Casey Baylor is? She's the girl I once told you about who rejected me at the age of eleven when I wrote her a passionate love letter."

Yes. She remembered the story. About the beautiful girl

who had dazzled him and then humiliated him in front of the whole school. That's who it was. And now, now that they were grown up, she was back to claim him. The unattainable goddess. The light in the airport seemed to dim for a moment. Casey. R.J. remembered the story about how much David had wanted her. She remembered that when he'd told her the story she'd felt jealous that she wasn't the one David had loved passionately when they were eleven, and when she told him that, they had laughed because they realized that when R.J. was eleven, David was three. People were bumping them as they pushed by.

"Our parents have known one another for years. Our backgrounds are very similar. She's as deeply involved in her family business as I am in mine."

And she's the right age, R.J. thought, the right religion, the right social stratum.

"Well, last night when I had dinner with her, after just these few weeks of getting to know her really well, I decided to ask her to—"

"Look," R.J. said, pulling her arm away from him now. "Spare me the details. You could have saved yourself a trip all the way out to the airport to say this. I'm sorry about your father, but at least you made him and yourself happy by having a reunion with the perfect woman. *Mazel-tov.* Nice of you to tell me that. I'm sure it makes you feel as if you're handling things properly. Well you're not. Because handling things properly would have been to call me when all of this started and tell me the truth, but not you. You're a leaver. A quitter. Someone who runs away from feelings and the truth. And the truth is that you saw me at dinner at your father's house and said to yourself: 'What in the hell have I done here? This broad is not gonna make it in my family. She doesn't impress my father.'"

David didn't even blink. It was as if she hadn't said a word. Instead, he picked up almost exactly where he'd left off. "So . . . I decided to ask her to let me confide in her, and she said please do, and I said, 'Casey, there is something I need to talk about. And that is that I am so in love I can't see straight, with a woman I met in Los Angeles several months ago. She's a crazy comedy writer who has a son and she's eight years older than I am, and she's as Jewish as I am Christian, and most of the time she's a raving maniac. And even though all I want to do is be with her forever, I'd be lying to you if I didn't say that there's a part of me that's afraid. Afraid because I know that no matter what I say or do, no matter how I wish with every fiber of me that it could be otherwise, the truth is that I can't make Eleanor Benning be other than the cold bigot she is, or stop my father from wishing I was with someone who is more like me, the way every parent does.' "

"Seven and a half years," R.J. snapped.

"Forgive me," David said back, then went on. " 'The people I've known all my life—some will understand, but somewhere without a doubt somebody will say something about Jews being pushy and someone will make some comment about her age, and you can put money on it that one of these sunny afternoons when I take him to play golf at the club, somebody will say something hurtful to her son and for the sake of the two of them, because I care for them both so much, love them so deeply, I've spent the last weeks worrying and thinking that maybe I should step out of their lives and not bring them into a world where I know that insult and misunderstanding is not a possibility but a certainty.' " There were tears filling his blue eyes, and R.J. ached with the effort to hold back her own as he went on.

"And Casey said, 'David, you haven't changed. You're still a jerk who does dumb things. Everybody knows that love like you're talking about happens once in a lifetime. And if you don't want to regret it 'til your dying day, you'd better grab that woman before she gets away.' But she was only telling me what I already knew. R.J., I love you, but I don't want our differences to destroy us."

R.J.'s face was stinging with heat as a voice somewhere again announced the flight for Los Angeles.

"I told my father this morning that I want to marry you," David said.

"And what did he say?" she heard herself ask in a voice that was choked with pain.

"Exactly what you'd expect," David answered. "He said, 'You have nothing in common.' "

"And what did you say to that?"

"I said, 'Dad, you couldn't be more wrong. We have everything in common. We each want desperately to be a part of a real family. We both long to have the kind of love and passion with a mate that our parents had with one another. We both care about children. Want to have one or maybe even two in our future. We want to be able to find a haven in each other from the slings and arrows of the world outside. I could go on for days about all that R.J. Misner and David Malcolm have in common.' "

Boy, could this man say the right things. R.J. felt as if she were breathing normally again for the first time in a month.

"So what did *he* say?" She was blinking very fast to hold back her tears.

"He blessed it, R.J. In his way. By not telling me I was making a mistake. By not telling me all of the reasons I shouldn't do it, but by telling me in his usual manner and with his usual five words or less."

"Which were?"

"There goes Greenview Country Club."

Neither of them could hold back a blurry, teary-eyed smile.

"R.J., I'm sorry I left. You're right. It was a lousy thing to do. But please, say you forgive me and that you'll marry me, because I can't let you go back to Los Angeles like this—"

But before R.J. could respond, a man's voice interrupted. "If you don't say *something* there, honey, no one's going back to Los Angeles, because I'm the pilot." And when R.J. looked around and saw the line standing behind the man in the blue pilot's uniform, she realized that she and David were blocking a whole group of people who were trying to board the plane.

As the two of them moved out of the way, David took her into his arms and they kissed. Happily, deliciously, they kissed. Then they heard the call on the P.A. system.

"United Airlines paging David Malcolm. David Malcolm, please come to the courtesy telephone." David looked afraid. He took her hand and moved her to a corner of the waiting area where there was a white phone and picked it up.

"Hello?" he said. "This is David Malcolm. Yes, I'll hold."

He put his arm around R.J., and as he pulled her close she could feel him shaking.

"Hello. Yes. I'm on my way." He hung up the phone and looked at R.J. "He's very bad" was all he said, and then he turned and left the airport, and R.J., feeling as if she had just awakened from a dream, heeded the last call for the flight to Los Angeles and walked back to the gate to board.

"When Jeffie was four years old, one day he told his father and me that he was going to run away from home," R.J. said, then looked down one more time at the note card she held in her hand. She wanted to be able to tell the story perfectly and she hoped that no one could see how nervous she felt and how she was trembling so terribly inside. "His father, trying to discourage him, reminded him that in order to survive in the outside world, there were certain things people had to do for themselves that four-year-old Jeffie still wasn't able to do. One of them was to prepare food, and another was to tie one's own shoes. Jeffie, still determined to make it on his own, thought about that for a minute and then said to Arthur: 'That's okay. I'll eat cookies and wear my slippers.' "

A giggle went through the crowd and Jeffie blushed.

"It's that same fierce independence, that same enterprising mind, that same sense of humor that characterizes Jeff today, and it's those characteristics which have helped him survive a terrible tragedy and enabled him to help me survive it too. That's why, on this day of his bar mitzvah, when he officially becomes a man, I want him to know that I believe he's already been a man for a very long time."

Jeffie, handsome in his gray suit, and relaxed now that his long Hebrew recitation was behind him, hugged his mother, and there was another laugh from the crowd as everyone noted how the thirteen-year-old boy towered over her.

"Congratulations, honey," she said to him.

"Thanks, Mom."

R.J. took a quick look out at the assembled group. She could make out only a few faces. Arthur's parents. Manuela and her husband in the front row. Eddie Levy and his wife, Sally, Harry Elfand and Josie. R.J.'s agent, Stanley Hoffman, and his wife. Patsy in full array—a low-cut silk blouse and a white suit with sequined lapels. There was a long pause. Then there was another murmur of approval as David walked to the microphone. He wore a yarmulke and a talis over his gray suit, which was the same as the one Jeffie was wearing because they had chosen them together. For the wedding, three months earlier.

Now David spoke: "Unaccustomed as I am to speaking at my son's bar mitzvah," he said, and everyone laughed. "God does work in mysterious and wonderful ways," he added, and then he put an arm around Jeffie. "I want you to know what a fine young man I think you are, Jeff, and how lucky I am to have you as my son, because thanks to your patience and understanding, I'm learning a lot about how to be a parent. You see, you've been a son for thirteen years but I've only been a father for a few months, and I need all the help I can get."

There was another laugh. Then David looked out at the assembled group.

"R.J. and Jeff and I are three people who have each been longing to have a real family for a very long time. And that's why you see three such happy faces up here, because we're thrilled to have found one another. For me it's especially great, because it isn't everyone who gets to have his first child come to his wedding. I didn't even have to wait the required time to hear someone learn to call me Dad. My son called me that right away."

There were a few giggles, and then R.J. looked out at the faces, and she spotted a few like Dinah, wiping her eyes, and Arthur's parents, who were holding hands and smiling through their tears when David embraced Jeff. Then the rabbi said, "Please join us in the social hall for Kiddush and then for the reception at R.J., David, and Jeffie's home," and everyone rose and began to chatter.

R.J. and her son and her husband stepped off the platform, and as they did, arms around one another, a few people near the back of the synagogue parted in order to allow the man who had been sitting in the back row of the room to move to the front. Determinedly but with the halting pace made necessary by his age and poor health, he made his way toward them. He wore a navy suit and there was a yarmulke sitting on top of his white wavy hair.

"Thanks for coming, Dad," David said, embracing his father.

Rand Malcolm patted his son as hearty a pat as he could, then kissed R.J.'s cheek, then turned to Jeff and shook the boy's hand.

"I'm very impressed, young man," he said.

"Thank you," Jeff said.

The driver was waiting, so while Jeff went ahead to the social hall, R.J. and David walked Rand Malcolm out to the car, and when he was on his way home to rest, hand in hand they made their way back to the social hall to celebrate.

# DON'T MISS
## THESE CURRENT
## Bantam Bestsellers

# THE LATEST IN BOOKS
# AND AUDIO CASSETTES

## Paperbacks

| | | | |
|---|---|---|---|
| ☐ | 28671 | **NOBODY'S FAULT** Nancy Holmes | $5.95 |
| ☐ | 28412 | **A SEASON OF SWANS** Celeste De Blasis | $5.95 |
| ☐ | 28354 | **SEDUCTION** Amanda Quick | $4.50 |
| ☐ | 28594 | **SURRENDER** Amanda Quick | $4.50 |
| ☐ | 28435 | **WORLD OF DIFFERENCE** Leonia Blair | $5.95 |
| ☐ | 28416 | **RIGHTFULLY MINE** Doris Mortman | $5.95 |
| ☐ | 27032 | **FIRST BORN** Doris Mortman | $4.95 |
| ☐ | 27283 | **BRAZEN VIRTUE** Nora Roberts | $4.50 |
| ☐ | 27891 | **PEOPLE LIKE US** Dominick Dunne | $4.95 |
| ☐ | 27260 | **WILD SWAN** Celeste De Blasis | $5.95 |
| ☐ | 25692 | **SWAN'S CHANCE** Celeste De Blasis | $5.95 |
| ☐ | 27790 | **A WOMAN OF SUBSTANCE** Barbara Taylor Bradford | $5.95 |

## Audio

| | | | |
|---|---|---|---|
| ☐ | **SEPTEMBER** by Rosamunde Pilcher Performance by Lynn Redgrave 180 Mins. Double Cassette | 45241-X | $15.95 |
| ☐ | **THE SHELL SEEKERS** by Rosamunde Pilcher Performance by Lynn Redgrave 180 Mins. Double Cassette | 48183-9 | $14.95 |
| ☐ | **COLD SASSY TREE** by Olive Ann Burns Performance by Richard Thomas 180 Mins. Double Cassette | 45166-9 | $14.95 |
| ☐ | **NOBODY'S FAULT** by Nancy Holmes Performance by Geraldine James 180 Mins. Double Cassette | 45250-9 | $14.95 |